❧ THE ❧
STARS
DISPOSE

Tor Books by Michaela Roessner

Vanishing Point
The Stars Dispose

~ THE ~
STARS
DISPOSE

MICHAELA ROESSNER

A TOM DOHERTY ASSOCIATES BOOK
NEW YORK

This is a work of fiction. All the characters and events
portrayed in this novel are either fictitious or are used
fictitiously.

THE STARS DISPOSE

This book is printed on acid-free paper.

A Tor Book
Published by Tom Doherty Associates, Inc.
175 Fifth Avenue
New York, N.Y. 10010

Tor Books on the World Wide Web:
http://www.tor.com

Tor® is a registered trademark of Tom Doherty
Associates, Inc.

Design by Lynn Newmark

Library of Congress Cataloging-in-Publication Data

Roessner, Michaela.
    The stars dispose / Michaela Roessner. —1st ed.
        p. cm.
    "A Tom Doherty Associates book."
    ISBN 0-312-85754-3 (acid-free paper)
    I. Catherine de Médicis, Consort of Henry II, King of France,
1519–1589—Fiction.   2. Medici, House of—Fiction.   3. Florence
(Italy)—History—1421–1737—Fiction.   I. Title.
PS3568.O3675S73   1997
813'.54—dc20   96-42995
                                                                CIP

First Edition: April 1997

Printed in the United States of America

0 9 8 7 6 5 4 3 2 1

This book is dedicated to:

My mother, Barbara Grutze Roessner,
and
Shadrach, the original Gattamelata

CONTENTS

❧ THE ❧
STARS
DISPOSE

PROLOGUE

April 16, 1519
FLORENCE, ITALY

A cat sat licking itself on the sill. The rich promise of prosciutto cooking in wine, buckwheat polenta steaming, spit-roasted hare, songbirds basted with mustard, and, soothing the senses, the subtler perfumes of distilled cinnamon water and simmering almond milk drifted up through the open window from the kitchen courtyard below. The cat paused in its grooming now and then to sniff out the window or to glance back, with a cat's typically amused expression, at the proceedings in the room.

We must look like the picture of the Three Wise Men, come to pay homage to the holy child, Ruggiero thought as he crowded with the other two men around the ornate inlaid cradle. The infant within glowed like a jewel.

The painting Ruggiero had in mind was not the one adorning the chapel a floor below them, where they had just baptized the baby. That fresco was by Benozzo Gozzoli and portrayed *The Procession of the Magi.*

No, he was thinking of *The Adoration of the Magi* in the church of Santa Maria Novella, executed by the divine Sandro Botticelli. The setting in that fresco was different. It portrayed a ruined excuse for a stable, while this—he glanced briefly around—one of the more modest rooms in the palace, would have pleased vengeful King Herod himself.

The subject also differed. Here the object of such intense scrutiny was a baby girl, not the Son of God.

But, Ruggiero thought, surely the expressions on the faces of himself and the other two men—the concern, the awe, the reverence—could have served as models for the Wise Men in Botticelli's masterpiece.

Ruggiero looked at the cat and smiled. Sunlight bathed its coat, causing the mottled yellow, russet, orange and ivory fur, framed by black velvet patches and stripes, to glow like different grades of gold. The cat blinked gleaming emerald eyes at him. The whole effect reminded Ruggiero of the nuptial bed of tortoiseshell inlaid with mother-of-pearl and ivory given to the baby's parents by the pope on the occasion of their wedding, only a year ago.

Beside him, Ariosto sighed. "Only a branch shows a little green in its leaves. And I am divided between fear and hope whether winter will leave it to me," the poet murmured.

His words broke Ruggiero's moment of tranquillity, a spell bounded only by the walls of this room with its purring cat, its comforting kitchen-borne smells, its sunlight, its healthy baby girl. How skillfully and sadly the flamboyant writer had summed up with a few words the child's situation—the last fragile greening on a venerable and declining family tree.

"Surely not the last branch," the third man in the room, Bazile the mathematician, interjected. "Don't forget Ippolito."

Ariosto waved his hand in dismissal. "A beautiful and bright child. He would have brought delight to both his grandfather, Lorenzo *Il Magnífico*, and his father, the gentle Giuliano. But since he is illegitimate, even if he flourishes, at best he'll be considered a grafting from the original tree."

"Well, then there's—" Bazile said, then thought better about continuing. Ruggiero the Old and the poet looked at their companion, who flushed. They knew who he was about to refer to. Recently a young boy had appeared in the camp of Cardinal Giulio de' Medici, himself an illegitimate family offspring. Everyone could well guess who his father was— the cardinal himself. But ugly rumors had begun to spread to the effect that the ill-favored, ill-tempered boy was a bastard half-brother to the angelic baby girl who lay before them.

Several doors away the infant girl's mother, Madeleine de la Tour d'Auvergne, lay desperately ill with puerperal fever. Elsewhere in the palace, the father, Lorenzo de' Medici, Duke of Urbino, grandson of Lorenzo the Magnificent, last of the legitimate line of de' Medicis descended from Cosimo, Pater Patriae, was wasting away at the age of twenty-seven from the combined effects of old war wounds and a dissolute life.

"Poor little *Duchessina*. What will become of you?" Ariosto whispered as he looked down at the baby.

Ruggiero and Bazile exchanged a glance. Together they had cast the infant's horoscope. What they had learned of Caterina Maria Romola de' Medici's near future anyone with knowledge and common sense could guess without the aid of the stars. Her parents would both die within weeks. Her great-uncle, Pope Leo of the fabulous tortoiseshell bed, would send an agent (most likely Cardinal Giulio) to fetch Caterina to Rome. There she would take her place as a pawn in the pope's political games, much as he had manipulated the lives of her parents.

"Do you know?" Ariosto asked the two other men. "Have the stars told you her destiny?"

Ruggiero bowed his head. "Astra declinant, non necessitat: The stars dispose, but do not compel." No one, not even Ruggiero the great astrologer and physician, or Bazile the famed mathematician, could predict with certainty the rest of Caterina's life. Ruggiero turned away. Sometimes his natural clairvoyance foresaw the future with the transparency and limpidness of the finest white wine, but only when there was no opportunity for the examined individual's life to fork awry. Therefore, he could usually only see into the very near future in detail.

But what he and Bazile had seen without question, with their arcane calculations, was that the stars would dispose in Caterina a true Medician nature of courage, intellect, taste, and refinement. That she would remain a pawn in the Great Chess Game for only a short while before beginning her metamorphosis into a queen. And that, no matter how her life twisted and turned, Ruggiero's life and those of his sons would intertwine inevitably with hers.

Ruggiero crossed the room to look out the window, hoping to avoid more of Ariosto's questions. He absently stroked the cat as he looked down into the courtyard. Below, a young woman crossed toward the steep steps leading up to the kitchen. She held a baby on her hip and trailed a toddler behind her. Looking up at the window she caught sight of Ruggiero and smiled. The toddler at her side followed her glance, focusing his gaze with a chubby small hand winged over his eyes, which were almost blinded by masses of rich red curls. He crowed and waved at Ruggiero. The astrologer gestured gently back with his fingers. "Don't dawdle, Tommaso," Ruggiero heard the woman admonish the child as she pulled him gently along.

Now why could not Caterina's family have been as peaceful, industrious and happy as those simple folk? Piera was the wife of Ruggiero's cook and master carver, Gentile. Ruggiero had asked her to return to the de' Medici palace to wet-nurse the *Duchessina* until the infant's fate was decided. Return . . . for Piera herself had been raised in the Medici household, her own parents pastry-makers and sauciers to the great family in its prime. When Gentile and Piera wed there had been great celebration in the culinary guilds, who considered the union a joining, in a fashion, of the great houses of Medici and Ruggiero.

And who was to say it was not true, in fact? the astrologer mused. Servants' quarters were usually rife with the bastard get of their masters. Piera's large, dark eyes bore a strong resemblance to those of the de' Medici family her parents served. And Gentile's frame and manner of moving were remarkably like Ruggiero's own father.

Ruggiero tickled the cat's chin. She responded with such slithery pleasure that she almost fell off the windowsill into the room.

"Must that beast be here in the nursery?" Ariosto snapped.

Ruggiero turned to the poet. "She is here for the little *Duchessina*'s protection," he said.

The poet paled and crossed himself. "Forgive me, Maestro stargazer. I didn't realize the creature was one of your familiars."

Ruggiero threw back his head and laughed. "Not one of *my* familiars. If she assists in magic at all, Gattamelata here would have to be counted responsible for the spell you claim yourself cast under every time you overindulge yourself eating lark-stuffed ravioli at my house. She belongs to my master carver's wife, who has consented to act as the *Duchessina*'s wet nurse for now."

Ariosto looked insulted. "*Gattamelata?* Your cook had the audacity to name a cat after one of the greatest *condottieri*?"

"Where is the insult?" Ruggiero teased the cat by tugging lightly at her whiskers. She reproved him by slapping his hand with a soft paw. "That *condottiero* was named himself after a cat. And what better name for this one? *Honey cat.* Her disposition is as sweet and smooth as bee nectar, yet in battle she is as brave, deadly and courageous as the general himself was. Piera says there is no better ratter in all the world—not terrier, tomcat or ferret. My cook insisted on bringing Gattamelata with her to protect the *Duchessina* from every kind of vermin. I only hope to God that Caterina may enjoy such fierce and loyal protection till the end of her . . ." He trailed off, thinking of the dark days and danger he had seen lying ahead for the baby no matter which way her life path turned.

Ariosto had come up beside him. The poet laid a hand on his arm. "What have you seen of her future?" He repeated his question.

Ruggiero hesitated. Ariosto was a favorite of Pope Leo's and therefore the pope's creature; a spy of sorts, whether he cared to think of himself that way or not.

The astrologer jerked his chin significantly in the direction of Madeleine de la Tour's room. "Of the child's parents, O poet, you have sufficient intellect and wit to guess their end."

Why not put an idea into Ariosto's mind? Both poet and pope would assume, coming from Ruggiero's lips, that it was what the stars ordained. "I have seen in her horoscope that Caterina will be raised as a good de' Medici. That the pope in his wisdom will fetch her to Rome to be raised by her aunt, Clarice Strozzi."

Across the room, Ruggiero saw a startled look cross Bazile's face. The horoscope they cast had said nothing so specific. What it foretold was that Caterina would experience peril during a siege (nothing new for a member of the house of Medici), and that, if she survived, she would marry a prince of French blood.

Ignorant of all this, Ariosto looked satisfied.

Ruggiero turned away so that the poet would not see him smiling down at the cat. What a divine inspiration. Clarice Strozzi! Now there was a de' Medici of the first water. Why had not God ordained that she be born the male in the family instead of her decadent brother Lorenzo?

Ruggiero's smile turned into a frown. Just as well to ask God and the stars why they had ordained Lorenzo the Magnificent die of gout in his prime, at only forty-three years of age. Just as well to ask why God had allowed Il Magnífico's clever and beloved younger brother Giuliano to be murdered in God's own cathedral during the Pazzi conspiracy. Just as well to wonder at all the misfortunes that taxed this brilliant shooting star of a family.

Ruggiero and Bazile had seen that the only future that would guarantee Florence's return to the noble and enlightened greatness it had enjoyed under Cosimo Pater Patriae and Lorenzo Magnífico was a future where Caterina remained in Florence, her childhood uninterrupted, her bond with her homeland and its people unbroken. In that future the astrologer/ physician and the mathematician had foreseen Caterina coming of age fully supported by Florence's *Signoria* and beginning a rule of political astuteness, prosperity, and intellectual and artistic flowering similar to, and then surpassing, that of the wily Isabella d'Este in Mantua. But with the imminent death of both of Caterina's parents, that path to the future was disappearing.

All at once Ruggiero felt helpless and ignorant in the face of fate, in spite of all his ability and learning. The cat nuzzled his fingers, hinting for more caresses. He obliged her and whispered, "Keep Caterina safe, little whiskered warrior. Keep her safe."

I

The de' Medicis

1

March 1527
FLORENCE, ITALY

Tommaso sat up straight on his stool in his corner of the kitchen, all attention. Standing beside the main worktable near him, his father, Gentile, stropped carving knives against the whetstone, then caressed each blade just once to a side against a leather strap.

"You don't want to disturb the sharp burr you've raised with the whetstone, but neither do you want any residue of metal dust to foul your first slices," the master carver explained as he placed two majolica plates, one large and one small, at careful angles to the edge of the table, next to the knives and the resting roast.

Gentile moved with an effortless but deliberate grace, every gesture suffused with ritual: the sharpening of the blades, the laying out of the implements, the manner in which he considered the waiting roast. It cast a sort of spell upon the proceedings.

Elsewhere in the kitchen all was the usual clamor and bustle as the cooking apprentices and scullery maids kneaded and pounded bread, rolled out dough for pasta, ground spices in pestles, and whisked sauces at the other workstations. A scullion checked a haunch roasting on the spit in the great fireplace. The ovens banked along the far wall opposite the shelves and smaller worktables were primed—the roasting oven heated to cook three fat capons and a frittata, the *fornaio* baking pastries for dessert (though most breadstuffs were cooked early in the morning), and, in the *salamander*, a platter of oysters enjoyed a brief bath of flame. Sacks lay piled high near the pantry door at the opposite end of the kitchen. The kitchen cat rustled among them searching for rats. Some of the younger Ruggiero sons who'd come looking to pilfer scraps of food were teasing Tommaso's littlest sister, Beatrice, as she sat struggling to shell peas with her fat five-year-old's fingers.

But the triangle of Tommaso the student, Gentile the master, and youthful Cosimo Ruggiero the proud provider of the roast formed an inviolable well of serenity in the chaotic flurry. It reminded Tommaso of the dense and holy tunnels of light that streamed down from the stained-glass windows and clerestories in the cathedral during mass.

"Examine carefully for the perfect angle before committing your hoisting fork," Gentile said. "If you are in the habit of dropping your joints of meat upon the floor you will find yourself swiftly laughed out of your profession and your proclivity for entertainment limited to eligibility in the jesters guild."

With a single swift clean motion, Gentile thrust the tines of the great fork deep into the roast and hefted it clear of the plate and into the air with such ease that it seemed to float there. A small lake of rosy juices was left behind in the platter. They exuded a dense, rich aroma. Tommaso's mouth flooded with saliva.

"But besides merely securing the joint, it must also be well and equally balanced. And just so too you, the carver, must be well and equally balanced. Your body must display an easeful and pleasing stillness; not only for the pleasure of the watching diners, but for your physical comfort as well. Although this is a substantial piece," he nodded to Cosimo, the responsible hunter, "you will often be called upon to carve far larger joints. Therefore you must arrange yourself to be comfortable in the task to avoid fatigue."

Tommaso saw Cosimo smile at the compliment. This was only the haunch of a young hind. It would have been considered far too small to present at a formal dinner, as the young master well knew. But Cosimo obviously appreciated Gentile's courtesy. Of late, Cosimo's studies with his father Ruggiero the Old had left him little time to develop the riding and hunting skills he'd shown so much promise at when he was Tommaso's age.

Tommaso returned his attention to his own father. He noticed how Gentile held his elbow in, close to his body, so that the weight of the haunch rested more on his ribs and hip than his left arm. His shoulders were relaxed. With his right hand, Gentile selected one of the knives. He began to turn the roast at a slow, steady pace. He slid the tip of the knife into the very top of the roast at the slightest of angles, so smoothly that its penetration was a surprise. Thin medallions of meat drifted like russet flower petals down onto the larger round plate, forming a precise roseate pattern.

"Bravo, maestro carver!" Cosimo applauded. Gentile acknowledged the compliment with a nod, not breaking his rhythm. When he reached the rarest middle portion he moved over to the smaller plate and pared three perfect slices onto it. Then he returned to the bigger platter.

He picked up a second blade and held it also in the right hand, separated by one finger from the first knife. The wafer-thin collops of meat now fell two at a time, closer together, altering the pattern on the plate to a twisting inward spiral. This time only an amazed sigh escaped from Cosimo.

When he completed the carving, Gentile picked up the dish the roast had been resting on. With a single clean motion he swirled the puddle of juices evenly over the slices, saving just enough to glaze the smaller plate. Selecting the last of his knives—a blunt wide blade—he dipped it into the salt cellar. A gentle scattering of salt and it was finished.

"Let the salt and juices soak back into the meat for at least three minutes," Gentile said as he tidied up. He poured a small bowl of rose water, set beside it a napkin, fork and knife. He gestured Cosimo to come over and presented the youth with the smaller platter.

Cosimo gasped. "How did you know? That is exactly the portion I would have chosen for myself, my favorite part of the roast. Thank you, good Gentile. I confess I've been mad with hunger since you began your demonstration." Cosimo immediately rinsed his hands in the rose water, wiped them dry on the napkin, and began to devour the paper-thin morsels.

Gentile didn't ignore Cosimo's question, but he addressed its answer to Tommaso. "How did I know? It is not enough that one has poise, balance, grace, skill and an impeccable presentation. You must know which portions of what quantity to present to your master, mistress and honored guests, and when. You can trust your instincts somewhat, but I advise that the wisest course is to study *those* you serve as avidly as *what* you serve."

Gentile set Tommaso to arranging the whetstone, a *tondo*, and a set of smaller carving knives and hoisting fork while he cut a tight, compact joint from a spit-roasting kid. "There," he said, presenting the much smaller cut of meat to Tommaso. "Let us see how much you observed. Don't concern yourself with the double-knife cut. Just the fundamentals."

Tommaso seized the fork in his left hand like a weapon and stared at the roast as if it were Goliath and he David. Where, oh where to stab the tines so he wouldn't disgrace himself? He looked up to see his father watching him, burly arms folded across his chest, face impassive except for one sardonically cocked eyebrow.

Tommaso thought a moment, blushed, and set the fork down. He went out into the kitchen yard. The chill March wind shocked his skin after the steaming heat of the kitchen. He rinsed his hands with a dipper of water from one of the rain barrels, drying his cold fingers on his shirttails as he reentered the kitchen. He didn't want his father to think him a grimy barbarian lout like a German or Frenchman.

After donning an apron he took his place at his workstation. This time he sharpened his knives carefully before he even thought of attacking the roast. A peek sneaked over his shoulder at his father assured him he'd made a better start this time. Gentile had turned away and was chatting with Cosimo, comparing the study of the arts they were each dedicated to.

"But think of the similarities, Maestro Carver!" Cosimo exclaimed in rebuttal to some point Gentile had just made. "As you yourself just demonstrated, cuisine isn't merely rending some natural object edible and plopping it before a diner. It is a ritual that entrances and focuses all the senses and intellect and wit, with lessons to teach and benefits to confer far beyond the obvious gross material one of feeding one's hungry body, important as that is.

"It is the same with astrology and the other occult arts. They are meant, when well mastered, to profit mankind in ways far beyond mere gain and superstition."

Aha, thought Tommaso. Cosimo was running aground on Gentile's doubts about—with no offense meant to Cosimo's astrologer father—the effectiveness and worth of mystical practices.

Tommaso tried to reexamine his roast with detachment. Where indeed should he stick his fork in? Somewhere near the center. He kept in mind that he'd have to lift the meat with that same motion and hold it up as long as it took him to carve it. Which might be a long time indeed.

The cat came out from behind the grain sacks, unsuccessful in her hunt. Tommaso thought that was probably because she was so pregnant she couldn't move with her customary swiftness. She sat at Tommaso's feet and stared up at the roast. She made it clear that if *he* couldn't find a use for that haunch, she could.

"Go away Gattamelata," Tommaso said. "I know exactly what I'm doing," he lied. "I'm just taking my time about it."

The cat wasted no more time with him and waddled off to beg from Gentile and Cosimo.

"So you see," Cosimo was continuing, "the occult arts do not differ from those sciences that are more concrete and obvious to us, like mathematics or medicine. They simply penetrate more deeply into those realms that exist beyond the comprehension of our immediate senses. At the same time they serve another purpose in elevating our sensibilities by piercing man's thick hide of complacency."

Tommaso thrust the fork tines deep into the haunch, turned the fierce downward force upward, and lifted. There!

Gentile mock-frowned. "You speak eloquently, young master. Who would not be disarmed by your words? But I only trust what I can see, touch, feel and smell. I'm a simple, practical being."

"Aha!" Cosimo crowed. "*You* prove my point with your subtle ploy of deceit posing as honest modesty. With my eyes I *see* that what you say is true. How you illustrate those virtues—simplicity, practicality—as you bustle about this kitchen! But I *know* them to be false. You are in fact a well-educated, sophisticated man. You attended public school, though I was not born yet to *see* it. You are well read and constnatly endeavor to add to your learning. In this case my eyes garner me less truth than my knowledge. And so it is with all the scientific arts, whether 'solid' or arcane."

Gentile threw back his head and laughed. "You are a miracle, young

Cosimo. Your father will have reason to be inordinately proud of you one day."

Tommaso stood with the sharpest knife in his right hand. What had he seen his father do? It seemed like magic, a technique veiled from the eye. Gentile had rotated the roast with his left hand. Tommaso remembered that. He set the knife down and concentrated on just turning the joint. When the action looked like what he remembered he picked up the knife again.

How had his father gotten the knife in? It had appeared to melt into the meat. Tommaso held the blade up to the joint. No, not stabbing. It wasn't that. He turned the haunch against the knife's sharp edge. The knife slid in. Yes! That was it! His heart leapt. He held the knife at what he hoped was an elegant angle and turned the roast round and round, the blade mysteriously invisible within it. That was the secret. The knife did not do the cutting. Rather, the meat cut itself against the blade as it turned. Dense, salty aromas steamed from the edges as he carved.

"There are so many cases to illustrate my point, from the obvious to the esoteric," Cosimo said in response to some further comment from Gentile. "We feel the wind, yet we do not see it. Dogs hear noises and smell odors that we cannot, yet we do not disbelieve them. Take your patchwork cat here." He stopped to feed a scrap from his plate to Gattamelata, whose plump body was balanced up on her hindquarters, begging prettily. "Have you never seen her startle or focus on something outside, or in a room where there appears to be nothing or no one? Can you be sure that she is not cognizant of some entity that you are not?

"The occult seems mysterious only because the physical senses you speak so highly of and rely on with such trust are in fact sadly developed in mankind, mere beggars' alms. The so-called 'mystic' realms are largely an extension of those parts of the natural world inaccessible to us. We are blind, deaf, dumb, clumsy, and graceless compared to the beasts of the field."

In spite of his initial triumph Tommaso was finding the roast rough going. It sat well fixed on the tines, but his thrust had not been as well centered as he'd thought. The collops peeled off onto the *tondo* in a lopsided fashion. Here and there lay a lovely slice, even a series of them, but they were uneven in size and shape. He could see how he should wield the knife to ensure uniform thinness, but he couldn't coordinate his movements to bring it off. He'd long ago given up any attempt at an elegant arrangement on the plate.

Sweat plastered his rust-chestnut hair to his forehead and dripped down into his eyes. After a furtive glance to assess that his father's attention was still on Cosimo, he quickly wiped his right forearm across his eyes. His left arm felt leaden, even braced against his side as it was. Paradoxically, the more he sliced away from the roast, the heavier it weighed on his arm. Sticky oily juices trickled down onto his left hand. As he approached the middle of the haunch the meat turned unruly, ripping away in shreds and chunks.

His father had already taught him a good deal about judging meat, butchering and jointing. So Tommaso knew that this haunch had never been destined for display on the sideboard—more likely chopped up for a modest dish like *mortrews*. And, as further proof, he had only to look at the humble wooden *tondo* his father had provided him, instead of a lovely ceramic majolica platter like the one Gentile had used for his own demonstration.

"So what is it that allows us to hold sway over the swifter, more graceful and sensate animals?" Cosimo tapped his head. "It is this. Our intellect. That which allows us to pierce what at first appears to be mystery. That which allows us to transcend our inadequate physical legacy. That which allows us to harness our emotions to noble purpose."

Tommaso looked at the *tondo* and the disastrous hunks of flesh heaped there. At eleven Tommaso was too old to cry, but he felt a deep despair that bore an uncomfortable resemblance to weeping.

"Almost done, are we?" Gentile spoke at Tommaso's shoulder. Tommaso turned toward his father slowly. There was no disguising what a calamity the exercise had turned out.

"Come, come. That woeful look may be premature . . . until after an assessment of your efforts," Gentile said as he released the hoisting fork and knife from Tommaso's hands.

The words gently teased, but Tommaso caught the slight grimace his father made as he used the knife to scrape the bottom of the joint off the

fork onto an empty *tondo.* Gentile then used the fork to pick apart and examine Tommaso's efforts. Once in a while he lifted a morsel clear to set
it on the second *tondo.*

"Here," he said, indicating some ragged chunks. "These are from the
middle. You did not let the cut rest quite long enough before carving.
Cleaning yourself up, sharpening your knife and composing yourself provided almost enough time. Just a few more minutes and next time you will
find it goes more easily." He smiled as though to assure his son that there
would indeed be another opportunity. Tommaso wasn't sure he wanted
one.

"Now these are quite nice." Gentile fished some of the tidier slices
from the bottom of the pile. "Perhaps somewhat uneven in shape, but that's
easily remedied. I'll teach you how to gauge the placement of the fork better. Just a little too thick, but evenly carved." Gentile set the fork down.
"You have an excellent eye, Tommaso. That is the most important thing"
—he shot a glance at Cosimo—"the ability to *perceive.* Never mind that we
don't possess eyes as keen as falcons. For this we don't need it."

Cosimo put his hand to his face to hide a grin.

Gentile turned back to his son. "You immediately discerned that I
didn't saw at the meat with the knife; that the 'secret' lies in turning the
joint against the blade, so that the weight of the meat slices itself. You also
noticed how I used my body to support the burden of the endeavor by
bracing my upper arm and elbow against my ribs."

He slapped Tommaso's left shoulder. "You may think your arm is sore
and tired, but that's nothing compared to the agony suffered by most apprentices when they start out. They don't *see* what I do"—Cosimo coughed
to cover a laugh—"and seem to think they should stand like this." Gentile extended the hoisting fork away from his body in a flamboyant, exag-
gerated gesture. "You would find that in this position even the mysteriously invisible occult roasts of Cosimo Ruggiero the Younger would
become monstrously heavy in a short while." He cocked an eyebrow at
Cosimo.

Tommaso stood speechless. His father was pleased with his performance.

Cosimo came up and slapped his other arm. "I'm amazed at your amazement, Tommasino," the youth said. "You've grown up all your life in this kitchen and always worked hard and succeeded at whatever your father has set you to."

"Just at chores," Tommaso said. "Chopping and stirring and mixing. Maybe some tasks that needed skill, but none that required artistry."

"The beginning of all apprenticeships is filled with awkwardness," said Cosimo. "I'll tell you what—since I've been privy to your lessons and discomfort, it's only fair that I return the favor. I'll arrange for you to attend one of the tutorings I suffer from *my* father. It would be good for you to see that all professions are difficult to master."

The hair stood up on the back of Tommaso's neck. He shook his head hard. No. His father might be cynical about their master Ruggiero's profession, but Tommaso was not. Too many times had he passed Dr. Ruggiero's laboratory or study and heard strange arcane sounds, smelled dreadful unidentifiable odors issuing from within.

"Thank you, good Cosimo," he stammered, recovering his manners. "But between school and my work and apprenticing here, I hardly have the time to trouble you . . ."

He was interrupted by Cosimo's laughter. The older boy clapped him around the shoulders again. "Dear Tommasino, you've turned white as sheep's cheese. How serious you must be to so greatly fear being taken from your studies," he said slyly.

"Don't distract or tease him," Gentile chided Cosimo. "You'll come to rue the day, for someday Tommaso will serve as *your* master carver and cook."

Cosimo's expression changed suddenly. He turned to Tommaso with a thoughtful look. "No, I don't think so, Gentile. I don't think Tommaso will be my carver after all. I think he is destined for greater service."

Both cooks, father and son, fell silent. No one, not even Gentile, could deny that Ruggiero the Old had a talent for prophecy and that his son had already shown similar promise.

But then Cosimo laughed again. Gentile and Tommaso both relaxed. No doubt the young master was just continuing his little jest.

"Tommaso, chop your exercise up fine for a dish of brewet," Gentile said as he tidied up the area. "Then I want you to measure out some spices your mother has asked for and take them to her. The Medici seem to have returned to Florence to join Cardinal Passerini with nothing but their hungry servants and more ecclesiastical sycophants."

"And their hunting prowess," defended Cosimo. "That will help keep their larders filled." He had just returned from a hunting trip with the Medici heirs to the de' Medici country estate at Careggi. "My own efforts"—he gestured to the roast slices Gentile had carved—"were modest compared to theirs. Ippolito brought down a boar, Alessandro speared a young stag, and even the newly arrived *Duchessina* killed two fine fat pheasants, though she's younger than your daughter Ginevra."

Tommaso felt a pang and Gentile looked further disgruntled. They both missed the tranquil Ginevra, whom Piera had taken with her to the Medici palazzo as a helpmate.

"It's a shame they can't net or spear something as precious as these," Gentile grumbled as he took down spice jars from a shelf. "Tommaso, dole out three measures each of cinnamon, marjoram, and powdered ginger; two measures each of cloves and nutmeg; one-half measure each of sandal and saffron, and don't forget to log them into the kitchen ledgers. Surely Pope Clement de' Medici will not want our household accounts to suffer. Either that or Ruggiero the Old can add the sum on the next time he bills the Medicis. You'll find silk packets to put the spices in next to the market basket."

Tommaso worked quickly, anxious to please his father now that Gentile's expansive mood, stimulated by the verbal jousting with Cosimo, was wearing off. Gentile complained and became gruff whenever his wife Piera was gone for more than a day. Piera had been helping out her parents at the Medici palace for a week.

Tommaso missed his mother too. He understood that his father assigned him the chore partially as a reward for his diligence with the carving lesson, rather than sending over a scullery boy or slave.

"You'll need these to take them over." Gentile thumped down a small leather satchel, a large-lidded carryall basket with shoulder straps, and a rough woven livery.

"What's the basket for?" Tommaso asked as he pulled the livery over his head. The spices would fit easily into the satchel.

"For this," Gentile said. He picked Gattamelata up, slid her into the basket and fastened the lid before she knew what was happening. Immediately, mournful soft wails wafted out through the wickery.

"Gattamelata? To the palace? Why?"

"Their kitchen has been in chaos ever since the pope sent Cardinal Passerini to take up residence. For more than two years now the mice and rats have been playing as much havoc with the Medici larder as the cardinal has with Florence's." The tone of his voice made it clear that Gentile considered the Medici kitchen's swarm of vermin to be no more than just retribution. "Your mother wants Gattamelata to have her kittens at the palace to provide them with new ratters."

Tommaso could tell that his father felt about the Medici much as he did—their needs and demands were unending. First Piera and Ginevra, and with them Pietro, the youngest child, and now even the family cat.

Tommaso stopped and kissed his sister Beatrice's forehead as he passed her. She smiled a woeful little smile. "Kiss Mother and Ginevra and Pietro for me," she said.

"I will," Tommaso promised.

"Tommaso . . ." Gentile said.

Tommaso turned at the kitchen door.

"Watch out for any Arrabbiati, son. Right now they hold a grudge against anyone they think aligned with the Medici."

2

⚜

Tommaso trotted in a deliberate manner through the narrow cobbled streets, dodging the occasional foraging pig or peacock. Guildhalls, apothecaries, dyeworks, counting houses, fireworks workshops, and hospitals loomed above him, their thick, imposing walls faced with stern granite or tiled geometric patterns of black and white, rose and yellow, green and pink.

From open windows high above the streets telltale aromas drifted down to Tommaso: the thick boiled stench of the dyeworks; the dusty yet sleek smell of the silk weavers; the deliciously hellish sulphur fumes from the fireworks *bottega;* the odors of spices and pungent medicinals from the apothecaries, so similar to those of Ruggiero the Old's laboratory that Tommaso shivered.

The aroma of food wove through all the other smells, for no Florentine would allow food, good food, whether artful or simple, to be far from hand. Tommaso smelled rosemary-trussed capon spit-roasting; the perfume of *arrosto morto,* with its lamb slowly cooking in a bath of red wine; the simple worker's hearty supper of bread and garlic soup. Tommaso thought of all the people he could not see but knew were there: all of them working, or talking, or resting, or eating, or arguing. To him, battlement-encircled Florence was like a great cauldron filled with a complex and

perfectly balanced and seasoned stew of all the good, rich, wild things like
mushrooms, artichokes, boar, hare, and woodcock.

The straps of the basket carrier chafed at Tommaso's shoulders. Now
and then he ducked into a church's portal to readjust them, eliciting a grumble from Gattamelata as she was shifted about.

"My apologies, *bella*," he murmured to her. He wanted to make himself comfortable before he crossed the river Arno and left the safety of his
neighborhood. After that, in these times, it would be unwise to stop until
he reached the de' Medici palace.

"Hey, small *furafante!* Yes, you—the one with hair the color of the Devil
himself. Why don't you come join us?"

Tommaso looked up from tightening the basket's straps to see a youth
calling to him from an alleyway just past the church.

He sidled by carefully. Behind the fellow who'd hailed him was a small
crowd of young men playing dice. Since the church was funded and pa-
tronized by the wool merchants' guild, Tommaso guessed that these were
apprentices with too much time on their hands before the spring shipments
of English shearings arrived.

"Where are you going so quickly? Come play a game or two," they
teased him.

"You are wrong to compare his coloring to Satan's, Paolo," a dark-
haired gambler called. "Rather liken him instead to *alchermes,* for he is of
the same hue and looks to be as sweet and intoxicating as that fine liquor.
And who knows? Perhaps as deliciously virtuous as the good monks who
distill it."

This induced screams of laughter from the group, since the monks
who produced *alchermes* were not particularly known for their chastity.
Tommaso blushed up to the roots of his hair.

"No, I stand by my first assessment," the one called Paolo said. "We
can see by your livery you serve the house of the mage Ruggiero. By chance
are you a spirit or imp? Stop for us then, we implore you. Surely you have
love philters and magical charms to bestow on us."

"Possibly I do," Tommaso, now well past them, called over his shoulder. "But clearly such handsome and able courtiers as yourselves would have
little need for them."

The entourage of gamblers cheered at that. Their leader swept off his cap to Tommaso.

This quarter of the city respected the Ruggieros, believing their occult talents protected the neighborhood and ensured its prosperity. Tommaso knew that although it never hurt to be cautious, here his livery would protect him from the *brigate*'s pranks. Elsewhere in the city it might have the opposite effect.

As always, customers crowded about the butchers' shops lining the Ponte Vecchio made passage across the bridge slow going. Burdened as he was by the bulky basket, it was even harder than usual for Tommaso.

But on the bridge he was still safe. Rival factions from all over the city mingled in peace, for the butchers did not like their lucrative business interrupted by frivolous quarreling. Their customers respected their wishes: Butchers got more daily practice wielding their cleavers and knives than the most competent swordsmen their swords. And the butchers loved the opportunity to exercise their skills to restore order in their quarter when necessary.

Tommaso considered himself especially secure. His family, enmeshed as it was in the intricately interconnected culinary arts, possessed many friends and relatives in the butchers' trade. In fact, he realized he should be edging toward the other side of the bridge because—

"Tommaso! Is that you, Tommasino? Come and give your cousin a dutiful kiss," a woman's voice called out from one of the open stalls. Too late, Tommaso groaned and ducked his head. His bright, distinctive hair had given him away.

The woman pushed her way out of her stall. Her customers made way for her. She seized Tommaso's arm. "What would your mother Piera say if she heard her eldest son didn't stop to pay his respects to his dear, delicate cousin Leonora?" she asked as she leaned her cheek forward for Tommaso to kiss.

The crowd around them roared with laughter. Cousin Leonora was as tall, strong, and well muscled as any man. Tommaso pecked her cheek quickly and then jerked his head away.

Of the eight women-run wild game shops in the city, hers was the only one that had never been harassed in any manner by the *Signoria*. In fact, she and her daughters had never been harassed by anyone, to Tommaso's knowledge. He'd once heard his father say jokingly to his mother that it was hard to believe there were men sufficiently brave to get children on Leonora—so perhaps the tales of her being a witch were true, and her girls were the offspring of spirits or demons. Piera had not seemed to find Gentile's jest amusing.

"You call that a kiss? Don't make me doubt that you are Gentile Arista's son. Now, *this* is how you kiss." She wetted his cheeks thoroughly. Tommaso squirmed. "And what you might also consider doing is . . ." She leaned forward to whisper in his ear. He braced himself for some obscene bit of doggerel.

"Watch your back, little one," she hissed. "Three young cutthroats have been shadowing you since you passed the sausage-maker's table. I don't recognize them, but one of them is sporting a red-hilted dagger."

Arrabbiati!

The crowd misread the shock on Tommaso's face. "Throw the fingerling back in the river, Leonora! He's too little. Cast your nets for bigger cod," a bystander catcalled.

Leonora released Tommaso. "I believe you are right. I could do with a larger catch."

Tommaso backed away from Leonora, casting his glance right and left, trying to make out who his pursuers might be.

"You!" Leonora cried as she seized a handsome but shabbily dressed young man. "Now here's one with a little meat on him!" The fellow wriggled in her embrace like a netted trout, looking as helpless as Tommaso had felt a moment before. Leonora swung the youth around, to the crowd's vast enjoyment, and Tommaso saw pinned against his side the shredded-red-ribbon-wrapped dagger—symbol of what the Arrabbiati would like to do to red-robed Cardinal Passerini, the pope-imposed tyrant of Florence.

Tommaso edged his way backward through the crowd. He made out two other ruffians who must be the first's companions; they stood in gaping consternation instead of laughing with the rest of the onlookers. Tommaso turned and hurried off.

The press of people thinned out. Tommaso was trotting at a good clip by the time he reached the end of the bridge. He headed straight for the Medici palace on the Via Largo, trying to make his strides as smooth as he could for Gattamelata's sake.

When he heard the shouts behind him he realized his mistake. He should have headed off immediately to a winding side street. His pursuers had broken free from Leonora's diversion. With the straight view down the broad avenue they'd easily seen his bright hair and the bulky basket.

Tommaso ducked into a side alley. At this point his pursuers did not know whether he was aware of their following him, nor for certain that the Medici palace was his destination. As physician and astrologer, Master Ruggiero served many of the city's great families. Tommaso could have been sent on an errand to any of them.

Tommaso changed his direction. He chose another narrow lane that gently curved away from the Via Largo. As he rounded the corner he saw the Arrabbiati farther down the alley he'd just left. They were moving slowly, pretending to examine a potter's wares. What would be the worst they'd do to him? Knock him down and steal the valuable spices? Box his ears and black his eyes? As long as there were shopkeepers present they'd dare no more. But if they threw him down, what would happen to the very pregnant Gattamelata trapped in the basket? And Tommaso knew that if it were dark and the streets deserted they might not be averse to killing a young errand boy as a warning to any who chose to deal with Cardinal Passerini and the Medici.

In spite of the chill of the spring day, which was intensified by the shadows of the tall buildings, Tommaso began to sweat. His hair stuck to his forehead and brushed against his eyes. He pushed it away with a curse. He felt a humming against his back. Strangely, impossibly, Gattamelata had begun to purr.

Tommaso moved as quickly as he could without seeming to hurry; his route followed an arc around the Medici palace. An aproned servant came out the back door of a shop with a bucket of gray water to wash away garbage piled up near the door. Ducking around the water sluicing over the pavement afforded Tommaso a clandestine glance back. The Arrabbiati trailed farther and farther behind. But they were still there. They had not lost interest in him.

Tommaso wandered along alleys he'd never seen before, that he hadn't known existed. They circled gently, like the curve of a perfect bowl. The farther along that curve they carried him the more nervous he became. He hadn't stopped to linger and play the way a boy using an errand as an opportunity to dawdle and avoid work might. If he kept circling until he rounded back in the direction of the palace, the Arrabbiati would know he was trying to evade them.

He began to peer into shop fronts, warehouses and homes, hoping to find one that he could pretend had been his destination all along. But everything was unfamiliar. He was as likely to seek refuge in a place sympathetic to the Arrabbiati as one aligned with the de' Medici. He couldn't risk it.

The sunlight as it washed across the buildings now angled from a different direction, telling Tommaso that he'd reached the halfway point of the great circle he'd been inscribing and was about to round back toward the bridge. He glanced behind him. The Arrabbiati were closing in, dodging around vendors and bullock-drawn carts. They knew he'd tried to trick them. Tommaso began to run. He thought he heard, faintly, the city lions roaring in their cages in the distant Piazza de la Signoria.

Where were the intersecting streets cutting inward to Via Largo? Even if he could find one, Tommaso knew he couldn't reach the Medici palace before the Arrabbiati overtook him, but at least he had a better chance of running into Medici supporters who would help him.

But in this quarter of the city all the alleys branching off the street seemed to turn away, outward toward the city walls. Tommaso winced at every jouncing stride, expecting a pained complaint from Gattamelata. Instead, her purr came more and more loudly through the basket's wicker. *Impossible animal,* Tommaso thought.

He stumbled on the cobblestones, cursing their roughness. The broader avenues enjoyed large, smooth stone pavers that would have provided better footing. At last Tommaso saw a lane turning in from the right ahead. Its mouth was jammed with people trying to make their way toward and from the heart of the city. His pursuers would catch him before he could fight his way through the crowd and escape down it. Tommaso edged along the far side of the street and kept running.

He passed two more intersections, each as crammed as the first. After the last one the street began to empty out. Tommaso didn't dare look behind him. His hunters must be closing in. Tommaso ran helplessly, forcing leaden legs to pump up and down. He was breathing so hard he could feel his lungs crushing against his heart.

Gattamelata's purr droned loud as a hive of bees. It reverberated against the sides of the basket, buzzed through Tommaso's back, his bones. Tommaso felt it filling and vibrating the very walls of the alley. It made Tommaso want to scream, if only he'd had the breath for screaming.

The geometrically contrasted colors of the facades looming over him no longer seemed representative of logic and order. They began to look like enormous, monstrous versions of the bright painted pebbles his mother kept for luck. Their gaudy patterns pulsed with barbaric vitality. Their brilliance hurt Tommaso's eyes.

Tommaso felt as though he were running through water. He gasped for air, each gulp drawing daggers into his lungs. His clothing was soaked with sweat. His leggings clung to his thighs. He rounded another corner. There, just ahead of him, was the Ponte Vecchio again, with the broad avenue leading up to it. If he could reach it he'd be amongst his own. He'd be safe.

He risked a glance back and almost stopped in surprise. The Arrabbiati were still chasing him, but they'd dropped far behind. But not so far that Tommaso couldn't see the looks on their faces: They were furious, frustrated and incredulous.

Tommaso turned toward the bridge again. His legs felt lighter with hope. They ran faster of their own accord.

Then, as if in a dream, an oxcart filled with oil casks turning onto the bridge jammed at the traces. The lead ox went down, dragging its partner with it. The cart overturned. The entrance to the bridge was filled with rolling casks and shouting, cursing people.

Tommaso could not believe it, even as he found himself running past the bridge, past his one chance at safety. The Arrabbiati would soon catch him. For a moment he almost hoped they would, or he would be doomed to run forever, round and round.

Over Gattamelata's irritating incessant purring Tommaso heard his hunters' swift footfalls now, closer and closer behind him. Just as he had been heartened at the sight of the bridge, so had they been heartened by the accidental blockade and picked up speed.

Tommaso reached the spot where he had first heard them shouting behind him, at the mouth of the street that would have led him directly to the Via Largo and the Medici palace. Tommaso had completed a perfect circle.

And at just that moment he seemed to fill with roundness. He felt as sealed and inviolable as a golden ring. He cut down the road, having nothing to lose. He looked back. Amazingly, the Arrabbiati stood there at the head of the street, glaring at him.

Gattamelata's purr trickled down to a mere hum that tickled almost pleasantly in Tommaso's ear. Casting frequent glances behind him, he trudged the rest of the way to the de' Medici palace.

3

He did not enter through the imposing front doors facing the Via Largo. Those opened onto the palace's lovely inner courtyard, whose array of pillars and arches had once been graced by Donatello's statuary.

Instead, Tommaso trudged around the corner and all the way to the back to a more modest but equally sturdy doorway. It was unbarred. He stepped into the kitchen courtyard and stopped for a moment to compose himself. His heart was still pounding, his breath still short.

The Medici kitchen yard boasted a garden, but it was much smaller than the Ruggieros'. This was often true of the newer, grander palazzi, whose space had been acquired by carving away smaller shops and tenements. Some had no garden or back courtyard at all and the kitchen—as was the case with the de' Medici palace—was integrated into the house. The Medicis' garden boasted at least a few fruit trees and a small plot of herbs and greens. Unlike the Ruggieros', it did not have a well. The Medici well lay directly under the palace, with shafts that led clear up to its roof, so that the upper stories had direct access to water.

From the honored lore of his mother's family, the Befaninis, Tommaso knew that, when the palace had been built, his great-great-grandparents had fought to have the kitchen built on the second, or "noble floor," accessible to the garden by a set of steep steps, rather than up in the garrets, which had been the fashion of the period.

The Befaninis won that battle. During later troubled times when the de' Medici fell out of favor and the Befaninis were asked why they continued to work for them, the family's traditional reply was, "For all their occasional follies, the Medici are wiser than you know. They listen to their cooks."

Today, laved with light by the retiring sun so that it appeared glazed with amber honey, the Medici kitchen courtyard looked as serene as a cloister. In spite of the chill, fruit trees delicately unfurled their blossoms. The herbs in the garden shone a healthy dark green.

Near the top of the steps leading up into the kitchen a slave girl sat plucking a pheasant. Her face was shaded by a battered straw hat and she wore a shapeless work smock far too large for her. Yet, gilded as she was by the dying light, she looked as beautiful, tranquil and blessed with grace as any of the angels bedecking the church of San Giovannino degli Scolopi next door. Every now and then she stopped in her work to take a bite of food from a plate perched on the step above her. The merry, busy kitchen noises floating through the open door behind her only served to counterpoint the quiet of the courtyard.

Calmed by the loveliness, Tommaso was at last ready to greet his mother.

The little slave girl didn't look up as he started up the steps, nor did it appear as though she'd move aside to make it easier to pass. Furthermore, she was doing a poor job of cleaning the pheasant; plucking dainty, ineffectual tufts here and there, a pretty cloud of down settling about her. Poultry should be cleaned by pulling out feathers in one small area straight down to the scalded skin, then enlarging on the bird's nakedness from there.

Tommaso noticed too that the plate she turned to so frequently to nibble from was laden with a nice portion of *cibreo*. An unpretentious dish, it was true, but far too fine to serve as a slave's snack, let alone on a plate of fine majolica rather than a wooden *tondo*. Even from where he stood at the base of the steps Tommaso could smell the subtle nuances of chicken livers and cockscombs resting on their bed of artichokes and knew that his mother had cooked the dish.

He climbed a few more steps. Still the slave ignored him. He studied her more closely. She was young, seven or eight, near his sister Ginevra's age. She'd probably been bought quite recently. Her skin was pale and waxy in texture. Because of the hat's shading brim he couldn't tell the color of her eyes. But since her hair shone a light gold under the dying sun's rays, he would guess them to be blue or gray. She must be a Circassian, and that was the clue Tommaso needed to explain her behavior.

The Medici, clear back to Cosimo Pater Patriae, had preferred Circassian slaves for their fair beauty and pretty ways, whereas many Florentines kept Tartars and Russians for their strong backs. The Ruggieros usually chose Greeks for their intellect and learning. Undoubtedly this poppet had come from Rome with the Medici retinue and, used to the ostentation and luxury of life in Pope Clement's extended household and still new to slavery, did not yet understand the reality of her status. Well, she'd learn otherwise quickly.

Another thought stopped Tommaso as he mounted the steps. Part of a slave's fate was to submit to love without choice or desire. What if she had been purchased to eventually satisfy the whims of the pope? Or, Tommaso shuddered, the whims of the pope's favorite, Alessandro, who the pope claimed to be Duchessina Caterina's illegitimate half-brother. Compassion touched Tommaso's heart. Let her enjoy her spoiled ways then, for as long as they might last.

The little slave finally bent her head toward him, no doubt curious about his erratic progress. A shadow slithered snakelike down and across her. She turned to look back up the steps. Someone stood silhouetted in the kitchen doorway. The setting sun cast a corona around his darkness.

"Intialo," the girl breathed in a low voice, almost a growl.

"So there you are. Not done with that pheasant *yet?*" The voice was young but harsh. The speaker stepped fully out into the dying light. Tommaso's skin prickled as though he'd been peppered with pins. For a brief moment he wondered if his thoughts had conjured the youth that stood at the top of the stairs. But his name could not be Intialo. About fourteen years of age, with overlarge flabby lips, frizzy hair, and an arrogant stance, there was no mistaking Alessandro de' Medici, of whom all Florence was whispering.

"No, I've just barely begun," said the slave.

"Leave off with that puny bird. Cardinal Passerini will be ready to sup soon. You know how he hates to be kept waiting."

To Tommaso's astonishment, the girl shrugged and returned to plucking the bird. It was no surprise when Alessandro pulled back his hand, threatening to strike her if he'd been close enough. "You would dare disaccommodate the pope's favorite theologian?" he roared.

"Theology is a poem, with *God* for its subject," she replied calmly, then muttered as an afterthought, "*not* Cardinal Passerini."

Alessandro turned white and jumped down a step toward her. The girl dropped the pheasant and leapt to her feet to face him, knocking over the plate of *cibreo*. It fell and shattered on the stone pavers below. Tommaso could see that Alessandro meant to push the girl off the steps to join the shards of majolica. Although the little minx deserved a beating, a forceful fall could break those fragile limbs or even kill her.

Tommaso found himself rushing up the stairs, any well-considered thoughts left behind where he'd been standing. "Messer de' Medici," he shouted. "Signore!" and then didn't know what else to say.

Alessandro and the girl stared down at him. The fatal moment was broken. From the startled expression on the youth's face Tommaso could see that Alessandro hadn't noticed him standing near the bottom of the stairs. Alessandro hastily pulled his hands behind him and scowled. "Is this some diminutive red-faced, red-haired demon from hell?" he snapped.

The girl giggled. "No, this must be Piera's son Tommaso. She's been waiting for him to bring some supplies for the kitchen." She peered at Tommaso mischievously from under the brim of the battered straw hat.

Now it was Tommaso's turn to stare. Her eyes were not blue or gray, but as large and moistly dark as a doe's. They looked exactly like his mother Piera's eyes. They were the eyes of a Medici.

"Come, turn around. I wager I know what's in the basket."

Tommaso did as she said. He felt like an imbecile. She wasn't a Circassian slave at all, but yet another of the de' Medicis' bastard get. He should have known. No slave, let alone one so young and a girl besides, could have quoted the immortal Petrarca. Theology is a poem, indeed.

No one could claim that the Medici were ungenerous to their bastards, at least those they chose to acknowledge. Pope Clement himself was an excellent example: his original given name was Giulio, reflecting that he was the "natural" son of the cathedral-assassinated Giuliano. His mother had been Guiliano's only official mistress.

Was this little wench a daughter of Clement's, get on some Circassian slave? Her looks were about right for it. In which case, Tommaso guessed, she was being groomed to become a lady-in-waiting to one of Rome's aristocratic families. That would explain her being assigned to learn kitchen duties. It would also explain her ineptitude.

But what about Alessandro's actions? Tommaso knew he had not mistaken the youth's hostility, or his intention to harm the girl. Had he witnessed rivalry between two of the pope's favorites?

The girl finished unbuckling the basket. Tommaso felt the weight at his back ease as she carefully drew Gattamelata out.

"Look 'Sandro, isn't she lovely?"

Tommaso, easing the carrier from his shoulders, ducked his head to hide a grin. In truth, dangling by her armpits from the girl's grip, her kitten-full belly bulging out and her flat little head sunk into her shoulders, Gattamelata looked more silly than lovely. As she was swung in Alessandro's direction she laid back her ears, bristled her fur like a hedgehog, drew her lips back over pink gums to expose snakelike fangs, and hissed. She reached out her front paws toward the youth, grabbing at him with fully extended claws.

Alessandro paled and backed hastily up the steps. "More demon spawn." He tried to make it a joke, but he looked shaken.

"Don't be silly, 'Sandro. She's here to catch rats. All the rats in the house. Even the biggest and most treacherous ones." It was clear that the girl hadn't mistaken Alessandro's intentions. "And just look at her. Any day now she'll have a fine litter. Then there will be lots just like her, crawling everywhere all over the house, ready to pounce when the rats least expect it."

Alessandro scrambled backward to the top of the stairs and almost bumped into Piera, who was coming out the kitchen door. Ginevra peered from behind her. "What is going on out here? Ah, Tommaso, at last you've arrived with the spices. I was beginning to worry."

Alessandro recoiled. He looked as afraid of Piera as he had been of Gattamelata. He muttered something unintelligible and ducked past her and Ginevra into the kitchen.

As soon as he vanished the little girl scooped Gattamelata up into a more comfortable position in her arms. She ducked her head to nuzzle the cat, who immediately started purring. The girl looked up at Tommaso from under thick eyelashes.

"Thank you," she murmured. "I knew you would arrive when I needed you." Tommaso wasn't sure if she meant him or Gattamelata.

"Come, you two," Piera scolded. "We need those spices to finish preparing dinner. Tommaso, you can stay and lend a hand to make up for your tardiness. And you, my *befanini*, can find a cozy safe spot for Gattamelata."

Again Tommaso was startled. Befanini—was this servant girl a relative of his and not a Medici after all? Then he realized that his mother had meant it as a fond sobriquet. *Befanini* meant "little witch" and was a kind of cake; a delicate biscuit spackled generously with colored pralines.

The kitchen was crowded. Besides Tommaso's grandfather and grandmother Befanini, his grandfather's mother, Angelina, and her brother, the grand pater Giacomo Befanini (who though ancient was still proud master carver of the house), and the regular scullery servants, a host of aunts, uncles, and cousins had come in from the Medici country estates to help. Tommaso didn't see how he, his mother, Ginevra, and the little Medici bastard could squeeze in, especially since his mother was almost as pregnant as Gattamelata.

But it was the food that truly filled the room to almost overflowing.

Almond cream soup with pigeon steamed in a warming tureen, waiting to be served as part of the first course. The smooth, rich taste of the almond cream married to the morsels of gentle bird would soothe the diners' palates and allow their appetites to take wing for the rest of the meal.

Pappardelle boiled in a pot nearby. When these wide, flat, venerable noodles, so beloved by the ancient Etruscans, finished cooking they would be drowned in a rich red sauce of rabbit and served alongside the soup, comforting those who had dined too lightly earlier in the day and arrived at the table in pain with hunger.

A spit-roasting boar took up almost the whole of the fireplace. This must be the beast that Cosimo Ruggiero said Ippolito de' Medici had brought down. It looked almost finished. Slabs of bread balanced on the grill below caught its aromatic, dripping juices. Tommaso saw no sign of the stag Cosimo said Alessandro had killed. It was probably hanging to age in the meat cellar.

The kitchen tables and benches were covered with serving platters waiting to be burdened with fried veal sweetbreads napped with eggplant sauce, buckwheat polenta flecked with green speckles of silver beet, pies stuffed to bursting with pork, eggs, sausage, and dates, grilled trout, milk curds sprinkled with sugar and cinnamon, mortadella served with boiled whole onions and *gobbi*, quince fritters, pear tarts, saffron jellies. Tommaso's belly felt filled just trying to inventory the feast. The Ruggieros often entertained lavishly, but nothing to match this. In all the times Tommaso had visited his mother's family in the Medici kitchens it had never been so crowded. This must match the days when Lorenzo the Magnificent fêted all Florence.

"The spices, the spices," Grandfather Befanini called out when he caught sight of Tommaso.

"The spices, the spices!" The rest of the clan took up the cry. Cousins banged knives on saucepans, scullery maids clacked spoons together. Tommaso blushed and bowed, held up the satchel his father had given him. Piera pushed him forward gently. "Help Father sort them out. Then make yourself useful. Afterward, you can join us in *la matta cena* before going home."

Tommaso looked around at the chaos again. Dining here would be a "mad supper" indeed.

Grandfather Befanini clapped him around his shoulders and drew him to the small table at the other end of the kitchen that served as the accounts desk. Tommaso described the contents and weight of each spice packet while his grandfather noted them down in his ledger. Tommaso looked at him out of the corner of one eye. His grandfather was in his late fifties. It never ceased to surprise Tommaso that such a tall, masculine-looking older man could look so much like his mother Piera, the epitome of feminine youth and grace. That trick of appearance was the doing of the sly, illegitimate de' Medici blood.

Tommaso felt a tug at his leggings. "Tommaso, Tommaso! Where is Beatrice?" He looked down into a small, round rosy face, two chubby little outstretched hands. Tommaso looked at his grandfather, who nodded his permission. "I'll take care of distributing the spices," Grandfather Befanini said.

Tommaso swept the toddler up into his arms. "Well, Pietro, she is hard

at work shelling peas and helping Father back at home. She told me to tell
you that she misses you."

"I miss her too."

"Have you been helping Mother here?"

Pietro rubbed his eyes with flour-dusted fingers. "I've been kneading
bread."

"And have you been a good boy?"

"Of course!" This was said so indignantly that even if their grandfather hadn't roared with laughter as he left Tommaso would have known
that his little brother had been, as usual, into all kinds of mischief.

"I see. Forgive me for doubting you."

Tommaso turned to a light tap on his shoulder. Ginevra stood there
holding the now-plucked pheasant. It was clear who had finished the task:
gold and auburn down clung to her as if she were some small angel. It only
added to the seraphic impression she always gave, with her serene demeanor,
rose-tinged porcelain skin, dove-shaped gray eyes, and doe-colored hair.

"How *is* Beatrice, truly?"

Tommaso laughed. "Well, in *truth*, she is woeful and glum out of all
proportion. You'd think her some wizened old hen instead of a five-year-
old. She misses Mother. She misses you. She especially misses fussing after
Pietro here."

Ginevra reached over to tidy Pietro's unruly brown curls. "You know
how inseparable they've been up until now."

Tommaso nodded. "Mother says that's how we were too when we were
that little."

"My big brother who protected me on one hand and tormented me
on the other."

"Protected? Tormented? You speak as though it were the ancient past.
I thought I still did."

Ginevra laughed. "How could I deny you the employment? You'll be
glad to know that I've been able to keep up on my studies, even without
you to help me. I've been privileged to help the *Duchessina* with her recita-
tions. You would be amazed at her learning, Tommaso. I think she knows
as much as Cosimo Ruggiero, yet she's a few months younger than me."

"Actually, I can well imagine," Tommaso said somewhat sourly, thinking how even the de' Medicis' bastard-get servants could quote Petrarca freely.

"Are Passerini and Cardinals Cibó and Ridolfi to be kept waiting on their supper because two of my children must stand and chatter?" Piera stood behind them with her hands on her hips, the de' Medici get peering around her. There was a frown on Piera's face, but her words were mild and her eyes smiled as she scolded. Although cooks must be discreet about their employers, Tommaso knew his mother disliked Cardinal Passerini as much as the rest of Florence.

"Ginevra, give me the pheasant and go wash up. You'll be taking in some of the dishes, so you two girls need to change before supper is served. Tommaso, put your brother down and help your cousin Umberto untruss the boar. After that you can clean and trim artichokes, then sweep up the broken plate in the courtyard."

"I found a nice place for your cat," the blond girl told Tommaso. "She's already nesting happily."

"Gattamelata is here?" Pietro crowed. "Where, where?"

"She's in the bread pantry."

Pietro raced off on chubby legs. "At least that should keep him out of harm's way until dinner is served," Piera sighed.

The two girls giggled and walked out of the kitchen with their arms around each other. Tommaso had another thought. The de' Medici get was probably being groomed to be the *Duchessina*'s lady-in-waiting. It made perfect sense, that the pope would keep family interests knitted tightly together by having an illegitimate cousin always at her side. Better that than let an outsider become her helpmate and confidante. And what about Ginevra? The two girls seemed very close. Tommaso's heart sank in his chest. Was Ginevra being trained to serve the *Duchessina* too? Would he lose his sister to the far-ranging de' Medicis?

Ginevra and the little blond girl stood in the middle of a room another floor up in the palazzo. As they changed clothes they took care not to let their dirty work smocks brush against any of the room's fine furniture.

Eight years ago this space had served as a nursery for an aristocratic orphaned infant. Now it boasted a canopied bed, an ivory-framed mirror, a rosewood stand bearing a chess set, a writing desk with an inlaid marble top on which sat a fine agate vase filled with flowers, some small but fine tempera panels depicting courtiers walking with their ladies in a garden and dancing at court, a multitude of chests and trunks, and several ornately carved chairs and stools.

Ginevra stooped to pick up and fold her discarded smock, then dusted stray flour from her gray woolen *gamurra*.

"Leave that for the maid," the little de' Medici said. "Come help me with this." She laughed. "I'm all tangled up."

"What did you think of my brother?" Ginevra asked as she pulled the garment over the other girl's head. The yellow-haired girl's reply was muffled by the clothing.

"What?"

The other girl pulled free. "I said, I think he has a good heart. He fairly flew up the stairs to intervene with 'Sandro on my behalf. He didn't know what to do when he got there—still, it was very brave of him. And, as it turned out, that was enough." Underneath the work smock she wore a sleeveless *gamurra* of honey-colored linen. The chemise trailing below was a rich peach hue.

She looked thoughtful. "He takes a while to think things through. He's not as bright and quick as, say, Ippolito."

It was Ginevra's turn to laugh. "In your eyes, no man is." She opened a chest. "Which sleeves do you wish to wear tonight?"

"The pomegranate-colored ones with the little seed pearls woven in. All right—a fair point on quickness, but I would say he is not as quick as you. But then, in my eyes few others—even Ippolito—are, except for your mother."

Ginevra flushed, both in pleasure at the compliment and annoyance at the slight to her older brother. She bowed her head as she threaded the sleeves' attaching ribbons through the slits in the *gammura's* arm holes.

"I'm not saying that your brother is dull," the other girl said hastily. "Simply that he seems one of those likely to mull a thing over, to consider it slowly from all sides before coming to a decision. Who is to say there is not, in the end, greater wisdom in such a path? And there is something else to him, something earnest and yet unformed." She giggled again. "But, until 'Sandro's arrival, I thought it would take him forever to climb the kitchen steps."

She touched Ginevra's cheek with light fingers. "And, like you, he is lovely to look on." She sighed and retrieved her hand, rubbing her palm down her own dull-complexioned cheek. "How it would help my future if I were as pretty as you or your brother."

Ginevra picked up a flaxen brush and began to dress the other girl's tresses. "How can you say that, Caterina? Don't you know how many women and girls squeeze lemon juice into their hair or petition the apothecaries for concoctions to turn their curls exactly the color of your own, as if lead could indeed be turned to gold? Or how many use those black pastes from the Orient to make their eyes appear as large and dark as yours? Our master Ruggiero has predicted you will grow tall and fair." Ginevra clicked her tongue. "Perhaps it would be wiser to ask God that you reach womanhood a little *less* attractive and striking."

The other girl threw back her head and laughed. "Oh Ginevra, you are so wily, who can flatter and yet chastise me back into modesty both in the same breath. You truly are my gossip. I think, for my soul's salvation, that I should never let you leave my side."

4

Sitting in a far corner of the de' Medici kitchen, Tommaso cracked egg after egg into a large copper bowl. Saffron yolks slid through transparent whites to bump against each other so gently that the way they foundered and broke upon one another, releasing swirls of color, seemed impossible. His mother had once told Tommaso to be careful of his friendships; that like the eggs they could be ruptured by the slightest of shocks.

"Here's a whisk for that," his cousin Umberto said, handing Tommaso a wire whip. Umberto pulled up a stool for himself. Balancing a bowl of porcini in his lap, the older boy cut the mushrooms into quarters against his thumb with a small knife.

The serving platters scattered all over the kitchen were now filled with food and laid out by course. The Befaninis and their helpers stepped back to make room as the serving staff bore away the first-course dishes to the great sideboard in the banquet hall for display.

Suddenly the servers bowed low as a stately woman swept in. She was dressed in a brown umber gown, its sleeves and matching waistcoat a dark blue velvet embroidered with gold thread. Three boys trailed her. They wore the same de' Medici livery as the other servants. But though they looked attentive and respectful, they also bore traces of resentment on their faces and didn't carry themselves like servants.

"That's Madame Clarice Strozzi," Umberto whispered in Tommaso's ear. "The boys are three of her ten sons. They've been put to squire's duty tonight as wine servers to the cardinals."

Madame Strozzi toured the kitchen. She sniffed at and prodded each dish in turn, occasionally beckoning for a small fork to extract morsels to taste. As each platter gained her nod of approval it was whisked away to the banquet hall by a server.

"Not even Madame Strozzi's dislike for Passerini will allow her to abandon the de' Medici tradition of hosting an excellent table," Umberto whispered again. "Pope Clement still retains some wits after all. In asking Madame Strozzi to return to Florence and manage the palazzo while Passerini is in control of the city, the pope has neatly arranged that the *Duchessina* remains safe, the Medici properties stay under the stewardship of the only Medici the *Signoria* have any respect for, and Clarice herself stays too busy too cause him any trouble. It's said she hates her cousin the pope as much as she scorns Passerini."

Tommaso was fascinated by Clarice Strozzi. She possessed a commanding presence. Her huge black de' Medici eyes, instead of the soft doe-dark of his mother Piera's, were fierce and watchful as a hawk's. When she completed her circuit, Tommaso felt all his relatives silently releasing held-in breaths: She had not rejected a single dish.

She reached the head of the kitchen, where the ancient master carver Giacomo stood at attention. Next to him his sister, Tommaso's great-grandmother Angelina, too frail to stand, perched on a stool like an ancient dull crow. And attentively beside her, her only child, Grandfather Befanani.

"Maestro carver and chef, the dinner is excellent." Clarice Strozzi's voice was rich and rounded with a meaty bite to its undertones. "I'm sure our blessed ecclesiastical guests"—the bite sharpened—"will be praising this repast for months to come. We are looking forward to a display of your carving skills as our midmeal fête."

Giacomo bowed low, his carving set tucked under his arm.

To Tommaso's surprise, Clarice Strozzi turned to his great-grandmother and took the crone's clawlike hands in her own soft aristo-cratic ones.

"And you, Angelina. Don't think it has escaped my attention how this kitchen, deserted and neglected by my family for so long, has nonetheless continued to flourish and excel under your benign guardianship."

Angelina cocked her head to one side as a dusty old bird might. A smile slid across her face and vanished, like the swift passing of a small cloud's shadow on a windy, sunny day.

Clarice looked up and met Angelina's son's de' Medici eyes. Grandfather Befanini nodded.

Tommaso shot a glance at Umberto, hoping for an explanation, but Umberto had returned to quartering mushrooms.

As soon as Clarice left the Befaninis leapt into action. The courses to be served later were shoved together. There was again space to work in.

One of Piera's sisters slid the boar-juice saturated crusts from the grill and tossed them into a pot hung over the coals. Then she drizzled olive oil over them. As soon as they steamed with a rich aroma she threw in vegetable water, chopped savoy cabbage, and leftover chickpeas to make a hearty bread soup.

Another sister's husband chopped fish to pat into *poltettina fritte* while Piera poured oil into a deep skillet to fry the croquettes when he was ready.

"I'll go heat our pans," Umberto said. Tommaso nodded. He beat the eggs till they frothed, then added the mushrooms and several handfuls of bright orange zucchini blossoms.

Umberto shouted "Ready!"

Tommaso poured the mixture into the frittata pans and stood by with several big *tondi*. When the frittate had cooked through on one side, Umberto slid them onto Tommaso's wooden plates. Umberto placed the pans over the plates and together the two boys flipped the frittate back into the pans. The pans were returned to the fire so that the other sides would cook evenly.

Medici-liveried attendants removed the second course of the aristocratic meal to the banquet hall, leaving room for the cooks to sit. Their wild rush of preparations culminated in perfect timing . . . their "mad meal" was ready to eat.

Plates were piled high with salads of wild herbs and spring greens, slices of a borage-savory spelt loaf, and cooked stuffed celery. Bowls of soup sent up plumes of aromatic steam. Umberto and Tommaso's frittate were slid from their pans at the moment of perfection. The puffy omelets stood stalwartly high, both sides evenly golden, their insides buttery soft. The fish *poltettina fritte* were crisp outside but melted hotly on the tongue.

All of the kitchen's wild clatter, laughter, and shouted instructions died away, replaced by the muted clicking of forks, knives, and spoons against plates and the contented murmur of serious diners concentrating on their food.

In the silence and self-absorption Tommaso studied his extended family. They were enjoying the satisfaction of good work achieved together; the reward of resting briefly and regaining strength from the product of their combined efforts; the warmth of camaraderie. This was what he usually felt—albeit on a smaller, more intimate scale—back at the Ruggieros'. This was what he and his father had been missing since his mother's return to the de' Medicis.

Piera passed around more of the soup. As if she guessed what Tommaso was thinking, she sat down and chatted with him briefly. He brought her up to date on gossip from the Ruggiero household. She asked him why he'd been so late bringing the spices. He made light of the chase. Why should he worry her needlessly? Undoubtedly the Arrabbiati had gone on to other pursuits. Tommaso told his mother only that he'd been harrassed by young blades. Piera looked at him skeptically. Tommaso knew she intended to interrogate him more fully, but the remains of the second course—roasts followed by palate-reviving pastel-colored fruit ices—returned under Great-Uncle Giacomo's supervision just then. The third course of boiled meats and stews was rushed out.

The kitchen help hurried to finish their own suppers. When the fourth and final course had been served it would be just a short time before the servers and wine stewards, forced to attend the entire banquet in mute abstinence, descended on the kitchen like locusts. Their dinner must be artfully contrived from the leftovers before they arrived.

Piera left Tommaso to start wrestling platter-strewn scraps into fresh new dishes. As she stood to go Tommaso felt a heavy gaze fall upon them.

He glanced up to find his great-grandmother watching. Tommaso dropped his eyes to his work. Of all his vast, extended family, the only member he did not feel completely comfortable with, who filled him with unease, was Angelina Befanini.

He did not know exactly why that was. Mute and barely present in the bustling kitchen setting, she posed no threat. But Tommaso felt her presence as a disquieting absence, a deep dark well that one could fall into if one came too close.

And there was another thing that bothered him, though he would have admitted it to no one, even himself. His older relatives were always comparing him to her. According to them, in her younger years her hair and coloring had matched his precisely. Even the timbre of her voice, though lighter, had supposedly been similar to his, as if she had provided the template for his existence.

Tommaso glanced over at her. The old woman had looked away. Her blank gaze fell harmlessly now on the great kitchen fireplace. He watched her with some dread. If her hair had once glowed the same auburn as his own, all that remained were rusty streaks staining straggling wisps of dull gray. Perhaps her eyes had once shone the same golden brown as his. If so, they'd faded badly to an eerie light ocher. And the things Tommaso felt defined his life—a fully present enjoyment of each moment and a strong desire to struggle and succeed—seemed entirely extinguished in every part of her being.

"Tommaso, if you've finished there, look lively. The guests are retiring from the banquet hall. The servers could use our help clearing the table." Umberto's voice cut through Tommaso's uneasy reverie. Tommaso leapt up and hurried after his cousin.

The banquet hall proved more chaotic than he expected. Due to the cardinals' sacred status the usual protocol for exiting the dining area had broken down. Instead of the ladies retiring first, the cardinals and their retinue led in withdrawing. Apparently they'd taken their time about it too, for the women still milled about.

Tommaso caught sight of his sister Ginevra among the gaily colored throng, a pretty gray dove flocking with peacocks. The girl she stood chatting with wore a gown as bright as a summer bouquet. The little aristocrat's elaborately braided and coiled curls were tucked into a crocheted cap of golden thread, while Ginevra's hair flowed smoothly and naturally from under a plain cap of white embroidered linen.

Ginevra saw Tommaso. She smiled and lifted one hand. The other girl turned with a sedate and regal air to see who Ginevra was waving to.

Tommaso's breath caught in his throat and his mouth hung open. He knew her at once and, finally, who she really was. He felt his face flushing so deeply that it must match her pearl-bangled sleeves of deep red. He tried to remember everything he'd said to her on the steps and in the kitchen. Had he insulted her?

Ginevra's hand dropped to cover her mouth. She was trying not to giggle. The *Duchessina*'s lips stretched in a widening grin. Tommaso knew that both girls had instantly understood the true nature of his flustered reaction. He snapped his mouth closed and bent over in a deep bow to cover his misery.

When he raised up, Ginevra's eyes were moist with suppressed tears of laughter, but the *Duchessina* had ceased smiling altogether. Tommaso's heart sank. She turned to face him fully. Her dark eyes grave, she returned his bow with a court-perfect formal curtsy. Then she favored him with a smile of such shy, sweet grace that he knew he was forgiven and that his embarrassment would stay her secret.

But then she frowned and turned to look over her shoulder. Tommaso followed her gaze. Alessandro hovered in the doorway, glaring at her. Tommaso shivered. There was such menace and hatred in the youth's face that Tommaso wouldn't have been surprised if Caterina crumpled and withered away under its force.

She didn't. She visibly straightened and returned it with a glare of her own, first contemptuous and then utterly dismissing. She swung back to Tommaso and smiled at him again.

Tommaso's breath caught in his throat.

The moon had risen to meet Florence's rooftops by the time Tommaso finished helping his mother's family clean up after the banquet and was given leave to return home.

He'd been in such a daze that he'd strapped the basket to his back and was ready to go when Piera reminded him that he also needed to take the accounting for the spices and the satchel. Clicking his tongue in mild reproval, Grandfather Befanini himself slid the satchel into the basket. Trying to hide his chagrin Tommaso hugged Pietro and his bemused mother good-bye, promising to give all their messages to Gentile and Beatrice.

He barely felt his feet touching the pavers of the Via Largo. The thoughts floating through his mind buoyed him like drifting clouds. What was it his father had said to him, several lifetimes ago earlier in the day? "Study *those* you serve as avidly as *what* you serve."

The upper classes of Florence often deigned to visit the humble confines of their kitchens and even made sure to know a little of the art of cooking. But never had Tommaso heard of an heiress forced to labor as a scullery maid. Why had she been set to pluck a pheasant on the back steps? Then he remembered that Cosimo Ruggiero said that *Duchessina* Caterina had brought down two fine, fat pheasants during the hunt, so the pheasant must have been hers. Even so . . . Tommaso thought of how familiar his mother and sister were with her, of her courage in the face of Alessandro's hostility. Why did Alessandro hate her so much?

But most of all Tommaso kept picturing Caterina nibbling at the plate of *cibreo,* distracted from her chore by her pleasure in the dish. Tommaso whistled a few bars of a happy tune. He already knew how to cook *cibreo* well.

That was his last thought before he felt himself lifted up off the ground and backward. He was thrown against a wall in a narrow, dark alley, knocking the breath out of him and abrading one side of his face. He slid to the ground. Kicks and blows began to rain down.

5

Did you think your charlatan of a master or the Medici tyrants he serves could protect you, little lapdog?" a voice hissed above him. A kick caught Tommaso solidly in the hamstring and he yowled.

"Take him farther in. We're too close to the road," another voice muttered. They grabbed Tommaso by his arms and the basket and dragged him down the alley. Tommaso couldn't see their faces in the dark, but there were five attackers altogether. The three Arrabbiati he'd escaped that afternoon had found reinforcements. Even if his leg wasn't numb and spasming from the kick he knew he couldn't scramble to his feet and get away from so many.

A flat-handed blow caught him alongside his wall-bruised face. Tommaso shrieked. The impact twisted him all the way around. He landed heavily on all fours. The cobblestones smelled of offal thrown from the windows above and urine.

An upward kick caught him in the stomach. The muscles there roiled in waves. He retched, coughed, vomited his entire dinner. Above him the Arrabbiati laughed.

"Do you think we mean to kill you?" one of them said. "Not at all. We want you alive to present our warning to your masters." A leisurely, almost soft kick pitched Tommaso forward into his own spew. The Arrabbiati laughed again. Tommaso curled tightly in on himself.

"Actually, I think it would be hard to kill you with a beating," the voice continued. "You're cushioned by a nice layer of fat, unlike honest, hard-working Florentines who are starving because of Passerini's greed."

The next kick was vicious. Tommaso was glad that the crushed remnants of the basket, still strapped to his back, protected him somewhat. He cried weakly, feeling no shame at all.

They pulled him up from the ground by the basket and used it to swing him around. Tommaso guessed that befouled as he was, the Arrabbiati had no desire to further lay hands on him. They swung him into the wall, against a rain barrel, then into the wall again. Tommaso moaned and closed his eyes. They spun him round and round. He was sure they'd eventually let him go to hurl down the alley or fly full force into the wall.

There was a sound of scuffling. The trajectory of his spin changed abruptly. He was yanked backward again, then just held dangling. He heard more scuffling and the sound of blows. Tommaso flinched, but none seemed to be landing on him. All at once the alley was dotted with light. Soon after that the commotion ceased.

The narrow corridor was filled with men. Several of them held torches. As light touched Tommaso's face one of the newcomers reached for him and Tommaso felt his unseen rescuer hand him over. His redeemer faded back into the shadows of the crowd, but not before Tommaso glimpsed a young, beautifully sculpted narrow face surmounted by huge, dark eyes.

De' Medici eyes, Tommaso thought deliriously. They are everywhere.

"So, Agostino, is this why you've come down from Carrara? To thrash children? Is this the kind of task that Francesco Carducci is setting his followers these days?" The bearded man asking the questions held one of the torches. Its light played over the dramatic, rough hewn planes of his middle-aged face.

The Arrabbiati that Cousin Leonora had delayed on the Ponte Vecchio stood wedged between two glaring, stalwart men. Tommaso's left eye had puffed up and swollen shut, but with his right he saw that Agostino's face also bore some damage. This cheered Tommaso considerably.

"Ser Buonarotti," the Arrabbiati stammered. He seemed unable to say anything more, whether because he could think of no excuse, or perhaps he was struck by awe. It was no small thing to be caught in such an act of cowardice by one of Florence's most famous citizens.

"Haul them off to the watch and hand them over," the older man said and turned away.

"*Ser* Buonarotti, please, for the love of my father!" Agostino finally found his voice.

The man whirled on him. "For the love of your father? If *you* loved your father you would have stayed home in Carrara and continued to honestly quarry marble."

"Would that I could," Agostino shouted as he struggled in the hands of his captors. "But thanks to Cardinal Passerini's tariffs and taxations, there's no work for honorable men in Carrara. Divine Michelangelo, should we stay there and quietly starve?"

The sculptor looked at him with contempt. "Better that than amuse yourself by beating innocent children. At least you would have saved your honor." With a wave of his hand he dismissed them. "Take them away," he told the men who held them.

When they'd gone the sculptor angled his torch so he could look at Tommaso. His nostrils widened, then pinched, and he winced back a little before his mouth twisted in a wry smile. "It looks from what's left of his livery that our young friend hails from the house of Ruggiero."

Tommaso nodded, his lips too bruised to answer.

From the rear of the cluster of remaining men, the good-looking young blood who'd rescued Tommaso spoke up. "I think I saw this boy earlier this very evening. He may serve the house of Ruggiero, but I believe he is one of the Befanini children."

Tommaso blinked in surprise. The youth must have been one of the diners at the Medici palace. Tommaso hadn't noticed him. But then, in his brief stint of clearing the tables, he'd only had eyes for the *Duchessina.*

"In that case, 'Lito, to you falls the task of telling those good cooks that one of their red-crested cockerels has narrowly missed being tenderized, filleted, and braised," Michelangelo quipped.

The men laughed at that. Tommaso might have joined them but his face hurt too much.

" 'Lito, were you seen by those ruffians?"

"I don't believe so. It was dark in here until you brought the torches," the youth said.

"Nonetheless, take Bernardo with you," the sculptor said. "It is clear that danger walks the streets tonight. Be careful before you venture out again."

Michelangelo Buonarotti turned back to Tommaso. "And now, what to do with you? Your wounds should be attended to and you need to be cleaned up. Can you walk?"

The fellow holding Tommaso up by his arm released his grip with an air of relief. Tommaso began to fall forward as his weight shifted to his injured leg. With a sigh the man hauled him back up again.

"Girolamo, give good Antonio a hand there," Michelangelo ordered another man. "The boy appears too damaged to make it home, whichever place that is. Our original destination is closer. Il Tribolino's *bottega* will surely have the means to lave and succor our little chef." He gestured to some other men. "And you two, go inform the house of Ruggiero."

Tommaso was glad to find that the workshop Michelangelo referred to was only a block away. And so, he felt sure, were the two young men who braced him under each arm and gingerly hoisted him along like an animate pair of crutches.

Girolamo was a stranger to Tommaso, but he recognized Antonio Gondi. The Gondis, a small banking family, were clients of *Doctore* Ruggiero. Tommaso had glimpsed Antonio there several times. With his high forehead and clear eyes surmounted by lightly etched eyebrows, Antonio possessed the look of a mild-mannered intellectual. Unfortunately, at this moment, those fine eyes were narrowed to slits and Antonio's small, delicate mouth pursed in distaste.

Wretched with embarrassment at his sorry state, Tommaso wished he could throw himself into the Arno to wash off the worst of the muck clinging to him. And if he should drown in the process, all the better. Every buffet and blow he'd received throbbed. So sharp was one particular pain in his side that he could barely draw breath into his lungs. With each step his body became stiffer and stiffer. Tommaso groaned. He had been saved by a party captained by one of Italy's most famous artists and he was hardly worth scraping off the offal pile.

"Here we are," the sculptor declared, pounding on a stout, iron-bound door. An apprentice let them in.

"Michelangelo." A slender man in his early forties hurried forward, dusting plaster flour from his leather apron. "I confess, I expected a somewhat larger company."

"Fear not, Tribolino." Michelangelo clapped his friend on the shoulder. "Your prospective patrons will find their way here, after they turn over a few errant Arrabbiati to the watch. Their appetite for beauty will only be whetted by a little adventure." The sculptor briefly described the encounter with the ruffians and the rescue of Tommaso. "So you see, before we can treat ourselves to a viewing of your latest work, we need your aid in succoring our young companion here."

Tribolino looked at Tommaso doubtfully. "I believe he needs cleaning up first." He clapped his hands. Several more apprentices appeared. Il Tribolino pointed to Tommaso. "Take him in the back and prepare a bath for him. He seems sorely hurt, so help him in the matter."

The apprentices took over the yeomen's duty for Antonio and Girolamo. With little enthusiasm they half-carried Tommaso through the high-ceilinged space, winding a circuitous route around huge blocks of plaster, half chipped away to reveal the cast bronze treasures within.

The kitchen was in a warren of rooms at the back. With the help of a stout-armed woman servant they rolled out a tub for Tommaso to stand in. They heated enough water in kettles to pour over him. When they saw the extent of his bruises they ceased to act so repulsed and gently scrubbed him. What he had suffered could be the fate of any servant or apprentice, even themselves. When he was bathed and dried they dressed him in worn but clean leggings and a smock and helped him back into the studio.

The compatriots of Michelangelo who'd been sent in search of the watch had rejoined the group. They all stood by a big burning furnace, drinking wine and talking. Small models of sculptures were displayed on workbenches around them. The air smelled of cold dusty plaster and hot burning wax.

Tribolino turned and saw Tommaso and his attendants approaching. "Aha, your victim returns. I believe he is presentable enough to suffer an examination now."

"Yes, whereas before *we* would have been the ones who would have suffered," Girolamo jested.

The others all laughed, except Antonio Gondi, who pulled over a stool for Tommaso to sit on. To Tommaso's relief, the young man's face had relaxed from distaste into kindliness.

Tommaso gasped as he sat. The pain in his side sliced straight into his lungs, cutting off his breath.

"Who shall do the honors?"

"I believe that should go to *Ser* Buonarotti. He is, after all, the master anatomist here," Antonio Gondi said.

Michelangelo drew up another stool to sit facing Tommaso. He put one hand under Tommaso's chin. Although the sculptor's fingers were coarse and rough-burred with calluses, he turned Tommaso's head from side to side with gentle, delicate movements.

"So, victim," he said. "How different you look out of that dark alley and into the light. Do you have a name?"

"Tommaso, son of Gentile Arista," Tommaso mumbled through bruised lips. "My mother is Piera Befanini."

Tribolino whistled and then chuckled. "A princeling of the culinary guild."

Michelangelo frowned at his friend. "I doubt *you* would be chortling if you'd endured as much pain as Tommaso here."

The sculptor touched Tommaso's face again. "Here, all the damage is on the left side only. The skin is thoroughly abraded, the lip split and puffy, and soon you'll boast a full spectrum of violets, blues and greens with that black eye. On the right side, nary a mark. In one person, turning from profile to profile, you could serve as a model for heaven and hell. On one side, an abused demon. On the other, an angel."

He cupped the back of Tommaso's skull with his other hand, his touch softly probing and almost sensual. "Have you felt dizzy, or like swooning?"

Tommaso shook his head slightly.

"No swelling lumps. That is good. What extraordinary hair and coloring you have." The sculptor brushed the unscathed side of Tommaso's face with his fingertips.

Tommaso suppressed a shiver. Michelangelo Buonarotti might be the most revered artist in all Italy, but he was rumored to have a strong, if discreet, preference for young men and boys.

Michelangelo smiled. "Titian would give a thousand of his beloved Venetian canals to have you pose for one of his paintings. I've never seen a better match to his ideal."

He pulled back the sleeves on the smock and examined Tommaso's arms. Purple bruises mottled the length of both of them. "You pulled them up to protect yourself, didn't you?"

Tommaso nodded.

"Neither seems broken, but I wager it will be weeks before Master Ruggiero gets any heavy labor out of you."

Although Tommaso relaxed as he realized that Michelangelo's gaze was intent but detached, he could not seem to rid himself of the incipient shiver. He whimpered when the sculptor tried to pull the smock over his head.

Michelangelo raised an eyebrow. He settled for carefully rolling the smock up as far as he could. With gentle fingers he probed Tommaso's side.

Tommaso cringed.

"A broken rib at least," Michelangelo murmured. He rocked back on his stool and ran one hand through his beard. "Your master is the physician, not I. The best thing would be to poultice and bind you, then send you home in a litter."

He gestured to Tribolino and asked for clean rags and an herbal poultice. "And you, Girolamo. Pour some of that mulled wine for the boy. He's shaking."

Tommaso's teeth were chattering now. Antonio Gondi threw a cloak over his shoulders while Michelangelo held a cup to his lips. The aromatic steam cleared Tommaso's head and calmed him before he'd drunk a sip. The hot liquid poured down his throat, filling him with warmth until he felt as though every vein ran with molten gold.

"There. Much better. Of a sudden you'd begun to turn to alabaster." Michelangelo motioned for a goblet for himself.

"We'll all be binding broken children ere long," said Girolamo, handing him one.

"I'm afraid you're right," said Michelangelo. "Agostino's means were wrong, but he had reason to complain. Desperate men take desperate measures. Pope Clement's policies are turning the *popolo* not only against himself, but the Medici family. And not only the Medici family, but against the papacy itself. He is blinding himself to other, grimmer alternatives looming on the horizon."

"The godless Germans," someone whispered into the silence that fell at Michelangelo's words. "Even now the *Reiters* march on Rome."

"Yes, and I'm afraid Clement will bungle it badly with them." An apprentice brought the supplies Michelangelo had asked for. The sculptor set them by his stool. He sighed. "How could one who showed such canny promise as a cardinal grow into such a bad pope? God, mysterious indeed are Your ways, but please show a bit more mercy for poor Florence. Drink a little more wine, Tommaso."

Tommaso drank till the heat of the liquor blazed in his face. Michelangelo slid the cloak from his shoulders and asked him to extend his arms. The sculptor began to apply the poultice to his ribs.

"It is Cardinal Silvio Passerini who is to blame for Florence's woes, not Clement," protested Il Tribolino.

"And who was it who inflicted Passerini upon us?" asked Michelangelo. "I know for a fact that Francesco Guicciardini, who is in the pope's confidence even more than you or I, wrote to Clement complaining of the cardinal's incompetence in managing Florence's affairs. He even called Passerini a eunuch! Yet the pope chose to turn a deaf ear. Now, why do you suppose Clement did that? Think on it for a moment."

He stretched and smoothed the wrappings. "Tommaso, I will bind you enough to support you, but no more than that. I cannot tell exactly where the ends of that broken rib wander about within you, so I don't want to press too strongly. Do you understand?"

Tommaso nodded. But as Michelangelo began to wrap him, pain shot through his side. He keened and clutched at the sculptor with clawed hands. Michelangelo rocked back on his stool in surprise.

Tommaso dropped his hands in embarrassment, then whimpered at the twinges even that small motion caused.

The artist ran a hand through Tommaso's hair. "It's all right, Tommaso." He swung off his stool and rummaged through a worktable. He came back with two plugs of hard brown wax. "Here, try this. I'll be as gentle as I can. Scream as much as you wish and grasp the wax as hard as you need to."

Tommaso concentrated on the texture of the dense, cold paraffin in each fist. He forced himself to let each agonizing pulse in his side translate into a desperate squeeze through his palms. By the time Michelangelo finished binding him he was panting with pain.

Michelangelo drew the cloak around his shoulders again and held more wine to his lips. "Rest a bit and we'll call for a litter to carry you home. You certainly will live, Tommaso, but your injuries are severe enough that Ruggiero should look at them as soon as possible."

"No need to call for a litter." One of the men who'd gone to alert the Ruggiero household had arrived while Tommaso was being tended to. "Messer Ruggiero is having one sent over. The boy's father will arrive with it shortly. Botello stayed on to show them the way. I would have gotten here sooner, but the household made us sit and tell the whole tale, and nothing would do but we answer every question."

He held up a big basket. "Then in their gratitude the kitchen staff loaded me up with this. My friends, we feast a second time tonight as a reward for our heroism!"

The group clapped and cheered. "Well done, Bembo!"

Bembo winked at Tommaso. "If those Arrabbiati had had the brains of donkeys they would have thought to ransom you for food rather than beat you."

Tommaso smiled lopsidedly around his split lip. He slowly unclenched his aching fists. The wax was warm, soft and pliable now. He pressed the two wads together into a single lump and picked at it aimlessly.

Most of the men crowded around the basket to see what morsels Gentile Arista had packed away as their reward. Antonio Gondi stood at one of the display tables, balancing a maquette in each hand. One was a model for a statue of the goddess Athena, the other for a statue of Mars. He looked from one to the other thoughtfully.

"I've been pondering your question all this while, Michelangelo," he said. "I confess I've come to no answer, for the situation makes no sense. Why would Pope Clement *deliberately* inflict a fool like Passerini on Florence? The Medici are still astute bankers. Such an action spites themselves as much as the rest of Florence. Besides, every last one of them loves this city. Tribolino here would say that they *are* Florence, as much as the stones in the buildings, the lions in the square, and the *Vacca* ringing in the campanile."

Il Tribolino nodded his head vigorously in agreement.

"Yes," said Michelangelo, wiping his hands clean of poultice on a scrap of leftover rag. "The Medicis love Florence. But they do not necessarily love Florentines. At least not Clement or his predecessor Pope Leo, or the *Duchessina*'s late father and grandfather."

He looked glum. "Popes Leo and Clement. Would that they were still the happy youths Giovanni and Giulio de' Medici I grew up with. When Giovanni became Pope Leo he did not forgive the Florentines for exiling them in their youth. Neither has Giulio. Beware, my friends. It is said that the lions in the square prowl restlessly these days. It's an ill omen."

"You would not speak in that fashion if 'Lito were still with us tonight," Antonio protested.

"No, I would not," Michelangelo admitted. "Ippolito is like the fine old de' Medici mold recast in good bronze once again." His eyes dropped to the floor. "Oh Lorenzo, why did you die so young?" he whispered, more to himself than to the rest of them.

The other revelers grew quiet. Of all those present, only the great sculptor had known Lorenzo the Magnificent.

Michelangelo looked up and regathered himself. "Besides honorable Ippolito, can you name me one other Medici worthy of the name?"

The men looked at each other uneasily. Even Tommaso knew it was Alessandro that Michelangelo referred to obliquely with such sarcasm.

"Well, there are the women," Bembo said haltingly.

"The *women?*" someone said.

"The little *Duchessina*," Bembo defended himself.

Tommaso's heart leapt.

Michelangelo shook his head. "An unproven filly. Soon enough the pope will find a way to betroth and marry her off to his advantage."

Tommaso's heart dropped.

"Then there's Clarice Strozzi," Bembo continued stubbornly.

"Clarice Strozzi?" Everyone broke into gales of laughter. Tommaso was scandalized, but the tension in the room was broken.

"Oh my, yes," Girolamo said, wiping tears from his eyes. He pointed to his genitals. "I often swear by the envy I suffer that woman, for she is far better endowed down there than myself."

Even Tribolino was laughing, though he tried to be stern. "Don't be disrespectful," he said.

"I'm not, truly. I may jest at her expense, but the very reasons I tweak her are the same reasons I would follow her willingly into battle."

"Just don't get in front of her on those battle lines if she gets irked with you. Have you ever been on a hunt with her and seen how she can shoot?" Bembo crossed himself. "The only person I have even more respect for is her husband Filippo. What courage that man must have to have gotten a leg up on her to father so many sons." He started to continue, but Antonio Gondi elbowed him and pointed to Tommaso.

"What? Oh yes, an innocent is present." Bembo clapped a hand over his mouth.

Michelangelo looked at Tommaso. "He doesn't look mortally offended. He probably knows more about sex than you do, Bembo. What is that you've got there, Tommaso?" the sculptor asked as the others roared at Bembo's expense.

Tommaso handed over the transformed ball of wax. "It's a pheasant," he said shyly.

"Indeed it is. A most excellent pheasant," said Michelangelo.

Almost without thinking Tommaso had shaped the *Duchessina*'s pheasant, as he imagined it must have looked trying to take flight to escape her.

"What is it?" Tribolino and some of the others crowded around. Michelangelo showed them the waxen bird.

"Where did you learn to sculpt like that?" Tribolino asked.

Tommaso felt bewildered. "I wasn't sculpting. I was just muddling about."

"Then how did you learn to muddle so well?"

"I've seen pheasants before. We cook them all the time. Usually I'm the one that dresses them out, so I know how their bones go, then the meat on top of that, then the skin and feathers on top of that. I was just copying what I know with the wax."

Il Tribolino looked nonplussed.

Michelangelo grinned. "Of course," he said. "It never occurred to me before, but all carvers and butchers *would* be natural anatomists. Gentlemen, it appears we did not after all come to the aid of a child, but rather a fellow artist."

Il Tribolino studied the small sculpture. "This is no small talent, young Tommaso. If you ever wish to explore the arts more fully you will always be welcome here."

Tommaso felt himself blushing again.

A pounding came at the door. "I'll wager that's the litter come to get you," Michelangelo said.

Before Michelangelo could turn away Tommaso snatched at his sleeve. "Wait, please," he begged the sculptor.

"What is it?"

"It's about the pheasant. The *Duchessina* caught and killed two such pheasants at a hunt."

Michelangelo looked baffled. "So?"

"It's important. *She's* important. She's only a little girl, but she did it all herself."

Michelangelo looked at Tommaso with a dawning light in his eyes. "I can see it's important to you, Tommaso. Are you trying to tell us we shouldn't discount Caterina Maria Romola too soon?"

Tommaso nodded his head, no longer brave enough to speak.

Michelangelo ruffled Tommaso's hair again. "You should not worry so. If *you* see such virtue in her, then others will too."

All the way home in the litter Michelangelo's touch lingered, not unpleasantly, on Tommaso's skin.

6

Cosimo Ruggiero could tell his father was concerned. Ruggiero the Old's movements were even slower and graver than usual as he went about the ornately oak-paneled room igniting tufts of herbs in the hanging censers. The study filled with aromatic nose-tingling fumes. Normally the great table in the center of the study was covered with weighing scales, apothecary jars filled with minerals or herbs, and all the other paraphernalia necessary for the preparation of medicinals.

But after Ruggiero the Old requested Cosimo clear away the bandages and medicines they'd doctored Tommaso with, the table lay sparsely decked with only two small oil lamps, several old manuscripts and a newer bound book of Euclidean geometry, a spate of academic implements, a single unlit candle, and a lump of phosphorus-saturated dolomite.

In spite of the way he'd jested with Tommaso earlier in the day and tweaked the boy for his superstitions, the fine hairs on the back of Cosimo's neck prickled when his father rolled around the great, round, purple-velvet-draped mirror from where it stood on its heavy oaken stand facing the wall near the window. Cosimo helped his father position the mirror so it would catch the moon's ermine light fully. Cosimo's breath caught, as it always did, when his father slid away the heavy fabric that covered the mirror, exposing the speculum's glossy black-glazed surface. The instant the moonlight touched it, it began to cloud over as though a fine silver dust was settling on it.

Cosimo shivered. He liked the cook's son and had been as distressed as the rest of the household by the attack on Tommaso. But it wasn't unusual for young toughs to gang together as *brigate* and vent their heated blood by bullying servant boys. Tommaso had survived the misadventure with cuts and bruises and a broken rib. Why had the incident engendered his father's more arcane preparations?

Ruggiero the Old drew a circle on the floor around the table with the lump of dolomite. As if he could read his son's thoughts he said, without pausing in his task, "Up until a few weeks ago there was never a time when someone under our protection and wearing our livery had to fear for their safety walking Florence's streets in the day or the night."

The circle finished, he stood and brushed his hands clean against each other. "Come. While the mirror charges, let us have a lesson." He gestured for Cosimo to sit beside him at the table and opened one of the books.

"Your education to this date has focused on language, history, mathematics, philosophy, anatomy, and physicking. You have also begun basic studies in those subjects most men deem impossible: knowledge and understanding of matters beyond the normal ken of our senses."

He sighed and stopped to gather his thoughts before continuing. "I have spoken to you before, my son, of the interconnectedness of all things; that God created this interweaving to achieve a divine and perfect balance."

Cosimo found himself distracted, as always, by the drifting phosphorescence rising from the circle's chalk. It floated up to form a gauzy wall around them. When it radiated through the smoke from the censers he saw lit up within the herbal fumes the figures of strange but simple creatures.

His father caught his glance. "I trust you do not fear *those*, my son. I've told you before that they are only the spirits of long-dead sea creatures. Aware of us they are not."

The luminous shapes wafting in the smoke believed they still swam in ancient seas. Cosimo tried to imagine what the place they thought themselves to be in looked like. How it smelled.

His father tapped the open astrology book gently to regain his attention. "They do serve, however, to illustrate my point."

Cosimo looked at the picture his father pointed to. A dizzying array of orbs intertwined there, meticulously rendered to appear transparent, revealing their structure.

"There are a multitude of spheres of existence besides our own. Most we cannot ever truly know. But observe"—the older man tapped the drawing again—"how they overlap and intersect. At those interstices they influence each other. Their gravities, like the Earth's and the Moon's, pull upon each other. And it is precisely those intersecting points and planes that we *can* know, by dint of meticulous study and research.

"With geometric laws we can construct the shape and size of an unknown form with knowledge of just a few points. Just so, once we learn to recognize these cosmological crosspoints, we can construe and apprehend whole other realms of existence."

Cosimo tried to guess what those preternatural points might be like. Far easier to imagine himself one of the chalk creatures, floating in a vast, warm, dark antediluvian ocean, the stars glimpsed only as wiggling worms of light through the heavy canopy of waves moving overhead, jostling against fellow sea creatures as playfully and simply shaped as himself: pinwheels, commas, cones, dashes, bristling globes.

Cosimo looked up to find his father watching him, waiting patiently for him to return from his reverie. Cosimo coughed in embarrassment and focused on the lesson again.

"By what means can we recognize those points of intersection, Father, if we cannot see them?"

"Sometimes we can contrive means to actually see them with a magnification of some sort." His father gestured to his reading glass. Cosimo remembered the first time his father had instructed him in observing a beetle under that glass. After initial revulsion he'd been fascinated. How much there was that he'd been unable to see with his unaided eyes.

"Another method is with some form of dye. Think of the way a whirlwind, in drawing up earth, stains itself with dust and reveals the nature of its innately invisible structure to us.

"Then there are other means: odors, noises, recognition of an interstice's 'personality,' heat or cold, and sometimes only by a crosspoint's af-

fect. I could take you to our family farm on a peaceful, quiet afternoon.
Still, you would be able to tell that a great wind had come through earlier
by the broken branches of the trees, piles of leaves blown into drifts,
knocked-over baskets, scoured earth, the frightened anger of the poultry."

Father and son shared a smile. As a small child, Cosimo had often
earned the farmwife's wrath by chasing and terrifying her chickens with
the fireplace bellows.

"But here is where my analogy becomes inadequate. Euclidean geometry refers simply to points in space—*places*, if you will." The older man
shut the book of mathematics and drew another volume squarely in front
of them. "The intersecting points between the realms can be *anything*: an
object, a sound, a person or creature, a moment in time, a ray of light, an
action—anything. And because these 'points' exist in more than one plane
they may have different attributes, appear as different avatars, or exist to
a greater or lesser degree in the different planes."

"Can you give me examples?" Cosimo asked, confused.

His father thought for a moment. "Something that exists as an active
creature in one plane of existence may express only the stable side of its
nature in our own world, appearing to us in the mute, solid form of a tree
or a boulder."

"Ah," exclaimed Cosimo. "Could that explain the ancient Greek leg-
ends of wood and nature nymphs? Daphne and the like?"

Ruggiero the Old smiled his approval. "Exactly." He pointed to the
drifting pelagic wraiths. "And they are a different example. What exactly
are ghosts and shades? Some are indeed leftovers of the dead—some slight
resonance left trapped in this plane while the rest has gone on to God's
celestial realms. Other like apparitions are the simultaneous appearances
of an entity in its own world and our own. More than likely the entity is
not even aware that part of itself is projecting into our dimension. Here,
let me show you."

Cosimo turned in his chair while his father laid five iron bars in a line
along the edge of the table so that the bars lay between the two of them
and the mirror near the window. "This will be our sea wall, so as to
speak," Ruggiero said. "Watch the speculum." He leaned forward in his
chair and, by stretching his arms out, could just reach to balance his mag-
nifying glass against the middle iron bar. The old mage began to chant a

series of phrases over and over. Cosimo recognized the words as Hebraic but didn't know what they meant—all his studies had been in Latin and Greek so far.

While they'd been speaking the black mirror had charged with moonlight. It glowed opaquely. Now, with each word Ruggiero the Old uttered, its silver gleam pulsed outward, creeping along and up the edges of the protective chalk circle. A strong but not unpleasant smell drifted through the room, like that New World spice vanillum poured over a plateful of salt. The air felt warm and muggy. The sea wraiths' swimming became agitated. Cosimo wouldn't have guessed that they'd sense anything in their delusional existence, but somehow they did.

Ruggiero the Old's chanting changed. The same words droned forth, but in a different order. The light from the mirror drew inward, dimming at the edges of the room. The sea creatures faded from sight, except where the censers' fumes still highlighted them. The mirror's reflected light tightened to a cone focused on Ruggiero's reading glass.

Cosimo leaned back uneasily, waiting for the concentrated beam to burn through onto the table in a flash of psychic manifestation. His father's words dimmed to a hum. Cosimo counted five heartbeats of absolute silence. Then his father began to sing.

It was a lilting, quiet tune, totally unlike the solemn chant that had preceded it, in a language Cosimo had never heard before. He hadn't known his grave, somber father could sing so sweetly. Something in his heart ached at the knowledge.

Ruggiero the Old finished on a drawn-out golden note as honeyed as any lark's trill. Instantly light flared from the mirror to the reading glass. But rather than burning through, it bounced off the glass surface back into the room, throwing up a corridor of radiance. A fresh new smell like that of growing wheat filled the study.

Cosimo gasped. His father raised his other hand, the one not steadying the reading glass, cautioning him to wait in silence.

They sat for what seemed a long time but was probably no more than minutes. Suddenly motion rippled through the passageway of light.

A man walked down the glowing corridor. Although he was large and strode deliberately, no sound of heavy footfalls, or any sound at all, reached

Cosimo's ears. The apparition was as colorless and transparent as the luminous sea creatures had been. Through the man Cosimo could see the study's heavy oak cabinetry. The man reached the far wall and vanished straight into it.

Ruggiero the Old began to sing again. The ephemeral corridor contracted to a thin line of light, then shrank to a hot blotch on the angled reading glass. Ruggiero's song slid into chanting. The cone of light poured back into the mirror like milk pouring into a bowl.

Ruggiero the Old set down his glass. "What did you just see?"

"A man translucent as water; appearing, walking, then vanishing."

The astrologer smiled. Cosimo knew the safe simplicity of his answer amused his father.

"But how did he seem to you? In what manner was he dressed?"

"He appeared a large man. As for his clothes . . ." Cosimo faltered. He'd never seen their like before—more exotic than even a Mohammedan's robes or brocades from Cathay. He could not begin to describe their intricate folds and pleats. And there was something about the man's build and manner of walking; and something different about the structure of his face. It had been long and strangely planed, as though in a distant past the man's ancestors had bred with animal gods.

Cosimo shivered. "I've never seen the like on this earth, nor ever think I shall."

His father nodded and smiled.

Cosimo felt somewhat reassured. "So what seems to be a ghost walking through a door without opening it might just be a . . . a fellow walking down an open street in his own world, unaware of his appearance before us?"

"Yes," said Ruggiero the Old. "Just as a man in a room with a mirror in it, hidden to your *direct* sight, might be clearly seen in the mirror through an open window or door. You do not actually see *him,* but you know for a fact he is there. This happens 'naturally' when a combination of factors occurs in both worlds. But I can achieve the same results at my convenience." He gestured to the moonlight-saturated mirror.

"So now I understand the whys and wherefores of ghosts and shades," said Cosimo. "How does this help us in our work?"

His father pointed to the moon. "You will never actually walk upon the moon, my son, but you know the impact it has upon you—without touching you it draws the tides of your blood."

He drew from the tidy pile of implements a square made of four ingeniously bolted together wooden rods. "Do you see the right side of this tool?"

Cosimo bobbed his head.

"And the left?"

Another bob.

"Do you notice that in no way are they directly connected?"

"Yes, Father."

"Yet observe what happens if I press on the left side of the frame." The left piece of wood bowed inward. Ruggiero the Old was bracing the rest of the tool to keep it upright. Still, Cosimo could see how the pressure pulled at the top and bottom pieces and the strain they in turn produced on the right-hand stick.

"Do you see?"

"Yes. The right side moves. It is affected."

Ruggiero the Old nodded. "This is an uncomplicated model of how our existence can be affected by worlds beyond our ken. And, just as importantly, how *we* can affect *those* worlds." The astrologer pushed on the stick again. "If this bending occurs in another realm and causes a dire flexing in our own, do you not suppose that there are those of us here"—he nodded at the flexed wood—"who will not take note of the problem, study its origins, and do what we can to remedy it at its source?

"Even if we cannot reach that plane directly, we have ways to observe it." He jerked his head toward the moon-soaked mirror. "And ways to affect it, especially through the adjoining planes.

"So might you not suppose that the inverse would also be true?" Ruggiero the Old began pushing on the right side of the frame until the left side flexed. "What if *our* realm is the one causing intraplanar tension? Surely our counterparts on the opposite strut will take whatever action they must to counteract the strain."

Cosimo was astounded. "There are those like *us* in other realms of existence?" He tried to imagine otherworldly mages.

His father chuckled. "Of course. But do not presume them to be anything like us—scholarly Florentine gentlemen clad in sober black *lucco*. But observe further." He picked up the framework and pushed on both the right and left sides. The connecting sticks at top and bottom bulged wildly. "What of the hapless inhabitants of the conjoining planes? See how they are affected. Will they stand helplessly by, or protect themselves from all this commotion if they can? And what if it is *we* who are the innocent binding rods, caught between two tumultuous planes?" He flexed both sides again, till the top and bottom were in danger of snapping. Cosimo flinched, waiting for the crack of angry wood.

Ruggiero the Old relaxed his hands and spared the framework. "This device possesses four equal sides. At any moment each one can take on any role: affector or affected, or both at once."

Cosimo tried to summarize the lesson out loud, as he understood it. "Here you've shown me four interlocking planes of existence, one of which is our own. There are agents in the other three that we may ally ourselves with or be on guard against, and who we must be careful of in regards to our own influence upon them. But you said that there were a myriad of worlds."

"Yes." Ruggiero the Old nodded gravely and flapped through the book in front of him. "I told you the frame was but a simple model." He stopped fluttering the pages. He'd turned back to the drawing filled with intermeshed spheres of all sizes.

Cosimo's heart weighted and sank to the bottom of his chest. For a brief moment he recalled the look of despair he'd seen on Tommaso's face earlier in the day when the boy realized the enormity of the task of learning his father's trade of roast-carving. He felt tenfold worse than Tommaso must have.

"It's impossible," Cosimo stammered.

A cold, dry smile briefly stretched his father's lips. "You are beginning to understand the depth of our undertaking," he said. He pushed a sheet of paper, a quill pen, and a small notebook of mathematical arcana at Cosimo. "First you start simply, with intangible equations. Now you know why your tutor Bazile is such a hard taskmaster. Soon enough you will obtain knowledge of words, places, and creatures to substitute for all those abstract x, y, and z's. You'll see those dreary equations take on life."

Ruggiero the Old paged back to the first geometric pictures he'd shown Cosimo at the beginning of the lesson: two lines crossing at one point; a line plunging through a plane; two planes intersecting; several planes intersecting along the length of a single line.

"Notice this particular configuration," he said of the last. "How it mimics the way the leaves of this book meet at the binding, making the binding the strongest, thickest part by virtue of its role as the locus point. We started by speaking of 'points' that enjoy existence in *two* planes, or realms. Be aware that there are interstices that share the borders of *many* worlds, the way this binding participates in the existence of all these pages. And like the binding, these loci are stronger than the planes they unite. These boundaries, in whatever form they take, must be treated with great care. They can be useful tools, powerful allies, dangerous foes, or the seams at which our reality can be held together or ripped asunder."

Cosimo shuddered. "Why are you telling me this now?" He shuffled the papers of mathematical equations. "Isn't this premature, when I haven't even begun learning, let alone mastering, the basics?"

His father closed his eyes and rubbed the space between his eyebrows wearily. "A year ago I would have looked ahead to this day and said yes, it is too early. But events are moving more swiftly than I'd hoped. It may prove necessary for you to recognize the influences of other realms before you have the means of controlling or even calculating them."

Cosimo finally understood. "An incident such as the stalking and attack on young Tommaso!"

His father nodded sad approval. "Exactly. The invisible whirlwinds from elsewhere have begun spinning again around the family de' Medici, picking up hapless debris at their edges, thereby making themselves known to us.

"What you must know from the beginning"—he picked up the book in front of him, snapped it shut, and shook the binding edge at Cosimo—"is that the little *Duchessina* is such a one as this. At her tender age I doubt she apprehends her true nature as yet. She may *never* experience a full understanding of her attributes. But as she grows older she will certainly comprehend some of it. It is our task to guide and help her. We must maintain as best we can the balance between the different realms of existence."

The older man picked up the iron bars rimming the table and stacked

them neatly. Cosimo was startled to see that they bore signs of salt rust.
They'd been clean when his father laid them down.

"You proclaimed our work impossible. There is some truth to your
words. Only God apprehends all, for everything is His creation. What is
required of us is but to try: with diligence to continually expand the borders of our knowledge and the ability to act with wisdom."

Ruggiero the Old opened the geometry book again to a drawing of a
perfect equilateral triangle. "God can be represented thus: infinite, yet tri-
partite in nature. The Holy Three: Father, Son, and Holy Ghost—the most
stable and perfect geometric structure. Three equal, interlocked parts that
form a single whole, a celestial balance. Balance, my son. It all comes down
to balance."

He nodded to Cosimo's paper and quill. "Let us start tonight with a
basic applied geometry lesson. Later we'll return to the mirror to see if we
can gain some insight into the events of the day."

7

In the de' Medici palace kitchen pantry Piera lingered after the rest of the staff, even her parents, had gone to bed. As she turned the rising rounds of bread dough, then re-covered them with damp cloths, she made a mental note to herself to add extra borage to the supper salad the next day for Ippolito's man-at-arms. He'd complained of sore and swollen joints in his hands. She'd also add more peony root and peach leaf to Cardinal Passerini's morning tea to try to calm the wretched, neurotic man.

From a narrow shelf so low to the floor that even the little scullery maids hated to stoop to it, she slid out a tray of luck stones. She'd painted them the night before with iron washes and herbal stains. Their otherness, their true structure, was revealed to her like bones pressing up through the flesh on starving horses. All she had to do was trace over those patterns with the paint to expose their other lives, the source of their luck.

She glanced out the open pantry door to the kitchen beyond. The Moon's full light poured in through the window, glazing every surface it touched with the thick smooth whiteness of cream. The kitchen was utterly silent.

"Bless my efforts, Holy Three," Piera murmured. "Mother Diana, Lady Aradia, and Little Kitchen Goddess." She slid the stones back into their hiding place.

In the coolest, darkest corner of the pantry she bent again, to a pile of fennel roots. She stacked them one by one on a nearby sack of spelt and picked up the burlap-wrapped bowl that had held them and a stoppered flask behind it. Piera unwrapped the dirt-encrusted burlap, freeing the flat round bowl. It was so dusty from the burlap and the roots that its color was indistinguishable. She carried the flask and bowl into the kitchen, washed the bowl with well water, dried it, and set it on the open windowsill. In the moonlight its true color shone luminously—a rich, satiny black.

Piera uncorked the flask. She sang a soft evocation and poured the bowl almost full with the strong-smelling murky water from the flask. The flowing water sheened silver as the moonlight struck it.

Unlike Ruggiero, Piera needed no specially prepared herbs burning in censers. The complex perfume made by all the day's cooking filled the room, superior to any incense. But she hesitated before proceeding to the next step. She needed to be relaxed and calm, to lay to rest the apprehension that had plagued her all day. And which had increased threefold since Ippolito had returned to the palazzo with news of the attack on Tommaso.

Her eyes narrowed. Too many old patterns repeating again, accelerating. She glanced at the entryway to the kitchen. Ancient Angelina huddled on her stool there, an almost invisible sentry. What Angelina had set in motion so many years ago was tangling together, netting Piera's children. Time was twisting into a knot.

Piera clenched her hands. Now was not the moment to think of such things. She pulled at the fine chain that hung around her neck and disappeared into her bodice, drawing up on it until the silver pendant at its end lay in her palm. She stroked it between her hands, blanking her thoughts to the same state of flowing empty clarity that Angelina lived in all the time these days.

The reflection of the Moon filled the bowl so perfectly that the bowl looked as though it was brimming with iridescent cream. Piera took up the flask again, poured a little of the water into her palm. "Undines, lovely undines, see what I have brought you," she chanted as she sprinkled the water from her hand into the bowl. Water from the river Arno back into itself.

The Moon in the bowl trembled and shivered apart as the droplets struck, then smoothed over again. Piera gazed into the bowl and whispered her offerings and desires.

Somewhere deeply below the Moon's reflection—far deeper than the bowl's shallowness could allow for—a dim shape stirred and moved toward the surface. Then another, and another, until the bowl's depths swarmed with languidly moving shapes. The Moon reflected in the bowl remained still.

They were not women, yet definitely female. And huge. The small circle of the bowl formed a window looking down and into another place, a world of water. A world, Piera knew, without a moon or any other bright thing in the sky.

But not altogether without light. The undines had beautiful blind-looking milky eyes that sieved in the faint glow emanating from the tiny plants and animals that floated thickly through their world. Some of the minisculae clung to the undines' sleek skins in a filmy layer, so that the great creatures' bodies glimmered like pearls, enhancing their resemblance to vast naked languid women. They swarmed in slow adoration to Piera's miracle gift to them of the Moon's full light.

Piera's breath caught in her throat. She felt the pang of a particular kind of hunger. How often at any time of day or night had she not also been summoned herself? Not to the Moon, of course. Not to any moon. Not to anything she could describe in words. Words applied to this world. The undines had nothing that would pass as the word for *moon* in their world, she was sure.

"And now, sisters, for your gift in return," she whispered to them.

Across town Ruggiero the Old and Cosimo sat in front of the great mirror in the study again. This time the vision they gazed on lay within the mirror, as solid looking and real as if they looked through a window.

"But what does it mean, Father?" asked Cosimo

Ruggiero the Old shook his head. "I do not know."

The mirror looked out on a lake. Floating on the water were statues of men and women, modeled in classical Greek style. But instead of being carved out of highly polished marble, they had been crafted somewhat coarsely from an unfamiliar, off-white granular stone. The lake lay so still and pure that it reflected the sculptures perfectly. Surrounding the lake in the distance were masses of foliage.

"Is it the past? The future? One of those other worlds?"

The old mage looked perplexed. "I cannot tell. I don't know why this image conjured itself for us."

At the same moment Piera looked down at the very same scene reflected in the moonlight-glazed eye of an undine. She waited. Long after the mage and his son had given up and put away their great speculum she sat before her small, simple one. At last she was rewarded.

A great hand, like that of a god, reached down and moved the sculptures about, rearranging them at will. Then all was still again. Sometime later a face as great as the sky loomed over the lake. The lake, reflected in the undine's eye, which was reflected in Piera's scrying bowl, itself suddenly reflected image after darkening image on its surface.

Piera passed a shaking hand over the bowl three times as quickly as she could to make the vision go away. She had recognized that looming face. She knew who the great hand belonged to and what the statues were made of. She could not, would not let herself think of the images that had risen to shift and turn so terribly on the waters.

Tommaso. She'd never even considered Tommaso. Everything had always indicated Ginevra as the sole Chosen. For five months after Caterina's birth, until she'd been taken away to Rome, Piera had nursed the two girls together: Caterina on one breast and Ginevra on the other. Piera had been so sure that the two girls' lives were irrevocably entwined. She was still sure of it now. All that time with the two of them drinking of her, until the three of them were as one. With Caterina's return Piera had found the bond yet unbroken.

When had things changed? When had the Little Kitchen Goddess taken Piera's oldest son also under Her protection? What did it mean?

✶ ✶ ✶

In her newly chosen bed in the pantry Gattamelata prepared to sleep. Her usual custom was to turn three times counterclockwise before lying down. But tonight she turned seven times widdershins, then seven times clockwise, then seven times widdershins again, full seven times each side to side before she settled to dream.

8

❧

"Please, Tommaso? No one else possesses your skill. Caterina will be utterly charmed."

Tommaso sighed and accepted the proffered loaf of marzipan. It was as difficult to refuse Ippolito as it was to resist the *Duchessina*. He took out a sharp knife and cut the almond paste into seven equal sections. Under the blade, it was as stiff as his ribs still felt.

Doctor Ruggiero insisted that he was mending quickly from the beating. To Tommaso the process seemed interminable. Deeming it unwise for him to attend public school until he healed, his father and Ruggiero had arranged for him to be tutored at the Medicis'; a neat arrangement that allowed him to accompany Cosimo, who had recently been assigned as one of the *Duchessina*'s teachers.

Tommaso took the first section of marzipan. He rolled it between his hands until it warmed and became pliable.

"This is her first *Calendimaggio* in Florence," Ippolito said. "We must make it special for her." The youth perched on the edge of the great kitchen worktable.

Normally Tommaso disliked people hovering over him as he worked. But besides the fact that Ippolito had rescued him, the de' Medici heir was so witty, kind and valiant that it was hard to resent him. Furthermore, he blocked the view of Angelina Befanini perched on her stool in the kitchen doorway.

"Excellent!" Ippolito proclaimed as Tommaso set the first completed sweet on the table. It had been transformed from a lump of paste into one of Gattamelata's kittens, all set to pounce.

Tommaso picked up the next marzipan plug. He'd mold this one into a kitten innocently washing its face with one paw, fit prey for the machinations of the first little sculpture.

Ever since his brief sojourn at Il Tribolino's, Tommaso found that with too much time on his hands he felt compelled to work a transformation on every raw simple thing he picked up. And since that which he had most access to was not clay or wax or wood, he'd become a whittler of hard cheeses, a molder of pastes and dough.

"I won't be able to color these," he warned Ippolito. "The colors would just run together and become muddy." Gattamelata's kittens were a wonder: seven of them, each as spotted and pied as their mother.

"Have you ever seen the like?" Ginevra had breathed when Gattamelata first proudly displayed her progeny.

"Only once before," Piera said quietly, as if she were talking to herself. Tommaso turned to look at her. The expression on her face had almost passed, so he could not be sure if it had been sadness after all.

Ippolito reached for the marzipan models, interrupting Tommaso's thoughts. "It's not their color but their liveliness that makes them so endearing," the youth said. "You've captured that spirit to perfection."

"Don't pick them up yet," Tommaso said hastily. "Let them dry thoroughly or they'll crumble when you tie them to the bough. Do you have the ribbons?"

"Right here," Ippolito said. He pulled some bright-colored streamers from his doublet. One of the real kittens leapt at the dangling temptation.

"Aha! This is for your toothsome double, not for you, I'm afraid," Ippolito laughed. He picked up the kitten with his other hand and waggled the ribbons just out of its reach, teasing it. The kitten clawed at them with happy enthusiasm. "Your mother Madonna Piera gave me some candied nuts to tie on. I already picked out a nice flowering branch."

Cosimo came in just as Tommaso finished the seventh candy kitten. A Ruggiero man-at-arms followed behind him. "The young ladies are finished with their lessons," Cosimo announced. "The *Duchessina* asked that we stop by Madame Strozzi's on our way home."

He bent to examine the marzipan catlings. "These are marvelous, Tommaso. Perhaps food is not your calling after all. We should consider apprenticing you to Il Tribolino, or perhaps *Ser* Buonarotti himself."

Tommaso flushed at the idea of working with Michelangelo. "These are just trinkets for the *Duchessina's* May Day bough," he said and nodded at Ippolito, who grinned and dangled the ribbons at Cosimo as if he, too, were a kitten.

Cosimo swatted at them good-naturedly.

"Did your mother physick you again?" Cosimo asked as they made their way to the Strozzi mansion a quarter of a mile away.

"As always." Tommaso made a face. Ever since the beating, whenever he visited the Befaninis in their kitchen his mother forced on him infusion after infusion of peony root, mater herbarum, bitter fuga demonum, and rowan.

"I tell her how I'm healing, the care you and your father lavish on me. She nodes in agreement even as she forces a third or fourth cup down my throat."

"Such is the nature of mothers," Cosimo said. He nodded over his shoulder at the laconic man-at-arms following them. "Enzio here accompanies us at *my* mother's bequest. And I cannot say she's wrong. Florence will remain in this state of tension until we hear that the emperor's forces have been turned away from Rome and defeated."

He sighed. "Tomorrow the young girls will dance to the music of lutes in the Piazza Santa Trinitá after finding decorated flowering boughs hanging on their doors. But I fear that this May Day will prove to be the most lackluster Florence has seen in many a year."

"True," Tommaso agreed, "but since this is the first the *Duchessina* has attended perhaps she'll enjoy it, having nothing to compare it to. It was chivalrous of Ippolito to prepare a *Calendimaggio* bough for his little cousin so she wouldn't feel neglected. I should do the same for Ginevra. Just because a girl is too young to have a sweetheart doesn't mean she wouldn't like a few decorated branches hung at her door."

Cosimo favored Tommaso with a curious glance and seemed about to speak, but they'd arrived at the Strozzi mansion, its corbels and spandrels adorned with the Strozzi family emblem of crescents and Fillipo Strozzi's personal insignia of sheep and falcons. "I'll be but a moment," Cosimo said as he pounded at the door. He unslung a purse draped by a long cord over his shoulder. "I have only to return some excess bangles to Madame Strozzi that Caterina and her ladies didn't need in adorning their May Day gowns."

Now it was Tommaso's turn to look at his young master curiously. Surely even the *Duchessina* would not request that the oldest son of the greatest physician and astrologer in the city act as a lackey to run her slightest errands. Tommaso wondered what else Cosimo might be transporting to Clarice Strozzi.

A servant opened the door and Cosimo entered, leaving Tommaso to stand loitering with the silent Enzio.

To a degree Tommaso understood why he'd been assigned as Cosimo's casual squire. The order of the day was strength in numbers. With stout-armed Enzio flanking them, the two boys retained at least some freedom to roam the city. Other menservants accompanied the two other older Ruggiero sons. Cosimo's mother had sent her younger children to the family country estate.

Still, Tommaso wasn't sure why he, of all the Ruggiero household, had been honored with the position of companion to the Ruggiero heir. Perhaps Ruggiero the Old felt badly for the injuries he'd suffered. This was likely. The doctor's sense of honor and obligation was strong.

Less explicable was Cosimo's sudden commission to the de' Medici palazzo as one of Caterina's tutors. Why would the sage cast his oldest son into the Medicean eye of the storm? But Tommaso was glad of the fact. It allowed him to see his mother and siblings on a regular basis. And the *Duchessina.*

The door opened and Cosimo slipped out, his light burden gone. Whatever Caterina had wished conveyed to her aunt—whether a note, an object, or a few well-chosen words—it had been quickly exchanged.

Unencumbered, Cosimo looked less somber. "Let's pass by the Piazza delle Signoria on our way home and see how preparations for the festivities are going," he suggested.

On *Calendimaggio*, once the young girls finished dancing to lutes at the Piazza Santa Trinitá, they paraded through the city to the Piazza de la Signoria. To honor them, colorful banners had been raised and stands erected for them to sit on to view the annual *calcio* tournament between the apprentices of the major guilds.

Tommaso looked across the piazza and nodded his approval of the decorations, the boys practicing for the tourney. Others were also watching, mostly young blades done with their own apprenticeships who felt it their duty to benefit the players with their expertise by calling out advice in the form of catcalls. Here and there groups of them were raising wagers on tomorrow's outcome.

"I hope the banking apprentices do well," Tommaso said. "It would be pleasant for the *Duchessina* if her family's traditional guild comports itself with honor. Will you play on the physicians' team, Cosimo?"

Cosimo shook his head. "Only if someone is injured. My studies haven't allowed me to throw around a *calcio* ball since last summer."

"Will Ippolito be playing? I'm sure Caterina would like someone from her family to champion her. It's nice how Ippolito has taken over the role of elder brother, since Alessandro seems to dislike her so much."

Cosimo raised his brows. "Surely you don't believe that fable, that Alessandro is Caterina's illegitimate half-brother?" He laughed at the confused expression on Tommaso's face. "Where is the mother that bore him—the supposed mistress of Caterina's father, Duke Lorenzo? Where was Alessandro born? As a child, he appeared suddenly in the midst of the papal household. It wasn't until after Duke Lorenzo's death that claims to his lineage were made on Alessandro's behalf. No, look elsewhere for Alessandro's true heritage.

"And as for Ippolito . . ." Cosimo hesitated. "Tommaso, your sentiments concerning pleasantries for your sister and Caterina are commendable and appropriate for an elder brother. But don't assume the same motives for Ippolito." He favored Tommaso with a meaningful glance.

Tommaso blinked in surprise.

"I don't mean to suggest that Ippolito's intentions are unchivalrous," Cosimo said hastily. "To the contrary, Ippolito and the *Duchessina* are close as brother and sister, and more besides."

Tommaso took Cosimo's meaning clearly. He was shocked. "But she is so young," he protested. "And Ippolito is sixteen years of age."

Cosimo looked grave. "Yes, the *Duchessina* is still a little girl," he agreed. "And certainly nothing untoward occurs between them. But Ippolito will not be ready to marry for twelve or more years. At that time Caterina will be eighteen, a perfect age for her to wed. And because they are so well suited to each other in interests, intellect, and taste, and are already so fond of each other, I'm certain the possibility of a match has naturally occurred at least to Ippolito."

Tommaso was stunned. Then he flushed as he realized why Cosimo was taking the time and effort to explain matters to him. Was he so transparent? Evidently so. Yes, he was smitten with the *Duchessina*. But not in the way that Cosimo thought. Tommaso didn't have the words to explain how he felt about Caterina.

"We should be getting home," Cosimo said. "I don't want my mother fretting after us."

They left by way of the Via di Leoni. In front of them, also moving away, was a band of youths, laughing and joking. In their midst was Alessandro de' Medici.

Tommaso looked at Cosimo uneasily. As someone intimate with the de' Medici heirs, Cosimo would no doubt wish to join Alessandro and his companions. If that were the case, Tommaso would stick close to Enzio and endure till they parted company.

To Tommaso's surprise, Cosimo slowed his pace and began an earnest, if one-sided, conversation with Enzio on the merits of swordplay versus the art of the spear. Every once in a while he'd cast a surreptitious glance at the group of youths ahead of them, an expression of distaste sliding over his features.

When had Cosimo become disenchanted with Alessandro? Tommaso still remembered how the apprentice mage had defended Alessandro to Gentile, praising the de' Medici's hunting skills. But perhaps a rift between them was inevitable, Tommaso reflected. Someone as decent as Cosimo couldn't long remain tolerant of Alessandro's behavior. In the few months since he'd come to Florence, Alessandro had become as famous for his rudeness, arrogance, and dissolute behavior as Ippolito had for *his* courtesy and charm.

By the time Alessandro's group passed the lions' cages fronting the street, Cosimo and Tommaso lagged well behind.

Used to being on constant display, the lions paced back and forth, making their customary grumbling and soughing sounds. But as Alessandro and his group approached, the lions fell silent. Their massive heads swiveled around as one to stare at the de' Medici heir. To Tommaso's amazement, as the youths walked by the great cats began to stalk Alessandro within their cages. Tommaso had never seen the like before. Seven sets of golden eyes widened and focused. Seven sets of heavy, wide paws held perfectly still, then moved one careful step at a time. By the time Alessandro's group passed out of sight the lions were packed together in a solid mass of tensed muscle and tightened talon at the corner end of the cages, pressed hard against the restraining iron bars.

Alessandro had seemed unaware of the lions' deadly focus. But Tommaso saw Cosimo shiver beside him.

9

May 13, 1527

There! No, there," Tommaso cried, dashing around a pillar. The kitten he chased bunched its fat little legs underneath itself to run, then skidded and slid, turning round and round on the sleek inner courtyard floor. Facing the other way, the kitten now decided to chase Tommaso, who lashed a long cord behind him for it to pounce at.

"I've got one," Caterina called. She swooped up one kitten into her arms, only to shriek with surprise and laughter as another one ambushed her, leaping onto her skirts and chimneying its way upward with a determined expression on its whiskered face.

"Hold still," Ginevra said as she unhooked the furry assailant from Caterina's smock and set it down.

Released, it laid back its ears, twitched its tail, and pounced at her instead. Ginevra jumped out of the way. Umberto, two slave girls, and Pietro were trying to encircle three of the other kittens.

Throughout the palazzo the adults had been subdued all day. Cosimo brought the *Duchessina* and Ginevra to the kitchen, announcing that Ruggiero the Old would be arriving shortly for an important meeting, canceling all scheduled tutoring. The rest of the Befaninis being busy cooking, Piera consented to continue the children's tutelage in arranging and hosting banquets.

But soon, weighed down by her pregnancy and the kitchen's heat, she decided to let the children go off and play. She addressed her little class of Tommaso, Umberto, Ginevra, Caterina, and two small slave girls. "Take the kittens and your little brother with you," she said. Only Ginevra paused at the doorway to look back at her mother.

Piera leaned heavily against the accounting table. She saw the look of concern on her daughter's face and tried to reassure her with a wan smile. "We'll be going home soon. The baby will arrive within a week or so and then I'd only be a burden here. In the meantime, let your heart be light for a while."

Ginevra took her mother's meaning. All of Florence lay under the burden of dark clouds, waiting to hear news of the emperor's march against Rome. May Day's festivities had been subdued. Only the *Duchessina* was innocently thrilled by the festivities.

Ginevra followed after the other youngsters.

"This way," Caterina whispered, shepherding them past the Great Hall, where the adults were gathered. "They're all in there—the cardinals and their men, Cosimo, Aunt Clarice, my ladies, Ippolito and 'Sandro—so there's one to bother us." They went farther along the hallway, past the family chapel, then down the main stairway, which bottomed out at the front inner courtyard.

The *Duchessina* released the kitten she carried. It scampered off to explore the statues and sarcophagi scattered about under the columned arcade. The other children followed her example. The game was on.

Ginevra leaned against one of the pillars, watching. She didn't set down the kitten she held until it insistently squirmed half out of her grasp. In the few months that she had known Caterina and grown close to the *Duchessina*, this was the first time Ginevra had seen the heiress allow herself to be a child.

Her mother Piera often teased them that they were like sisters because they'd shared milk at her breast during their infancy. Ginevra felt instead that they'd grown close because they shared a weight of responsibility far beyond their years: Caterina as the sole true heir to a great family, the locus around which great events would turn; and she, Ginevra, as the repository of all Piera's training, hopes, and plans. A pivot point that, though unseen, might prove to be as important as the *Duchessina*'s. And part of her heritage from her mother was to know, deep in her bones, how closely her fate was linked with the *Duchessina*'s.

Ginevra's shoulders bowed. So often of late she'd felt overwhelmed, though she took care to show it to no one. How could Caterina run about so care free? Couldn't she, of all people, feel how they rested in the eye of a storm? At any moment horrendous gales of change might strike.

And for all her Mother Piera—spells and potions and scrying, nothing could stop those winds from blowing. They would come. Ginevra shivered. And finally understood Caterina. While the stillness lasted, this might be their last opportunity to be children.

Caterina was laughing hysterically as the kitten climbed her skirt. Ginevra bent to release it, dodged it as it turned on her, then joined the others.

It seemed only moments later that one of the slave girls held up her hand. "Listen," she said.

They heard faint sounds of doors opening and closing upstairs. The adults might be sending to the kitchen for refreshments, or the meeting might be ending.

"Perhaps we should get ourselves and the catlings back to the kitchen," suggested Umberto. The others looked at each other, then deferred to his seniority. Not only was Umberto the oldest, he was also the only one of them to have lived his entire life in the Medici palace. He knew exactly the boundaries of space and etiquette.

"Two of the kittens are missing," said Tommaso. "They're still too little to be left running loose down here."

One of the slave girls peered about. "They're not here. Maybe they've run up the stairs."

Clutching the kittens that had been accounted for, the children mounted the steps.

Ginevra rested midway, trying to frame a still quiet spot in her mind, as her mother had taught her. If she could, the kittens would fill that space, revealing their location.

Tommaso's triumphant hoot jarred her from her walking trance. "I

found the *furafante*," he called. "The little demons went seeking religion."
Ginevra hurried the rest of the way up the steps. Her older brother stood
at the door of the chapel.

The children crept into the de' Medicis' private holy space. Fra Lippo
Lippi's *Virgin Adoring the Child* glowed at them from above the altar. Flanking it were Gozzoli's two enormous murals of exulting angels. Around the
body of the chapel marched another mural depicting the procession of the
Magi. Even little Pietro was hushed by the sacred beauty of the place.

The kittens were not so respectful. They were playing up on the altar
and had already knocked over a silver chalice and a candlestick.

Before the children could act, one pounced and chased the other the
length of the altar. The would-be prey balanced for a precarious instant
on the altar edge, then launched herself into the air. She just barely managed to hook her claws into the enormous carved, wooden screen that stood
near the wall between the altar and the pulpit. The pursuer didn't hesitate
and also leapt, but fell short to the floor. She immediately started scrambling up the screen after her sister.

Umberto groaned. He pried the assailing kitten loose and handed it
to Caterina. The kitten perching on top of the scrim hissed at him.

"Come on down, little mistress," Umberto crooned. The tiny cat responded by flattening her ears to her skull and growling.

Umberto muttered an oath back at it.

"Don't swear in the chapel," Caterina reproved.

A pounding resounded at the front doors below, loud enough for them
to hear clearly one floor up. The children started.

One of the slave girls peered out of the chapel down the hallway.
"Someone is coming down from the great room to answer that."

"Quick," said Caterina, handing the kitten she held to Umberto. "As
soon as they've passed take the catling and Pietro and run to the kitchen.
Ginevra and I will stay and catch the last one. If we're found here I'll say
I came in to offer a prayer to my parents' souls. Tommaso, stand guard at
the door."

Ginevra was amused at the alacrity with which Tommaso obeyed Caterina. But both boys hesitated at the door.

"From the voices, it sounds like Ruggiero the Old," Tommaso reported.

"Then run, now," Caterina hissed. "Before they mount the stairs."

Umberto slipped his entourage of slave girls, Pietro and kittens out the door.

It took Ginevra and Caterina only a moment to right the candlesticks and chalice and straighten the altar cloths.

"Come down, little one," Ginevra cajoled the kitten. "Come down and play with us."

The kitten mewled piteously, then hissed again.

"Let it have a moment to calm itself," Tommaso called.

"But do we have a moment?" Ginevra asked, turning to Caterina.

"If Ruggiero the Old has just arrived, surely they'll confer for a while," Caterina said. "Perhaps, as Tommaso said, if we leave the kitten alone for a moment it will compose itself."

Caterina wandered off a few paces till she stood before Gozzoli's mural. She looked up at it. Ginevra thought Caterina looked wistful. But when she went to the heiress, Caterina smiled and put an arm around her.

"Look, my gossip. I've been told I was baptized under this very painting, so that all my life I would be looked after by the three great Wise Ones, as has every true de' Medici since the dawn of time. See here where Gozzoli painted my great-grandfather as the youngest of the Magi?" Caterina pointed to a handsome youth clad in a magnificent golden tunic and scarlet leggings, sitting astride a prancing white charger.

"He was still young, and both his father Piero and grandfather Cosimo Pater Patriae were still alive—see, they are here, and here, in the painting. Yet Gozzoli seemed to have looked into the future, for how else could he have known that Lorenzo would grow to be the wisest, bravest, and most brilliant of my family?" Caterina's face glowed with pride.

She really is beautiful, thought Ginevra. Why does that fact seem to hide from the world?

Ginevra glanced over the painting. Surely those three anonymously pretty girls were meant to represent Piero's daughters, Lorenzo the Great's sisters. And where was Piero's wife, the renowned Lucrezia Tornabuoni? If she had been represented truly Ginevra knew the aristocratic Lucrezia would have closely resembled her own mother Piera—it was from Lucrezia that the family inherited what had come to be known as "de' Medici eyes."

"Of course, Great-Grandfather looked nothing like this youth," Caterina sighed. "Perhaps I assign too much to Gozzoli's talents after all."

Ginevra had to nod in agreement. The adolescent in the mural boasted pale even features and curly honey-colored hair. Lorenzo *Il Magnífico* was swarthy and dark haired. His famously twisted sardonic features bordered on ugliness. Yet such had been the strength of his charm and personality that it was said that once met he was nearly irresistible.

"And here are all the others," Caterina prattled. "Lorenzo's sisters, Gozzoli himself. See how Gozzoli wrote his name across his hat, so you couldn't mistake him?"

Tommaso left his post and came to stand behind them.

"And that young boy over there on the other white charger is Giuliano." Caterina's voice hushed respectfully as she spoke of Lorenzo's younger brother, disgracefully murdered in the cathedral in the prime of his youth. The *Duchessina*'s attention drifted back to Lorenzo. "Oh, Great-Grandfather," she said sadly. "Why did you die so young and leave the family adrift? You were only in your forties. Did the Wise Ones stop watching over you?"

But Ginevra could not keep her eyes off the portrait of Giuliano. He was as inaccurately painted as his older brother in the same manner of trading light for dark, but the gentle features may have been painted close to true. He was known to have been the handsomest of the de' Medicis of his day.

Ginevra's eyes filled with tears. Her thoughts echoed Caterina's words. Oh, Great-Grandfather, why *did* you die so young—only in your twenties—and so horribly, in the church? If you had lived, would you have acknowledged any of us, as you did your other bastard, who now parades about as pope? She wondered if Tommaso knew exactly where the Medici blood in their veins came from.

"Someone else is at the front door," Tommaso said, as more pounding brought both girls out of their reverie.

The door was opened immediately, as if someone had been waiting there, expecting a new arrival. Footsteps marched up the main stairs. "Master Ruggiero wants you to wait for him and the others in the chapel." The voice belonged to the house steward.

"We've got to get the kitten down," Caterina said urgently.

With the new commotion the little cat looked even less disposed to descend than before.

Tommaso stood on tiptoe and held out his hands. The kitten stretched her neck toward him, tiny pink nose flaring as she sniffed at him. Then, to Ginevra's amazement, it scrambled backward until it was low enough for Tommaso to grab it.

"Why did she come to you and not to me?" Ginevra asked.

Tommaso grinned. "You spend so much time in the *Duchessina's* company that you no longer smell deliciously of the kitchen the way I do," he said, handing the kitten over to Caterina.

Just then the footsteps stopped outside the chapel.

Ginevra grabbed Caterina and Tommaso and pulled them behind the only nearby cover in the chapel—the altar—just as the chapel door began to open. Someone entered. The chapel door closed shut. Only a single pair of shoes could be heard pacing impatiently back and forth on the marble floor.

In silence, the children tried to get as comfortable as they could in their hiding place. Caterina was wedged in the middle, a situation Ginevra was sure did not displease her brother. Caterina seemed to be straining to hold in a fit of giggling. Ginevra was not similarly amused. If they were caught behind the Medici holy of holies, it would not be on the little heiress that blame would fall.

Two more people entered on anxious, hurrying feet. "What news of Rome?" The nasal, high-pitched voice belonged to Cardinal Passerini.

"I cannot say until my master arrives," said First Shoes.

"By God, you *will* answer the cardinal," shouted the third person. It was Alessandro. He sounded as much frightened as angry. "Give us news of the pope or I'll beat it out of you," he cried. There came the sounds of a brief scuffle.

"Hush, hush, Alessandro," Passerini nervously soothed. "Forgive the youth, *Ser* messenger. He's distraught with concern for his mentor."

Ginevra looked over Caterina's head to her brother. Tommaso raised his eyebrows in response, as surprised as she. It would have been impossible to imagine the haughty, flighty cardinal apologizing to any servant.

The doors opened again and more people filed in. Ginevra closed her eyes and concentrated on the sounds. She recognized Ruggiero the Old's deliberate tread and Cosimo's too, pacing his father's like a shadow. After that she could not be sure, but she guessed a total of four or five newcomers had entered the chamber.

"What news do you bring us of Rome?" The voice belonged to Clarice Strozzi.

For a moment there was no answer, until Ruggiero the Old spoke. "It's all right, Lazaro. You may answer. I had you come here to report directly to these people, the heart of the Medici here in Florence."

He knows, Ginevra realized. He knows all or most of what Lazaro is going to say. And he's known it for a while, perhaps even days.

She felt Caterina stiffen beside her. She glanced down. The *Duchessina* no longer looked amused. Her face was white and strained. Caterina had also understood the meaning behind the mage's calmness. She had to be furious that at such a moment she, the one true de' Medici heir, had been sent off to take cooking lessons and play with kittens.

"The news . . . it is not good," said Lazaro, still hesitant.

"The pope! Is the pope dead?" Alessandro's words were a shrieking caw.

"Clement is yet alive, or at least was when I left Rome."

Ginevra could not tell whether the slight edge of scorn in the messenger's voice was directed toward the pope or Alessandro.

"On May fourth that French deserter the Duke of Bourbon reached Isola Farnese," Lazaro continued. "From there, a mere seven miles from Rome, the duke sent word that the city would be spared if sufficient ransom could be raised to appease the imperial troops.

"The pope refused. He had finally turned his attention to the task of defending Rome. To that aim he appointed Renzo da Ceri to lead and organize the city.

"But the citizens would not support him. They prevented da Ceri from blowing up the bridges over the Tiber. Some of the great families would have even sent envoys to try to make a separate peace with Bourbon, if da Ceri had not stopped them. The capitol bell rang, but few Romans left their homes to join the troops."

Lazaro paused, as good messengers do when their news needs time to be absorbed. All of Italy knew how Rome chafed under Clement's rule, much as Florence suffered under the incompetence of Cardinal Passerini. But not to respond to the call of a city's great bell—it was inconceivable.

"In the end, da Ceri had scarcely more than eight thousand men to defend Rome's walls."

"What is this about Bourbon?" Ippolito asked. "I thought that fearsome ancient German George von Frundsberg led the *landsknechte*."

Ginevra shivered. Von Frundsberg, a devout Lutheran, wore a massive golden chain around his neck. It was reputed he'd said he intended to strangle the pope with it with his own bare hands.

"He proved to be *too* ancient," Lazaro said. "When he considered leniency in the attack on the citizens of Rome his troops rounded on him. He suffered a stroke and had to be carried away."

"Ah, good news, then," said Alessandro. He too must have been thinking of the heavy gold chain.

"Not really," said Lazaro glumly. "The imperial troops arrived in Isola Farnese as ragged, filthy, and hungry as beggars and as fierce as demons. I believe they could have torn our brave Florentine lions to shreds with their bare hands. By the time Bourbon sent messengers with ultimatums to the pope, the ransom for sparing Rome was so great that Clement could never have met it, even if he'd wished to.

"On May sixth they attacked. Although initially repelled by the papal gunners, Bourbon's men eventually succeeded in mounting scaling ladders against the walls."

"How can that be?" protested Ippolito. "It's an easy matter to push those things off."

"Mists rising from the Tiber hid their actions. It seemed that even the river conspired against the city. Afterward, gates were flung open from inside, breaches blown in the walls, and the enemy rushed in. The only good news was that Bourbon was shot. The Prince of Orange got him away to a nearby chapel, where he died. Now Orange leads the troops."

"But the pope, the pope?" Alessandro was in agony.

"Saved by the Bishop of Nocera, who talked him into making a run for it along the stone corridor that bridges the apostolic palace to the safety of Castel Sant' Angel. The bishop held up Clement's robes so he could run faster, and even flung his own purple cloak over the pope's head so no enemy in the streets below would see and recognize him by his white *rochet*.

"Then the drawbridge was drawn up, the corridor barred, and the rest of Rome left as prey for the German and Spanish jackals. *They* had the luxury of resting the remainder of the day. The next morning the sacking began."

Lazaro paused. When he finally continued, his voice was so hushed that Ginevra could barely hear him from behind the altar.

"At least eight thousand people were slaughtered the first day alone," he said. "The most wealthy survived—those with unbreachable palazzi like fortresses. The merely rich found themselves ransomed, then tortured when the money was delivered. The *reiters* drug the poor out into the streets and butchered them for sport. Priests were forced to desecrate the cathedrals. *Reiters* gambled on church altars, wagering for the rights to strip nuns naked and rape them on those very altars. Baptismal fonts were filled with monks' blood.

"By the second day I saw mothers throwing their children to their deaths from the roofs of tall buildings and then leaping after to avoid being taken. On the third night I scaled down the wall of the Castel Sant' Angel and escaped to come report." He muttered a curse surely never heard before in the chapel. "Would that I had left weeks before. What I saw . . . what I saw . . ."—he began weeping—"no decent man should have to see. An orphanage burned with all its children screaming within it. The ill and crippled pulled from their hospital beds and hacked into unrecognizable heaps of flesh.

"The Spanish and Colonnan troops showed some restraint and only looted, but the Germans are mad soulless beasts."

"The pope, is he yet safe?" persisted Alessandro.

"Yes, of course. Or, at least, was when I left." Lazaro's voice was angry, irritated. "It would be hard for the enemy to get a clear shot at him, even should he be unwise enough to visit the outer battlements, for he is constantly surrounded by that chattering monkey Benevenuto Cellini, who I am ashamed to acknowledge as a fellow Florentine. Cellini is so busy dancing around His Holiness, boasting of his great deeds defending the *Castel*, that he has little time to actually defend it."

"What about Cardinal Farnese?" asked Passerini.

"Still alive, no thanks to Cellini. That idiot rolled a cask of stones down almost on Farnese's and another cardinal's head."

"And what about—" Ippolito started to ask. Names began to fly through the air as fast as a flock of dark crows as Lazaro's audience asked who had and had not survived.

Caterina's fingernails dug into Ginevra's arm. Ginevra bit her lip against the pain. Caterina must be in agony to know the fate of the children who had been her playmates in Rome. But she was condemned to silence by her exclusion from the meeting. Ginevra watched the anger smolder in the *Duchessina*'s eyes. If they could see that look, she thought, they would be afraid to treat Caterina like a helpless pawn.

"And Isabella d'Este?" asked Clarice Strozzi.

"Your dear friend is not only safe, she triumphs and is declared a saint by many," said Lazaro. "Weeks before the invasion she ordered her palazzo fortified, walled in all the windows and portals, hired armed guards, and laid in provisions. Then she invited in all she knew. They came. I hear that almost two thousand people have found refuge with her, including the ambassadors of Venice, Ferrara and Urbino."

"She'll not be able to hold out long supporting that many," muttered Passerini.

Clarice's laughter held relief but no joy. "She'll not have to, now that she's survived the initial invasion. Those Mantuans always safeguard their bets. Her youngest son, Ferrante, serves in the Italian division of the imperial army. He'll get her out of Rome safely."

To many of the anxious queries Lazaro hesitated, then said, "I do not know. Perhaps they are safe, perhaps not." He hinted instead, telling them of more anonymous atrocities, until, finally, they were silenced.

"Lazaro, take your well-deserved rest," Ruggiero said gently. "We thank you for your bravery in risking all to reach us. Would that the news were kinder. But at least now we know. Food is waiting for you in the kitchen."

After the messenger left, the sage addressed the others. "I now ask of you the impossible—to forget the fates of fond friends and allies in Rome. There is nothing we can do for them now. Soon all Florence will know this news. With Clement a powerless prisoner in Castel Sant' Angel, the position of every de' Medici in Florence becomes precarious. The *Signoria* will act soon."

"Ser Ruggiero is right," said Clarice. "Like Isabella d'Este, we should have begun planning weeks ago. Through my husband we can send for mercenaries to add to our meager forces. I suggest we adjourn to the *studiolo* to begin drafting letters."

When the adults left, the three children slowly unfolded themselves from behind the altar. At some point Tommaso had pried the kitten away from Caterina. It lay asleep in his arms. Ginevra watched her brother stretch his aching arms carefully so as not to awaken it. She thought of the way they'd been playing with the kittens such a short while ago, as happy as children anywhere. She looked at the dazed expression on Tommaso's face, the flinty look in Caterina's eyes, and knew that the three of them would never be children again.

"Did you notice that Messer Ruggiero was the only one who did not query the messenger?" Caterina asked harshly. "Yet he doesn't lack respected colleagues in Rome he's concerned about."

Ginevra nodded. Whatever arcane measures Ruggiero the Old used, he'd gathered all the information he needed before his messenger's return. Lazaro's report had been for the benefit of the others, or at most a concrete confirmation of what Ruggiero already knew.

"We'd best go," Tommaso said softly. "We don't want to be missed with the house in such a state."

As they went out Caterina paused again at the painting of the Magi. "The three Wise Ones have abandoned Clement and turned against him, though he still has his own evil protection. All those innocent people suffered in his stead." She turned to Ginevra with tears in her eyes. "Will the Wise Ones abandon me too? Will they abandon Florence?"

Ginevra squeezed her hand to comfort her. "You are true to your blood. The Wise Ones are with you."

But as they entered the hall from the chapel, Ginevra heard the Florentine lions roaring in confusion in their distant cages. She shivered. Never had she felt so cold.

10

Tommaso hurried through the stone-paved streets as he had so often the last few days, catching his heel once in a while on the pavers in his haste. Since the affair in the chapel tutoring had been canceled; likewise cooking lessons and elaborate banquets for visiting guests. Tommaso now spent much of his time running messages back and forth between the Ruggieros', the Medici palazzo, and the mansions of other Ruggiero clients and allies.

Tommaso wore the prevalent uniform of uneasy times—a plain brown livery decorated with a crude wood-block print of a Florentine lily or lion on the chest and back. As soon as news of the sack of Rome spread, Florence became as agitated as a frothing, choppy, discontented sea. Every faction was at risk. Every faction needed anonymity.

That morning the *Signoria* had ordered the Vacca rung. Unlike Rome, when Florence's Senate ordered the great bell tolled through the streets, all the adult male citizens rallied to the Piazza de la Signoria. The formation of a *Balia* was approved.

This emergency committee met most of the day, then released its decision: The Medici's claim to Florence as a duchy was terminated.

To cheering crowds it was announced that the city would once again become a republic. And the young de' Medici heirs? As a gesture of compassion, they'd be allowed to remain in Florence as average citizens and favored with exemption from taxation for five years.

Gentile's face was closed tight as an unyielding oyster when he returned from the piazza with the rest of the Ruggiero household men in midafternoon. He handed Tommaso the anonymous livery.

"Run as fast as you can to the Medici palazzo. Tell your mother to have her and the children's things packed and prepared to leave. I'll follow behind within the hour with men-at-arms and a litter to carry her. Doctore Ruggiero has already given his approval. My wife will not give birth in that place."

He handed Tommaso a spit-iron from the rack by the fireplace. "Let no one stop you. If anyone stands in your way, strike him across the shins or knees with this. Hard."

The change of regimes was already having its effect on the streets. The artisans, who several weeks ago had started lackluster preparations for the St. John's Day midsummer festival, romped rejoicing through the streets, anticipating more funds in the public coffers for the celebration. This year the St. John's Day celebration at midsummer would be spectacular, laying to rest the memory of the lackluster *Calendimaggio.*

The alleyways were nearly blocked by the traditional tableaux and relics, and the juggernauts that carried and displayed them. Workmen swarmed everywhere—painting, gilding, restoring. Their patched-up efforts rolled, lurched, or hobbled down the streets to determine what further repairs might be needed. Tommaso found himself caught in the midst of a parade of the almost sound, the almost mended. All about him acrobats and dancers warmed atrophied muscles, singers atrophied larynxes.

An enormous mask, tall as three men standing on each other's shoulders, bobbed to and fro, flanked by a troupe of prancing choristers. When the great face turned in his direction, Tommaso saw that it belonged to Saint John the Baptist himself. What had appeared at first to be a ruff garnishing the mask's neck proved to be the fateful platter of St. John's destiny. The mask needed further renovations. Its paint and lacquer, abraded down to the supporting wickerware, looked as decayed as the eroded flesh of a corpse.

More masks, puppets, and disguised performers crowded in behind Tommaso. Since they traveled in his direction, Tommaso let himself be swept along.

Buffoni and *arlecchini* whirled round and round and flipped head over heels over head over heels in continuous cartwheels, laughing maniacally. Masqueraders pranced in grotesque parodies of court dances, disguised with the frozen faces of beautiful girls, unctuous churchmen, and gallant courtiers.

An *obby oss* bobbed by, capering with a strange dignity. The hooded androgynous figure was masked by a large horse puppet suspended from its shoulders fore and aft, so that it appeared to be riding the toy beast. But in fact it was its own two legs protruding below that provided the graceful canter.

The *obby oss* beat a steady, implacable rhythm on the round taut sides of its ostensible steed, as if on a drum.

In a piazza somewhere ahead fireworks began bursting. They must have been an old batch. Usually fireworks burst into glorious iridescent shapes of girandoles, Catherine Wheels, pinwheels, and fizgigs, followed by spent swaths of subtle color washing down the sky. But these pyrotechnics strafed the sky in stuttering shapeless flares of a white so bright their brilliance scorched Tommaso's vision. He could see nothing in between flashes, making it seem that there were two kinds of light. They alternated white and black, white and black. Tommaso moved haltingly through a landscape entirely leached of color.

The practicing revelers appeared to be trapped by each instant of stillness, each phosphorescent flicker. This made the masqueraders' progress horribly eerie. Under Tommaso's bedazzled gaze it looked as though they were changing. In quick, stark glimpses the *arlecchinis'* faces took on the empty hard whiteness of skulls. The *buffonis'* flesh and features grew twisted and lumpy, till they appeared less costumed men than strange beasts from another world altogether.

The *obby oss's* drum thrummed the beat of the failed fireworks' flashing—the stroke of the beat and the cadence of the light the same. Tommaso stumbled, feeling dizzy and ill. He thought he was suffocating. Suppressing a mounting panic, he traced air flowing into his lungs with each breath but still suffered the curious sensation that he was inhaling nothing.

Then he knew what caused that perception: There were no smells. No sulfur stench of fireworks, no musty scent of costumes stored away too long, no reek of sweating masqueraders, none of the aromas of cooking that made up Florence's background perfume. That was impossible! Tommaso's panic overwhelmed him. He pushed through the strobing throng, his fire iron held before him as a shield so that he wouldn't have to touch any of the apparitions.

Think! Think of odors! Tommaso silently screamed at himself. He thought salty—of prosciutto cooked in wine and served with capers. He thought unctuous—of eggplant stewed in almond cream, topped with *mortrew* custards. He thought spicy—of Neapolitan cinnamon cakes and medlar tarts dusted with ginger and saffron. He thought tart—grape pulp laved with lemon ice. He thought bitter and peppery—a bed of arugula garnished with chopped silver beet. He thought *dulceforte*—sweet-and-sour—roasted rabbit drowning in a piquant honey vinegar sauce.

His mouth flooded with saliva. *If I cannot smell, at least I will taste,* he told himself.

His mouth saturated with flavor. The lights flickered and faded behind him. Shouts replaced the *obby oss*'s drumming. Tommaso smelled garlic and lamb cooking somewhere nearby—real garlic, real lamb—and realized he was being carried down the Via Largo by a crowd of ordinary angry citizens.

"Take back what was wrested from us unfairly!" a woman just behind Tommaso cried. "*Make* Passerini return his pope-sanctioned booty!"

A stout man to Tommaso's left jeered. "Forget the money. Every last florin departed for Rome and Clement's coffers months ago. If the cardinal's family chooses not to ransom him, we'll have to take satisfaction directly out of his skin."

"Ransom?" someone ahead shouted. "Use the young pope-spawn to retrieve Florence's wealth." This suggestion met with great cheering.

Tommaso fought his way to the side of the crowd. The mob was set on plunder. It reached the Medici palazzo's front doors. Under Michelangelo's directions, in the last few days the first-floor windows had been

walled up and the great door barred shut. For the moment the crowd contented itself with screaming insults up at the few papal guards and de'
Medici retainers peeking from upper-story windows.

Was this all there was to protect the building? Soon the throng would
tire of threatening and start searching for timbers to ram the door with.
What could Passerini be thinking? Why didn't he act—if nothing else,
come to the window and try to calm the crowd with meaningless promises.
Tommaso edged the rest of the way out of the mob and ran.

The Strozzi palace was a quarter mile away. It too was well fortified.
But when Tommaso flung himself shouting against the door the watchman recognized him and let him in quickly. Inside, the atrium bustled with
preparations. Pikes were being oiled and sharpened, helmets and armor
cleaned, the barrels of arquebuses carefully checked. Many of those readying themselves were young, barely men—Clarice Strozzi's older sons and
their friends. Tommaso saw the second Ruggiero son—Cosimo's younger
brother Lorenzo—strapping on a saber and a dirk, though he was only a
few years older than Tommaso.

Tommaso leapt up and down, shaking his arms and flinging his bright
hair to draw their attention. "The Medici palazzo is under attack!" he
screamed. "A throng just arrived and they're intent on plunder!"

His words cut through the din. There was only a scant second of
stunned silence before the household leapt into action. Piero and Leone
Strozzi grabbed Tommaso under his arms and rushed him up some stairs.

"Wait . . . but . . ." Tommaso said, his feet scrabbling to reach for the
ground. The youths didn't waste any breath explaining what they were
doing with him until they burst through the door to a sitting room and
deposited him in front of Madame Clarice Strozzi.

"The Medici are under attack," Piero announced to his mother. "This
one brought the news." He rounded on Tommaso. "Speak!" he com-
manded.

Tommaso described the situation in as few words as possible. Clarice
Strozzi snatched up a small box on her desk and was striding out the door
before he finished.

"Muster everyone but the household staff," she said over her shoulder to her sons. "Tell them to bar the way after we've left. That should

suffice. At least Florence neither wishes nor dares attack the house of Strozzi yet."

In the courtyard she briskly inspected several helmets, then carefully slid one on her head over her coiffure and lace cap.

"Mama, will you next take up a halberd?" Leone asked, unable to suppress a slight smile.

"I don't need to. I handle a dirk very well—I prefer close-in fighting." Clarice refused to bandy humor with her second son. "In my girlhood, after Florence banished my father and all of us along with him—including those donkeys fated for Popedom, Giovanni and Giulio—I learned to master the small blade. I had to."

Leone's smile faded from his lips.

"The helmet"—his mother patted her head—"is for protection against the stones and other hard projectiles rabble are wont to throw. No one has exemption from that sort of haphazard attack."

Tommaso danced from one foot to the other, trying to fit some words in, to finish his report. "Madame Strozzi, the house . . . the house."

She stopped and looked at him. "Yes?"

"When I left, the mob was gathered at the great front doors. They would expect the garden wall and gate on the other side to be completely barricaded, but there are several hidden rear entrances. May I suggest that we not only avail ourselves of them, but take a covert route getting there, so as not to alert the crowd in front?"

Clarice Strozzi looked offended and drew back. Tommaso flinched. Then she leaned forward with a savage smile. "You have a bright mind, little cockerel. You may make no such suggestion because that occurred to me the moment you delivered the news. That is why we are not only going to follow a stealthy course to the Medici mansion, we are even going to leave by one of *this* palazzo's hidden exits."

She frowned. "However, one more thought does occur to me. Marsalino!" she shouted. The watchman looked up from buckling armor on one of the men-at-arms. "Someone may have seen this boy arrive. And it might eventually occur to that poltroon Passerini to send someone from within the palazzo out one of those hidden passageways to run to us for help. When and if they arrive, let them in and keep them here. Contrive to make all here seem busy so that it will appear we haven't left yet. We may gain some advantage that way." She threw on a cape, turned on her heel and headed down a corridor; men-at-arms, sons, allies, and Tommaso scrambling after.

Even having to detour from the most direct route, they approached the de' Medici property in short time. Tommaso opened his mouth to direct Clarice Strozzi to a door hidden behind the ivy. He snapped it shut when she headed straight for the entrance and was glad he hadn't spoken. Piero Strozzi and Lorenzo Ruggiero wrestled with the ivy till it parted, revealing a thick door of walnut with a great iron keyhole.

"We'll have to pound and shout to alert the household to let us in," said Lorenzo Ruggiero uneasily, brushing away some cobwebs. "If the crowd around the corner hears us we'll have to defend ourselves all the way in."

"Surely not," replied Piero Strozzi. "There will be men stationed in the garden in case it occurs to the mob to scale the back walls. They'll hear us easily."

Clarice Strozzi ignored both of them. From a pocket in her cloak she produced the small box she'd gathered from her desk before leaving. Inside was an ornate key and a small flask of oil. She dabbed some oil on the key, then worked the key into the lock.

"It's been years since this door has been used," she explained. "Some months ago we tested it on the garden side, but obviously could not do so outside without drawing attention. So the lock may still be rusty here."

She wrestled with it briefly. The key turned, eliciting scratchy protest from the lock. Clarice pushed. The door opened two thirds of the way. Piero Strozzi entered first, then helped his mother through. Tommaso followed after Lorenzo Ruggiero and Leone Strozzi. The men-at-arms backed in after him.

The door opened only so far because it bumped into a carefully pruned apricot tree. On the garden side the door had been overpainted to look like a faux portal, adding charm but not utility to the garden. The illusion was further heightened by the tree planted in front of it. No one would have guessed that it was a real entrance and that fully armed soldiers could enter and squeeze past the tree. Which might explain the grim faces of the kitchen scullions, stewards, and Medici men-at-arms, armed with cleavers, pikes, and arquebuses, that stood in a circle just past the tree.

Beyond them at the top of the kitchen steps stood one of Piera's sisters, Vittoria, waving at them to enter quickly and quietly. As Tommaso ran up the stairs he glanced over his shoulder. Clarice Strozzi was handing over the key and box to Lorenzo Ruggiero and posting a few of her men to join the guard in the garden.

"My father will arrive shortly with a litter for my mother," Tommaso whispered to his aunt when he reached her. "As soon as he sees the crowd out front he'll double back here. Tell Lorenzo Ruggiero to watch for him and let him in. My mother is . . . ?"

Vittoria hustled him inside. "In the sleeping quarters, lying down," she said. "I pray with all my heart that Gentile arrives quickly. Piera's time is soon. I will go warn Lorenzo Ruggiero. You go to your mother. You'll have to pack her and your little brother's things for her. She hardly has anyone attending her—just Mother and Maddalena. Everyone else is standing guard or preparing to defend. Where is Umberto? We sent him out through the wine cellar just a short time ago."

Tommaso marveled at Clarice Strozzi's foresight. "We'd already departed the Strozzis'," he told his aunt. "I saw the crowd from the street and ran to the Strozzis' to alert them. Don't worry about Umberto. The Strozzi watchman will let him in and keep him there in safety."

A slave girl a little younger than Ginevra was holding a fretful Pietro at bay before the laying-in room, trying to distract him with games. Pietro crowed with delight to see Tommaso. He clung to his older brother's livery as Tommaso went through the doorway.

Tommaso untangled himself from Pietro's grasp. "I'm sorry, Pietro. You can't come in here now."

Pietro promptly burst into tears. "I want to see Mother," he sobbed. "Why do you get to go in?"

Tommaso knelt before him. "I can't stay long either. You're going to have to be a big boy today, Pietro. We're going home and I'll need your help in packing things up. All right?"

Pietro's sobs subsided to sniffles. He tried to nod manfully and stepped aside to let Tommaso pass.

Piera looked lost lying alone in a high, broad bed meant to sleep a family of four or five or a whole raft of kitchen help. Grandmother Befanini perched on the bedside, wiping Piera's clammy forehead with a damp cloth. One of the cousins, a girl of almost marriageable age, waited in attendance with a basin of water. The only other person in the room was Great-Grandmother Angelina Befanini, perched on a stool in a corner. The room should have been bustling with sisters, female cousins and scullery maids.

Piera raised her head and feebly smiled at Tommaso. Tommaso's heart felt as though it would burst with pity. Her smile was as radiant as ever, but he'd never seen his mother so weak. When she'd given birth to Beatrice and Pietro she'd stayed in the kitchen kneading bread and chopping vegetables until minutes before her delivery. He rushed to her side, stretching across the great bed to clasp her hand.

"Mother, what is wrong?"

"Nothing. I'm just tired. I'm saving my strength for the baby." Piera glanced up at her own mother. Grandmother Befanini nodded and moved away.

"Maddalena, go get clean rags. We may need them soon," Grandmother Befanini instructed the cousin.

"Father is coming," Tommaso told his mother. "He should be here any moment to take you home."

"Even with that throng outside?"

So she knew. "Yes. When he sees them he'll come around to the back. I was sent ahead to pack your things—yours and Pietro's and Ginevra's. Clarice Strozzi and her men are here—they'll keep order," he tried to reassure her, though he wasn't sure if even Madame Strozzi could quell the anger he'd witnessed.

Maddalena walked back into the room with an armload of clean clothes. "Vittoria just told me," she said. "It was Tommaso who had the foresight to fetch the Strozzis."

Piera smiled and stroked Tommaso's hair. "You are a good boy. And so bright." An expression passed over her face that Tommaso couldn't decipher, except that part of it was regret. "I wish now I'd thought to . . ." she started, then shook her head. "Too late, too late," she whispered to herself.

Tommaso looked across the bed to his grandmother, who just shrugged. Behind her, Great-grandmother Angelina tilted her head in one of her inhuman birdlike gestures, Tommaso shivered

Piera squeezed Tommaso's hand. "Ignore my mood." She struggled to raise herself onto the pillows. "Maddalena," she called to the cousin, "my husband arrives shortly to escort me home, so I hope that you won't be needed after all. Be so kind as to pack Pietro's and my things." Piera turned back to Tommaso. "Ginevra won't be coming with us just yet."

Tommaso couldn't quell his stricken expression. His mother squeezed his hand again. "Don't look like that, Tommaso. The *Duchessina* needs her more than we do."

Tommaso didn't want to tell his mother how he'd felt the anger rising like heat from the crowd outside, but he couldn't help himself from blurting, "What if it's not safe here? Neither the *Duchessina* nor Ginevra should stay here."

Piera shook her head. "As long as the two of them are together they are secure."

"Then let Master Ruggiero bring Caterina into his home. That would be safer yet," Tommaso said, shivering again, thinking of the demons the old sage could undoubtedly unleash to patrol the property. All of Florence hummed with rumors of how it must be just such arcane measures that allowed Lazaro the messenger to escape unscathed from the pit of hell that Rome had become.

"Would that could be," sighed Piera. "But Messer Ruggiero retains more power by maintaining a stance of at least partial neutrality." She slid back under the covers. Tommaso ached with guilt for tiring her further. "Tommaso, we have but little time. Please fetch Ginevra, and quickly. I need to speak to her before your father comes."

Ginevra and Caterina would be cloistered away, anywhere on this floor or higher.

Tommaso glanced into rooms as he raced down the hallway. The hereditary de' Medici staff seemed better prepared than Passerini's men. Under the head steward's guidance, pages and scullery maids hauled buckets of water into each room and drew drapes back from casements; it might occur to the rabble to stone the windows and pitch flaming brands through them. Men-at-arms hid behind the bunched-back curtains, their arquebuses primed, ready to light and fire. And behind them other servants clutched long cudgels. If scaling ladders were raised against the house the stout staves would push them away. Kitchen staff roamed everywhere, armed with fresh-sharpened butchering knives. Among them Tommaso spied Grandfather Befanini and Great-grand-uncle Giacomo.

As Tommaso passed the main stairway he saw Clarice Strozzi in the inner courtyard below, directing her men, ordering defenses fortified throughout the first floor.

Tommaso headed for the stairway to Caterina's room, one more floor up. But as he passed the closed door of the grand *studiolo* he heard the muffled sounds of people arguing.

Past the *studiolo* a narrow hallway veered to the right. Tommaso turned down it. It led to the door of a servant's pantry. Tommaso opened the door carefully and stepped in. On the opposite side an open portal offered back access to the *studiolo*. The portal was obscured by a tapestry hung two arm lengths out from the *studiolo* wall. In this manner servants could enter and depart the *studiolo* discreetly, without having to make a grand entrance through the room's front doors.

Tommaso listened for a moment till he thought he'd determined everyone's placement in the room. Then he slid behind the curtain and sidled in.

Of the debaters, only Ippolito noticed Tommaso. His eyes flickered over him with no change of expression and without losing the rhythm of his argument. "We cannot do *nothing,*" the youth said as he paced the room. "You're going to have to take action one way or the other. You know which action I prefer."

Alessandro, his back to Tommaso, responded in sneering tones. "What you wish is not action at all. I say barricade the block, send for Strozzi armaments from outside, ready every wagon and equipage we have from within, and crush the rabble between the two forces till every last one of those rogues is dead. Then identify the bodies, banish their families, appropriate their property."

"I'm not sure that would be politic," Passerini said nervously, glancing over his shoulder at the noises of the crowd pressing up through the thick glass window. The cardinal sat huddled behind the room's enormous walnut and serpentine desk.

Ippolito and Alessandro strode back and forth, circling and glaring at each other like a couple of unproven tomcats negotiating their first fight.

Only Caterina sat perfectly still, perched in a brocaded gilt chair like a tiny queen set on a great throne. She looked straight ahead, her face frozen. Behind her two ladies-in-waiting clenched handkerchiefs, as nervous and pale as the cardinal. To her right stood Ginevra.

Tommaso shifted from foot to foot and tried to catch his sister's eye. This dialogue had obviously been going on for some time. There was no indication of when it might end. He doubted the participants knew that Clarice Strozzi had arrived and taken control of the situation. How was he going to extricate Ginevra?

Passerini waved his long, pallid hands like two fluttering wounded birds. "There's only so much I can do. My alternatives are limited. His Holiness made the three of you my charges and your safety is my first responsibility."

Tommaso realized, to his amazement, that the cardinal feared the imprisoned pope in far-off Rome more than the irate throng outside, who even now were screaming how they would like to tear Passerini limb from limb.

"This is outrageous." Ippolito pounded his fist on the desk. Passerini flinched. "Those people are Florentines and we are Florentines."

Tommaso noticed this pointedly excluded Passerini, a foreigner. Ippolito further barred the cardinal with his next words. "We are Medici. We have never been ashamed to be as one with the rest of Florence's citizenry. Better to be a member of the *popolo* here than an aristocrat in Rome. I say accept the *Signorias'* offer proudly."

"Surely you jest, cousin," snarled Alessandro. "Do not count me as one with that rabble outside."

"We must decide. We must decide," fretted Passerini. "We can barricade ourselves in here as His Holiness has done in Rome and await God's intervention. Or we can contrive to flee to safety and bide our time until fortune's reversal."

Tommaso despaired. The minutes were slipping by. In spite of his mother's wishes, he tried to think of ways he could smuggle *both* Ginevra and Caterina out of this room and this mansion. Perhaps if Caterina were dressed as one of the slave girls—it had fooled *him* once, after all.

The doors to the *studiolo* crashed open. The cardinal turned white and began to slide down behind the desk.

Clarice Strozzi strode in. Her sons followed, and behind them several Strozzi men-at-arms. "So, this is where you've been cowering."

She marched over to the windows and flung them open. The jeers and shouts of the mob poured through unmuted. Clarice turned on the cardinal.

"You should listen to that, Passerini. It is music of your own composition. It is you who have brought things to such a pass, with your incompetence and petty betrayals. This is not the way things were managed by my ancestors. With benevolence and gentleness *they* gained the steadfast loyalty of their fellow Florentines, so that the city stood behind the Medici through all adversities." Clarice's voice boomed through the room, filling it. They all quailed back. All but Caterina and Ginevra.

"And *you!*" Clarice rounded on Alessandro. "Your despicable and dishonorable behavior has betrayed the secret of your birth and confirmed to all the world that you are not true de' Medici. And not only you—but because of the monstrousness of your parentage—Clement too. Clement, wrongfully pope and now rightfully languishing in Sant' Angel."

Alessandro's hand went to his sword in its scabbard. Before he could draw it, Clarice was within his guard, her drawn dirk at his throat. Her sons were only an instant behind her, flanking Alessandro tightly.

The din from the street below had entirely ceased. Tommaso easily imagined hundreds of ears straining upward to catch every last syllable of Clarice Strozzi's tirade.

Alessandro neutralized, Clarice went to stand at Caterina's left side, facing the cringing men.

"Why are you surprised that all this day have turned against you? Leave! Leave this house to which you have no claim. Leave this city that has no regard for you. In this dark hour the family honor depends on me and Caterina."

Passerini looked almost relieved, now that his mind had been made up for him. He began snatching papers from the desk; papers gaudy with the heavy papal seal. Whatever directives Clement had been sending him, the cardinal knew he'd be ill advised to leave them behind to fall into the *Signorias'* hands.

Ippolito looked stricken to be included with Passerini and Alessandro. He reached out to Caterina, but Strozzi men were pulling him and Alessandro out the door, urging them to make haste. Alessandro was glaring hatred at Clarice Strozzi over his shoulder as he was tugged along.

Tommaso took advantage of the commotion to sidle near his sister. He tugged at her sleeve. "Ginevra, please come with me. Mother's time has come. She needs to see you before Father fetches her away." Tommaso invoked a silent prayer that somehow Gentile had found a way to get into the palazzo.

Caterina turned in her chair. "Piera has gone into labor?" Tommaso nodded. By now it surely must be true.

Caterina clasped Ginevra's hands in her own. "Go to her. You see what is happening here. Who knows when you will see her again? Who knows when I will see her again." Caterina's eyes filled with tears, shocking Tommaso.

"My gossip," Caterina said, "you will know where to find me when you are done."

Ginevra nodded gravely. Then she and Tommaso ran for the kitchen.

Tommaso noticed absences in the house. Though larger sculptures and heavy paintings were still in place, everything small, fine and easily portable had disappeared. Gone were the Persian vases carved from semiprecious stone, smaller marble busts, bronze medallions, etched crystal bowls meant to hold armfuls of flowers on their silver and enamel stands, and the small sculpture carved from the thighbone of the giraffe given to Lorenzo the Magnificent's private zoo by the Sultan of Babylon, after that gentle animal had finally died of old age. Tommaso wondered where Clarice had ordered them hidden.

In the kitchen all was chaos. Gentile had arrived, escorted by young Cosimo and several of the Ruggiero menservants, some wearing the Ruggiero colors and others the general Florentine livery. They stood in a cluster, arguing with Vittoria and Grandmother Befanini. Great-grandmother Angelina kept trying to hand a carrying basket to Gentile, who distractedly kept pushing it away. The litter lay in the entryway to the laying-in room, surrounded by carrying baskets and a light trunk. A strange odor hung in the air: It smelled like a simmering blend of vinegar, roses and freshly killed game.

Maddalena was piling up some of the baskets, almost in tears. She pulled Ginevra aside. "Your mother's water has broken, and still your father insists on taking her away. This is madness. She could deliver in the streets, in the middle of all those lunatics outside. You must speak to him."

Gentile heard Maddalena. "Ginevra? Is that you? Gather your things and get ready to depart. Where is Pietro?"

"Ginevra?" Now Piera's voice came weakly from the room. "Please, I must see you."

Ginevra turned one way and the other, torn between the two. She threw Tommaso a beseeching look, but Tommaso barely saw her as he cast his gaze looking about for Pietro. Where was his little brother? Where was the slave girl who was supposed to be attending him?

"Pietro?" he called. "Father, he should be right here." Tommaso and Gentile locked gazes: The toddler might be wandering about unprotected. At any moment the crowd outside could break in and storm the hallways. "Find him, Tommaso," Gentile said harshly.

Tommaso tried to think of where Pietro and the slave girl might have gone. The little slave would probably prefer to go into hiding—someplace safe like the chapel, perhaps. But Pietro would want to see the excitement. He couldn't stand to be left out of anything. The question was, of the two, who was more in control? If the slave girl were still in charge, they would not have left their post before Piera's door.

Tommaso rushed through every room on the front side of the mansion. Pietro would try to find the best view possible. But each room was still being guarded. The men-at-arms wouldn't let small children loiter.

When Tommaso finally found them he cursed himself. He and Ginevra had passed by the two fugitives on their way to the kitchen. The children were hiding in the space between a display cupboard and the sides of the generous niche the cupboard had been placed in. The cupboard was at the top of the great staircase leading down to the inner courtyard. It gave a wonderful view of the proceedings below.

Tommaso hauled Pietro out first, then offered his hand to the little slave girl. She flinched back from him. "I'm sorry, *Ser* Tommaso, but he wouldn't stay. I tried to make him mind, and then all I could do was follow after him."

Pietro was pulling on Tommaso's arm, craning to see down the stairwell. Tommaso looked over his shoulder. Clarice Strozzi, still helmeted, had ordered the front doors opened and was standing at the foot of the staircase, talking to a delegation of *Priori* from the *Signoria*. The scarlet-and-ermine-robed senators seemed to be straining to look officious but instead appeared nervous about the mob pushing at their backs.

With their shields Clarice Strozzi's men struggled to hem in the crowd pressing in behind the *Signoria*. As Tommaso watched, the rabble finally pushed through at the sides. The men-at-arms realigned themselves to secure the courtyard itself, but looters streamed away down the side halls. How long before they discovered the rear stairway leading up to the kitchen?

Tommaso turned back to the slave girl. "There is no time for this," he snapped. "Please yourself. Either stay and hope that none of the mob finds you here by yourself, or come with me." The girl grabbed at his hand. Tommaso pulled her out. He lifted Pietro to perch in the crook of his left arm with that single smooth motion he'd worked on so hard with his roast carving. Clutching the little slave girl with his other hand, Tommaso hobbled as quickly as he could toward the kitchen.

As they passed a narrow stairway that led up to the third-floor suites Tommaso heard someone rushing down it. He veered to make room and looked up. Cardinal Passerini, cloaked in anonymous black, descended on them with the look of a starving crow swooping on carrion. Behind him Alessandro bumped down the steps, trying to manage a number of parcels.

"There you are!"

Tommaso glanced about, wondering whom Passerini was addressing. But then the cardinal grabbed his right shoulder, almost dislodging Tommaso's grip on the slave girl.

"I believe I heard you mention that a pregnant woman is to be spirited out of here? Your mother, yes?" The cardinal's fear-fueled grin was terrifying. Tommaso froze like a trapped rabbit.

"He's kitchen help," said Alessandro. "Push on to the kitchen. That's where she'll be."

Push on they did, Passerini propelling Tommaso and the little ones before him as if he were a ship and they his prow.

Gentile stood at the door to the kitchen, waiting anxiously for Tommaso and Pietro. When he saw them in Passerini's hands he blanched. The cardinal shoved past him.

Ippolito sat at the worktable talking urgently to Cosimo Ruggiero. He was still flanked by Strozzi men-at-arms. He looked up in surprise at the cardinal's entrance.

Two Ruggiero menservants stood by the back door holding the litter, which was filled with a cloud of bed linen. Tommaso could just make out his mother's dark hair turning restlessly from side to side under all the fabric. Ginevra and the Befanini women hovered about her. A Ruggiero page was trying to hoist as many packed parcels as he could onto himself.

"Ah, Ippolito, there you are," Passerini said. "Excellent. Not a moment too soon. Put that litter down, my good fellows," he addressed the Ruggiero servants. "You," he said to the man hoisting the head of litter, "hand me your livery. You won't be needed after all. And you," he ordered the other man, "give your livery to *Ser* Alessandro here. Ippolito, get a livery for yourself from one of the others." He turned to the page struggling to balance Piera's parcels. "Drop those things. We have more important items for you to carry."

Ippolito shook his head slowly, his face angry. The two litter bearers looked at each other in confusion. Before they could act, Gentile stood between them and Passerini.

"So you think you're going to hide behind my wife's suffering to escape? Then, in a few blocks, when you've cleared the danger, take to your heels and leave her lying helpless in the streets? You shall not touch her."

Passerini stood nonplussed for an instant. He finally chose to pretend Gentile didn't stand there before him, hadn't spoken. "I am a cardinal," he said to the litter bearers. "The Medici heirs must safely flee. Lay down your burden."

"Stand fast!" roared Gentile.

The silence that engulfed the room was leavened only by Piera's pain-racked panting.

Let us go, Tommaso silently prayed, listening to that wrenching sound. *Dear God, please just let us go.* He slid Pietro out of his arms to the floor and readied himself to leap to his father's aid. The little slave girl had long since fled for cover.

"They will not abandon your wife, Gentile." The soft, clear voice belonged to Cosimo Ruggiero. "They'll have to accompany Piera all the way to my father's house. Only there will they be able to borrow the swift horses they need and money for traveling. The rest of our men will surround them so that no one will recognize them."

His words broke the spell that froze the room. Still, Gentile put out his hand to stop the cardinal. "Not him." He spat on the floor. "I'll not have him near her."

Cosimo looked about the room. "What about Ippolito? Will you trust Ippolito?"

Gentile looked at the young man. "Yes," he said reluctantly.

Tommaso watched the emotions struggling in Ippolito's face. He knew the youth didn't want to leave Florence, the Medici palazzo, or Caterina. But faced with a rescuer's duty, especially the rescue of a helpless woman, he could not refuse. His nod was as reluctant as Gentile's "yes."

A flurry of preparations followed. Liveries were pulled on over *luccos* and Passerini and his charges pulled their cowls up to shadow their faces. Gentile tried to grab Ginevra out from the middle of the cluster of cousins. Tommaso was reaching down again for Pietro, thinking gratefully of Cosimo Ruggiero's quick wit and agile diplomacy, when he felt something pushing against him. He turned in annoyance.

Great-grandmother Angelina stood there with the carrying basket she'd been trying to thrust onto Gentile earlier. It was much like the one beaten off Tommaso's shoulders by the Arrabbiati. Angelina pressed it into Tommaso's arms. Hair raised on the back of his neck when he felt something moving around within it.

"It is only She," Angelina reassured him, "and all of Her children but two. That is all we need left here to protect us."

Tommaso stood for an instant in slack-jawed amazement when he realized Angelina's enigmatic words meant that the case carried Gattamelata and her kittens. Tommaso nodded at his Great-grandmother but was afraid to let go of Pietro long enough to sling on the pack. He looked down to find his little brother cowed and silent, clutching at his leggings. "What is the matter, little *furafante?*"

"Papa . . . so scary."

Pietro had never seen their father angry. Neither had Tommaso, for that matter. Tommaso squeezed his little brother's hand to reassure him, then let go just long enough to hoist the basket onto his shoulders.

Ippolito had not taken his place yet at the head of Piera's litter. He was busy loading up someone with all the baggage. To Tommaso's amazement, the individual disappearing from sight under the parcels like an overladen donkey was none other than Passerini. For once the cardinal was making himself useful. Tommaso had to grudgingly admire the man's resourcefulness. No one would ever guess that the arrogant cardinal would stoop to act the laborer as a survival strategy.

In the meantime Alessandro had taken up his post at the foot of the litter and hefted the back poles. His nostrils were drawn and pinched in distaste. The strong smell Tommaso had noticed earlier must have been that of Piera's broken water, for the scent radiated from her like a strong, hot perfume. Alessandro and Piera were whispering at each with a hatred neither bothered to disguise.

"You seem in some distress, my lady," Alessandro gloated.

"Only for a short while, in the bearing of yet another child to thwart your kind. I've used the luxury of my lying-in time to begin to knit you a lovely garland of black hens' feathers and hemp. Don't you feel your time here growing thinner, Intialo?"

Alessandro paled but recovered quickly. "Patience, my lady." His smile bared all his teeth. "You wouldn't want me discomfited. I might slip carrying you down those steep steps to the garden."

"It would be worth my death to see the crowd outside tear you to pieces," Piera hissed.

As if conjured by her words, the mob at last found its way to them. Gentile and rest of the Befanini men rushed to the kitchen's entrance. The crowd paused at the bottleneck pass the door presented—a pass lined with sharp, competently wielded carving knives.

"Let us through," someone shouted.

"Proceed as you wish, at your own peril," Grandfather Befanini shouted back.

"Who is that you have there?" asked a tall man, craning his neck to see over and past the others. He pointed at the litter. "Do you mean to cheat us of one of the Medici brats with a ruse?"

Passerini and Alessandro hunched further into their cowls.

"That is my wife, who is about to give birth," Gentile said. "Let us leave in peace, unless you want the death of an innocent woman and her unborn child to stand between you and the gates of heaven when you face God on your judgment day."

"Let us see her then. We can decide for ourselves how big her belly is!"

Tommaso looked for a safe place to cache Pietro. If the crowd breached the doorway, his father and grandfather could kill any number of them, but eventually they'd be pushed backed and overwhelmed. After that, anyone who stood in their way—anyone who lost their footing and fell or who was as small as Pietro—would be crushed in the surge.

Out of the corner of his eye he saw his mother struggling to sit up in the litter. The litter rocked to and fro, almost unbalancing Alessandro and Ippolito, who had at last taken hold of the front poles. "Look at me," Piera gasped. "For pity's sake, look at me." But she couldn't raise herself and the crowd couldn't hear her. It began to press forward.

And abruptly halted. Tommaso rose onto his toes to see past the shoulders of the kitchen defenders just in front of him. Like curdled milk, both sides had drawn back. In the middle stood Angelina Befanini.

Gone was her dimness. She bristled like a gaunt old heron defending her nest. "You would threaten a daughter of the Befananis?" Her strident caw was a curse. "You would risk the wrath of the ancient Sacred Three? Foolish Florentines! Even now the demons of other realms have slipped their leashes and stalk toward Florence. Yet you menace a beloved attendant of our Holy Mother just when you need Her protection and guidance most. She will turn Her back on your disloyalty."

Angelina began to spin about counterclockwise in rickety circles. "You will die horribly in the streets, bloated and blackened," she wheezed. "You will die horribly in the streets, bloated and blackened. You will die horribly in the streets, bloated and blackened. And we shall do nothing to save you."

Three times made it a curse. And all of them knew too well what bloated and blackened presaged. Many of the men twined their thumbs in their fists in a *mano en fica*, muttering a prayer against the evil eye. They shrank back farther. In the silence Piera's panting groans could finally be heard.

"Let them go," the tallest man muttered. "We want Passerini and the Medici brats, not a pregnant woman and a broken-down old *strega*."

Gentile gestured to Ippolito. The litter trundled down the garden stairway as the mob fled the other way out of the kitchen and back into the mansion proper.

Tommaso held Pietro fast. He looked over his shoulder as he followed the others out the door. Angelina Befanini still stood in the middle of the kitchen, her brief return to angry consciousness fading, her eyes dimming to confusion. Ginevra stood beside her Great-grandmother, bracing her as the old woman seemed to collapse in on herself. Ginevra smiled sadly at Tommaso and framed the words "good-bye" with her lips.

Tommaso nodded to her and hurried down the steps.

Negotiating the litter through the clandestine garden door was difficult. But as soon as the party reached the street Gentile snatched the back poles of the litter from Alessandro. "I couldn't hear your words, but I could well see the manner in which you were speaking to my wife. De' Medici or no, if you were not still a beardless youth I'd thrash you right here in the streets, then leave you to the mercy of the mob."

Piera screamed in pain. "*Ser* Arista, we must hurry," urged Ippolito. They pushed forward, almost running over the pavestones.

Alessandro stood for a moment in confusion, exposed and afraid. Cosimo Ruggiero grabbed several parcels from the overburdened Passerini and thrust them at Alessandro. "Hold these up high on your chest, shadowing your face." Cosimo threw the edge of his Ruggiero-heralded cloak over Alessandro's shoulders.

"The get is just like his sire the pope," Tommaso heard one of the Ruggiero menservants say to another. "Both, as they take the coward's route, protected by the concealing cloak of one more noble than himself. It's a shame our young master won't get to share in the Bishop of Nocera's fame."

"Hush," said the other man. "Not many Florentines would applaud young Cosimo's bravery. Pray for his sake they never find out."

The way from the Via Largo to the Ponte Vecchio was crowded with throngs convening toward the Medici palazzo. Pushing against them was akin to fish swimming against the tide. Tommaso was all too conscious of Pietro's clinging to him, of the basket of cats dragging on his back.

By the middle of the bridge traffic cleared enough for the group to pick up its pace again. Tommaso wedged his way to the front of the litter. Piera was panting—her eyes closed, her face very white. Over his shoulder Ippolito murmured to her, "We'll be there soon, good lady. Take heart. Wait but a few more moments."

Piera whimpered. "I can wait but I don't think this child can. It's battling its way out of me."

Tommaso lifted Pietro awkwardly up into his arms and ran ahead toward Cousin Leonora's. He knew she'd drop her business to help his mother. But when Tommaso drew abreast of her stall it was closed. Tommaso slid Pietro back down to his feet. Like all the rest of Florence, Leonora must have decided to take part in the commotion, one way or the other.

The door to the Ruggiero palazzo opened just as the entourage approached it. Ruggiero the Old himself ushered them in.

"Hurry, hurry," he waved them through.

"Piera is almost . . ." Gentile gasped, just as Passerini shouted, "Our horses, where are our horses?"

"This way," Ruggiero the Old said, guiding the litter down a hallway. "My wife has a room all prepared, and several of your relatives showed up, insisting they would be needed."

Gentile and Ippolito carried the litter through an open doorway. Tommaso squeezed his eyes shut in relief at what he saw there: a bed as big as the bed at the de' Medicis', with the efficient Madame Ruggiero waiting at its head, hordes of bustling women servants and scullery maids, basins of hot water, piles of clean linen, and, at the foot of the bed, smiling, holding both of her arms out, Cousin Leonora flanked by three of her daughters.

The door shut behind the litter.

"I am a cardinal!" Passerini screamed. "You would put a servant's needs above mine?"

"For the moment, her needs are greater than yours," the old physician said. He looked the cardinal up and down. "I think it unlikely that you'll be giving birth in the next few moments. Compose yourself, *Ser* Passerini. You'll be safe here for at least this hour—ample time to ready yourself for departure. You will escape handily. This much I have foreseen."

Passerini looked less nervous. Alessandro merely looked sour.

The door opened again. "Out! All men out. We have work to do, and Piera has left us precious little time in which to do it," came Leonora's voice. Gentile and Ippolito pulled out the empty litter.

Ruggiero gathered the three fugitives together. "My steward has packets readied for you, including sufficient funds to cover your journey. My fastest horses are being saddled even now. You'll find them out back."

"But how can we repay you?" asked Ippolito. "The pope is a prisoner in Sant' Angel."

"Although you are His Grace's wards, you are also de' Medici. Clarice Strozzi will reimburse me from the family estates." Ruggiero smiled dryly. "Thank you, however, for asking, Ippolito. Now you should begin your preparations. My steward will lead you to your horses."

Gentile clasped Ippolito's hand as the youth drew away. "Bless you for your help, good Ippolito. Consider the Arista family always your allies." He was almost weeping.

Tommaso felt Pietro leaning against his leg as heavy and stiff as a log. He looked down at his little brother. Pietro's chubby face was strained. What a distressing day for him—separated from their mother, almost overrun by a mob, seeing their father consumed by unrestrained wrath, and now, though safely home, that same strong father so distraught.

"Father, I'll take Pietro to the kitchen and get him settled," Tommaso said.

"Yes, of course, thank you," Gentile said, distracted. He slid down to sit on the floor, his back braced against the wall opposite the doorway.

In the kitchen Beatrice pounced on Pietro and Tommaso. "Where have you been?" she scolded. "They said you were home. But you weren't here. Where are Mother and Father?" She looked around accusingly, as if the pots and pans and fireplace were guilty of hiding her family from her.

Tommaso smothered a smile. In the absence of her mother and older sister, Beatrice had tried to become the mistress of their little domain. At five years of age the kitchen was still the entire scope of their home to her.

"Mother is busy producing our next little Pietro," he reassured her.

"And Father is waiting on her. But I *did* bring back some other members of the family, a few whom you haven't had the chance to meet yet."

He took off the basket, laid it on its side on the floor, and opened its lid. Gattamelata stalked out scornfully, obviously displeased at the rough ride she'd suffered. The five kittens tumbled out afterward, probably thinking it had all been some sort of new game.

Beatrice squealed with delight. When Tommaso left the kitchen his younger siblings had forgotten him completely. They were busy playing with the kittens and Pietro was trying to find enough grown-up words to describe to Beatrice all his grand adventures in the Medici mansion.

Gentile still sat slumped in the hallway. He looked up as his oldest son returned.

"She's had the baby and *it* must be well—I can hear it crying." Gentile's face was tired and drawn. "But they haven't come out and told me anything. I don't know yet how Piera—"

The door opened. Leonora peered out. "Gentile? Could you come here?"

Gentile leapt to his feet. With his broad back filling the doorway Tommaso couldn't see into the room. But whatever Leonora murmured to him too quietly to be heard over the baby's crying, it must have been good news, for Tommaso saw his father's shoulders lift, his back straighten. Gentile reached out as Leonora handed him something. The squalling grew louder. Gentile turned around, a small squirming bundle in his arms.

"Look, Tommaso." Gentile beamed. "Your mother has given you not only a new sister, but practically a twin." He drew back the covers from the baby.

Tommaso was appalled. The baby bore a thick thatch of tufting scarlet hair, as if flickering fires haloed her head. The bright red color matched her wizened face. Its intensity matched her angry screams. Tommaso hoped the baby didn't really look like him.

Because, to him, the infant bore a terrible resemblance to Angelina Befanini as he had last seen her in the de' Medici kitchen—even down to a similar confusion in the eyes. But this tiny new thing was gripped by a rising, rather than fading, fury.

11

❧

That night Gattamelata slipped out the open kitchen window. She wound through the streets and crossed over the Ponte Vecchio, its stalls shuttered and quiet but still wafting the rich smells of the raw meat sold that day to her fine, delicate nostrils.

On the far side of the bridge she trotted to the Via di Leoni. Other cats watched her from windowsills and alleyways, but none challenged or greeted her. As she approached the cages behind the Piazza de la Signoria she finally encountered other cats, trotting in the same direction. By the time they'd assembled before the lions' cages there were thirteen of them in all. Like some great pride, the guardians of the portal to Florence—the seven great cats behind the bars and the coven of little ones in front—faced to the south and east, the direction from which the gathering shadows had begun to pool together and flow into Florence.

12

First week of June, 1527

Cosimo peered out the window of the antechamber at the fields and lovely rolling hills that lay beyond Florence's great walls. Flocks of birds flew like songs. Young crops glowed emerald green with the flush of first growth. It was as if even nature rejoiced at the lifting of Pope Clement and Passerini's yoke.

Then the young mage dropped his gaze to the streets just below him. At first glance the activity there appeared to mimic the countryside's prosperity. Florence was preparing itself to celebrate all summer long, starting with the annual grand fête in honor of Florence's patron saint, John the Baptist, on June 24.

Artisans gilded giant models of castles in the streets, where they would dry more quickly in the sun. The castles represented the many towns under Florence's jurisdiction. In huge cauldrons blocks of wax melted for casting into votive offerings. Refurbishers worked on the great chariots that would bear the city's most sacred relics in solemn procession. The relics, safely stored away, included a thorn from Christ's final crown, a nail from the cross, and the thumb of St. John himself. Costumes far more elaborate than mere clothing were under construction. Clothiers stretched newly dyed fabrics over struts so large and ornate that entertainers had to crawl inside to wear them.

There was much for Cosimo to see from his vantage point: craftsmen, costumers, street artists, and pantomimers. But there were others mingling among the ebullient, bustling Florentines. Wolves with serpents' tails glided between the renovated juggernauts. Raven-headed men in strange garb stood watching. Their beaks, split wide in enigmatic smiles, revealed canine fangs.

Cosimo knew through his father's tutelage that both of these sets of creatures came from a world called Amon and could tell of things past and future. Their presence was ominous but no surprise; of course they would have appointed themselves observers to the unfolding events here.

But there were others less neutral than the Amonons who prowled the streets. Cosimo saw gray shadowy shapes lurking—monstrous-visaged scurrying things; bone-faced revelers; entities so transparent they could only be glimpsed in brief shiny glints, like the sunlit angles of cut crystal goblets. Even with all his training Cosimo could barely make out that these last appeared to be riding stiff toy steeds, beating on their mounts' sides as though they were drums.

Could his fellow Florentines see any of the otherworldly visitors? It appeared that some noticed a few of them: the raven men and bone faces. They must assume the creatures were garbed actors preparing for the festivities. But Cosimo felt sure that most of the other visitors were completely invisible to the eyes of ordinary men and women.

However, the Florentines certainly saw and reacted to the rats that dashed in and out of alleyways and about their feet. Cosimo would have liked to have laughed as a stout gilder hopped about trying to stomp a bold rodent. But Cosimo couldn't. He knew others who would laugh at death but he was not among their number.

What did his fellow citizens think of the growing throngs of rodents? This Cosimo did know—he'd heard them talking. They thought the pests had been drawn by the promise of abundant festival food as surely as all the itinerant troubadours and entertainers had been drawn by the promise of employment. Cosimo knew this not to be the truth. The rats arrived in Florence to serve as steeds as surely as the drum-horses served as steeds to the *obby oss*. But the rats would not be ridden by mages from another land. They'd be ridden by the Eternal Executioner Himself.

"What's taking them so long?" Tommaso asked at his shoulder, startling Cosimo from his reverie. The young cook's voice sounded uncharacteristically fretful. Cosimo glanced at him. Tommaso was gazing past him at the scene below.

"We've been waiting quite a while. Why did they summon us if they didn't need us?" Tommaso retreated from the window. "And what do they want us for?"

"I'm sure they'll call us soon," Cosimo assured the younger boy. "And then we'll find out together what this is all about." He looked one last time out the window, his unease increasing. Why did he have the impression that Tommaso's nervousness derived from the goings-on outside, rather than the cryptic summons from their respective fathers?

But that could not be possible. Tommaso lacked the requisite training. Nor did the occult tradition run in the boy's blood. Or did it? Gentile looked at Tommaso curiously. He seemed to remember a rumor of an old Ruggiero servant/master pairing. Had it been his grandfather? His great-grandfather? The Aristas had served the Ruggieros in the kitchen almost as long as the Befaninis had served the de' Medici. It was certainly possible, even probable.

"How is your sister Ginevra?" Cosimo asked, studying Tommaso. "How does she find convent life?"

Tommaso shrugged, his eyebrows drawn together in an expression of annoyance. "Peaceful enough, I suppose. She works hard to help the *Duchessina* keep up her studies. It's difficult. The nuns of the Convent of Santa Lucia are salt-of-the-earth types. They aren't enthusiastic about higher learning. It's too bad the *Signoria* chose to send the *Duchessina* to Santa Lucia rather than to the Murate."

Tommaso's gaze kept drifting out the window. Was it Cosimo's imagination, or did the boy shudder? "Ginevra never complains," Tommaso continued, "but I know that to her alone has fallen the burden of keeping the *Duchessina* calm and tranquil in these uncertain times. With Madame Strozzi refusing to leave the de' Medici palazzo, Caterina is isolated from her family."

Cosimo nodded in sympathy. "It's a shame that two innocent young girls should have to bear the burden left by Passerini. But if Clarice Strozzi leaves the palazzo the *Signoria* will use the opportunity to further plunder the family assets. Caterina is enough of a de' Medici to understand that."

Just then, Enzio opened the door to the study and waved them inside.

Cosimo noticed Tommaso's shudder as they entered the room and the manner in which the boy cast surreptitious glances at Ruggiero the Old's occult accoutrements.

Cosimo looked at the company gathered within with some surprise. Whoever he might have guessed would be assembled, it was not this group. There were the two fathers, of course: his own, putting on the pleasant face that Cosimo knew hid grave concern. And honest Gentile, not bothering to conceal a certain air of misgiving.

It was the two others whose presence puzzled Cosimo. Why would Michelangelo Buonarotti and Il Tribolino require an audience with young Tommaso? Or himself, for that matter? Il Tribolino appeared as ill at ease as Gentile. Michelangeo, of all those present, was the only one who looked truly nonchalant. He leaned against the wall next to the great velvet-covered speculum, picking at his cracked fingernails and calluses with a dining dirk.

"Thank you for your patience," Ruggiero the Old addressed the two youths. "Tommaso especially, please forgive the delay. It was necessary— the four of us have been deciding a turn in your future. The greater the time and care invested in negotiating this decision, the better you will fare in the coming months."

The old man glanced over his shoulder. Whether at the speculum or Michelangelo, Cosimo could not tell. "I foresee that with the Medici largely in exile and Florence returned to republican rule, the call on my house to provide entertainment will abate for a while, with a subsequent slack in the kitchen's duties. At the same time, looking to the farther future, it has been brought to my attention, Tommaso, that you exhibit strong artistic talents."

Il Tribolino nodded solemnly in agreement. "On the unfortunate occasion of Tommaso's visit to my studio his gifts were noted. I told him then that he'd always be welcome back."

Out of the corner of his eye Cosimo saw a small smile cross Michelangelo's lips.

"Therefore we've decided to assign you to the *bottega* of Nicolo de Pericoli, also known as Il Tribolino, for a period of no less than one year and no more than three. During that time you shall wear two hats, so to speak.

"The first will be as one of Il Tribolino's apprentices. Your training

will be in the sculptural disciplines, as those most conducive to imple-
mentation in the culinary arts.

"Now, so as not to let your primary skills lapse during this period,
the other 'hat' you'll wear will be as a journeyman cook. You'll work hand
in hand with Il Tribolino's housekeeper. Though a good woman, Il Tribolino says she manages to produce only the most basic fare. It is hoped
that your knowledge will expand her skills."

Gentile's face bore a grudging look of approval. Cosimo guessed that
this was the condition that had won the master cook over.

"You'll need to work hard, but I don't believe you'll find the labor un-
manageable—at least not the cooking duties," Ruggiero the Old said. "Il
Tribolino's workshop is much smaller than our household."

"And our tastes far less refined," Tribolino interjected. "Your father
assures us that you are more than capable of managing the food needs of
a *bottega* such as ours."

Tommaso turned to his father with a look of amazement. Cosimo was
amused: Caught in making a blatant compliment, Gentile blushed as
brightly as his son.

Gentile waved his hand in an offhand manner. "I confess that you've
mastered the basics and are developing adequately in the more refined as-
pects of the art. I concur with *Ser* Ruggiero that a post of greater but still
limited responsibility might be of benefit to you at this juncture. And with
the increasing emphasis on frippery in dining presentations, developing
your artistic talents could serve you well in the future.

"However . . ." Gentile paused to frown at his employer, "I do not understand *Ser* Ruggiero's timing in this manner. The Medici may have suffered another reversal of fortune, but they are not my master's only clients.
Many of those others now see *their* stars rising as the Medici's fall. Florence prepares to flourish and celebrate. *I* foresee for the House of Ruggiero *more* of a need to entertain, with subsequent demands on the kitchen
and its help. In which case I'll need my son's two good hands."

Cosimo knew that normally his father would enjoy Gentile's logical
protestation. But the old mage only favored his cook with a strained smile.
"I'll compromise with you, good Gentile," the old man said. "If your fore-
cast proves correct and mine false, we'll arrange with good Nicolo here to
borrow Tommaso back."

Gentile looked chagrined, no doubt realizing the challenge he'd laid down to his master's field of expertise. But he also looked bewildered.

As he should, Cosimo thought. Gentile's reasoning had been flawless. But the cook, armed only with his intellect, could not know what Ruggiero, imbued with arcane knowledge, had discerned. The apprehension Cosimo felt earlier returned. His father had told him only a little of what the future portended. But with his own meager skills Cosimo saw the phantoms gathering in the streets, felt the weight of the future gathering dark and heavy on the horizon.

"Tommaso, you do not look entirely happy," Ruggiero the Old observed.

"I'm grateful for this excellent assignment," Tommaso said. "Any reluctance you observe is only due to leaving my current duties unattended. My mother has been weak since the birth of the new baby. My sister Ginevra continues to accompany Caterina de' Medici in her confinement in the Convent of Santa Lucia. I am the only family member dispensable enough to take the time to visit my sister and make sure her needs are met."

Cosimo marveled at Tommaso's subtle diplomacy. In the guise of Ginevra's dutiful brother, Tommaso enjoyed fairly free access to the Convent of Santa Lucia. He'd developed into the main conduit of information between the Ruggieros and Caterina. His tactful comments reminded Ruggiero the Old of his clandestine assignment.

"Excellent points that I've already considered," said the mage. "Therefore, to ease the burden on your mother and compensate your father for the loss of your able hands, I'm in the process of purchasing a suitably trained slave from the Vespucci family.

"As for your obligation to your sister, your concern is commendable. Rest assured. Because your apprenticeship will be one of double duty, you shall be compensated with extra leisure. That will leave you time to visit your parents here *and* your sister in Santa Lucia."

Ruggiero the Old's message was as subtle as Tommaso's: The boy would be expected to stop by the Ruggiero household to pick up messages for Caterina before visiting the convent.

"And an added benefit," the sage continued, "one that your father approves of, is Il Tribolino's custom of continuing his apprentices' formal education."

"I strive to emulate the example of Lorenzo the Magnificent," Tribolino chimed in, "who provided the same for the students of his arts school."

Gentile had been nodding in approval, but his face suddenly soured.

"With such advantages, I can only declare myself fortunate, pleased, and willing," Tommaso said.

"Then all that remains of this issue is to draw up the bonding papers and finalize a few details," Ruggiero the Old said. "You'll move to good Nicolo's *bottega* tomorrow. Cosimo, I requested your attendance at this meeting because I'd like you to act as second to this arrangement. Should any matter arise regarding Tommaso's apprenticeship, if neither myself nor Gentile is available, you will stand as official arbiter. Do you agree to this responsibility?"

"Of course, Father." Again a hidden message. Ruggiero the Old was knitting Tommaso and Cosimo's lives closer and closer together in the service of Caterina de' Medici.

"Then the two of you may go. Cosimo, tomorrow you'll help Tommaso move his things. And I'll summon you back here when the papers are ready to cosign. *Ser* Buonarotti shall serve as our witness."

Michelangelo nodded to Cosimo. His catlike smile had not changed throughout the entire proceedings.

Cosimo waited to speak until he and Tommaso walked down the hallway far enough to be safely out of hearing of the men in the study.

"You seem pleased to move on to Il Tribolino's," he said.

Tommaso nodded. "And you are surprised by my reaction. Please don't take offense, good Cosimo. I love this place. I consider it my home. And your family is the finest employer in all of Florence."

"But this new venue will provide you with new friends and opportunities," Cosimo suggested. "And perhaps a chance for adventures away from your parents' watchful eyes."

"Certainly, as you say, new opportunities," Tommaso agreed. "Ever since the night Ippolito and *Ser* Buonarotti delivered me from the Arrabbiatis' beating, my hands have hungered to create delicacies not merely for the palate but for the eye as well. Il Tribolino provides me with perhaps the only chance I'll ever have to learn the skills I need.

"But as for adventures, lately I've had enough to last for years." Tommaso shivered, paused. His eyes looked haunted.

Cosimo's earlier apprehension returned. They came to the back door of the mansion. The kitchen lay directly across the courtyard. From it issued a high-pitched keening, like a kettle whistling furiously. The hairs on the back of Cosimo's neck prickled erect at the sound of it.

Tommaso looked glum. "And I may as well confess it. For the first time in my life I'd rather live apart from my family. My mother is so weak that it cuts my heart to see her. My father worries himself to exhaustion looking after her. Pietro and Beatrice have retreated into their own little world together. I've tried, but I'm no comfort to any of them."

The shrieking came again, louder.

Tommaso made a sour face. "And always, always, that infant screaming her lungs out. You'd think her a demon from hell. So, Cosimo, since I can be of no use to my family just now, I'd rather take the coward's route and hie myself away for a while."

Cosimo chuckled. He felt relieved. What he'd supposed, for just a brief moment, to be precognition on Tommaso's part was simply the dread any eldest son felt for his family at the onset of difficult times.

He clapped his hand on Tommaso's shoulder. "Don't task yourself with the coward's flail. Even your father finally looked pleased at your new position, despite his objections. Although I must confess myself surprised at how he scowled at the mention of Tribolino's extra schooling. I've never known Gentile to be less than enthusiastic for higher learning."

"It wasn't the education he objected to, but the mention of a Medici— Lorenzo the Magnificent," Tommaso said.

"How strange for someone whose family has been in the service of my family for generations to be anti-Medicean." Cosimo kept his tone light, as if this potentially dangerous topic was nothing more than cause for mild amusement.

"He's not," Tommaso defended his father. "His objections are of a personal, not political, nature. You know how enamored he is of my mother, how devoted to our family. But whenever the Befaninis or the de' Medicis themselves call, my mother returns instantly to the palazzo on the Via Largo. Now my sister has vanished into the service of Caterina Maria Romola. And even I . . ." He shrugged and let it go at that. "My point being that wherever he turns, my father sees the Medici taking his loved ones away or putting them at risk. That was why he was grateful when Ippolito helped bear my mother's litter home. Ippolito was the first Medici to put himself at risk for *our* family."

"And you, Tommaso . . . How do you feel?"

"I understand perfectly how my father feels. And yet . . ." Tommaso blushed. "And yet I confess myself to be one of the Medici-beguiled members of my family."

The baby screamed again, a sound of pure raw fury. Cosimo tried to smile at the appalling noise. Tommaso shuddered.

"Have they named her yet?" Cosimo asked.

"Yes. Luciana. She'll be christened this Sunday. But already my mother's pet name for her is *Melata*—*Honey*—after our sweet-tempered cat." Tommaso shook his head in disbelief.

13

The person in Il Tribolino's workshop Tommaso most feared meeting was the cook in whose kitchen he was to be thrown; the grown woman to whom he, a boy not quite yet twelve, was supposed to give culinary advice and aid. When he and Cosimo arrived that first day they'd been escorted to the back of the *bottega*.

In hindsight, Tommaso didn't know why he'd been surprised to find the cook to be none other than the stout-armed woman who'd prepared his bath and helped Tribolino's apprentices clean him up after the Arrabbiatis' attack.

They entered the kitchen to find her rolling out dough for pasta. She looked up, beamed, dusted herself off rather inadequately, and grasped Tommaso's hands in her own floury ones.

"Aha! My new colleague! I've been berating the master for years to find me a partner. And at last, as I face my dotage, he *finally* acts to ease my burden.

"I am Elissa Pecorino, daughter of Calandrino and Emilia Pecorino. The Pecorinos trace their lineage back five generations—my grandfather Pasquino, his father Tedalefo, his father Antigono Jacopo, and his father Rinaldo—to the Pecorinos of Radda en Chianti, where my family excelled in the making of the cheese whose name we bear, not to mention excellent ricotta and *marzolino* also. My mother's parents were Ricciardi and Gianetta Sedani. My mother's sister, Constanza, bore a daughter, my cousin Leonora. And since Constanza married an Arista, Leonora is also your cousin. Therefore, we can also consider each other to be cousins of a sort. Would that I had known that the night you came to us so sorely wounded." Finishing this litany, she crushed Tommaso in an embrace that was indeed reminiscent of Cousin Leonora.

"You could not have treated me more kindly even if you had known," was Tommaso's muffled response.

After that they got on famously. Since she was responsible not only for cooking but also for laundry, cleaning the back living quarters, shopping and managing all accounts pertaining to the apprentices, Elissa Pecorino was glad to relinquish as much of the kitchen work to Tommaso as possible.

Conversely, Tommaso had anticipated a friendly reception from the other apprentices. They were, after all, boys close to him in both age and social station. But they'd surprised him by remaining cool. He was now two weeks into his apprenticeship and still unable to win them over.

The three older boys distrusted him because he came from nowhere to step directly into their level of work and schooling. The two younger boys resented him because although he was nearer to their age, he was allowed to practice on small sculpting assignments of his own alongside the older apprentices while they cleaned up the studio and carried in buckets of water and loads of oak for the foundry.

The living arrangements in the *bottega* were also different than Tommaso expected. Unlike most master artists, Il Tribolino did not live in the studio. He'd married well and lived with his wife and children in a home not far away. Therefore, he was present only at the midday supper. All the other meals were cooked for the apprentices, the one journeyman sculptor and Elissa Pecorino. In spite of Il Tribolino's claims to desire more refined food for his studio, in truth, the simple, hearty, and nourishing comestibles Elissa Pecorino had cooked all along were what was called for.

Since he prepared so much of their food, the other apprentices didn't dare quarrel with Tommaso or torment him unduly. The older boys were at least civil to him. Tommaso wondered if that might also be because they had helped clean him up the night of the beating and knew he'd already suffered his share of hard knocks.

Yet none was friendly to him. When he came to bed late at night after cleaning the kitchen, long after the rest of them had retired, he found that the five of them contrived to sprawl out so completely that there was no room for him in the huge bed they all shared. He was forced to sleep at their feet at the bottom of the bed. At least the summer evenings had turned warm enough that Tommaso survived in spite of the lack of covers.

On his second visit home Tommaso sat down with his father and told him how matters stood.

"And again, what is it that you do? Beyond the work as an artist's apprentice, what service do you provide there?" Gentile asked.

"I prepare and cook food for them," Tommaso replied.

"For whom, exactly?"

"For Madonna Elissa Pecorino, the apprentices and journeyman, and, at midday supper, also Master Tribolino."

"So . . . you cook food for people?"

Tommaso's brow furled in confusion. What could his father be getting at? "Yes. You know that is what I do. You taught me those skills yourself."

"I taught you how to prepare *food*, yes. You do that well, Tommaso. But that is only half of it. You must develop your skills in the second part of the equation. That art you see demonstrated in this household and of which I have spoken to you. But I cannot teach it to you. You must develop your own abilities. It matters not what delicacies you prepare if you are blind to those you prepare them for."

"Food . . . people," Tommaso said slowly. "Are you saying that I must know those I serve as well as I know the food I serve them?"

His father smiled. "Master Ruggiero purports to discover the hidden mysteries of the world. But if you, my son, learn well this important lesson, you will not only gain renown as a chef, you may also find at your disposal the key to unlock the mysteries of the human heart, for a heart happily nourished opens more easily."

Tommaso returned to the *bottega* thinking of his father's words. At the midday supper he planned the courses with an eye to pleasing Il Tribolino. The rest of the day he and Elissa served good, hearty, anonymous meals.

He'd been neglecting the most formidable weapon in his arsenal to win the friendship of his fellow apprentices.

The baking bread still smelled barely cooked, like raw yeasty dough. Tommaso paced back and forth in front of the oven. Never had he known a loaf to take so long to finish. Elissa Pecorino glanced up at him from the kneading trough. "Is this a new foundry experiment?" she asked politely. "Perhaps the friction of the air, as you pass by more and more quickly, adds to the *fornaio*'s heat?"

Tommaso grinned sheepishly. "I hadn't thought of that. Do you think that might be true? If so, I could make a case that anxiety, not necessity, is the mother of invention."

Elissa's laugh was warm and comforting. "And who would not be anxious before submitting their first formal assignment to the master? I believe your loaf is ready at last. Perhaps you could cease your pacing and liberate it."

The bread did smell done. An aromatic steam issued from the *fornaio*, as heady with the scents of saffron, cinnamon, cloves, and coriander as with the usual golden smell of baked bread. Kitchen cloths wrapped around his hands, Tommaso pulled it out. He slid a thin sharp knife gently along the sides, then let it rest for a few minutes. Finally he turned it upside down on a *tondo* and carefully pried at it until the bread released and fell into the plate. Tommaso examined his work and sighed with satisfaction. He placed the *tondo* near the hearth to keep the bread warm.

"Tommaso, hurry to finish your work here. The master wants us together for our critique." Salvatore, one of the older apprentices, stood at the kitchen door.

"I'll be right there," Tommaso said. "I have only a pot to finish cleaning." He dropped the still-warm pewter pan into a wash basin. "By the time the rest of you have set up your pieces I shall be there."

Salvatore cast him an impatient look and left.

Tommaso hurriedly scrubbed the pewter pan. He thrust it for a few moments back into the still-hot *fornaio:* That was the quickest way to dry it. Then he pulled it out, his hands battened again in cloths, and ran into the studio, his heart pounding. This would be his first critique of a completed assignment.

The three older apprentices' pieces sat well displayed, each on a separate stand and flanked by their makers. The two younger boys stood nearby: Although they were not yet allowed to work on their own pieces or complete assigned projects, they still attended the evaluations so that they might develop their critical eye. Vittorio, the journeyman, was adjusting an armchair into a comfortable position before the pieces. As soon as he finished, Il Tribolino sat down in it and settled in.

There were no display stands of appropriate size left. Tommaso propped up his piece as best he could on a workbench, setting it in a near upright position by placing a heavy chunk of plaster behind it. He noticed the stifled scornful smiles on the other apprentices' faces.

"Now that we are all present," Il Tribolino said, nodding toward Tommaso, "let us begin. The lesson at hand consisted of modeling a casting for a die suitable for producing a run of large medallions, as I demonstrated for you. Such items are popular and, when you have established studios of your own, may well prove to be your economic mainstay while you await assignments of larger commissions. This exercise also allowed you, in a smaller format, to practice bas-relief sculpting, so that perhaps someday you might compete for such glorious consignments as Ghiberti's inspired Baptistry doors."

The apprentices smiled as expected. Il Tribolino was a kind man. His humor, while not sidesplitting, was pleasant enough to acknowledge.

Il Tribolino stood and walked over to the first piece. "Ah, Gherardo. The Annunciation. Your devout parents would be proud of your choice. Or are you cleverly looking to a future of religious patronage? Perhaps in the manner of my gossip Benevenuto Cellini, who strikes such medallions for the pope?"

Gherardo ducked his head and grinned.

"So much for theme," said Il Tribolino. "One can hardly fault such holy inspiration. Now . . . the artwork itself. Your composition is weak—the figures do not fit as nicely as they might within the circular form."

Gherardo's grin dropped from his face.

"On the other hand, the modeling is quite fine. Both your Virgin and angel are nicely proportioned. The relief work is well done—the finished cast piece should exhibit excellent contours and sense of shadow. Do not worry unduly about the composition. You will learn.

"As for the technical assessment . . ." He picked up the piece and examined it closely. "A fine job. Your investiture burned out well and you've cleaned the mold properly. It will make a fine casting.

"Salvatore, I believe you are next?" So he went to each in turn. Salvatore's die illustrated a scene from the myth of Daphne and Apollo. Bertino had settled for a simple bust in profile, in the ancient Roman style.

"And now for our newcomer." Il Tribolino had to stoop to look at Tommaso's piece on the bench. Its depth was much greater than the other dies'.

"Our little cook has delusions of grandeur," Gherardo laughed. "He must expect to attract patrons richer than Cosimo Pater Patriae to fill such a fat thing with a casting of gold or silver."

"Perhaps he confused the vocabulary of the *bottega* with that of the kitchen," countered Salvatore. "Tommaso, a medallion should be more the thickness of a flat bread wafer than a cake loaf."

Il Tribolino waved his apprentices to silence, but his brow creased as he picked up Tommaso's effort. "Let's examine its artistic merits first. Ah, another classical theme. A depiction of the goddess Ceres, if I'm not mistaken."

He peered into its depths. "And nicely done, as best I can make out. The Mother of grains and agriculture—an appropriate theme to your calling, Tommaso, but I know of few bakers wealthy enough to commission you for such a piece. Still, quite excellent for a first effort. Your composition is well balanced. The modeling is a little hard to see because of the die's depth, but appears well done.

"Technically . . ." Il Tribolino sighed. "I fear your fellow students are right. The sides of the mold are a little uneven and likely to crack under the heated brunt of the molten poured metal. It is also far too deep. No one would ever commission such a thick medallion. Besides proving unnecessarily expensive to cast, the resulting piece would be of such a thickness as to contradict the concept and technical accomplishment of bas-relief. With such a thick chunk of metal, you might as well simply make it a full sculpture in the round. I'm afraid we'll not be able to cast a sample from it, as we will the other dies here." Il Tribolino gestured to the pieces set on the display stands.

"But it already has been cast," Tommaso said. "With your permission, I will be happy to fetch the finished piece for your assessment, so that you might comment on it more fully."

Tommaso slipped out of the circle of astonished faces. In the kitchen he picked up the fragrant bread on its *tondo* and hurried back into the studio. He set it down on the bench next to the die.

The dough had risen and filled perfectly into the mold, so the resulting bas-relief in the baked bread bore flawless witness to Tommaso's modeling skills.

Ceres stood in the middle, flanked by bound sheaves of wheat. Her hands extended outward in benediction over a procession of cattle, horses, sheep and goats. The sun rose over her right shoulder, the moon over her left. The bottom of the die had toasted the bread perfectly in highlights of gold and shadows of warm brown, so that the chiaroscuro effect of a well-done bas-relief was perfectly satisfying.

"Yes, Master, the mold's sides are irregular. I hope, with more experience and skill, to correct such problems in the future. And I know my die is too deep for precious metals. But that is because I will never work in the nobler elements, like my colleagues here, but rather in materials far more transient and humble. I chose a depth appropriate to the medium to be cast. And yes, my design would only appeal to a baker's patronage. But I disagree that a baker would not part with a few florins for such an item. With a such a loaf pan he could please his customers' eyes as well as palates and declare at the same time his wares uniquely his own. Perhaps he might come to commission a different design for each kind of bread he bakes. And then, indeed, I might prosper."

At that, everyone laughed. Il Tribolino nodded his approval.

"Now, shall we conduct one last critique?" Tommaso asked all of them. "The obvious one for such a piece?" He grasped the edge of the loaf to begin to break it into pieces.

"No, wait." Gherardo put out his hand to stop him. Tommaso knew what he felt. The bread was truly beautiful. How could anyone with art in their soul bear to destroy it?

Tommaso tore off the first piece and put it in Gherardo's hand. The bread's steaming interior, flecked with spices and studded with raisins, released an even headier aroma.

"To compensate for the sadness of executing one's art in transitory materials, there is the satisfaction of knowing that just as pleasing duplicates can be easily and quickly cast, or should I say baked?" Tommaso said as he broke off and passed pieces to all of them. As casually as he could, he watched each in turn for their reaction.

He'd hoped to accomplish much with this simple loaf of bread. He wanted to prove to the other apprentices that he was their equal in skill and talent, yet at the same time reassure them that he constituted no threat to their artistic futures. Had he succeeded? It seemed to Tommaso with each bite they took that the edge of their reserve toward him melted away a little.

Since his discussion with Gentile, how hard Tommaso had studied each of them in turn! The youngest apprentice, Pagolo di Arezzo, seemed happily lost in another world as he ate his piece. Tommaso smiled to himself. The bread was from a recipe for *panina gialla*. Lucious with raisins and spices, it was typical of the baked goods from Arezzo that gave that area its name of "the sweet Aretine land." Tommaso had guessed the youngster, apprenticed away from his birthplace, might be homesick. As Pagolo eagerly accepted a second piece of the *panina*, Tommaso knew he'd found the opening to at least one heart.

14

In the cloisters of the Convent of Santa Lucia two girls sat in the shade on a stone bench playing cat's cradle with a long piece of hemp cord, chanting as they changed its patterns and handed it back and forth to each other. Some of the nuns who passed them frowned to see them at idle play. But, because the girls were not novitiates, there was little they could do. Other nuns smiled, remembering how they had played the weaving game in their own childhoods.

"The Well."

"Cat drinks from The Well."

"Cat turns into Lion."

"Lion climbs The Ladder."

"The Ladder's climbing changes into Candle's flame arising."

"Candle's light fades before The Sun."

"The Sun catches Death."

The two girls looked at each other, sighed, and began again.

"The Well." Ginevra strung the universal opening of initial loop about her hands and secondary loops around her fingers.

Caterina studied the pattern. She dove her fingers in, reweaving it. She slipped the new configuration onto her own hands. "Light glinting in The Well gleams like Diamonds." The pattern drew out to a set of gem shapes strung tight between two supporting lines.

"Diamonds are part of the pattern of Snake's endless tail." Ginevra's choice shifted and multiplied the diamonds into scales.

The girls looked at each other with hope. The snake catches its tail to become the endless hoop of regeneration.

"Snake flees before Two Foxes."

"Two Foxes catch Two Squirrels."

"An Arrow finds them all." Caterina looked up with tears in her eyes.

"Arrow catches Death." Ginevra wove the only figure possible. "Again. We'll do it again until it comes out right. Start with our strengths and our allies."

"The Well."

"The House by The Well."

"Twelve Men come to The House." They both thought gravely for a moment who the twelve men might be. Each intersection in the string figure represented a person, a place or an event.

"Twelve Men carry Money."

"The Money flies, well spent, on Bird's Wings."

"The Bird's Wings fly, in turn, on Lightning."

"The Lightning brings . . . Death."

"We must stop this," said Ginevra. "We cannot avoid Death. It *will* come. That being so, we must focus on the goals at hand and let Death take His due." They started over.

"The Well."

"The Well reflects Twin Stars." Their hands clasped and they gazed into each other's eyes as they transferred the twine. They knew well just who the twin stars were.

"Twin Stars hidden by Storm Clouds."

"Not Lightning," hissed Caterina. "Not Lightning again."

Ginevra nodded. "Storm Clouds . . ." Her fingers darted in and out. She drew the loops onto her hands. "Storm Clouds bring rain to Little Fishes."

Caterina crowed and went to work feverishly. "Little Fishes are caught and cooked in The Cauldron."

For the first time Ginevra looked hopeful. The Cauldron was the sign of one of the Wise Three, the Great Mother who was also the Cook.

"The Cauldron's cooked feast feeds the Cat." Even better—another of the Wise Three.

"Cat goes raiding the Bird's Nest."

"Bird's Nest built of Sprigs of Rue." Better yet.

"The Bird herself watches, perched on a Sprig of Rue."

"Bird is threated by The Hunter."

They looked at each other soberly. There were only two possible transfers. Death, or . . .

"Bird flies away," Ginevra finished. "I'm sorry, Caterina. That's the best we've been able to do. From here we can go to Bird flies away to a Far Land. Then end on Far Land At Peace."

Caterina looked at the design in despair. "I know. Bind it up, Ginevra, and send it to your mother. She must know."

15

That same afternoon Piera sat nursing her new baby in the Arista family sleeping quarters in the Ruggiero palazzo. She shifted Luciana from her right to her left breast, then caressed her sore nipple with weary fingers. How was it possible that she, who had nursed both Ginevra and Caterina simultaneously, who'd given such a sturdy start to Tommaso, Beatrice, and Pietro, now produced barely enough milk to feed one tiny, unhappy baby?

In her months at the de' Medici mansion Piera had been so busy helping her family and teaching Ginevra and Caterina that at times she'd forgotten her pregnancy, only remembering when her bulk rudely intruded. Now Luciana acted the part of abused starved outrage, as though punishing Piera for neglect suffered in the womb.

Piera looked down at the baby. How had her other three looked? Oh, she remembered well. Drowsy, sleepy eyes. Contented gentle sounds halfway between dove's coo and cat's purr.

Not this one! Luciana's eyes bulged awake, almost crossed. She suckled so hard it felt as though she were trying to draw Piera's entire breast in through her tiny mouth. All this feeding and still she remained so small. And so very angry.

"Oh, Melata," Piera breathed. "I almost fear to go looking for your stone."

With her spare hand Piera picked up pattern-stained pebbles that she held in a pile in her lap. She drew them forth one by one, fondling each of them in turn in her palm, calling them by name. "Caterina. Ginevra. Tommaso. Beatrice. Pietro. Gentile. Cosimo . . ." The list went on and on. Small though the pebbles were, the pile was heavy. "Stay near each other. Stay safe under the watchful eyes of The Three."

She picked up a boldly marked pebble that perched alone on the chest next to her. "Ippolito, come join the others as quickly as you can, for your own and their protection." She placed it with the others in her lap and passed her hand over the pile seven times before setting it apart again. As soon as she grew stronger she would have to search for Luciana's stone.

Besides Luciana's, one other stone was missing from the pile. Across the courtyard, in the mansion itself, under a stairwell, Piera had hidden a small box inlaid inside and out with the "ever-watching eyes" of round slivers of black and white onyx. A strand of bright blue beads was wrapped tightly about the box. The strand was secured with an intricate baffling knot. Inside the box lay a dull brown stone on which Piera had long ago stained a pattern in saffron orange.

She'd hidden the box on the day she'd been summoned back to the Medici palazzo. She'd taken care that the other pebbles always remained with her, far from the imprisoned pariah stone.

And so it was that Alessandro de' Medici had begun to be willed apart from the others. And he'd felt it, clearly. He hadn't known how she'd done it or why. But he'd sensed that the power came from her and he hated her for it. It had been hard at the palazzo, feeling his malignance hovering, trying futilely to encircle her, Ginevra, and Caterina with its poison, trying to break her influence on him.

The only time she'd weakened was when she'd let herself see how much pain he suffered. What mother could see something young in such confusion and anguish and not respond? But then she had but to think of whose child he was, and she remembered that he really was not a child, though he and his clandestine father the pope might think so. He was only a flesh skin filled with an evil shadow projected from another world. The shadow Intialo.

"That is the lesson," she murmured to Luciana. "For enhancements or summonings, take a bit of something and put it back into itself. Thus, when one is spit-roasting beef, you always baste it with its own juices. In calling the spirits in the water, I sprinkle a bit of water from the river Arno back into itself.

"But if you want to subtly poison something, take a bit of that something, corrupt it, and *then* put it back in.

"That was how Alessandro came to be. The specters who stand against Florence got the bit of de' Medici seed they needed through the seduction of Cardinal Giulio de' Medici. They corrupted it with their own seed and decanted it back into a vessel that was born as Alessandro, who serves them as their tool."

Piera sighed. That vessel, and Giulio's obsessive pride in his illegitimate patrimony, were the only obstacles standing between Caterina's and Ippolito's union.

"And I fear to say this, *Melata,* my sweet," she whispered to her newest child, "but those two dark peaks may yet prove unsurmountable to us."

Throughout the city it was the custom for kitchen crews to retire as early as possible. When dinner had been cleared away and the kitchen cleaned, all the cooking staff, from master carver down to the most humble scullery slave, sought sleep as soon as they could. The next day they would be the first Florentines to stumble from their beds, before the sky had lightened enough to give even a hint of impending morning: Fires needed to be laid, water set to boil, rising bread turned once more before the daily baking, and any produce lacking in the pantry purchased at the open-air *mercato.*

That night, when Gentile and the rest of the kitchen staff lay asleep, Piera crept into the kitchen, Gattamelata following her, rubbing at her heels and purring. Piera held the pebbles in a sack in one hand and Luciana balanced against her hip with the other. She put down the sack just long enough to light an oil lamp, then slid the pebbles into her own special cauldron set at the edge of the firepit. She sprinkled seven herbs over the pebbles—rowan berries, St. John's wort, mater herbarum, rue, vervain, Solomon's Seal, and zedoary. "For clear sight, protection against all evil, death to all evil," she whispered. Luciana crowded and chortled, rare sounds of delight from the petulant baby. Piera decanted a pitcher of well water into the cauldron and left the herbs and pebbles to steep, as she had every night since the end of her laying-in. Gattamelata curled up by the hearth to guard the cauldron.

The next morning Piera rose before the scullery maids. She fished out all the pebbles. She hung the cauldron with its herb-saturated water over the hearth and added a little cinnamon oil and honey. When the morning fire was set the pot would provide the first tea of the day for the entire household.

Then she took the pebbles and arranged them in groups around the kitchen: Caterina and Ginevra together on the windowsill. Herself, Gentile, Piero, Beatrice and the Ruggieros in a tidy pile out of the way near the hearth. Tommaso, who until recently had been part of the Ruggiero household heap, now perched just a little farther along the sill from Caterina and Ginevra. Other small mounds were set inobtrusively here and there.

No one would disturb them. The scullery maids and journeyman cooks knew them to be luck stones of some sort. They sometimes crossed themselves when they came upon the pebbles, but who would meddle with the kind of luck the Ruggiero household enjoyed?

16

June 23, 1527

Tommaso lay down his carving knife and frowned. The huge pile of celery root shavings dwarfed the finished piece that sat next to it, a tiny white satyr.

"What do you think, Madonna?" he asked Elissa Pecorino.

She reached over his shoulder and picked up the figurine. "What a sly-looking little creature. You've quite captured his roguish nature. And how clever of you to finish him with just the right rustic touch."

Tommaso glumly scraped the celery root shavings into a large bowl of lemon water. "You flatter me. The roughness in technique was not by design but by inadequacy. I've listened to Il Tribolino and Michelangelo rhapsodize about the joys of discovering the form hidden in the material, but the glyptic techniques elude me. I'll never master stone or wood. I'm far more comfortable with building up a piece from clay or wax."

"Or almond paste or dough, or casting molds of pudding or aspic," Elissa Pecorino pointed out. "We who cook are used to working with soft pliable materials. You've had your lifetime to make yourself comfortable with them. Carving away from hard substances is foreign to our nature. You must allow yourself the time and patience to develop new skills. I promise that you will excel someday."

"I pray you're right." Tommaso picked up a chopping knife and held out his hand to her for the satyr. "I'd better slice him up and add him to the rest before the root starts to discolor."

Elissa Pecorino held the statuette back. "I'm going to keep him. I prefer he satisfy my appetite for good company rather than my appetite for food." She perched the satyr on a cornice above the fireplace.

"He'll start to turn yellowish and nasty within the hour," Tommaso warned.

"Yes," Elissa Pecorino agreed. "And dry out and draw in a little, becoming leathery in the next few days. He'll come to look the very image of an old faun. We'll let time supply the polish you feel you lack, Tommaso."

"When Michelangelo was only a little older than me he carved a copy of an antique bust of an old faun so exquisitely that Lorenzo Magnífico sang its praises," Tommaso said wistfully.

"True. But first Lorenzo criticized it. Michelangelo tried to improve on the original by carving his version with an open and smiling rather than closed mouth. Lorenzo pointed out that young *Ser* Buonarotti's execution lacked a certain realism—old people never retain all their teeth, something any cook could have told him. It was only after Michelangelo knocked out a front tooth that the sculpture earned the great Lorenzo's praises. Michelangelo was still learning, as you are now. That's why you're here, yes?"

Tommaso nodded, considerably cheered.

"And since the episode of the *panina gialla* you seem much happier here, more at ease," she added.

Tommaso nodded again. In the days since the critique the other apprentices had begun to accept him into their company. Tommaso enjoyed the budding camaraderie, the hard work in the studio, the challenges that Il Tribolino set them, and the stimulating company of the clients and other artists who dropped by.

"So much happier," Elissa Pecorino continued, "that you no longer rush away to the Ruggiero palazzo on your afternoons off, as you did when you first came here. Sometimes it seems as though you contrive tasks to linger here." She cast a significant glance at the pile of celery root shavings.

Tommaso followed her look, jumped up, tore off his apron and grabbed his Ruggiero livery from where it hung on a peg. "I'm late!" he cried. "I completely forgot. Why didn't you say something sooner?"

He struggled his way into the livery. "Just steam the celery root shavings in a little water until tender. Then braise them in some olive oil."

Elissa Pecorino held open the kitchen door to the alleyway behind the studio. As Tommaso dashed out he called over his shoulder, "Scatter two pinches of *dragoncello* over and mix in. The result will make a perfect bed for the salt cod you're baking."

Tommaso dodged past long streamers and banners as he ran. Tomorrow was St. John the Baptist's Day. Juggernauts stored in side alleyways gleamed with gilt and bright fresh colors. The streets overflowed with revelers, entertainers, and ordinary working Florentines. Nowhere did Tommaso see the apparitions of the weeks before. To Tommaso it felt like the blessed quiet after a storm.

A small brown shape darted under his feet. Tommaso cursed and broke stride long enough to launch a kick at it. If the phantoms had disappeared, the rats had not. They swarmed everywhere.

Tommaso slowed as he approached the Ruggiero palazzo. He was ashamed to admit it, but he now felt more comfortable at the *bottega* than in his own home. Whenever Tommaso returned he dreaded the sight of his mother's pale drawn face, the concern he saw in his father's eyes, Luciana's incessant crying, and Ginevra's absence.

He slid in the broad back door to the kitchen outbuildings. Before the overthrow of Passerini the door had been locked for fear of the Arrabbiati. Gentile had complained bitterly of the inconvenience that caused in unloading goods into the storerooms. Now that the *Signoria* ruled once again, Gentile felt safe enough to leave the entryway unbarred.

"Forgive my tardiness," Tommaso sang out as he passed the storerooms and walked down the hallway toward the kitchen. Only one person was there to look up and greet him; the new slave girl purchased from the Vespuccis sat in a chair at the far end of the kitchen, before the courtyard doorway, grinding spices in a mortar. Tommaso's forced smile relaxed into real warmth. "Filomena, where is everyone?"

As the slave rested the pestle in the mortar and looked up, sunlight slid across her features, highlighting golden brown skin, a small snubbed nose, and long, narrow eyes that should have been dark but instead sparkled a startling light blue. She was a few years older than Tommaso; he guessed her to be thirteen or fourteen. Though only a slave, she carried herself with a serenity that reminded Tommaso of Ginevra. "They're in the garden. Go on out. They're expecting you."

Tommaso stood in the doorway and looked out. A ring of fruit trees and curving rows of salad greens and leeks circled a knot-shaped bed of herbs, which itself encircled a well. The herb bed was Piera's special domain. It supplied Ruggiero the Old's pharmaceutical needs as well as the kitchen's culinary ones.

Gentile and Piera stood together directing the rest of the kitchen help in turning over sprays of young basil, *dragoncello*, and sage on slatted drying trays. Baby Luciana squirmed in Piera's arms. Beatrice and Pietro batted a *calcio* ball along the ground between the fruit trees, squealing with excitement. Gattamelata lay cleaning herself in a patch of sunshine in front of a row of leeks. Nearby, her five kittens played with the carcass of a young rat, flipping it into the air and then pouncing on it.

"There you are! What a day to be late." Piera's words scolded, but, as Tommaso trotted over to her, her eyes smiled. For the first time since the birth his mother looked like herself again—although her face was still too thin, her cheeks glowed brightly and her voice was strong.

"I'm sorry." He kissed her on each of those rosy cheeks, ducking over where she held Luciana. At close quarters the baby's whining ceased to blend in with all the background noises and took on its usual distinctive colicky pitch. Tommaso grimaced. Luciana had taken so much out of his mother—it almost seemed as though Piera had dwindled.

"Look at this," Piera said, backing up from him and shaking her head. "It's only been a week. Is it possible you've grown more? Tommaso, you're nearly as tall as I am."

Tommaso felt relieved. He patted himself down with both hands. Could that be it—that he was taller, not his mother smaller?

Gentile came up to put his arm around Piera's shoulder and for the first time Tommaso noticed that his father didn't loom over him as he had just a few months ago.

Gentile laughed. "Why are you surprised, Piera? His birthday is just a month and a half away. By this time next year he'll have passed you by and begun catching up to me."

"Tommaso! Tommaso!" Pietro ran over with outstretched arms. Tommaso swung him up in the air. Beatrice followed right behind. Tommaso had to swing her too.

"If I've grown so large, why don't these two seem any smaller or lighter?"

Gentile ruffled his hair. "Because they've grown too, of course."

Tommaso felt a brief, not unpleasant dizziness. For the shortest span it seemed as though time held its breath. Everything held absolutely still for a pure, golden moment: The garden bathed in summer sunshine; the heady scent of drying herbs; the kitchen staff bent cheerfully to their work; his family, happy and together; and besides the herbs, another smell lingered in the air like young, freshly gathered honey. The perfume was accompanied by a pleasing buzzing sound like the drone of grazing bees.

Then Tommaso felt the dizziness return. The humming sharpened, became irritating, resolved itself into Luciana's perpetual whine. Everything began to move again and Tommaso felt the gap in the tableau— Ginevra's absence.

"We mustn't let you linger here," his mother said. "The girls are expecting your visit." She climbed up to the kitchen, Luciana bouncing against her with each step.

Tommaso started to follow, but almost tripped as the cat rushed underfoot. In Piera's return to the kitchen Gattamelata anticipated the possibility of a tastier snack than common rat. The kittens, now better than half their mother's size, bounced after her. Tommaso turned in at the end of the little procession.

By the time he trailed into the kitchen behind them his mother was putting a corrected embroidery sampler into a small satchel. Tommaso knew that, as usual, a slim packet of letters would be hidden in the sampler's lining and stitched into place. Piera also placed in the satchel some small *Castagnaccio* cakes, new wine-colored silk ribbons for attaching Ginevra's sleeves to her *gammura,* and a lacy summer cap—the treats any mother might send a well-loved daughter. Tommaso slung the satchel over one shoulder, kissed his mother's cheeks again, and turned to go.

"Wait, that's not all," Piera said. "Hold this." She handed him a lidded carrying basket. She stared down at Gattamelata and the kittens thoughtfully, then scooped one of the catlings up.

Tommaso's eyebrows lifted as she popped it into the basket. "I swear to you, Mother, no one in all of Florence transports cats as much as I do," he protested.

"Listen to your complaining!" Piera said. "Tomorrow is the feast of St. John the Baptist. For generations the de' Medicis fêted the entire city on this day. Caterina must commemorate it apart from both her city and her family, with only your sister for company. Those drab nuns at Santa Lucia will do nothing to help her celebrate." Piera sighed. "If only the *Signoria* could have found it in their hearts to send her to the Murate. The sisters there would have been far kinder to her." Piera's mood became brisker. "In honor of the day the kitten is a gift for her—a small protector all her own. The nuns can hardly object; I hear Santa Lucia is infested with rats."

Since he was only a servant, Tommaso met his sister inside the delivery gate to the convent garden. Caterina was usually allowed to accompany Ginevra. When he saw the two girls Tommaso was glad that Piera had sent along the surprise gift.

Ginevra and Caterina sat together so quietly on the stone bench set just inside the gate that they might have been carved in a piece from the same granite as the bench. The scene would have made as lovely a sculpture as any in Il Tribolino's *bottega*.

And just as still. It brought to Tommaso's mind that instant he'd experienced less than an hour ago in the Ruggiero garden. But that moment had been filled with life transfixed. Looking at Ginevra and Caterina, it seemed as though he'd caught a glimpse of them frozen in eternity with only each other as company.

The kitten, Tommaso thought. The kitten will bring them back to life.

"You're so late, we were worried you weren't coming." Ginevra stood, breaking the spell. Her words were mild, but in her eyes Tommaso read rebuke. "How could you, on today of all days?"

"I'm sorry," he said. He scuffed his shoes and dropped his gaze. He didn't want to see similar disappointment in Caterina's eyes.

"It's all right." At least Caterina's voice was forgiving. "Your apprenticeship keeps you so busy that we're lucky you get away at all. I know how the burdens of responsibility can steal away the hours."

Tommaso thought about the celery root satyr and felt even guiltier. He handed the satchel to the girls. Ginevra pulled out the embroidery sampler and gave it to Caterina. The *Duchessina* rubbed it between her fingers, feeling the thickness of the packet of letters in the lining. Ginevra took out the treats from Piera and smiled.

"I'm sorry you can't be with your family for the festival," Tommaso said. "But because of that, surely the Magi are keeping especially close watch over you."

Tommaso meant his words to have a gallant effect. He was horrified when Caterina's eyes filled with tears.

With far less grace than he'd intended he hastily pulled the basket from his back. "So our mother sent a present. She said it would be a small protector all your own." He yanked the kitten out. "I'm certain this guardian will prove more entertaining, charming and affectionate than some withered, dour, old wise man from the East."

To Tommaso's relief, Caterina's nascent tears melted into giggles. She held out her arms for the kitten, then hugged it tightly. It squeaked in indignation.

"And should the nuns here disapprove"—Tommaso leaned over and whispered conspiratorially—"our mother hinted that a word might be put in their ear about their dreadful rat problem." He looked up to see Ginevra nodding her approval and knew he was forgiven.

"I'm going to name her Balthazar," Caterina said. She stroked the kitten's chin. It responded with a purr astoundingly large for such a small cat.

"Balthazar is a male name," Tommaso pointed out.

"That's true. Then I'll call her Balthazara," said Caterina.

"It's good you brought that basket," said Ginevra. "We have a somewhat larger bundle than usual to send back with you." She glanced about to be sure no nuns were watching, then reached behind the bench and pulled up a small canvas sack. Tommaso took it from her. Whatever was inside the bag was knobby and ungainly. Tommaso set it in the bottom of the basket. On top of it Caterina set the satchel, holding that week's newly stitched embroidery sampler, with its hidden outgoing packet of letters.

In the distance the Vacca chimed, just once. They all jumped, startled.

"A too-early call to matins," Tommaso joked. "The *Prioris'* pages imbibe too much *alchermes* again, no doubt in honor of the St. John."

Neither of the girls laughed. Ginevra took his hands. "Tommaso, not to chide you, but you were late. Almost too late. Please hurry the things we gave you back to Mother. Take shelter tonight, but do not fear too much. Remember that the Three Wise Ones keep watch over *all* the de' Medici."

Tommaso looked straight into his sister's eyes, but he didn't understand what she was trying to tell him. Her hands on his simultaneously begged him to linger and pushed him to go.

It wasn't till he was halfway back to the Ruggieros' that he remembered his mother's dark eyes and that de' Medici blood ran in his veins too.

Piera, squalling Luciana welded to her as usual, and the slave Filomena were working alone together in the kitchen when Tommaso returned. Tommaso could hear Gentile out in the garden calling instructions to the rest of the staff.

"Did Caterina like her gift?" Piera asked.

Tommaso passed his mother the basket. "Indeed. She named it Balthazara in honor of her family's traditional protectors."

It was good to see his mother smile again.

"There's another sampler for you to correct, and also something unexpected, mysterious and lumpish."

Apparently not unexpected to Piera. She reached straight into the bag. Curious, Tommaso leaned over for a better look as she drew out the enigmatic object. He frowned, puzzled. It was a piece of light rope, hardly more than a cord, gnarled with knots.

Piera eagerly spread it on the kneading table and examined it as if it were the foretelling entrails of a sacrificed sheep. Her brows drew together in a confused expression.

Tommaso was about to ask her why Ginevra would send her such a thing when he felt that something was terribly wrong. It took him an instant to realize what had shocked his senses.

It was a sudden absence of noise: Luciana had stopped crying. Tommaso, Piera, and Filomena stared at the baby. Luciana wore the strangest expression Tommaso had ever seen on an infant's face—one of terrible and deep calm.

Tommaso and his mother looked at each other. At that instant the Vacca began to toll in a long series of chimes.

All the new roses in Piera's cheeks drained away, leaving her looking as though she'd been carved from the palest ivory. Tommaso was sure he appeared the same. Although that particular pattern of the bells had never rung before in his lifetime, he knew—as did every other citizen—what the chimes announced: The plague had come again to Florence.

In a simple cell at the Convent of Santa Lucia the two girls huddled together on the bed they shared. "It has begun," Caterina whispered. She held Balthazara close to her.

17

August, 1527

Cosimo paced his father's study with fretful strides as he filled the censers with lichen and Dittany of Crete. Below the open window a procession of penitents wailed their way through the night, crying their petition to God to have mercy and spare them. Cosimo wondered how many of them had reveled the night before, only to awaken to the first warning signs of *gavóccioli* swelling in their groins or armpits.

Cosimo turned the great speculum at an angle where it would catch the most moonlight. He turned to his father for approval. Ruggiero the Old looked up from where he knelt on the floor and nodded.

Cosimo took advantage of his father's attention. "Those in charge are always blamed for catastrophes. The *Signoria*, having dispersed most of the Medici and taken control again, head the government just in time to be blamed for the onset of the plague.

"If the mages of those other realms—those 'affectors' of whom you speak, the opposite struts in the framework of existence —plot to deprive Florence of a rebirth of glory under Medicean rule, what does it profit them to send the plague and thereby weaken in all ways the enemies of the de' Medici family?"

Ruggiero the Old continued to slowly draw his chalk circle on the ground, careful not to knock over a small bowl beside him. "Because for the affectors to regain balance in their own plane the destruction of the

Medici must come from within the family itself to be complete. An apple, bruised from the outside, can suffer a single cut to remove the blemish and still prove good eating. But the apple with a worm hidden inside soon rots away entirely.

"Come stand within the *usurtu*, my son. It is almost complete."

Cosimo uncovered the speculum and went to stand behind his father. The older man finished the circle. He constructed a second enclosure by drawing a pentagram about them, its points touching the edges of the circle.

"For the affectors to achieve their goal, Clement needs Florence helpless at his feet. That is the reason for the plague."

"Why then have we helped him?" Cosimo protested.

His father picked up the small bowl. Liquid garnet glowed within— pigeon's blood. Ruggiero the Old began to trace symbols on the floor with it.

"If Florence is to experience glory under the Medici again, then there must be Medicis to glory under. It is to protect the *Duchessina* and the other, forgotten members of the family that we act. Unfortunately, the affectors have twined these individuals' fates so closely with Clement's that they cannot yet be separated.

"Today we endeavor to turn that circumstance to our advantage. I mean to bind Caterina even more closely to Clement so that his freedom hinges on hers. She will become the key to the lock that binds him, though no one will perceive the relationship except the two of us. Until she is released, he will remain a prisoner too and his plans thwarted.

"Face the window, Cosimo, and gaze out on the night sky. Focus your attention on the Great Bear's very heart, the star of Meraks, and repeat the stanzas as I chant them."

Cosimo followed his father's singsong evocation, asking Meraks to join them. The speculum filled with light like a pitcher filling with milk. It spilled over into the room. Cosimo shuddered as the smoke from the smoldering Dittany of Crete began to coalesce into a vast shape.

"Sister-eyes."

Piera always heard the voice just as the spark before her flared larger, distinguishing itself from all the other myriad stars embedded like jewels in the black velvet of the night.

"Sister-eyes." The placid echoing tones signaled she'd almost reached her destination. The rumpled, sable sky she'd soared through straightened itself and lightened, bleached by the glow of the orb she glided toward.

"Sister-eyes, I've been expecting you. It's been a long time since you visited me." Within the glow, edges of light outlined a great form.

"Greetings, Marax."

The form coalesced into the image of an enormous, molten-colored being with a flat, almost human face and a body like that of a reclining bull.

"A stargazer called you recently." Her statement was only nominally a question.

The creature nodded. "*Your* stargazer. When both of you have need of me you always follow him, never lead. You are wise, Sister-eyes."

Piera smiled. "Yes, Great Daemon. Thus I know of Ruggiero's visits but he does not know of mine."

"Except that he never 'visits,' " the Marax said. "Always he calls my form to him, in the way of all stargazers. Only you know how to speak my name properly, in the old way, and do me the courtesy of coming here."

"He is old among our kind," Piera said. "The journey would be hard for him, even if he knew how to set out on it. His ways are different from mine. He never learned to fly."

"The journey is hard for you," the Marax pointed out. "I fear each time that your little shell will not receive you when you return to it." The creature's eyes were enormous, limpid, tranquil, even in concern. Piera knew that when it called her "Sister-eyes" it bestowed great honor on her.

"I do not mind the stargazer's ways," the Marax assured her. "The journey is swift and easy for me, and he is always cordial enough."

"Did he ask for much? Did he gift you in return?" Piera asked.

"No need for gifts, not from him or from you this time. It is a matter of mutual concern. He only asked, as always, of the patterns in the stars. You will ask for more."

Piera nodded. "But before I ask of that, I have other questions: What did Ruggiero want to know? I have never asked you about the stars before, and how it is you read them."

"Regarding the stars, the advantages I have that you lack are perspective, distance, and a sort of vision most of your kind are not heir to. Your stargazer does not understand my attributes in this matter. He believes I exist in another sphere of existence.

"In fact, I live in the same plane as yourselves, but we are very distant from each other. Therefore I can look upon your world as you cannot.

"But besides that, I have the ability to see into other realms. When I gaze at your sphere I perceive it shimmering with those overlapping existences. Yours I see most clearly, of course, since it is also my own. But I also see through it to the others. It was of these the stargazer asked."

"Why was this of mutual concern?"

"Because the machinations of another planar realm will influence and eventually shift our plane. And so, although so distant from you, in the end it will affect me also. It is a matter of of great concern. If your stargazer had not called me soon I would have evoked him."

"What did you set him to do to cure this ill?" Piera asked.

"I told him how to tether one part of your realm to another part to hold the whole in place. I don't believe the knowledge will help you, however. Just as he never learned to fly, you lack the talents he is proficient in."

"But you can tell me of other matters."

"Yes. The small hard nuggets of matter that house the essences that you and I both see so well . . ."

"My stones," whispered Piera.

"Look after them well and fix them in place by any means you can. Your enemies will try to reach through to your plane to move them."

"What about the other attributes you know of? What herbs should I . . . ?"

"The green alive stillnesses of your world have little influence in this matter yet, other than to provide you with wings for your flight."

Piera sighed. The long hard journey had garnered little of use so far. There remained only one last attribute within the Marax's domain: the gift of the knowledge of familiars.

"Do you see new helpers for our cause? Familiars who may be approaching?" she asked. The Marax could detect and negotiate all three kinds: the spirits of the dead, the elementals, and the creatures of the world.

Piera expected little help here, for her own talents for perceiving and binding familiars was excellent.

The Marax surprised her. "Yes. I sense one who is developing and has almost arrived. A powerful familiar—one who will ultimately grow beyond even your power to control, for it is already bound directly to one of the Three Wise Ones. But you can guide it for a while. Watch for its coming."

Piera's heart leapt. She knew of whom the Marax was speaking. "Great Daemon, I bid you farewell, then. Soon I will bring a fledgling with me on these flights."

The sharp combined odors of the poultice stung in the back of Piera's nostrils and woke her. They blended into one acrid stench, but she could still make out the individual parts: smallage, cinquefoil, belladonna, thorn apple, and wild celery. Piera held her breath, knowing what would come next.

The headache struck like a blow from a stonemason's hammer. Piera whimpered and clutched at her temples. The pantry floor was cold against her back. She couldn't lie here long. She'd risked much for this flight. At any moment Filomena might rise to start the kitchen fires.

Piera moaned as she rolled to her hands and knees. She had to keep her wits about her. The herbs of flight could poison a baby. The first task was to find a healthy wet nurse—not an easy task with the plague raging. It would be days before the herbs were cleansed from her body and she could feed Luciana again. By then her breasts would have dried.

But, in spite of her pain and worry, Piera smiled. "Ginevra," she whispered to herself. "My daughter will be all I've hoped for. Even the Marax has seen it."

18

Tommaso and Elissa Pecorino ladled food onto platters as fast as they could. Tommaso swore as he tripped over a begging Melchiora. "Go out and catch a rat," he ordered the small cat. "That's why my mother gave you to me." When the Vacca tolled the arrival of the plague his mother insisted on giving him one of the kittens too. To honor Caterina's choice for her kitten, he'd named his after another of the Three Wise Men.

Melchiora mewed and sat up on her hind legs so prettily that Tommaso relented and fed her a scrap of chicken from the *minestra* and gently pushed her out of the way with his foot.

The other apprentices rushed past, carrying dishes into the studio. Sideboards had been hastily thrown together: planks laid across several empty armature stands. Such "mad suppers" had become common of late—not just in Il Tribolino's *bottega*, but Tommaso guessed across all of Florence as the plague threw all into confusion.

He and Elissa brought in the last two dishes—the chicken *minestra* and a fish pie. The other apprentices lined themselves up in attendance along the back walls.

The studio looked much as Tommaso had first seen it, on the night of his beating. Guests perched casually on benches and uncarved marble blocks, wine goblets, and faces crimson from the foundry's glow.

But now Tommaso knew all the players in the tableau. There were several art connoisseurs, including two of his rescuers, Bembo and Girolamo. Other artists had also dropped in: Francesco Lippi, the goldsmith grandson of that ribald and lusty friar-painter Fra Filippo Lippi; the wood-carver Il Tasso; two of Michelangelo's apprentices and his assistant Antonio Mini; the painter Andrea del Sarto, who was waited on by one of his own apprentices, a youth from Arezzo, Giorgio Vasari.

"How is your family, Tribolo?" Tasso was asking as Tommaso set down his platter. The wood-carver waved his empty wine goblet. Salvatore, the closest apprentice, rushed over to fill it.

"They are well," Il Tribolino said. "They've been waiting out the plague at my wife's father's estate near Volterra. In her last letter she wrote that her father fears the illness might spread toward them. They will soon flee to Sardinia till it passes."

"Why did you not join them?" Girolamo asked. "What does her survival benefit her if you perish here?"

Tribolino shrugged. "She is good-looking, still young enough, obviously fertile, and from a wealthy family. If I should die her father will be happy to marry her to someone from a more illustrious family than mine.

"It's true that if I fled I might not contract the plague . . . but then again, I might, for who knows where this calamity will end? I do know for certain I'd risk the loss of the commission for the bronzes for the Medici villas at Cestello and Petraja. And if I did that, I could lose this studio, and then my livelihood. I'd rather my wife came back to my corpse to grieve over than that I should run to her father for protection."

Bembo raised his glass to Il Tribolino. "Well said, Maestro. And a pox on those who call you a cautious, timid man."

Il Tribolino glanced sharply at his guest, not entirely appreciating the play on words.

Thankfully, someone knocked just then on the front door. Bernardo opened it a crack to peer out. Then he swung it wide. Two more visitors entered, their noses buried in bouquets of flowers and herbs.

Il Tribolino hailed them. "Greetings, Rosso and Pontormo. As usual your timing is impeccable: The *matta cena* has just been laid out. Unless, of course, you'd rather dine on those nosegays."

The painter Rosso Fiorentino handed over his cape and flowers to

Bernardo. "It may come to that, good host, if only to sweeten our organs. My very being feels fouled. The stench in the streets is overwhelming. Corpses lie piled like cordwood in the Piazza del Duomo. No one has yet taken down the blue canopies glazed with stars for the St. John the Baptist's festival. They're falling apart into tatters, making it appear as though the very heavens weep for Florence."

He looked around. "Where is that good banker, Antonio Gondi? Not here? I'm not surprised. No doubt out investing in the future monied elite of poesy-mongers and grave diggers. Don't you agree, Pontormo?"

His friend shrugged, both a response and to rid his cape into Bernardo's waiting arms. Pontormo was a shy man of few words.

"What news of our disappeared companion, the good youth Ippolito?" Tasso asked Rosso.

"None, though rumors fly that he and his evil shadow Alessandro could be hiding at any of the de' Medici country estates: Careggi, or even as close as Poggio a Caiano, though I put my money on Caffaggiolo. That place is like a fortress.

"Give us drink, drink, and more drink." Rosso gestured for goblets for both himself and Pontormo. "Curse the plague. I never expected to live long anyway."

"Fortunately or unfortunately, our good host here does not subscribe to total abandonment of the senses in the face of disaster," said Bembo. "It seems he wants to continue working, so that if he doesn't erupt in *gavóc-cioli*, turn black and die, he'll still be able to someday show up his father-in-law."

"You must be saved from such folly," declared Rosso. "And the best way to do *that* is to deprive you of your workers. Young Salvatore," he beckoned the apprentice over, "as I've entreated you before, stop wasting your colorist talents on this dusty sculptor and apprentice at my *bottega* instead."

Tommaso saw Salvatore cast a look at their master. It was true that the apprentice had a way with pigments.

When Salvatore saw that Il Tribolino looked merely amused at Rosso's baiting he said, "I might have been tempted, *Ser* Fiorentino, but since you say you expect only a short life span, it would profit me little to join you."

The guests shouted with laughter at this.

Tommaso cut the fish pie into wedges. The revelers crowded around the table as the apprentices filled *tondi* for them.

Someone pounded loudly at the front door. Since all the other apprentices were busy serving, Tommaso went to open it.

"Listen to that racket," Girolamo said. "Whoever it is must still be healthy."

Tommaso peered out. The man who stood there was handsome and of roughly Rosso, Tasso, and Pontormo's age—mid- to late twenties. He sported a forked beard almost identical to Michelangelo Buonarotti's, except fuller. Tommaso had never seen him before.

The man squinted at him through the crack in the doorway. "Ah, a new apprentice, I'll wager. Tell Nicolo that 'Welcomeness Itself' waits at his door."

Tommaso turned to catch his master's eye. "*Ser* Tribolino," he said, "there's a man here who—"

He got no further. The fellow used his lapse of attention to push past him.

Tribolino jumped to his feet. "Benevenuto! My gossip! God's own goldsmith!" The sculptor embraced the newcomer. Francesco Lippi and Il Tasso also leapt up and swarmed him.

"Benevenuto Cellini." Francesco Lippi pounded the man on his back. "For the love of the Holy Mother, what brings you home to Florence at such a dangerous time?"

Benevenuto Cellini cocked an eye at him. "What is danger to me? Nothing. Did I not only survive the sack of Rome but also emerge covered with glory?"

Tommaso remembered hiding in the de' Medici chapel and hearing the messenger Lazaro's bitter words concerning the boastful goldsmith.

"Even the dread *Reiters* know to fear the plague," Bembo pointed out.

"But not I," said Cellini. "I encountered Signor Plague four years ago in Rome, closed quarters and grappled with him, yet survive just as you see me."

"Benevenuto speaks the truth," Rosso Fiorentino said. "He came to visit me shortly thereafter at Cervetera to recuperate. I saw the healed sores myself."

Il Tribolino gestured to Tommaso to fetch and fill a glass for Cellini.

"If facing down the plague no longer challenges you, what brings you here?" asked Tasso. "Is business in Rome slow after the sack? We hear your greatest patron remains a prisoner."

"Pope Clement is still restrained in Sant' Angel," Cellini admitted. "His surrender was honored, but he cannot leave until he pays his ransom. Two thousand troops remain to secure him. The rest of the imperial army has scattered, fearing a spread of the plague and because they've eaten every scrap of food remaining in the Holy City.

"The rest of us are now free to go about our business. And even without the Pope's immediate patronage, business is good in all ways. General Orazio Baglioni wishes me to become a captain under his command. And I am turning away commissions right and left: Many less courageous and talented goldsmiths died during the sack—their shops of course being the first places the plunderers visited. So by God's hand the cognoscenti of Rome are forced into more discerning taste. I tell you, Tasso, when we walked together to Rome all those years ago, you should have stayed. You'd be a wealthy man today."

Tasso shook his head. "It was a grand adventure, and a right one for two nineteen-year-olds. But I don't regret returning to Florence. It's bad enough facing the plague here, but the plague *and* a sacking by *Reiters?*" He made a face.

"Well, the plague is why I'm here," said Cellini. "I wished to see if my father and siblings were well. And I wanted to let my father see in person that I'd survived the fall of Rome. When I told him of my success and handed over to him a substantial quantity of *scudi di moneta*, for the first time I believe he was actually proud of me. He urged me to leave immediately for Mantua to pursue my art, rather than take up my military appointment."

Cellini helped himself to some frittata and *torta di verdura* from the serving table. "This is what I need—hearty fare for the next leg of my journey. Antonio," he addressed Michelangelo's assistant, "where is your noble master? In spite of the love I bear all of you here, after my father, Michelangelo is the one man I hope most to see on this brief sojourn. How could you be reveling without him?"

Tommaso noticed that Cellini's voice had changed from what must be its customary arrogant tones to something quite different. He remembered how even the goldsmith's beard aped the master's.

Antonio Mini licked crumbs from his mouth and grimaced. "He drove us from the studio this evening in one of his snits. He changed the plans for the new sacristy yet *again,* which put him in a terrible mood." Antonio shook his head. "Then we suffered the misfortune of a visit from Leone Strozzi. The young cavalier felt it necessary to point out that the almost-completed figure of Giuliano de' Medici looks nothing like Lorenzo the Magnificent's younger brother."

"To which," Baccio, one of Michelangelo's apprentices, said, "the master snapped out in reply, 'So? A thousand years from now, nobody will want to know what he really looked like.' Young Strozzi slunk out of the studio with the rest of us. I dread working tomorrow."

"You can always send Giorgio over in your place," Cellini said.

With a sullen look Giorgio Vasari slid further behind his master, Andrea del Sarto. The youth had been promised an apprenticeship to Michelangelo, but when the sculptor had unexpectedly been called to Rome at the very beginning of Giorgio's training the boy had been passed on to Andrea. Everyone knew that although Giorgio's relationship with his new master was cordial, his pride smarted from the exchange and he still longed to be called to the side of the greater artist. From the safety of the shadows he glared at Cellini.

Antonio Mini tactfully diverted attention away from Giorgio Vasari. "Tribolo, perhaps you could help us. Send young Tommaso over to our master in the morning with some of this excellent chicken *minestra.* Michelangelo loves it cold. It would vastly improve his temper to break his fast in such a manner."

"Not to mention that the sight of Tommaso always changes his vinegar straight to honey," Baccio muttered with a grin into his wine.

This aside was not lost on Cellini. The goldsmith pivoted around to look at Tommaso and held out his goblet for a refill. Tommaso had to come close to pour the wine for him. He blushed under Cellini's scrutiny. It was true he'd never once caught a glimpse of the master sculptor's infamous bad temper, save for the time Michelangelo had rescued him from the Arrabbiati.

"So this is your new apprentice?" Tommaso wasn't sure what he read in Cellini's intense gaze. Perhaps some jealousy, a certain calculation, and interest deflected.

"Tommaso comes to us from the Arista family, who serve the house of Ruggiero. His mother's family has been in the employ of the de' Medicis for generations," Tribolino said. "To those of us indentured to the muse of Art, such a lineage is impeccable."

Tommaso saw grudging approval in Cellini's eyes.

"Tommaso is both apprentice and cook," Tribolino added. "He's proving excellent in both occupations. Unusual for one of only eleven years of age."

"Twelve," Tommaso corrected his master before he could catch himself.

Il Tribolino's eyebrows rose. "I'm sure the apprenticeship papers said eleven."

"They did." Tommaso was sorry he'd managed to draw even more attention to himself. "I turned twelve last week."

"You should have told us," said Michelangelo's assistant. "We could use any cause for celebration in these times. To mark another year is to laugh in the face of the plague."

"August," said Pontormo. "Born under Leo, the sign of the lion." They all turned to stare. Any words were rare words from the artist.

"Most propitious for a Florentine," said Rosso, "since those great cats, along with the lily, are the very mark of the soul of our city."

"To mark the occasion—perhaps a week late, but it's just as well since I hadn't arrived yet anyway—I hereby name thee Gato Tommaso Leoni," Cellini said. The goldsmith raised his goblet in a toast. The other guests cheered and drank.

"And such a fine mane you sport, Ser Leoni." Cellini teased his fingers through Tommaso's locks. Tommaso felt his face turn redder than his hair, red as the wine they drank.

"And beautiful coloring and features," Cellini continued, thoroughly enjoying Tommaso's discomfort. He addressed Il Tribolino, "When Rome recovers its social milieu you must let me borrow him for a prank. Remember your old compatriot Michel Agnolo da Siena, whom you worked with on Hadrian's tomb? He hosted wonderful salons and required all artists to each bring a lovely lady to the banquets.

"One night, as a joke, I prevailed on my Spanish neighbor's son, a beautiful youth called Diego only a little older than Tommaso here, to dress up as a maid and accompany me. If you lend me Tommaso I'll do the same with him. The affair would be a masterpiece of jest, for no one would suspect me of attempting the same prank a second time."

"Aha! You said *attempting*," Tasso challenged Cellini. "So your first effort was less than a success."

"On the contrary." Cellini waved his hand in dismissal. "Diego was so lovely and so well coached by me that all the men present lusted after my lovely 'girl' and all the real women chafed with jealousy. When the secret was at last revealed Michel Agnolo had me hoisted onto the other guests' shoulders and paraded about in triumph."

Il Tribolino's guests crowded around the goldsmith for more details. Tommaso took advantage of their interest to hand over his wine bottle to Bernardo. He gathered up the serving platters that had been emptied of food and fled with them to the kitchen. As he dropped the plates into the wash basin he shuddered, regretting not a bit that Cellini would be leaving Florence the next morning.

19

Piera woke with a start. The light in the room had halted between night's blackness and morning's lightness. Something was wrong. She held very still, listening. Stretched out against her left side Gentile was breathing deeply, not quite snoring. On her right side, Beatrice and Pietro curled together, their intermingled breaths fluttering as softly as moths. A heavier, coarser exhalation came from the kitchen: Filomena was pumping the bellows to start the fire.

Piera drew back the covers and slid from the bed on the children's side, covering them again quickly before they awoke. She listened again. Nothing. Perhaps it was the lack of noise that had disturbed her.

She slid off her night shift, sighing at the fresh semen stains. Ever since she'd stopped nursing Gentile had begun mounting her again each night. Moving against her in stealth and silence in the crowded family bed, she felt the full force of the longing and passion he'd curbed the months she'd been gone.

Piera felt ashamed. For the first time since their wedding she didn't return that passion. She didn't want to be touched. And she did not want to be with child again so soon. She knew she was at risk—the herbs she might have taken to prevent conception were too dangerous to her health after the trying delivery of Luciana. And the concoctions she put on her skin for flight further added to the peril.

She lifted her arms to pull on a sleeved slip and her *gammura.* More semen slid down her leg. Piera shivered.

She skirted some chests and the washbasin and let herself out of the room. Across the hallway was another, smaller sleeping chamber. She peered in.

The bed there had seen an almost complete change of occupants in recent months. In February it had slept Ginevra and two scullery maids with room to spare.

Now Ginevra slept in a cell at the convent with Caterina de' Medici. Atlanta, one of the scullery maids, had been recalled from her term of service by her worried parents at the beginning of the plague. She'd rejoined them in Prato, perishing when the epidemic engulfed that town too. Only the other scullery maid, Massolina, was left, sleeping soundly in the middle.

Ginevra's space was empty but newly rumpled—Filomena now slept there. Cousin Leonora's oldest daughter Francesca lay on the side that had been Atalanta's. Cradled in one of her arms nestled Luciana, in the other Francesca's own baby boy, Paolo.

Piera closed the door noiselessly. She was lucky to have Francesca move in as Luciana's wet nurse, but she couldn't help the pang she felt when she saw how peacefully Luciana lay in Francesca's arms.

Piera glanced down the hallway to the menservants' sleeping chambers, the storerooms, and beyond them the back door out to the street. Whatever had disturbed her didn't emanate from that quarter.

The kitchen looked peaceful enough. A fire blazed nicely in the hearth; water in the great cauldron was beginning to simmer. The kitchen door stood ajar. Through it Piera saw Filomena drawing more water from the well in the garden courtyard.

The kitchen and its outbuildings stood between the Ruggiero mansion and the rising sun. As the sky began to brighten it cast the shadow of the smaller building onto the larger.

Piera saw Filomena turn toward the mansion, then drop the bucket she'd been filling. The slave's motions seemed as slow as those in a dream. Something was making small, sharp distressed cries from the direction of the palazzo. Piera was out the kitchen door and past Filomena before the slave could respond.

Gattamelata was coaxing one of her daughters down the path through the herb garden with anxious chirps. The half-grown kitten was doing its best, but its hindquarters kept buckling under, lurching it from one side to the other with each step. Blood smeared the coats of both cats.

Piera scooped up the kitten and ran back to the kitchen. "Wrap her in these," she ordered Filomena, handing the slave some clean rags. "Keep her warm."

Piera cleaned the kitten's wounds, treated them with an herbal salve, and bound them as best she could. The injuries weren't the punctures of another cat, or the tearing a dog might inflict, but rather the slashes of a rodent's teeth. They sliced into but didn't completely sever tendons in the little cat's hind legs. If she didn't die from shock, she'd recover. But she'd always be lame.

While Filomena put the kitten in a basket and covered it with more rags to keep it warm, Piera looked over Gattamelata, who'd never ceased her anxious pacing and murmuring. Unlike the kitten, most of the blood on Gattamelata was not her own. Other than some shallow cuts she was unharmed. She hissed when Piera washed her wounds but didn't otherwise strike out or struggle.

Piera breathed deeply, consciously slowing her heart's pounding. Now that the crisis had been revealed she could calm herself.

The sky's color began to brighten from light gray to clean blue. The sun was about to rise. From the back rooms came the noises of the kitchen help readying themselves for work: water poured into washbasins, clothing chests slammed open and shut as work garb was drawn out.

Piera looked at her own small cauldron hanging at the edge of the fire pit. She didn't have much time before the kitchen became crowded. She reached into the cauldron for the pebbles, swishing away the steeping herbs that had risen to the top of the well water she'd poured in the evening before.

Her hand scraped the bottom of the pot. The pebbles weren't there. She glanced at Filomena, but the slave was beating oil into soaked and simmered millet. No, surely the slave wouldn't have touched the stones.

Piera's gaze dropped to the other side of the hearth. There was the pile of stones, just where it should be at this time of the morning.

Her breath caught in her throat. Had she gone walking in her sleep, her unconscious body loyal to the chores of protection? She picked through the pile. Here was her stone, and Gentile's, each of the Ruggieros', Luciana's new pebble, Massolina's and the others. All but Beatrice and Pietro's.

Piera willed herself not to panic. Tommaso's stone lay just where it should, on the windowsill. And a little farther, in its proper place, was Caterina's. But Ginevra's stone wasn't next to Caterina's. It was gone.

In the background behind her Piera heard the noises of the kitchen help entering and starting about their chores. But all she was truly aware of was blood hotly thrumming in her ears like a boiling waterfall.

She looked under the bread-kneading trough and on top of the spice jars. She ran her hand along the surfaces of cutting boards and work tables, as if her fingers would be able to see what her eyes could not. The noise in the kitchen waned as one by one the staff stopped what they were doing to stare at her.

"Mistress, what are you looking for? Can we help you?" Massolina asked her.

Piera waved the girl away. "No. Continue your duties. The household will want to break its fast soon."

She kept searching. There, there they were. Under the worktable, in the wedge formed by a sack of millet and a sack of buckwheat leaning against each other. Beatrice, Pietro, and Ginevra. Ippolito's stone lay opposite, around the curve of the sack of buckwheat.

Piera rocked back on her heels. She felt foolish with relief. There was no harm done. Someone must be playing a jest on her, tweaking her for what they thought her superstitions. Perhaps one of the apprentice cooks, on a dare from the others.

She stood up, dusted herself off and washed her hands in a washbasin. She left the wayward stones where they were. They were safe enough. She'd discover and confront her jester with them later.

Gentile shepherded Beatrice and Pietro into the kitchen. He still glowed from last night's pleasure. He beamed at Piera. Then he frowned when he saw how far behind preparations for the morning meal lagged.

"One of the kittens came in sorely injured," Piera explained. "We had to physick both her and Gattamelata." Out of the corner of her eye she saw Filomena and the rest of the kitchen help cast glances at each other.

Beatrice and Pietro ran to her for their first kisses of the morning. Piera hugged them to her fiercely, thankful that they were happy and well. "I'll assist with the serving to make up the time," she told Gentile.

Francesca came in bearing the two infants. She led Pietro and Beatrice into the garden to keep them out from underfoot.

Soon cool slices of pale green and butter-yellow melon, warm bowls of millet pulses, a pitcher of almond milk, figs marinated in wine, *pinocchiata*, trout poached in goat cream, and small individual cakes of *berlingozo* lay assembled, ready to serve. Piera supervised who would carry what to the sideboard in the dining room. Then she picked up the last pewter platter holding the well-browned *berlingozo* and followed at the end of the procession.

The culinary parade entered the palazzo and wound its customary route to the dining room. Unlike the whitewashed walls of the kitchen compound, the walls throughout the mansion boasted beautiful inlaid wood patterns, with a narrow plaster strip just below the ceiling sporting decorative frescoes. Piera noticed cinquefoil-shaped patterns of dark red pawprints tarnishing the matching parquet floorboard as they passed. The bloody prints backtracked down a side hallway.

Piera stopped and began to tremble. Nobody in the breakfast procession noticed when she fell behind. That hallway twisted about and led to the side stairway, skirting about a little-used storage space under the stairwell there.

A wave of vertigo washed over Piera. *Berlingozos* started sliding down to the floor. The pewter platter went crashing after them. Before it had finished bouncing and clattering Piera was running down the side hall to the stairway.

In front of the stairwell lay the biggest rat she'd ever seen, at least equal in size to the kitten that had challenged it. It would have been pure white but for the dark wine stains of blood spattering its coat.

Piera pushed it aside with her foot and opened the stairwell door wide. Dim though it was inside, enough of the morning's light entered that she could see that the dust inside lay undisturbed. The onyx-inlaid box sat just where she'd left it months ago, in a niche in the stair's joinery.

She snatched it down. Her hands trembled so badly that at first she couldn't unknot the tangle of blue beads binding it. She yanked at the strand. It broke, scattering bright beads everywhere. Piera lifted the lid on the box. It was empty.

As she raced back out toward the gardens and the kitchen she passed Filomena bent over the spilled *berlingozos*, picking up each cake and setting them on the righted platter. Filomena's eyes widened and she crossed herself as Piera sped past.

Piera stumbled in the garden. She went down on all fours, dirt grinding into her palms. Her feet caught in the hem of her *gamurra* as she came up. She stumbled again.

When she reached the kitchen she threw cooking pots about, pushed kneading tables aside, climbed up to peer behind the contents of the highest shelves. Nothing. Alessandro's stone didn't reveal itself anywhere.

Shaking with fear, Piera approached the sacks of grain where her children's stones huddled together. She looked around the sides, on top of the worktable they were stored under. Perhaps what she looked for lay behind the sacks?

She pulled at the bag of buckwheat. A dull brown stone, stained with patterns in saffron orange, fell from where it had been wedged between the sacks and landed right in the middle of the three pebbles waiting below it.

Piera backed away, silent for a second. Then she began to scream. An instant later Gentile's arms wrapped around her.

20

Late September, 1527

The funeral became larger and larger as it wound through the streets. It had started with one priest holding one cross leading two biers, each with only a handful of mourners behind it. Their muted chanting rose as faintly as smoke into the chill, pearly predawn light.

At almost every crossway bearers turned in to join the procession, their biers often holding several corpses. If they waited till a priest could be found to lead away their clients individually the streets would have filled with rotting bodies long ago. The situation was worsened by the fact that in spite of their supposed divine connections, the clergy were dying off as fast as everyone else.

By the time it reached the Ruggieros' district the procession filled the street, turning it into a moving river of dead bodies. Few additional mourners had joined the cavalcade, so the hushed lamenting was overwhelmed by the shuffling of the bier bearers' feet.

Tommaso turned off from where he lurked near the end of the procession. The few other citizens out on the street averted their faces from Death's parade. It was unlikely that Tommaso would be seen or recognized.

Tommaso doubted that Il Tribolino would punish him, though it wasn't his day off. He'd only been given permission to go early to buy some fresh produce at the open-air *mercato*.

If Tommaso were caught out, however, at the very least Il Tribolino would report his truancy to his father and Ruggiero the Old and he'd lose these opportunities to slip away.

Tommaso skirted around the walled corner of the Ruggiero property and past the back door to the kitchen compound until he arrived at the garden gate. He knocked five times rapidly. The latch clicked open. Filomena slid out.

"I was beginning to think you wouldn't come. The others will rise in a few moments."

"I'm sorry," Tommaso said. "Fewer and fewer peasants bring in their produce. It takes me longer to pick through and find the goods I need. If I return to the *bottega* with nothing I'll lose my chance to slip away. How is she?"

Filomena shook her head sadly. "Two nights ago I would have said she was better. Your father accompanied us on a walk by the Arno in the evening so she could take in some fresh air. Of late she's tried to deny her madness in every way. As if to prove those pebbles mean nothing to her, she skipped one into the river. She seemed almost gay afterward, like herself again. Yet the very next morning when I rose to start the bread-baking, I found her awake before me, weeping over her piles of stones."

"And Master Ruggiero can still find nothing wrong with her?"

Filomena peered back through the gate to make sure no one else was about before answering. "No, but he believes the circumstances surrounding the birth of Luciana weakened her constitution, leaving both mind and body vulnerable to melancholy. He fears she might become even more fragile, especially in these times." Filomena glanced down the alley fearfully, but no mound of corpses greeted her eyes. Either the power or the luck of the Ruggieros seemed to be holding fast. As yet there were very few cases of the plague in this small sector of the city.

Filomena shivered. "My mother's people believe there is another whole world beyond the veil completely equal to this one, except that it stands in opposition. If there is drought here, they suffer flooding. If a sheep-herder enjoys happiness and prosperity here, his counterpart lives in misery and poverty there. I look at poor Florence and think that in another land beyond our ken people are enjoying unprecedented good health, joy, and long life, all bought at our expense."

Tommaso looked at her, desperate to reach out to comfort her. "Il Tribolino must let me out of my contract," he fretted. "I'm needed here at home."

"What would you do here?" Filomena asked. "So many have died, fled the city, or hide in their homes that *Ser* Ruggiero never entertains anymore. We only cook for the family and the other servants. Pietro and Beatrice would be comforted to have you back, but it might make your mother worse, to think her condition so extreme that you had to break your apprenticeship for it. What does your sister think of how bad things have become?"

"I don't know," Tommaso replied. "When I first brought the news of our mother's collapse, both Ginevra and the *Duchessina* turned pale as milk. Since then I've told them as little as possible, other than Mother is a little better or a little worse, as the case may be. Still, such is the bond between mother and daughter, every time our mother suffers an episode I swear that somehow Ginevra knows."

Filomena bowed her head. "Then perhaps it is kinder to say as little as possible."

It occurred to Tommaso that Filomena had never had the chance to know her own mother long. It seemed to him the height of cruelty that one so lovely should have to suffer slavery.

The skin of her cheek looked like warm gold in the first true light of the morning. Tommaso felt a sudden urge to press his lips there, let them gently sink into that softness.

He flushed with shame. Filomena had been kind and helpful to him. Would he repay her by taking that which any could take from a slave? Someone would someday. Perhaps soon. But it would not be him.

"I must go, and you must go back inside," he said hastily. "Thank you again for meeting with me. I'll come again in three days on my afternoon off, so you won't have to risk meeting me."

"Wait." Filomena caught his sleeve as he turned to go. "I haven't told you everything." Her voice was both anxious and reluctant.

He looked at her.

"First . . ." She looked as though she could barely force the words out. "I believe your mother may be pregnant again."

Tommaso gasped. "But Master Ruggiero examined her. Surely he'd notice."

Filomena shook her head. "She's not long into it. The symptoms would be masked by those of her illness. Another of her sex is more likely to notice, this early on. But there is more."

She hesitated again. She looked so fearful that Tommaso began to feel afraid. "What is it, Filomena? Tell me!"

"I scarcely dare, for it makes me doubt my own sight and sanity. When we were out walking by the river the other day, the pebble she skipped across the water sank into the middle of the Arno. It was one of her patterned ones, a plain brown thing with orange lines marked on it. But I would swear that the next morning when I found her collapsed over her pile of stones, it was there among them."

21

The third week of October, 1527

"If you have grown so tall so fast, what must your sister look like?" Piera asked. Piera's wrist seemed so thin, the bones in her hand so fragile that Tommaso's own hand shook as he took the weekly packet for Ginevra from her.

He tried to smile reassuringly. "You must try to get better faster so that you can visit Ginevra yourself," he said, feeling ashamed of himself. He wanted to leave as quickly as he could and dreaded returning here after visiting with Ginevra and the *Duchessina*.

The atmosphere in the Ruggiero kitchen was as heavy and dense as the oppressive smell of a meal cooked too long. Pietro and Beatrice played together contentedly by the hearth, as he and Ginevra had played in years long passed. But the other servants seemed uneasy. There was no sign of Filomena. Or of Gentile.

"Where is Father?"

Piera looked distracted. She waved her hand in a vague gesture. "He's been in and out of the mansion all day. Perhaps he consults with *Ser* Ruggiero on the declining food supply." Her gaze sharpened. "Does there seem to be enough food in the Convent of Santa Lucia? Has the *Duchessina's* kitten been catching rats?"

The desperate expression in her eyes made Tommaso apprehensive. "I'll ask her," he promised his mother.

As he strode down the hallway past the sleeping quarters and store-rooms to the back door he racked his brains for words to offer up to Ginevra. It was always Caterina now who asked how Piera fared. Ginevra just stood back behind her young mistress and looked at Tommaso with eyes filled with dread.

Tommaso slammed the door to the street open and launched himself out onto the street.

Someone grabbed his collar from behind and yanked him firmly back-ward. As Tommaso fell, feet scuffling for purchase on the stone paving, he knew again the same helpless plunging in his heart he'd experienced when the Arrabbiati grabbed him. He whirled around, half stumbling, breaking his assailant's grip.

Gentile stood there, looking surprised. The hand he'd grabbed Tom-maso with was still outstretched. The other hand grasped Filomena's arm. A burlap sack was slung over Gentile's shoulder.

"Hold to, boy. Don't you hear when I call you?"

"N-n-no. Forgive me, Father. I was moving in haste with my thoughts elsewhere." Tommaso glanced at Filomena. Had Gentile discovered their clandestine meetings? Tommaso knew the conclusion, however erroneous, that his father would draw. Filomena's eyes were full of fear. Tommaso's heart sank.

"I've been waiting for you." Gentile's voice was harsh. "Today I ac-company you to the nunnery. I wish to see my daughter." He turned to Filomena and gave the slave a shake. "Do what I have told you to do. Be sure no one sees you."

This shocked Tommaso more than anything else. Never had he seen his father treat one lower in station in such a fashion.

Filomena nodded. She fled through the back door.

Tommaso's mind was a jumble of confusion as he hurried beside his father through the streets. By the time they reached the convent he was out of breath.

The weather had turned cold. He no longer met the girls in the gar-den. A bony, middle-aged nun ushered the two of them into the kitchen.

"I've come to meet with my daughter on an urgent matter," Gentile told the woman. His voice was brusque, barely civil.

"I'll send Sister Dominica to fetch the girls." The nun waved her fingers and a novice glided out of the kitchen.

"While she does that, you and I shall have a private talk." To Tommaso's amazement, Gentile grasped the sleeve of the nun's habit and drew her down the hallway after the novice. Tommaso peeked after them, watching until they disappeared at an intersection in the corridor.

A minute or so later the novice appeared at the top of the hallway, escorting Ginevra and Caterina. Tommaso scrambled back from the doorway.

"Father is here. He seems angry," Tommaso blurted out as the two girls entered the kitchen. A welcoming smile died on Ginevra's lips.

"You did not see or hear him?" Tommaso asked. "I thought he might be going to meet you on your way from your room."

The girls and the novice looked incredulous at the idea of a man wandering through the convent.

"No," Ginevra said. "Sister Dominica brought us here straight from saying our catechisms. Why did Father come?"

"I do not know. He's very curt. I've never seen him this way. Perhaps he seeks to bring you home to help care for Mother."

Caterina paled and clutched at Ginevra's hand. Ginevra patted her. "If such is the case, surely I'll only be gone for a short while, until she's better."

Tommaso looked over his shoulder. Sister Dominica had gone back to her chores. She was sliding rounds of freshly risen dough into the bread oven with a long-handled paddle, paying little attention to them. Tommaso handed the weekly packet to Caterina, who slid it into a pocket in her *gammura*.

Footsteps clattered down the hallway—one set belonging to a large person with a long stride, the other to a lighter person, whose feet pattered rapidly in an attempt to keep up.

Gentile burst into the room. The burlap sack swung from one hand. It was two-thirds full. The nun fluttered in behind him. Her face was strained. The little novice turned. Seeing the look on Gentile's face, she flattened herself to the wall next to the oven.

"You're here. Good. You're coming home with us," Gentile told his daughter. He handed Tommaso the sack. "You'll carry your sister's things."

"Am I to take care of Mother?" Ginevra asked. "Then, when she's well, I'll come back to accompany the *Duchessina,* yes?"

Her words halted Gentile. He looked from one white-faced little girl to the other. His blustering momentum began to visibly drain away.

Now Tommaso understood his father's strange behavior. Whatever task Gentile had set himself, he'd laid and lit a fire of fury to his actions to carry him through to the end without stopping.

Ginevra's quiet, frightened words had stopped him.

Gentile opened his mouth to speak, then closed it. He glowered at the nun. "Tell her," he ordered the woman. He pointed a finger at the *Duchessina.* "She will be the one left behind. Tell her."

The nun put her hand to her mouth and shook her head. With her other hand she made the sign of the cross.

Gentile swore an oath. The nun gasped and crossed herself again.

Gentile turned to the two girls. "This morning, when I bargained for fresh game on the Ponte Vecchio, I happened on one who delivers goods to this convent. He told me that as he brought a cartload here before dawn he came upon a doctor leaving, who had been summoned secretly in the night. The doctor would say nothing, but by keeping his ears open my friend ascertained the truth."

Gentile looked over his shoulder at the nun with the force of unforgiving judgment in his eyes. "The plague has come to this place. One of the sisters is dying of it even as we stand here."

The little novice dropped her bread paddle. Its clattering on the tile floor seemed to echo endlessly.

Gentile dropped to one knee before Caterina—not in a gesture of humility but rather to bring himself face-to-face with her.

"I'm sorry, *Duchessina.* I would do anything to take you away too, but I have no jurisdiction over you. I can only save my daughter. I spoke to my master and informed him of your peril. Even now he prepares a petition to the *Signoria* for your release to a safe haven."

Gentile rose to his feet. Standing, he loomed over her. Caterina was trembling, her eyes as deep and black as flood-filled wells. Guilt washed over Gentile's face as he looked down at her.

"You cannot know how filled with misery I am," he said, his voice now very soft, "to leave you here alone, afraid, and in danger. For the love you bear my daughter, please understand that I must save her." He gestured Tommaso toward the door. Then, grasping Ginevra's hand, drew her away from Caterina.

"Messer Arista." Caterina's voice quivered, but she spoke strongly. "You are correct in your assumption that I am afraid. But I am afraid for Ginevra, not myself. If you take her from me, it is she who will be in danger, not I. My safety is assured. For *her* sake, please do not separate us."

Gentile shook his head sadly at her delusional plea. He had to pull Ginevra through the doorway.

Halfway across the convent courtyard Tommaso looked back. The kitchen door was still flung wide open. Caterina stood alone in the middle of the room. Her hands covered her face as she cried. Even from this distance Tommaso could tell that she wept not from fear but from grief.

Gentile started walking fast and picked up speed as they neared home. Ginevra's and Tommaso's legs were no match for their father's longer stride. Tommaso had to trot to keep up and Ginevra was reduced to a scrambling run. As they dragged behind Gentile, Ginevra's eyes asked Tommaso a thousand questions. Tommaso had to shake his head. He knew none of the answers. All he knew was that their father was expanding his courage again as he accelerated his pace. What did their father intend to do next?

Gentile slammed through the back entry to the Ruggiero kitchen compound. He pushed open the door to his and Piera's sleeping quarters as they passed it. "Are you finished in there yet?" he demanded.

From where he stood Tommaso couldn't see into the room. He heard no one answer, but Ginevra looked startled, and whatever Gentile saw there evidently satisfied him.

In the kitchen itself, all heads were turned toward their entrance in a frozen tableau, alerted by the racket they'd already made. Tommaso had but an instant to take in the scene: the two young apprentice cooks—Ottaviano the journeyman chef and Massolina poised over their tasks; Piera sitting on a stool picking through a bowl of porcini in her lap; Beatrice and Pietro playing at her feet; Cousin Francesca perched on a worktable, nursing Luciana and her own baby Paolo; and Gattamelata and her catlings grooming themselves under the big worktable.

Gentile pushed Ginevra in front of him toward Piera. "The Medici rule this family no more," he said. "I cannot let their fate destroy the lives of my family, the lives of my children. No one is allowed to do that, not even the Ruggieros we serve."

Piera opened her arms to Ginevra, her face bewildered. "What are you talking about?"

"This day I found out that plague has struck the Convent of Santa Lucia."

Piera clasped Ginevra to her tightly, her already waxen face turning even whiter. "What have you done?" she whispered.

"Rescued my daughter from probable death. And I intend to rescue as many of the rest of my children as I can." Gentile turned toward the back hallway. "Filomena!" he bellowed.

Tommaso heard a door open. Then Filomena appeared, a filled burlap sack under each arm.

"Did you get everything?" Gentile asked her.

Filomena nodded, her terror-stricken eyes fixed on Piera.

"What is all this?" said Piera.

"Half this city or better may die," said Gentile. "If I could, I'd send every person in this kitchen away to safety. At least it is in my power to protect some of my children.

"As soon as I learned the plague had breached Santa Lucia I went to Dr. Ruggiero and informed him. He'd already instructed Old Taddeo to take the oxcart to the estate near Pistoia to stock up on produce, since fewer and fewer peasants are willing to risk entry to the city. *Ser* Ruggiero has given his permission that Ginevra, Beatrice, and Pietro may seek refuge at the estate with my father's family."

Piera stood up, still clutching Ginevra. "No!" she shouted. "You cannot do this!"

"Yes I can!" Gentile shouted back. "And if you were not so weak and ill," Tommaso heard accusation in his father's voice, "I would be able to send you to safety with them."

"What safety? Did fleeing Florence save poor Atalanta?" Piera threw the death of the other kitchen maid at Gentile.

They stood glaring at each other. "Francesca," Gentile said without breaking his locked gaze, "I cannot compel you to go, but I can offer it to you—refuge for yourself, your son, and our Luciana."

Cousin Francesca backed up toward the door to the courtyard, her arms filled with the babies, shaking her head no.

Gentile couldn't see her mute response but knew what her silence meant. "Very well. That is your choice. Massolina, take the little ones around to the front. Old Taddeo has held off on leaving until I could retrieve Ginevra. Filomena, take the sacks with all their things."

"No!" Piera screamed. "You are wrong. It is here, only here that they are safe." She tried to lunge past Gentile. He grabbed her. Beatrice and Pietro, quiet and terrified until now, burst into noisy tears and tried to hold onto their mother.

Gentile fended them off.

Piera, now sobbing too, wilted. "At least let me hug them good-bye," she wept.

Tommaso saw cracks open in the hard edifice his father had constructed to support and protect himself through this course of action. And through those cracks Tommaso glimpsed the utter misery Gentile was suffering.

Piera embraced the little ones until Gentile pried them away. He directed Massolina and Filomena again to take the children out to the oxcart. The maid and slave girl moved quickly, obviously relieved at the chance to leave the kitchen.

Piera had turned to Ginevra, to this daughter she hadn't seen in months, whispering fevered advice and kissing her cheeks. With both hands Piera pulled upward at a chain around her neck, drawing forth the silver crucifix that nestled so deeply in her clothing that Tommaso had never caught more than a glimpse of it. It swung clear. Piera lifted it to settle onto her daughter's neck. "For protection," she whispered.

It never reached its destination. There was a sudden, violent motion and then it was spinning up and through the air, hard and fast, hitting with a hard crash against the side of the bread oven.

"No more of your superstitions!" Gentile stood between the two, all of his fury returned. His fists were clutched and upraised. For a dreadful instant Tommaso thought Gentile might strike Piera. Gentile's whole face was clenched, teeth bared and eyes shut tight. His hands shook as he forced himself to lower and open them. When he was done he was panting.

"I've closed my eyes and closed my eyes for you, but I cannot tolerate it anymore. You think me blind? But for your foolishness you would be the strong woman I married, and you and Luciana could also be on your way to safe haven." He took Ginevra's wrist and pulled his daughter toward the door.

"Wait!" As they turned at her cry, Piera glanced frantically around the kitchen. She snatched up one of the young cats from where they hid under the worktable. She held the kitten out. "At least let Ginevra take the kitten. To remind the children of home. They are so frightened right now. For comfort. And there are so many rats in the country."

She looked so pitiful standing there.

Ginevra looked up at Gentile, adding her plea to her mother's.

Tommaso saw that Gentile was ashamed of his outburst, already deeply regretting it.

"Yes, that would be fine," Gentile muttered.

Ginevra cuddled the kitten in her arms. Gentile took his wife's face gently in his hands. "I'm sorry, *Bella*. I must do this. Get well enough to travel and I will send you to them. I've asked *Ser* Ruggiero to negotiate with Il Tribolino to try to get Tommaso released from his apprenticeship soon, so that he too can be safe."

With every word Piera dwindled more.

"Now come with me to see them off."

Ginevra tried to smile at Tommaso, a sad, wan little gesture with her lips. "When next you see Caterina, tell her that I have a cat too now. Tell her I'm naming it Casparina. That way we'll have all three of the Magi at our disposal."

Tommaso nodded, though with Ginevra gone he doubted he would have the opportunity to see the *Duchessina*.

They left. What was left of the kitchen staff became suddenly busy, bustling about and speaking in hushed voices.

Tommaso picked up his mother's crucifix from the floor. It was of an unusual ornate design. Its shaft and arms seemed to form the trunk and two main branches of a tree. At its foot was a fish. The Greek sign for

Christ, no doubt. A key was affixed to one of the side branches. The key
to the kingdom of heaven. The trunk was topped in clusters of three-
pronged leaves, with a waxing moon caught in its boughs. *A growing Moon,
symbol of rebirth and the Great Mother's strength.* The thought came unbidden into
Tommaso's mind. Startled, he almost dropped the crucifix. He shook his
head to clear it.

A piece had been broken off the end of the other arm by the impact
against the oven. Tommaso searched until he found it. It was a silver flower
head—it looked like vervain. He set it against the jagged end of the crucifix arm. It fit perfectly.

Tommaso slid the crucifix, its chain and the broken piece into a
pocket. He could easily repair it back at Il Tribolino's studio. Surely that
would comfort his mother.

22

Tommaso leaned back against the stone railing of the bridge of Santa Trinitá and looked up. The waning Moon, two thirds full, glowed through a light froth of clouds. He murmured a verse from today's lesson:

> How can that be, lady, which all men learn
> By long experience? Shapes that seem alive,
> Wrought in hard mountain marble, will survive
> Their maker, whom the years to dust return.

He'd never looked closely at such a night sky before, though he must have seen hundreds just like it, even in his short life. Tommaso was entranced by the way the silvery vapors gathered, shifted and rippled about the moon. They might have been dancing around her. And they reminded him of something, but he couldn't quite remember what.

> Thus to effect cause yields. Art hath her turn,
> And triumphs over Nature. I, who strive
> With Sculpture, know this well; her wonders live
> In spite of time and death, those tyrants stern.

These days everything seemed transitory to Tommaso, from the food he prepared, so quickly consumed, to the dying thousands who seemed, in their turn, mere fodder for the plague. Working on the great sculptures at Il Tribolino's, he was consoled by the heavy massive permanence of their beauty. They'd outlast time itself.

Tommaso took what comfort he could from the poem's words. They were part of a sonnet Il Tribolino had read while Tommaso and the other apprentices worked at buffing and polishing a completed bronze.

Even surrounded by pestilence, Il Tribolino saw no reason to discontinue their education. "As long as you are alive you can learn," he declared. "Memorize these lines well. They are the work of a great man. I expect you to be able to recite them back to me with meaning on the morrow."

> So I can give long life to both of us
> In either way, by color or by stone,
> Making the semblance of thy face and mine.

Tommaso chanted the next stanza. He glanced upriver to the Ponte Vecchio, usually well lit and bustling even at this hour. But it, like all of Florence, was dark and plague-stilled.

Tommaso shivered. It wasn't enough to constantly fear a painful pestilent death, but now he must worry about his divided family and the terrible tension between his parents. And yet, he felt so many other things as well these days. His fascination with and complete immersion in his studies at the *bottega*. The heat and bashfulness he experienced every time he saw Filomena. He felt like a too-full pot set over the fire.

His mouth twitched in a crooked grin. That's what the clouds around the moon reminded him of: a rich broth simmering, its fluids billowing, striving to come to a boil.

It was just as well he wasn't fated for the classical arts. With such a mindset he'd only prove a buffoon. How did the last stanza of that sonnet go?

"Centuries hence when both are buried, thus—" he began.

A voice at his shoulder finished for him,

Thy beauty and my sadness shall be shown,
And men shall say, "For her 'twas wise to pine."

Michelangelo had come up beside him as silently as a cat. The sculptor said the lines with such feeling and familiarity that suddenly Tommaso understood that the "great man" who had written them stood before him.

"I've taken you unawares, young Tommaso. You must no longer fear the Arrabbiati, to linger about so late. Have you grown so tall in the last months that you believe yourself proof against their blows?"

Tommaso shook his head. "Not unless I was armed with my sharpest cleaver. There are surer weapons against assault in these times. If surprised, all I have to do is double over, groan with pain, and clutch my armpits as if they were swollen and tender. Any ruffian, even one drunk and half blind, would be sore put to lay a hand on me."

Michelangelo smiled. "You're always so quiet at Tribolo's, lurking in the background with your pots and pans. I had no idea you possessed such wit. Why do you linger here, at night and alone? Who knows what unwholesome vapors might waft your way?"

"*Ser* Tribolino gave me leave to attend late Mass after supper. I stayed to light a candle . . ." Tommaso hesitated. It seemed inappropriate to chatter on to someone as distinguished as Michelangelo about his family's troubles.

"My sisters and little brother were sent away from Florence yesterday. I lit a candle for their safe journey." He didn't mention he'd also lit a flame for his mother's health and another for his father's troubled heart. "When I came to the bridge the moon caught my eye. I can't seem to take leave of its image, either in the sky or in the waters."

"Ah, you have an artist's soul to match your good looks."

Tommaso grimaced under the compliment. "I wish that were true. All I've uncovered with my gazing is a cook's simple soul. What art I may do in life is destined by my own nature to consist of the humblest and most transitory materials, unlike those of which the sonnet speaks. For when I stare at the clouds boiling about the moon, what I see is a rich hearty soup simmering."

Michelangelo threw back his head and laughed. "And who's to say you aren't right?" He peered up at the sky, then leaned over the water to study the reflection there.

Tommaso studied the artist as the artist studied the clouds and the moon. Michelangelo was only of medium height, quite a bit shorter than Tommaso's father Gentile. Yet his genius, which he bore so casually, made him seem a much larger man. He was lean and tough with muscle. No softening of fat showed anywhere on his body. His face was broad browed, well lined, of the type called noble, except for the crushed, flattened nose. His hair and beard were cut short, black with a salting of white throughout. Tommaso couldn't see his eyes well at this angle or in this light, but he remembered them well from the night that Michelangelo dressed his wounds. They were light amber, shot through with flecks of blue and dark gold.

Michelangelo rocked back from the bridge's railing. "Don't ever chide yourself for a too-plain imagination, Tommaso. It would never have occurred to me to see a good *zuppa* cooking in the clouds. But, now that you have let me see through your eyes, I see it plainly. It was there all along.

"Surely you know that Lorenzo the Great's finest poetry dealt not with gods or heroics or love, but with the simple honest pleasures of Tuscan life: farming, fishing, watching one's flocks, pressing grapes for wine, sitting down to country feasts."

He clapped a hand to Tommaso's shoulder. "All of this talk has made me hungry. Would you happen to have something like that moon soup simmering away at Tribolo's hearth? Yes? Then let me accompany you back to the *bottega*. I need to speak with Tribolo anyway about some marble he's trying to order."

Back at the *bottega* it turned out that Michelangelo was not the only one suffering from hunger pangs. As Tommaso improvised and chopped up silver beet, savoy cabbage, and sausage to add to a basic broth, Melchiora wrapped herself around his ankles, yowling.

"If you're so starved, go catch yourself a fat rat," Tommaso scolded her, even as he relented and fed her little morsels of the sausage. "Hush. You'll awaken Elissa Pecorino."

Usually dainty, Melchiora wolfed down the scraps as if she hadn't eaten in a week. But even the food didn't quell her anxiety. Tommaso was forced to pick her up and hold her in one arm as he stirred the soup.

"You'd think you were my awful baby sister Luciana," he told her. "Mind you don't shed any fur into the soup. Michelangelo has been kind so far, but don't forget that he's famous for his temper."

Tommaso stirred the soup carefully, checking the surface to make sure there really were no cat hairs floating there.

Out at the river he'd seen simmering soup in the clouds. Now he saw clouds boiling about each other in the depths of the soup. The clouds seemed to take on shapes and forms, as clouds are wont to do. Here there was a coiling dragon, there a Florentine lily. Tommaso fancied he could make out faces that he knew: Ginevra's, which shifted and thinned to become Piera's. This was boiled over by Gentile's face, then Pietro's and Beatrice's.

The steam lifting off the soup suddenly seemed too rich and dense. It thickened inside Tommaso's nostrils. He felt dizzy and far too hot. *Something is wrong. Something is terribly wrong*, he thought.

Tommaso jerked upright away from the hearth and dropped the cat. His skin was cold and clammy. He yanked off his shirt, felt frantically under his armpits. Nothing. He checked carefully for bruising, then felt along his groin. Nothing. Weak with relief, he slumped onto a bench and crossed himself. Not the plague. Not yet, at least. Then why had he felt . . . ? He pushed the thought out of his mind. Shivering, he pulled his shirt back on. Why not such imaginings? The plague was here, looming in the background of everything.

23

November 3, 1527

Piera woke again early hoping, yet scarcely daring to hope. She felt Gentile stiffen beside her and, with lidded anxious eyes feigning sleep, watch her depart. She knew it drove him wild that she continued her rituals. But shame for his outburst when he'd sent their children away and fear for her health kept him silent and brooding.

She also believed he'd finally guessed she was pregnant again. Though only early into it, she was gaunt enough that the slight roundness to her belly had begun to show. If he had guessed, Gentile must be wounded that she hadn't told him yet. Piera felt heavy not only with the new child, but with all the trouble that lay between her and her husband.

Even so, her heart beat more quickly as she entered the kitchen, like a bird struggling to raise itself into flight. No matter where she'd moved her children's stones—Ginevra's, Beatrice's, and Pietro's now all together—the next day Alessandro's was always among them, like an ugly cuckoo's egg.

Three days before she'd risen to face her morning vigil with dread. And had found a miracle. Alessandro's stone was nowhere to be found. It wasn't where she had cloistered it the night before, bound with blue beads high on a shelf. But neither was it near her children. She'd searched and searched, but couldn't find it anywhere. Each day since it had stayed disappeared. Would this morning be different? It had first vanished on Shadow Day—

what better day to be rid of an evil shadow? She held her breath and began her inventory.

Ginevra, Beatrice, and Pietro remained together, an innocent and inviolate trio. By the hearth the Ruggiero mansion pile of pebbles accounted for itself. Tommaso's stone lay where it always did, alone on the windowsill.

Since the children had been sent away Piera had been experiencing a terrible uneasiness. Now she allowed herself to feel weak with relief. She sat down heavily on a stool. When she regained her strength she'd go back in the bedroom, crawl between the covers and allow herself to enjoy Gentile's warmth beside her until it was time to rise.

Filomena came in and offered a subdued "Good morning" as she set about feeding the fire. When Piera favored her with a smile the slave looked startled, then beamed.

Have I changed so much? thought Piera. *Now that we're safe perhaps I can retrieve myself.*

She was so distracted with relief she'd failed to notice that Ippolito's stone was missing too, no longer nearby, protecting her children.

It was late that same day that Old Taddeo returned from the holdings near Pistoia. Gentile, Ottaviano and the kitchen boys helped the old man unload sacks of grain and almonds, casks of walnut oil, rounds of hard cheeses, and baskets of onions and pears into the storage area. The women had to begin preparations for the household's supper without them.

Afterward, Gentile entered the kitchen all smiles, seeming well pleased with himself. Smugness was not a trait he often indulged in. When he did, Piera found it irritating. But today it was so pleasant to see the weight of guilt and fear lifted from his shoulders that she forgave him.

"Everyone gather round and pour yourself whatever cheers you most. I have good news." He pulled an envelope from his pocket and waved it at them. "Taddeo says the children have been delivered safely to the estate and are well and happy. He delivered to me this letter written by Ginevra, which I'll read aloud for all to hear."

Gentile pulled up a chair and swung a leg over it, so that he sat back to front in it. He broke the seal on the letter and began to read.

"My dearest family, know that we have arrived safely and are under

Uncle Vincenzo, Aunt Costanza, and Grandfather Arista's kind care. It will take at least another day for the farmhands to gather together the items Messer Ruggiero requires, so I have time to write this letter and send it back with Taddeo.

"Pietro and Beatrice love the farm and are already enjoying themselves. Uncle Vincenzo takes Pietro with him to mind the sheep and Aunt Costanza has set Beatrice to feeding and minding the chickens and guinea fowl, an avocation Beatrice seems particularly well suited to and which grants her no small degree of contentment. As for myself, I am helping out as best I can in the kitchen."

Gentile paused and smiled. Piera knew he was painting himself a picture in his mind of the children settled in and happy. Then he continued.

"As soon as we arrived I decided to try not to lose too much ground in my studies by beginning to teach the little ones the rudiments of reading and spelling. Beatrice strives earnestly, but Pietro is really too young for the task. He begs me to just read stories aloud without making demands of him. I always relent, since I count such practice as being to my own benefit.

"We are healthy and content, but I have one sad and upsetting occurrence to relate. I hesitate to write it down, but Old Taddeo assures me that if I do not tell you of it, he will, and I would prefer to relate the episode in my own words."

Gentile stopped. He glanced up at Piera nervously. She knew he was loath to continue. She glared at him in answer.

He cleared his throat.

"It occurred on the journey here, as we passed through the edge of the Mugello. We were crossing a bridge over a stream when we heard the noises of a hunting party in the hills the stream fed down from.

"One of the hunting party broke clear of the trees and rode toward us. To our great astonishment the hunter proved to be Allessandro de' Medici. He positioned his horse at the foot of the bridge, blocking it so we could not pass. He began to jest. Perhaps he thought himself witty, but his comments were rude and cruelly mocking.

"Pietro, brave little warrior that he is, stood up on his seat in the cart and soundly scolded Alessandro. This made Alessandro furious. He rode up beside us, leaned over on his horse and reached out to strike Pietro.

"Now, since we had left Florence with no container to carry Casparina in, I had let the two little ones take turns carrying her. Of all of us,
she seemed the calmest on the journey. It gave Beatrice and Pietro comfort to hold her."

Gentile's voice dropped low as he read this. Piera could barely hear him.
He was remembering why his children were so upset when they left Florence.

"At the time of the altercation on the bridge, Pietro happened to be
carrying Casparina. As Allessandro struck at my little brother, Casparina
also struck, clawing Alessandro's hand and drawing forth long lines of
blood there.

"Alessandro screamed an oath. He snatched back his hand and stared
at it. Then he grabbed Casparina and with one motion snapped her neck
and threw her into the stream.

"At this Old Taddeo rose up and I think would have beaten Alessandro with the reins to the cart. If he had done so, who knows if Alessandro would not have broken his neck and hurled him into the waters too?
Then we would have been quite alone and defenseless.

"Just then, the rest of the hunting party burst out of the woods, at-
tracted no doubt by our cries. Ippolito led them. When he saw what his
cousin had done he was horrified. He chastised Alessandro bitterly.
Alessandro just laughed and rode off.

"Ippolito stayed and searched for Casparina, but the stream had carried her body away. He escorted us the rest of the way to the farm before
taking leave of us, being much ashamed by his cousin's actions.

"So now we are safe, but saddened by Casparina's loss. We miss her
for another reason too. So much of the harvest this year must be sent to
Florence because of the plague that Grandfather Arista says there will
barely be food enough to survive the winter. And there are rats everywhere,
attacking all that is left. The farmhouse has only one tomcat. He is very
old and can barely hunt.

"I pray this letter finds all of you well and in good health. Please remember us in your prayers, as we remember you in ours. Your loving
daughter, Ginevra."

There was utter silence in the room when Gentile finished. He looked
up at Piera guiltily. She saw him but didn't meet his eyes. Now she knew

why Alessandro de' Medici's stone had been hovering over her children. And why it had left. It had accomplished its task. It was only a matter of days now, weeks at most.

"But they are there, and safe from the plague," Gentile said at last.

Piera said nothing. She was frozen, impaled by the dagger of ice that had been driven into her heart. And she knew she would never be able to drag that dagger out or melt it.

24

The third week of November, 1527

Difficult as it was to fly through the stars and keep her bearings, Piera found it even harder to skim over the Tuscan landscape with no more than a new shard of moon to guide her. But she flew strongly, her purpose a hard wind at her back, her thin body lark-bone light. The unguents spreading through her pulse points beat her along like sturdy wings. And the way was familiar—she'd flown it at least once a week since the arrival of Ginevra's letter.

Northward and westward she flew. At last she glided over a too-quiet farmhouse. No lights showed in its windows. Freshly dug graves pockmarked the ground behind it. Like a shadow, Piera slid within the house.

"Mother? Mother, is that you?" Ginevra's voice was weak. "It's so dark here."

"That's because it's night, darling daughter. And your grandfather has only lit a fire in the fireplace. He's fallen asleep and it's dwindled to the embers." Piera was glad there was so little light. She couldn't have borne to see her daughter's ruined body clearly.

"No, Mother. It's much darker than that."

Piera's heart beat as hard as a bird's. Far away she felt the chill sensation of cold stones against her back. She had almost not made it in time. "Tell me about the little ones."

"They both died today. Mercifully, Pietro went first, early this morning without pain, although his body was black with bruises. He just looked surprised.

"But Beatrice died horribly. She was in agony. The *gavòccioli* under her arms were huge and hurt her terribly. I did my best—I made her herbal teas as you taught me, but they only helped a little.

"That was when Grandfather started drinking and turned away. He's not asleep, you know. He stayed sober only long enough to bury them both. He said it took so little effort to dig such small graves, after the big ones for Uncle Vincenzo and Aunt Costanza and the farmhands. But so many graves to be dug in only four days!

"Grandfather told me that the plague had touched him lightly when he was young and now spurns him, though he cried and begged it to take him too. Tomorrow he'll bury me."

"Hush. Are you in pain?" It took all of Piera's strength to keep the weeping from her voice.

"I was, but as it grew darker I left that behind. Now I feel as though I'm changing—that I'm shedding this body to become something else."

"That's why I'm here. To help you, my love," Piera said. "I wanted and planned so much for you. Those dreams have been betrayed, but I promise it will not end for you here."

Piera woke to the sounds of someone moving around the kitchen. She was late in returning—Filomena was already awake and starting her chores. Piera had left her bed in the middle of the night when Gentile slept soundly beside her. Piera knew she now had to move quickly to avoid detection.

But when she tried to raise herself, the cold pantry floor seemed to pull at her. Gasping with effort, all she could do was stare up at the ceiling as the inevitable pain crept up from her spine to envelop her skull in a throbbing mantle. The flying unguent burned at her pulse points. Piera at last felt what she hadn't noticed before: She was lying in a puddle of warm, thick liquid.

Dark plumes of smoke seemed to drift before her eyes. A persistent low drone filled her ears. She sensed rather than saw Filomena enter the pantry. And only dimly heard when the slave girl began to scream. At last

Piera finally understood that she'd lost more than three children that night.

People were moving about her. She felt herself being lifted. She recognized the powerful arms that held her, lifted her. Gentile's. Why did they tremble so? Her head lolled backward. As she was carried away she saw, upside down, the small pile of stones that had been her children.

Two of them were crumbled entirely to dust. The third, Ginevra's, was no longer dove colored with strong black markings. It bore no markings at all and had changed in color to a pure, deep, glowing scarlet.

25

❧

November 30, 1527

"Good, I'm glad you're here." Gentile clapped Tommaso on the shoulder.

Tommaso squirmed a little. Whenever Gentile waxed jovial Tommaso feared his father had at last succeeded at releasing him from his apprenticeship. Tommaso fingered the repaired crucifix in his pocket. If his father knew what he'd brought for his mother Gentile might not welcome him so.

Or perhaps he would. Filomena said that Gentile was frantic to bring his wife back to good health. Since the miscarriage anything that might cheer her won his favor. Piera hadn't left the bedroom since the morning she'd been found lying on the pantry floor in a pool of blood. Cousin Francesca had moved in with her to care for her. Gentile now slept in the men's quarters until his wife healed. *Or died.* Tommaso pushed the thought away.

Filomena had told him that Gentile spent every spare moment concocting delicacies to woo Piera's appetite and put flesh back on her bones. But Tommaso guessed that if anything cured her, it would be the foul-smelling infusions Cousin Francesca concocted and fed her a spoonful at a time.

There was so much tension in the kitchen, once such a happy place. All the other servants glided as soundlessly as they could around Gentile.

Besides that, Tommaso noticed how Filomena tried to sidle away whenever Ottaviano drew near her, and how often the journeyman placed himself in her path.

Tommaso felt miserable with helplessness, wanting to save Filomena.
Perhaps if he spoke to Gentile, who after all was lord of the kitchen. But
Gentile was too distracted with his own problems. Tommaso doubted he'd
intervene.

But even if Ottaviano could be kept at bay, Filomena would only fall
prey to someone else. The older Ruggiero boys were of an age to make
use of a slave girl. Tommaso was almost sure that Cosimo was too much
of a gentleman to abuse her. But Lorenzo, the second son, though blithe
and charming, would probably show no such scruples.

In the end, Tommaso knew the real reason he could not act on Filomena's behalf. Because he himself wanted her in just that way. Every night
of late he'd been sweetly tortured by dreams of her.

"I just received a letter from the farm. It's written in my father's hand."
Gentile spoke sharply and Tommaso realized he'd been caught staring after
Filomena. He flushed.

"Do you want me to help bring Mother in to hear it?" Tommaso asked.
"Or should it be read to her in the bedroom?"

Gentile glanced in the direction of the sleeping quarters. "No. Let us
read it first. Then we'll take it to her."

Tommaso remembered the first letter from Ginevra with its upsetting
news of Alessandro de' Medici. Gentile wanted to spare Piera in case there
was anything unsettling in this letter.

Gentile broke the seal. "My dearest," he started strongly. Then his
voice trembled and broke, "and now only son." Gentile stopped reading
aloud. His eyes traveled silently down the page, filling with horror.

One by one the sounds in the kitchen died away as everyone stopped
to watch him. Gentile's hands shook. The letter dropped to the floor.

Tommaso picked it up. "My dearest and now only son," he read in a
whisper. "May the Lord God in His infinite wisdom show you love and
compassion.

"In the last week, one by one, we have buried the farmhands. Then,
with my own hands, I laid to rest my only other son, your half-brother
Vincenzo, and his wife Costanza, who was pregnant with their first child.

Yesterday I buried your two little ones and today your beautiful daughter Ginevra, who, in this last month before the plague trespassed here, filled our house with such tranquillity and joy.

"I had hoped God would at least be merciful enough to spare her, but He was anxious to gather her goodness back to Himself. I alone remain, not spared but cursed. Praise God that your sisters married away from this place and that your stepmother died painlessly five years ago.

"It may be several days before I can find anyone alive and brave enough to pass through this afflicted region and who would be willing to carry this sad letter to you.

"I pray each day that it finds you, Piera, and your remaining children still alive and well.

"Your father."

Tommaso heard a gasp behind him. He pivoted around. Standing in the hallway entrance were Cousin Francesca and, leaning on her, his mother.

The sound had come from Francesca, standing with her hand clapped over her mouth. Piera stood white-faced and calm, completely unsurprised. Before Tommaso's eyes she seemed to straighten and grow stronger, while Gentile curled in on himself and shrank, like a spider fallen into the fire.

She already knew, Tommaso thought. *It's only what she expected. She's just been waiting to hear.*

A week later, on December 7, the *Signoria* relented. On that night Cosimo Ruggiero and Piero Strozzi escorted Caterina de' Medici through Florence's empty streets to her new home in the Murate on the other side of Florence. From almost that moment the plague began to abate.

Two days after that, on December 9, Pope Clement finally escaped from the Castel Sant' Angel. In much the same manner as his creature, Passerini, he disguised himself as a servant and fled with a single peasant as his companion.

In their great scrying mirror Ruggiero the Old and Cosimo watched the pontiff, clad in tatters and hiding behind a long false beard, make his way slowly to Orvieto in a humble farm cart.

"Is it done?" Cosimo asked bitterly. "Thousands upon thousands have died in this plague. Has the piper at last been paid enough in the coin of Florentine bodies? Has balance been achieved between the worlds?"

Ruggiero the Old looked at him with ancient weary eyes. "Oh, my son"—he shook his head—"the battle has just been joined. We only have a year, at most two, before the next onslaught."

26

January 5, 1528

Cosimo Ruggiero watched Michelangelo Buonarotti, pacing before the window, watch Tommaso Arista walk almost aimlessly down the avenue beneath them.

The young cook was walking away from his weekly rendezvous with his family. His shoulders were hitched up so high that his bright hair wavered like a timid flame about the hood of his winter cloak; a small brave lie to its owner's obvious dejection. Even gawky with adolescence and depression, Tommaso cut a beautiful figure as he wandered through the lace-like snow gently layering and thickening on Florence's streets.

"Tomorrow is the Feast of the Magi, the foremost festival in the de' Medici family calendar. But this year they'll host no glorious pageant and cavalcade," Michelangelo stated the obvious. "How will the poor little *Duchessina* celebrate the day?"

In spite of the artist's long association with the legendary family, Cosimo was surprised by the question.

"Her aunt will visit her in the morning," he replied. "Then Clarice must leave to spend some time managing Strozzi affairs before returning to the de' Medici palazzo. You know Madame Strozzi cannot leave it for a single day. The *Signoria* watch it always, ready to move against her and the family. So I'm afraid the *Duchessina* will pass the rest of the day alone, but for the company of the nuns. Why this sudden interest in the heiress?"

Cosimo kept the tenor of his voice neutral, conveying none of his own connection to Caterina.

Below, Tommaso moved so slowly, so reluctantly, that Michelangelo had paced back and forth any number of times, always unconsciously trailing his hand down the velvet drapes covering the great scrying mirror as he passed it, before the boy disappeared from view.

"I've had it on good account, from two very different people whom I admire and respect, that she is a member of the family to look out for—one with much potential," Michelangelo said. "Thank God there is someone left in the family besides Clarice with such quality."

Cosimo's eyebrows rose. Most of Michelangelo's current commissions derived directly from Pope Clement de' Medici.

Michelangelo understood his expression. "Anyone raised at Lorenzo the Magnificent's table as Giulio was would have developed a good eye for art and the desire to possess it. Although both admirable attributes, they do not guarantee wisdom in regards to political issues nor righteousness in moral matters. Artists employed by such individuals are under no obligation to ascribe nonexistent virtues to their patrons."

"But perhaps, in the interest of continued employment, those artists best refrain from public critiquing of such of their patron's qualities as fall outside the aesthetic arena," Cosimo observed.

"Of course," said Michelangelo. "That is why I speak of such things only with trusted friends." He looked at Cosimo pointedly.

The apprentice mage was flattered. It was clear from Michelangelo's inflection that there were those the artist counted as friends whom he would *not* trust with his opinions.

"We physicians and astrologers speak cautiously under just those same constraints," Cosimo concurred.

"Good. We understand each other," Michelangelo said. "Now as to what brought me here: This matter of the Epiphany and a certain little girl's enjoyment of it . . ."

"How can my family help you?" Cosimo asked. "Is it a matter for my father? He should be home from his physicking rounds soon."

"For how *I* intend to brighten the *Duchessina's* day, I need no help," said the artist. "I know what to do, and I'm on excellent terms with the sisters of the Murate. But knowing of your family's fondness of the child, I had a suggestion on how you might make her solitary celebration a little happier. And although he must be informed, we don't need your father's attendance on the matter, as you are bonded to deal with it. It will only be necessary to call at Il Tribolino's this afternoon."

Cosimo was intrigued. "Go on," he said.

January 6, 1528

Tommaso shifted on his seat next to Old Taddeo nervously. He glanced over his shoulder at the sacks of grain and casks of walnut oil that *Ser* Ruggiero was donating to the Murate. The oxcart had almost stalled several times in the deepening snow. Tommaso feared the casks might jar against each other and crack open.

"Are you sure I shouldn't get in back to hold things steady?" he asked Taddeo.

The old man shook his head. "What you're guarding up here is more important. And we've almost arrived."

Tommaso looked at the pile he held braced in his lap. The topmost item was a sheet of paper protected in an oilskin envelope. When Cosimo had arrived at the *bottega* yesterday, only shortly after Tommaso had returned there, with the request that Tommaso accompany Taddeo to the Murate on the Feast of the Magi to unload some supplies, Il Tribolino had immediately understood the true agenda of the errand. The artist rushed to complete a small ink sketch. "Should you happen to see the *Duchessina* . . ." he told Tommaso.

"I doubt I'll lay eyes on her, Master," Tommaso said.

"That's all right." Tribolino patted Tommaso's shoulder. "Then just ask the sisters to pass it along."

Then, when Tommaso had returned to the Ruggieros' this morning, both the old mage and Cosimo handed him several packages for Caterina.

And, finally, just as the oxcart was loaded and ready to leave, Piera came out of the kitchen with a tightly lidded pot wrapped in layers and layers of cloth. "This should stay hot till you reach the convent," she said.

Tommaso reached from his seat to lift it up. Looking down on his mother in this way he saw silver scattered through her hair that he was sure had not been there before. It matched in color the chain peeking up at the back of her neck. A poor trade indeed—her crucifix back, but not her children. Still, she'd seemed grateful when he'd given it to her.

As he took the pot from Piera, Tommaso avoided, as always, looking at her directly. For whenever he did he had to fight the urge to burst into tears. Physically, Piera had much recovered, but behind her dark eyes lay unquiet ghosts of loss.

Tommaso knew from Filomena that his parents were still estranged. Things had reached such a state that they no longer attended Mass together. Piera and Cousin Francesca went to morning Mass. Gentile accompanied the rest of the kitchen staff later in the day.

Ashamed at not meeting his mother's eyes, Tommaso settled the pot into his lap. Warmth pooled out across his thighs. Even through the cloth a rich aroma reached him. He had to smile when he recognized it.

"Let me guess," he said. "You'd like to be sure this is received by a certain golden-haired girl."

Piera smiled back up at him. Somewhere, behind all her haunted grief, Tommaso glimpsed the mother he remembered.

"You're prophetic, my son. Perhaps Cosimo Ruggiero may find competition for his future career under his very nose."

It was so good to hear his mother jest again that Tommaso mustered a laugh, although the hair on the back of his neck shivered erect.

The Murate's grounds were lovelier and far more extensive than those of the Convent of Santa Lucia. Several novices opened the gates, led Taddeo and Tommaso to the storerooms and kitchen and directed the unloading of the cart. Tommaso noticed that their habits were woven of a finer grade of cloth than those of the nuns of Santa Lucia, their voices more cultured, their manner simultaneously warmer, more open and refined than that of their plebeian sisters across town.

In the kitchen, in honor of the feast day, courses were being prepared of such delicacy that they might have been intended for the Medici banquet hall itself.

Finished with their task, Tommaso turned to the nun managing the kitchen, an elderly, plump woman with a kind face.

"Sister, with your permission, I have in my possession some gifts for one in your charge: Caterina Maria Romola de' Medici. They were sent by those who love and care for her. Would you see that she receives them?" The nun's cheeks became even rounder when she smiled.

"Please, call me Sister Teresa Lucrezia. I think that a responsibility you should discharge yourself." She clapped her hands. Two of the novices hurried away. A few moments later they returned, flanking Caterina between them.

The *Duchessina* wore a brocaded *gamurra* the color of a pink rose, over a white underblouse embroidered with flowers. Her sleeves were of a cream brocade whose pattern matched that of the *gamurra* and were tied to the dress with gold ribbons. What a change from the drab face she'd had to put on at Santa Lucia! With her hair floating loose about her shoulders like spun gilt, Tommaso couldn't imagine a more beautiful picture.

"Tommaso!" she squealed in a most un-*Duchessina* manner and ran to him like any little girl.

Tommaso wanted to pick her up, hug and whirl her about as he would have Ginevra or Beatrice. At the last moment he remembered himself and settled for dropping to one knee before her and clasping her hands.

"*Duchessina . . .*" he started, then stopped, his heart too full to say anything more.

"No. Up, up." Caterina tugged at his hands. "You are my gossip, beloved friend, not my servant."

But when he stood, her mouth gaped open in amazement. He'd grown even taller since they'd last seen each other, on that terrible day when Ginevra had been taken away. Caterina, on the other hand, had hardly grown at all since then. Tommaso towered over her like one of the adults.

Caterina giggled and tugged at Tommaso's sleeve. "I amend myself," she said. "Down, down. Not to humble yourself, but you've sprouted so in height that I feel as though I'm conversing with a tree."

Several of the nuns laughed at the scene. The kitchen supervisor beckoned and stools were drawn up for Tommaso, Caterina, and one by the hearth for Old Taddeo.

"That's better," said Caterina, settling herself in. "It's so good to see you and know you're well and safe." Her face saddened. "Cosimo Ruggiero told me about Ginevra. It's so wrong. She should be here with me now."

Tommaso gestured hastily. Even to hear Ginevra's name spoken twisted his heart with grief. "Please, do not speak of that, or think on it, today. This is an occasion for rejoicing. I've brought tokens of friendship and respect for you." He handed her the packages one by one.

Il Tribolino's sketch was of a nativity scene with the Magi gathered about the manger. The artist had adorned the Bethlehem stables with the six *palle* of the Medici coat of arms.

Ruggiero the Old's gift was a homily, illuminated and hand-scribed on a wooden panel. Caterina made a face. "Astra declinant, non necessitant," she read. "Must he always remind me?"

But Cosimo Ruggiero's gift brought her back to smiles. It was a silver perfume bottle.

"And what is this?" she asked as Tommaso handed her the smallest package, a little velvet pouch. "Who is it from?"

"I don't know. *Ser* Ruggiero didn't say," said Tommaso.

Caterina drew forth a small object bound in paper. She unwrapped it. It proved to be a golden brooch in the shape of a lion. Caterina smoothed out the paper that had held it. Words were written on the paper's reverse side.

"On this, our family's special day, remember that my thoughts always pace about and guard you, like the lions in the piazza. Your loving cousin, Ippolito," Caterina read. Her hands trembled so as she tried to put the brooch on that at last one of the nuns pinned it to her *gamurra* for her.

Tommaso's heart filled with both admiration and jealousy at Ippolito's devotion and resourcefulness. It could not have been easy to smuggle the brooch into Florence.

"And there is one last present," Tommaso said. He peeled away the layers of cloth from the still-warm pot. "My mother sends this to you, with her love." He lifted the lid. Seductive vapors wafted out.

"*Cibreo!*" Caterina exclaimed. "This brings back the happiest memories. You must share some with me."

The nuns brought them both bowls. A portion was offered to Taddeo, who pointed out that he got to taste Piera's bounty on a regular basis.

He asked if he might be treated instead to some of the pastries the convent was famous for.

While they ate Caterina asked for news from outside. She told Tommaso that her cat Balthazara had adjusted well to their new home. Although the Murate suffered from very few rats, the nuns had made it up to Balthazara by spoiling the cat with choice morsels.

"I cannot believe how quickly you came when you were summoned," Tommaso told the *Duchessina*. "Have you been taking lessons from Cosimo Ruggiero in prophecy?"

"Not at all," said Caterina. "All morning the nuns have been whispering among themselves, keeping secrets from me. I discerned that someone was expected to visit me. I never dreamed that it was you, Tommaso."

"Young Master Arista was not the only one whose appearance we anticipated," the elderly nun interrupted. "Someone else arrived even earlier and has been here all along. And that wonderful pot of *cibreo* is not, after all, your last gift today, *Duchessina*. If you've finished there, dress warmly and come with me."

A novice held out a thick *'sbernia* for Caterina to wrap herself in and a pair of fur-lined gloves for her hands.

"You are invited too, Master Arista."

"Thank you, Sister Teresa Lucrezia," Tommaso said, quickly donning his winter cloak.

The nun led the two of them out the kitchen door and around to the back of the convent, where a garden spread all the way down to the Arno. It offered a stunning view not only of the river but of the mountains surrounding the Florentine valley.

Even blanketed in snow, the pattern of the garden's plantings pleased the eye with its arrangement. The regular mounds of perfect white smoothness looked like a topiary display formed of sugar loaves.

A group of nuns clustered around the upper rim of the garden, pointing at something below, talking among themselves in hushed, delighted tones.

That something was a someone, walking toward them from the middle of the garden. Tommaso was shocked to recognize Michelangelo Buonarotti.

The sculptor's face was red with the cold. His hazel eyes sparkled. He wore a short jacket, thick hose, long buskins of dog skin, and leather gloves. He extended a hand to Caterina.

"Your timing is impeccable, Duchessina. I have just finished."

Caterina placed her hand in Michelangelo's and allowed him to lead her down into the garden.

There, in the middle, sat the Three Magi. Their task to bear witness to the Christ Child over, they had set down to feast. A banquet lay before them. Behind them the beasts that had borne them and the servants who handled the beasts also dined. A camel bent its head between splayed legs to nibble at straw. A palfrey and a riding ass nudged against each other for feed.

But it was the Magi who drew the eye. One was old with a long impressive beard, wearing a tall Byzantine hat. Another's features were Moorish. He wore a turban and in age was hardly more than a child. The last was Asiatic, his face strongly catlike. Their faces were both holy and merry, full of joy at their accomplished mission and appreciation for the repast set before them.

And such a repast! Pheasant and suckling pig, peacock and lark. Tureens of soup, tall bottles of wine. Great bowls of summer fruit.

And the most amazing thing of all: The whole scene lacked even a speck of color. It came to life from the blankest of palettes—that of purest white. It had all been sculpted from snow.

Caterina clapped her hands in wonder. "*Ser* Buonarotti, this is a miracle."

"Many winters ago, not long after Lorenzo Magnífico's death, we had a heavy snowfall much like this one," said Michelangelo. "I went to the de' Medici palazzo and in its courtyard built a snow sculpture for your grandfather Piero and his two little children—your father Lorenzo and your aunt Clarice. At the time I thought it a fine thing. But I believe that today I may have surpassed myself in this medium."

With a cry of delight Caterina left their side to run around the sculpture. The nuns above scurried down like a line of quail to join her.

Michelangelo looked at Tommaso. "This sculpture is for you too. Now you know that there is no material too humble, too transitory that it cannot be transformed into art, even great art. And if it is transitory, whether it be of snow or of food, then so much the better, in spite of what I wrote in that sonnet. For then we know that, like life itself, we cannot afford to take it for granted but must love and appreciate it during the brief time it is with us."

27

April, the Wednesday of Passion Week, 1528

Tommaso sat on a block of marble and fidgeted. "When did you say your master would be back?"

The stonemason's apprentices looked up from tidying the yard and shrugged. "Soon, as we told you. He's as anxious as you and ourselves to get to the cathedral."

Tommaso squirmed. He was supposed to meet his family to attend the Matins of Darkness with them. But just as he was leaving the *bottega*, Il Tribolino had begged him to stop at the stonemason's. The man was storing some fine Carrera marble for Michelangelo. After months of negotiation Tribolino had talked the sculptor into selling him several blocks.

"Mason Ridolfo departs right after Easter to work on building the new library in Livorno. If he doesn't sign the release now it may be months before I can claim the blocks," Il Tribolino explained.

Il Tribolino never made unreasonable demands so Tommaso reluctantly agreed.

"There will be plenty of time for you to reach the Ruggieros' before the service," Il Tribolino assured him.

But his master didn't know that the stonemason had been called away from his yard. Tommaso could do nothing but wait and fret.

With the advent of spring and the cessation of the plague, many Florentines returned to the city from self-imposed exile. Business picked up at the *bottega* as families commissioned works to be donated to the churches as their thanks to God for being spared the plague.

As a result, Tommaso hadn't been able to visit his family in several weeks. Even worse, he'd missed several of his clandestine meetings with Filomena. When he'd been able to resume them, the slave girl didn't appear. Undoubtedly she'd given up on him. Tommaso had hoped to arrive home early enough before the matins to draw her aside and explain.

At last Ridolfo arrived. He was impatient with hurry. His temper didn't improve upon Tommaso's presentation of the contract papers.

"Where is your respect for God, Christ and the Church?" the mason growled. "It probably means little to you, but *I* don't want to be late to the cathedral."

Tommaso bit his tongue and said nothing. The mason scanned the papers and signed the release form.

"So now I can tell my master all is settled and the blocks can be hauled to his studio next week?"

"Nothing of the sort," Ridolfo said. "I've signed the release. But Michelangelo, as the actual owner of the stone, must now co-sign that too. If you hurry you might catch him. Bring the release back to me for my verification and *then* the bargain is done."

Tommaso's heart sank.

"But don't bring the papers back till later. My apprentices and I will be at the matins and then go to dine afterward," the stonemason reminded him.

Tommaso ran all the way to Michelangelo's studio. The sculptor and Antonio Mini were just leaving.

"We are only just barely going to make it on time ourselves," Michelangelo told Tommaso as he pressed the document up against the stone wall to sign it. "Why don't you come to the cathedral with us?"

"I promised my family over a month ago that I'd attend with them," Tommaso said. "Besides"—he indicated his grimy work garments—"I need to change my clothes—at least a fresh waistcoat and jacket."

Michelangelo shook his head. "As you wish."

Tommaso ran all the way to the Ponte Vecchio. He'd wanted to be with his family during this service, especially by his mother's side, because its melancholy ritual reflected too much the course their lives had taken of late.

In the cathedral, the service began.

Tommaso thought about his little brother, Pietro. If Pietro were still alive he'd have trouble, as always, not becoming restless in the church.

At the cathedral, an acolyte snuffed out the first of the myriad candles lighting that holy place.

As Tommaso crossed the bridge he remembered Beatrice. How, though so little, she'd always chosen to take the mantle of responsibility on her small sweet doleful shoulders.

Another candle was extinguished.

The road on the other side of the Ponte Vecchio lay clear all the way to the Ruggieros'. Tommaso was tiring, but he wouldn't slow his stride.

His mind filled with images of Ginevra: the Ginevra he'd teased as a youngster; Ginevra playing with Gattamelata; Ginevra shelling peas in the kitchen; Ginevra huddled with Caterina de' Medici on the stone bench at Santa Lucia.

The light of an exceptionally bright candle flared briefly before it was smothered.

Tommaso reached the Ruggiero storeroom door. As soon as he opened it he knew he was too late. There were no sounds of preparation, no impatient calls to hurry up. The kitchen compound was silent.

He searched through the chests in the sleeping quarters until he found the new waistcoat the Ruggieros had given him as a New Year's gift, to be worn when he visited. He borrowed an old but clean jacket of his father's, though the sleeves hung long on his arms and its shoulders lapped well over his own.

Taper by taper the candles were dimmed. The cathedral began to sink into gloom.

It was as Tommaso bundled together his discarded dirty clothes that he realized the compound was not entirely silent after all. From somewhere came a dull, muted, rhythmic pounding.

Did someone remain after all? Perhaps Filomena. Most likely Filomena, left to knead bread or pound spices in preparation for the evening meal.

Tommaso slid out of the bedroom and down the hall. There was no one in the kitchen after all. But the sound was louder there and accompanied by gasping, as if someone were injured nearby. The door to the pantry was slightly ajar.

In the cathedral, only a single small candle remained lit on the altar. Its flame wavered weakly. In the darkness the congregation began to beat the stone floors with willow rods, raising their voices in lament.

A narrow wedge of light fell through the door into the pantry and onto Filomena's face. Her eyes were closed, but not tightly enough to hold back the tears that slid down her cheeks. Her face was rigid with pain as it was jerked back and forth by the motion and force of whoever lay on top of her, grunting and crushing her into the grain sacks. But past her pain was resignation. It was not the first time she'd suffered like this.

Ottaviano! Tommaso reached behind him, fumbling for a cleaver from the chopping block.

His movement cast a shadow over Filomena's face. Her eyes flew open. When she saw Tommaso she cried out, a wrenching sound. Immediately a large hand covered her mouth, in a gesture so automatic that Tommaso knew that it was not the first time her cries had been stifled.

Tommaso recognized that hand all too well. He slowly put the cleaver down. It did not belong to Ottaviano the journeyman. It was the hand of his father.

Tommaso ran and ran, aimlessly at first. The streets were so deserted he might have imagined the plague had returned. He couldn't go to the cathedral now and face his mother. He couldn't go to Tribolino's *bottega*. At last he returned to the one place he knew was empty—the stonemason's yard. There he collapsed on a block of marble.

After a long time he was vaguely surprised to feel tears slicking his cheeks. What was there left in him to make tears with?

"There is no sight so sad as that of an angel weeping."

Tommaso opened his eyes. Seen through his tears Michelangelo's face as it bent over him shimmered and wavered.

"Nor no sight," Michelangelo's voice caught, "so beautiful."

He put his hands on Tommaso's shoulders, bent over further, and gently kissed the tears from Tommaso's cheeks.

Tommaso sobbed, reached up, and drew the sculptor to him.

II

The Siege

28

November 8, 1528

"It's your fault we must work so hard," Elissa Pecorino said, only partly
in jest.

Tommaso looked up from the stuffed boiled veal breast he was garnishing with dried flower petals. "What do you mean?" He valued her good
opinion and couldn't imagine what he'd done to pique her.

"Before, when I offered nothing here but plain, honest cooking, this
bottega hosted no more than its fair share of soirees. I didn't mind the extra
work because when the other studios took their turn I'd get those nights
to myself in compensation. But in this past year you have made Tribolino's
parties as renowned for their cuisine as for their conviviality. Everyone
wishes to revel here all the time," she grumbled.

"Ah, but before there was only one of you to do the work. Now there
is another of you, in the person of me." Tommaso kissed her cheek.

When Elissa Pecorino swatted at him with a stirring spoon, mock-
scowling, Tommaso could tell her mood was improving. He couldn't resist needling her with a small torment.

"And what did you do with those nights of respite, Madonna? Go to
an extra Mass? Surely the clergy are not so handsome, charming, and attentive as our guests. Would you prefer some dry prelate to time spent with
Tasso, or Giuliano Bugiardini, or Bugiardini's assistant, Marcantonio?"

Of late the reserved Marcantonio was paying Elissa Pecorino a good deal of attention. Things had gone so far that they'd had to spring apart several times, flustered and disheveled, when Tommaso entered the kitchen unexpectedly.

Elissa Pecorino harumphed. "Well, at least there's one less person to feed tonight. Bugiardini has sent his assistant off to Livorno on some business."

Tommaso had to grin at the obvious reason for Elissa Pecorino's being out of sorts. "I'm sure Marcantonio did not go willingly."

Elissa Pecorino sniffed with disdain. "As if it's any concern of mine that he left." She fixed Tommaso with a gaze as sharp as any falcon's. When a small smile played about her lips Tommaso knew he was about to pay for his impudence.

"I cannot believe how our master's so-called friends ill-use him," she said. "Not caring a whit at the way their merrymaking eats into his profits. And the one who should stand as their model in good behavior instead sets the worst example. *Ser* Buonarotti never hosts a get-together, never invites his friends to drop in or set at his table. He begs off visitors to his studio saying his work is too humble in its unfinished state to be seen. So what kind of a friend is he to our good Tribolo, to put our master in the constant state of having *his* unfinished and unpolished art seen by all?"

Tommaso writhed under these scornful words delivered with such happy relish. Elissa Pecorino knew he couldn't bear to hear the least criticism of Michelangelo. But, by virtue of his relationship to the great artist, Tommaso couldn't say a word in Michelangelo's defense.

The community of artists had reacted with kindness and uncharacteristic discretion to Michelangelo and Tommaso's affair. The earlier jibes about the sculptor's attraction to the young cook ceased completely as soon as they actually became lovers. But that discretion had to be matched by an equal silence and complete lack of display of public affection between Tommaso and Michelangelo.

Apparently satisfied by Tommaso's downtrodden countenance, Elissa Pecorino decided she'd exacted enough revenge. She relented a little. "Of course, in his favor, where *Ser* Buonarotti goes, so follow all those lapdog patrons—sniffing and fawning at his heels like dogs not allowed in the house. And since our master Tribolino is the sort of softhearted man who *does* allow hounds in his home, he's reaped the benefit of their patronage.

In the end I suppose a balance is achieved between what they eat in food and what they spend on art."

Tommaso could have added that another result was that several artists who'd once been only friends of Michelangelo now joined the wider social circle. Artists like Bugiardini and his heretofore bashful assistant Marcantonio. But, on reflection, Tommaso decided it best not to bring up that subject again.

He struck another tack. "At least for this event the money doesn't come out of household accounts," he pointed out.

"True," she admitted. "Frankly, I think you apprentices quite mad."

The idea had been Salvatore's. In honor of the feast day of the four martyred stone-carvers, Saints Simpronian, Claudius, Nicostratus Castorius and Simplicius, Salvatore proposed that the apprentices band together to fête their masters. For months they'd saved from their wages, pooling *soldi* until they garnered enough for an evening's worth of decent wine and the banquet provender Tommaso proposed. Skits were concocted and rehearsed, speeches prepared, art contests arranged.

Originally an event intended only for the artists themselves, some of the patrons caught wind of it and begged to participate. Rosso Fiorentino and Francesco Lippi intervened on their behalf.

A small group of patrons would be allowed to attend, but only as onlookers or in whatever role the apprentices chose for them. In addition, they were required to donate to the proceedings, both to cover the extra food and wine they'd consume and to otherwise ease the burden on the apprentices' meager pockets. Michelangelo himself supervised the choice of patrons, limiting the selection to those who were not only wealthy and influential connoisseurs but who could enjoy the proceedings without intruding.

Tommaso set the last flower petals in place on the veal breast. He stood back to view his work while he beat the egg-white froth that would glaze the petals in place. "Our master doesn't think us mad. In his opinion, what started out as a lark turned into a judicious enterprise."

Il Tribolino used the occasion, as usual, to lecture his charges. "In this fashion you have captured the goodwill and attention of future patrons, before you've even begun producing mature works. Their interest will be kindled to follow your enterprises in the future."

"What about those not invited?" asked Gherardo. "Won't they remember us with ill will and resentment?"

Il Tribolino waved his hand in dismissal. "A very few, perhaps. But only at first. Their rancor will fade before the desire to be included in future events. You will find clients vying for your favor: a circumstance infinitely preferable to its reverse—the more common state of affairs, which finds artists groveling at their customers' doors like beggars pleading for alms."

Elissa Pecorino looked over at Tommaso's efforts at decorating the veal with grudging approval. "Our master's wisdom is that of wisdom in hindsight," she pointed out. "The original impulse, as I recall, was to both tweak and impress your betters. All other benefits that might derive had to be pointed out to you young blades by those same noble, willing victims."

Tommaso bit his lip to keep from blurting out that he and the other apprentices might not be the only ones to gain reward from the evening's proceedings. That would raise Elissa Pecorino's curiosity. To his relief, just then several youths walked in.

"Where do we put our masterworks?" Annibale, one of Rosso Fiorentino's apprentices, asked.

Tommaso pointed to a large covered crock. Annibale stood with his back blocking their view and slid several objects into the lemon-infused water within the container.

"You needn't be so secretive," Tommaso said. "I promised I wouldn't look until the judging. Why should I spoil my own pleasure in the guessing?"

"I'm sorry," Annibale apologized. "I don't doubt your honesty, Tommaso. It's just that the rivalry in our *bottega* reached such a ridiculous intensity in this matter that we've lost all trust in each other."

"Your distress will end soon," Tommaso said as he stood up and wiped his hands. "I'm done here for now. Let's see how preparations proceed in the studio. Don't fear that someone will peek in the crock to guess at or injure your or any other work when they slip their own in. Elissa Pecorino is here and she's in a mood to damage any transgressor." Tommaso was already sidling for the door as he spoke. He dashed through it as Elissa Pecorino's stirring spoon whistled through the air, just missing his retreating back.

The studio was better than two thirds transformed. Banners graced the high ceilings. Evergreen boughs camouflaged tool cupboards and work spaces. Tommaso and the newcomers helped several other apprentices wrestle planks onto crates to fabricate a more formal table than the usual sideboard. A second, smaller table was constructed on a makeshift platform to seat the designated "honorary shades"—the select group of patrons.

More apprentices arrived, bringing props and costumes for the skits and extra stools, *tondi*, and bowls for the banquet. At last some of the journeymen and assistants appeared. To free the apprentices for performing the entertainments, they'd agreed to exchange places with their juniors and serve as the wine bearers and servers for the evening.

Not wishing to run askance of Elissa Pecorino's unpredictable temper, Tommaso asked two of the younger boys to take the borrowed plates to the kitchen and rinse and dry them. He threw drapes over the tables and set each place with the requisite bowl of water for rinsing the hands and two napkins—one for wiping the hands and the other for the lap.

At last Salvatore clapped his hands. "Time grows short. We barely have time to judge our little competition. Tommaso, will you bring in the submitted pieces? And Battista, while he does that, set the interim name tags about the table." Battista, one of Bugiardini's apprentices, hurried to set scraps of paper on the table.

The crock in the kitchen was almost filled to the brim and heavy. Tommaso asked Pagolo di Arezzo and Tasso's apprentice Benedetto to help him drag it in.

"Judging will be decided by consensus," Salvatore declared. "Remember, the standards for this contest are the same as those governing this entire event. Each piece's portrayal of its subject matter should incite onlookers to mirth—including the subject himself. This last is most important, for your art should not wound or offend but generate in its subject a happy willingness to be part of the jest—in fact, to feel left out if he were not gently tweaked. In this fashion, my gossips, we hone both our wit and our ability to understand the complicated hearts of patrons, all to the better service of our art."

He coughed ostentatiously. "And the quality of execution must, of course, maintain the usual standards of excellence.

"Now, to review the rules: To ensure no ill will between apprentice and teacher, no one was allowed to portray his own master. Each apprentice had to execute at least two pieces, both to get a feel for the medium and so we would have plenty to judge from.

"Tommaso, would you do the honor of distributing the works to the appropriate setting? In the meantime, perhaps *Ser* Antonio Mini would be so kind as to fill our goblets with a little wine. Let us toast our own enterprise."

Tommaso worked quickly, pulling white lumpen objects from the crock, blotting them briefly, then identifying them as to which named scrap of paper they belonged to. Benedetto and Pagolo di Arezzo ran to deposit each of the pieces to its appropriate place. When they finished, Antonio Mini handed them half-filled cups of wine.

"A toast!" Salvatore cried. Everyone raised his tumbler. "To Tommaso Arista, for the inspiration for the first of tonight's proffered delights. Until Tommaso arrived in our midst, we humble sculptors thought ourselves limited to working in marble, bronze, wood, clay and wax. But through his example we've come to discover a whole new world of materials to work with."

Everyone laughingly cheered. Tommaso blushed to the roots of his hair and hid his face in his cup as he drank.

"Now, on to the judging," Salvatore proclaimed. They all circled around the table. "Our first place-setting will host Messer Jacopo Pontormo. I see we have three submissions to pick from."

Set above the plate were three small busts, each a portrait of Pontormo and carved from either a celery root or fennel bulb. The first was a simple but skillful caricature, elongating the artist's already lengthy features until they closed in on themselves like a door, making him look even shyer than he was. The second was a fantasy of Pontormo as animated and lively, mouth open in the manner of the perpetually loquacious. Shouts of approval greeted this rendition. The third pictured Pontormo in the style of his own drawings—big-eyed and pensive. Although subtly rendered, it paled in comparison to the second entry.

"But our choice must derive from the rules of the contest, not our moblike pleasure," Gherardo pointed out.

"True. Let us critique the favorite in that light," Salvatore agreed. He picked up the second entry. "First, would this piece embarrass or affront its subject, or cause him delight?" He looked at Realdo, another of Rosso Fiorentino's apprentices. Pontormo had no apprentices of his own, but Rosso's students knew him better than anybody.

Realdo looked thoughtful. "Although he's quiet, Pontormo is keenly observant, with a good heart and a quick enough wit. I don't know if he'd be flattered by this piece, but I'm sure he wouldn't take offense. And I'm certain he'd appreciate the skill with which it is executed and the imagination it demonstrates."

"It's decided, then," said Salvatore. "This shall serve as Pontormo's placard." He set the root-bust down and crumpled the temporary paper scrap name tag. Then he picked up the rejected pieces and gave them to Tommaso, who slipped them back into the crock.

"On to our next guest."

And so they proceeded around the table. The teacher-guests included the woodcarvers Tasso and Carota; the goldsmiths Francesco Lippi, Piloto, and Benevenuto Cellini; the painters Andrea del Sarto, Rosso Fiorentino, Pontormo, and Giuliano Bugiardini; and the sculptors Michelangelo, Rafaello da Montelupo, and, of course, Il Tribolino.

Benevenuto Cellini's setting was crowded with six entries. The vain goldsmith's flamboyance begged for satirization.

One submission was an artfully carved parody of Cellini's habit of aping Michelangelo. It looked exactly like the greater artist but for its fawning expression and uncrushed nose.

Another bust of Cellini could have been the portrait of a demon. Its tongue lolled and eyes leered—the very picture of venal lust, arrogance, and stupidity. The apprentices fell silent before such a cruel exaggeration.

"This one would make a fine gargoyle on a cathedral," Salvatore finally said with great tact, "but perhaps falls short of the criterion of aiming not to offend."

Out of the corner of his eye Tommaso saw Giorgio Vasari turn his head away. Cellini had returned to Florence at the end of the plague to find his father and all his other relations except for a brother and sister dead from the disease. Since Vasari's father had also died of the same illness in Arezzo, Tommaso thought the older artist might at last extend a hand to the younger in sympathy and friendship.

Such was not the case. If anything, Giorgio became even more the butt of Cellini's jokes. To make matters worse, with his father dead, Giorgio was now the major provider for what was left of his family: a heavy burden for an apprentice to bear who was still several years away from an assistantship. At the same time, every enterprise Cellini ventured into proved profitable. By the looks of the celery bulb caricature, Giorgio Vasari's resentment had at last crossed over into hatred.

In the end the bust chosen was the one that commented on Cellini's mimicking of Michelangelo.

Michelangelo was to be seated next to Cellini. His was the last place-setting decided on. Not surprisingly, the great artist was as popular a subject as Cellini, but for entirely different reasons. Portraits crowded his place-setting.

One was so enamored, so flattering, that when Salvatore presented it for judgment, Michelangelo's apprentice Ascancio shot Tommaso an incredulous look.

Tommaso shook his head emphatically in response. He would never submit such a transparently adoring proof of his feelings for Michelangelo.

Ascancio looked relieved.

Tommaso let out a long-held breath. In truth, he *had* tried to carve Michelangelo's likeness. And had succumbed to just the same sentiments as the bust being considered. But, unlike the author of the sycophantic piece, Tommaso understood the limitations his love placed on his abilities. He'd chopped up his efforts into a stew and chosen another artist to portray.

The best of the homages to Michelangelo was not only clever in concept but also in execution. A stalk of the plant had been left attached to the root. A long arm with a pointing finger had been carved from the stalk. The root ball itself formed the shoulders and head of a figure familiar to all of them: Michelangelo's portrayal in the Sistine Chapel of God giving life to Adam. It was one of the most widely copied paintings in all of Italy. Facsimiles had made their way to almost every art *bottega* across the country as a teaching tool. Only in *this* rendition the face of God looked suspiciously like Michelangelo's.

Tommaso knew that whoever carved the piece had to have been one of the later arrivals that afternoon, undoubtedly by design. It was laid right near the top of the crock, so there'd been no chance that the fragile stalk would be snapped off by other pieces being placed on top of it.

The apprentices couldn't praise the work enough. "As the master himself says, the form arises, as it should, from the constraints of the material," Ascancio pointed out, indicating the arm-stalk.

"And if anyone can be said to have given the spark of life to the arts as God has to man, it would be *Ser* Buonarotti," murmured Giorgio Vasari. Suddenly Tommaso knew just who had carved the besotted version of Michelangelo.

"But wait, wait," Bertino cried. "Excellent as this maquette may be, it lacks one thing. And that one thing is not the fault of its maker."

"What can you possibly be talking about?" asked Salvatore.

"Context," said Bertino. "Tommaso, do you have a bowl or container that upended would stand at least so high and provide a flat base at least so wide around?" He indicated the sizes with his hands.

"I think so," Tommaso said. He hurried to the kitchen and returned with a crock of about the right dimensions.

"Excellent. Now observe." Bertino upended the crock and placed it off center to the left and above Michelangelo's place-setting. He set the sculpture of Michelangelo on top of it, with the arm pointing to the left. Then he slid the portrait of Cellini that had been approved to the right of the goldsmith's setting until the forehead of that bust rested just below Michelangelo's outstretched finger.

"There you have it," Bertino declared. "The spark of creativity conferred."

All the apprentices screamed with laughter.

"But first we must be sure those tweaked will enjoy at least some small portion of our amusement," Salvatore cautioned, wiping tears of mirth from his eyes. "I deem the apprentices of both these artists the best equipped to decide on the seemliness of this arrangement."

"We're sure our master will find the, er, concept entertaining." Baccio spoke for all of Michelangelo's apprentices. Antonio Mini approved from the sidelines.

Paulino and Cencio, Cellini's apprentices, were laughing so hard that they had to prop each other up to reply. "Seemliness? By all that's holy we are the ones who will suffer the aftermath. Our master will claim this as an acknowledgment by the entire Florentine art community that he is indeed Michelangelo's true creative heir. We'll never hear the end of it."

"All the settings are decided," Salvatore said. "Tommaso, take away the rejected pieces."

"I'll need a good portion of these for the salad," Tommaso said. "Is there anyone here so attached to his efforts that he can't bear to see them chopped up?" He saw hesitation in some of the apprentices' eyes. But in the end they all agreed no sacrifice was too great for the banquet.

"Let us see who the winning competitors are," Salvatore said. "Please stand by your work." He himself went to stand by the bust chosen to represent Andrea del Sarto.

To everyone's surprise, Tasso's apprentice Benedetto was responsible for the Michelangelo-as-God portrait. "It was much like carving soft wood," Benedetto said modestly. "And using the stalk was akin to retaining a branch or two on the trunk of a tree for carving."

Tommaso went to stand by the winning Pontormo portrait. Donato, an apprentice of Francesco Lippi, was responsible for the busts selected for both Cellini and Rafaello da Montelupo.

All in all, the older youths garnished most of the honors. But from Andrea del Sarto's *bottega* Amerigo da Sienna, the youngest of all of them, had carved the chosen bust of Il Tribolino. Tommaso watched Giorgio Vasari flinch when he realized he'd been bested by one of his own juniors. It was proving a disheartening day for the Arezzan.

"Now, to judge the most excellent of the excellent, we shall let our betters choose," Salvatore declared. He placed a small purse in the middle of the table. "Remember, not a word of who carved whom until after their decision," he warned. "Now we must hurry. They'll arrive any minute."

Everyone moved quickly to finish the preparations.

From toasted slices of bread, Tommaso had earlier cut heraldic shapes appropriate for each guest. For the patrons, these would serve as the only indication of their place at table. Tommaso directed Annibale and Battista to place each toast silhouette in an empty soup bowl and put them at the proper settings.

In the meantime, he chopped a number of the rejected root busts into julienned strips. He tossed the slivers into a cauldron of simmering water. While Tommaso did that, Elissa Pecorino brought a pot of oil almost to boiling. She began to gently slide artichoke fritters into this seething bath. The fritters bobbed about, gilding quickly.

"They're here," Gherardo called through the kitchen door. "You must emerge long enough to greet them, Tommaso."

Tommaso looked at Elissa Pecorino, hesitant to desert her. But her good humor had returned entirely with all the excitement. She shooed him out of the kitchen.

The guests arrived almost en masse.

"They've all been over at Rosso's, drinking to work up an appetite," Gherardo murmured to Tommaso.

Salvatore clapped his hands to get everyone's attention. "Before you sit down to table, I wish to make a toast to inaugurate the festivities," he said. The journeymen distributed goblets to the guests and filled them. The apprentices helped themselves from jugs of cheaper wine.

"First, a toast to the 'Four Crowned Ones,' the noble stonecutters who set us an example by giving up their lives for their faith and their art."

The ensemble cheered and quaffed their first sip.

"Next, a toast to honor you, our masters, who strive so hard to teach us. All we are today we owe to you," Salvatore said with a wink, "as we hope to amply demonstrate this evening."

This was met with laughing groans by the artists as they lifted their goblets again.

"Let the festivities begin. You may now approach the table. I believe you'll find it easy to tell where you are to sit."

The raised dais for the patrons was deliberately situated past the larger table for the artists so that all would have the chance to pass by and observe the place-settings. The satirical busts were greeted with cries of delight and surprise by the artists. They circled the table to examine and comment on each parody.

As expected, this granted Tommaso much-needed time. He drained the now tender fennel and celery root strips and spread them out to cool. Then he and several other apprentices carried in platters heaped with the crisp amber artichoke fritters, wild boar sausages wrapped in pastry, fried sage leaves, and pork jellies.

The other apprentices were organizing themselves for the entertainments to follow. While Salvatore explained how Tommaso had been the inspiration for the first *sotelty* of the evening, the guests seated themselves. Tommaso flushed and hurried back to the kitchen for the soup.

Annibale and Cencio held the cauldron while he ladled a hearty chestnut-and-leek broth over the heraldic crouton in each guest's bowl. Tommaso was glad the cauldron was half emptied by the time they had to climb up to the raised platform the patrons' table perched on.

Cosimo Ruggiero, the youngest at that table, leaped to help them lift the soup up. Of late Ruggiero the Old had encouraged his son to enter society. Cosimo had begun to charge small fees for his physicking services, and his father supplemented his income with an allowance so Cosimo could commission small artworks and join the ranks of connoisseurship. Michelangelo had suggested that it might be politic to invite a member of the illustrious and well-connected Ruggiero family to the fête.

The other patrons consisted of the familiar trio of Bernardo, Girolamo, and Bembo, plus Antonio Gondi, Bartolommeo Bettini, and Federigo Ginori.

"So, young Cosimo, is this how the Aristas feed your family nightly?" asked Federigo Ginori.

"We always dine superbly," Cosimo said, smiling at Tommaso. "But not with such artistry and wit. Those qualities appear to be uniquely Tommaso's."

One of the apprentices blew a horn, signaling the beginning of the next entertainment. The apprentices from the studios that dealt only in the plastic arts, and those of the painting studios, had challenged each other to a duel: each student had to produce a piece in the opposite's medium, to often hilarious results.

Tommaso was glad he was too busy in the kitchen to hear the amused criticism. He'd executed a Last Supper in tempera on a wooden panel for the exercise. He'd been amazed at the difficulty of the task, especially in the choosing and laying down of the colors.

The artist guests got into the spirit of the event and, unsolicited, collected money for a small purse. The "winners" consisted of both the best and the worst paintings by sculpture apprentices and the best and worst maquettes by painting apprentices.

"So, what did you learn from this exercise?" Russo Fiorentino asked the participants.

"To have more respect for another's art," Donato admitted grudgingly. "Even if, or especially if, it is in a material unfamiliar to me."

Several of the *bottegas*, such as Michelangelo's, produced sculpture, paintings, drawings, and architectural designs besides. Those students, deemed to have an unfair advantage in the previous competition, had been required to compose songs, or, if unmusical to an offensive degree, sonnets in honor of the occasion.

Tommaso heard only bits and pieces of these as he organized the next course to be carried out: *papparadelle* with hare sauce, savory spelt cake, eggplant frittata, celadon-green stuffed savoy cabbage rolls. He was happy his work on the banquet excused him from the scrutiny of performance.

As it was, Tommaso suffered a distracting if exquisite torture every time his duties brought him near Michelangelo. It was agony to be so close and not be able to touch his lover, to have to pretend to barely know the sculptor. And all the while Benevenuto Cellini hovered on Michelangelo's other side, peering over and watching for any interchange between them with a carrion bird's interest.

Tommaso focused on his work, the entertainments, the conversation at the tables during the lulls between amusements, anything to divert him from thoughts of Michelangelo's presence.

"Clement may yet regret not granting Henry a divorce," Piloto said. "The English king proclaims himself 'Defender of the Faith,' but I've heard he'll leave the church to marry his twelve-fingered *strega*."

Tommaso set down one of the three serving plates of cabbage rolls he carried and kept moving around the table, setting the rest down and then picking up emptied platters.

Il Tribolino snorted. "What did King Henry expect? His Holiness had just made amends with Emperor Charles. Did Henry expect Clement would then turn about and kick Charles's aunt Catherine of Aragon from Henry's nuptial bed? If King Henry wanted cooperation from the pope, he should have indeed 'defended the faith' when Charles sacked Rome. Who would any reasonable man side with: An emperor who has proved that the sentence for disloyalty is the death of thousands, or a petty, vacillating, ineffectual barbarian despot? The loss of Henry's goodwill and faith is the loss of nothing at all."

"Are we surprised by King Henry's lack of reason?" Cellini sneered. "This is, after all, the monarch who invited, from all of Italy's artists, that arrogant fraud Piero Torrigiani to come to his court."

Several of the other artists coughed and cast anxious eyes at Michelangelo. Cellini may have brought up Torrigiani in that fashion to curry favor with *Ser* Buonarotti, but *any* mention of the expatriate artist who crushed his nose in his youth tended to aggravate Michelangelo.

Giuliano Bugiardini quickly turned the subject back to its original intent. "It may be we who should petition King Henry for support, which perhaps he would grant in retaliation for Clement's refusal to give him his divorce. We'll need whatever aid we can find now that Clement is back in power on the papal throne. Everything I've heard from Florentines living in Rome is that Clement thinks of nothing but vengeance for the exile of Alessandro and Ippolito."

"This is true," Michelangelo confirmed. "You all know my assistant who manages my Roman studio, Pietro Urbino. Urbino writes that matters have gone beyond rumor into common knowledge that Clement negotiates with his former nemesis the emperor to bring about Florence's downfall."

"The Medici have always been driven from Florence, only to return to greater glory. What Florence must plan for is the best way to negotiate that return with as little damage as possible," Il Tribolino insisted.

"I am no seer like young Maestro Ruggiero over there"—Michelangelo nodded at Cosimo sitting at the patrons' table—"but there is no question in my mind that that is what the future portends, one way or the other. So while we can, let our hearts be light and allow ourselves the enjoyment of our apprentices' creative genius."

"Michelangelo, you especially should enjoy it while you can. You know if Florence is marched on that the *Signoria* will call upon your engineering skills for the city's defense," Rafaello da Montelupo pointed out.

As Tommaso hurried away from the table, his arms filled with platters, he gestured frantically at Salvatore with his eyes to start the next presentation. The mood had become too serious.

The next set of dishes was the most splendid and needed the most work, but Tommaso stole away from his kitchen duties long enough to watch a farce that poked fun at Benevenuto Cellini.

The sketch concerned the residents of a particularly isolated convent anticipating the visit of a new bishop. The apprentices were wrapped in drab robes and headdresses in a reasonable approximation of convent garb.

One of the "nuns"—played with winsome falsetto charm by Pagolo de Arezzo—proclaimed in an aside to the audience that "she" had a female cousin living in a nunnery in Naples who was so tall and muscular that this cousin could easily pass as a man. "Nun" Pagolo coerces this relative—portrayed by one of Piloto's apprentices, a burly youth named Pierino—to come visit disguised as the expected bishop. Pagolo, of course, must first coach Pierino on the fine points of pretending to be a man, mimicking in perfect counterpoint Cellini's account of his own instruction of his attractive neighbor, Diego, on how to play the part of a winsome young woman.

The great surprise of the play was what a good actor Pierino proved to be. Rawboned as he was, he made a perfectly believable large, homely nun, dripping with initial piety, reluctant to deceive his "sisters" in the faith.

But, in the transformation to spurious bishop, instead of simply reverting to his own masculine behavior, Pierino maintained the illusion of a woman—and an unworldly one at that—struggling and finally succeeding in "her" efforts to render such a convincing portrayal of a bishop that the other nuns were quite smitten by "his" robust charms. At the end of the sketch, when all was revealed, the nuns lifted their two deceivers on their shoulders and paraded them about the banquet hall in triumph, exactly as Cellini had said he'd been honored by Michel Agnolo da Siena.

By the play's finish, Rosse Fiorentino was choking so hard with laughter that Carota had to pound on his back so the painter wouldn't collapse. Everyone else was bent over double from the hilarity and wiping away tears from the corners of their eyes.

Cellini received the skit with good spirits, taking it by way of an homage more than a mocking. "Ah, good Pierino," he proclaimed. "What a tragedy you aren't fairer of face. With your talent as my tool, what pranks I could concoct to play on the stuffy Romans."

As if this were a signal, several of the patrons rose at their table and began tossing *soldi* to Pierino. He demonstrated yet another unexpected ability as he leapt up and caught each one.

The only person who looked remotely discontented was Bugiardini. "Would that Pierino displayed equal skill in preparing fresco plaster and applying pigment," he grumbled. "After tonight, I have to believe that his father apprenticed him to the wrong trade."

Rafaello da Montelupo's squash-headed apprentice, Zuccone, stood up to sing a ribald ballad concerning fictitious events that befell Tasso on the occasion of Tasso's return home alone to Florence after his youthful trip to Rome with Cellini. The events were so explicit and lusty that if they had really occurred Cellini might have well wished he'd returned to his native city with his friend.

Tommaso used the time to pull some of the other apprentices in to the kitchen to load them with the next course. As soon as Zuccone's last notes died away, Tommaso's crew trooped their way to the banquet table, bearing casseroles of baked broad beans, pot-roasted pigeons cooked till their skins shone a glossy sienna nesting on a bed of steamed *verdura*, sauteed *gobbi* and silver beet, *femminelle* crabs from Orbetello napped with a *dulceforte* sauce and gracing a bed of saffron-tinged risotto flavored with their own madder-colored roe, and the salad of julienned fennel and celery root tossed with walnut oil and arugula.

Tommaso himself staggered in with the centerpiece, the garnished breast of veal. Since the piece was entirely his own creation, he'd refused any help carrying it. The artists gathered around and the patrons came down from their table to see this new *sotelty*.

"The Four Crowned Ones themselves, surrounded by all their symbols and devices," said Giuliano Bugiardini. "A lovely example of portraiture, Tommaso. Who would have thought one could achieve such nuances in flesh tones with such an unusual medium?"

Tommaso had used his struggles in executing the tempera panel to learn how to better manipulate color. For the veal breast, he'd applied dried flower petals to the meaty canvas as one might dab dry pigment on a fresco, building up blocks of color, then fixing them in place with the thin "varnish" of beaten egg white.

Tommaso beamed at such praise coming from an accomplished muralist like Bugiardini. But it was the clandestine look of pride on Michelangelo's face that made his color deepen till it matched the brightest roses on his culinary palette.

"Truly, it's a shame to sacrifice this work to such a base desire as our hungry appetite," said Rosso Fiorentino. He turned abruptly. "What *are* you doing, Pontormo?"

The shy draftsman had slid away from the table to fetch some supplies. He was peering over Rosso's shoulder, drawing rapidly with colored chalks in a notebook.

"If we do not tonight destroy this work for our pleasure, it will become exceedingly unpleasant in a day or so," Pontormo pointed out. "Better that it be recorded for posterity in a medium less subject to decay."

The other artists agreed. They stepped back to let Pontormo finish his sketch. Then Tommaso scraped the petals aside, hoisted and carved the roast as he'd been taught, with the basic single-knife style. He regarnished the platter with some of the flowers before serving the meat.

At the end of this course, Salvatore called for everyone's attention. "Now that our guests have dined on a visual as well as edible feast, I believe this constitutes an excellent moment to beg them to judge our humble group efforts in this exciting new domain of artistic comestibles." He gestured to the sculpted root portraits at each setting.

Then he picked up the purse of coins from where it had lain in the middle of the table the whole evening. He turned to Il Tribolino as the hosting artist. "What say you, Master?"

Il Tribolino stood and took the purse from his apprentice. "I say it's the least we can do in repayment for tonight's festivities. Messers, let us appraise these examples of a new art form and render our judgment."

The other artists rose and circled the table again, this time with an eye to assessing the best of the apprentices' efforts. Then they gathered in a group at the far end of the studio to confer in hushed tones.

After several moments they beckoned Salvatore to approach them.

"The portrait of *Ser* Buonarotti, this matter of its interaction with the bust of Cellini; was that the conception and execution of a single artist?" Andrea del Sarto asked.

"No," Salvatore told him. "Two different apprentices made the portraits, and a third conceived of the interaction between the two."

"Aha!" Andrea del Sarto looked at his fellow jurors. "It appears that our clear-cut winner is not so clear-cut then."

They huddled together for a while longer, heated mumbling followed by a clinking of coinage.

"We have come to a decision." Andrea del Sarto spoke for the rest of the master artists. "Your purse will be divided equally between the author of Michelangelo's portrait and the author of Pontormo's portrait."

Tommaso and Benedetto came forward to stand in front of their respective works and share the purse. To his surprise and secret pleasure, Tommaso noticed that greater cries of astonishment met Benedetto's accomplishment than his own. He was more accepted as an artist than he'd known.

"Benedetto's work would have won first honors alone if he had been responsible for the witty way it was put to use," Piloto said. "Who *is* responsible for that bit of cleverness?"

Blushing almost as much as Tommaso was wont to do, Bertino stepped forward to take credit.

"Ah, good Bertino. For your acumen we have gathered together another small purse. We feel that such sagacious sensibility has as much to do with great art as blows from a chisel, dabs with a brush, and copious amounts of sweat," Il Tribolino said as he handed Bertino a handful of coins, beaming to see yet another of his own apprentices gathering honor.

"Now we would like to find out who else is responsible for our likenesses," said Andrea del Sarto.

The rest of the chosen apprentices stood before their pieces. After watching Donato try to scurry back and forth between Cellini's and Rafaello's busts, the patrons collected a purse of their own to award him for garnering double honors.

The artists returned to their seats at the table.

"What I am curious about," said Rafaello, "is if these are the most successful entries, what did the others look like?"

"Yes," agreed Piloto. "I'd dearly love to see them. Not for further judging. We wouldn't even ask who their creators were, not wishing to embarrass them, but simply for amusement's sake."

"I have them back in the kitchen," Tommaso said. He saw Salvatore turn pale and frantically gesture at him. "It would be my pleasure to bring them forth for your perusal." Tommaso smiled reassuringly at Salvatore, who appeared ready to faint.

Tommaso, Battista, and Cencio dragged the crock into the studio. Tommaso pulled out the pieces one at a time, dried them on a cloth, and passed them around to the artists.

"There are a few missing," he conceded. "I sacrificed some to make the salad."

When it became clear that Tommaso had edited out the most offensive or controversial of the portraits, such as Vasari's of Cellini and Michelangelo, the color began to return to Salvatore's face. He mouthed his silent thanks to Tommaso.

Tommaso left it to Cencio to return the root busts to the crock when the guests finished scrutinizing them. There was still the last of the food to be readied.

As Tuscan tradition warranted, the *dolci* course was the most modest. Cold baked honeyed figs, grapes sprinkled with *alchermes*, perfectly ripened medlars and melon slices lay well arranged on their trays. Tommaso would have preferred serving all fruit, but, in deference to the occasion, he'd fried the simple *cenci* fritters that were traditional back to ancient Roman times and baked a large batch of *brigidini* wafers and also a *castagnaccio* cake, which he garnished with fresh ricotta cheese.

Long-faced Zuccone came in to fetch one of the platters, shaking his head. "That goldsmith!" he said. "I wondered how long he could bear others garnering the lion's share of attention."

From the way Zuccone spoke, Tommaso knew the goldsmith the other apprentice referred to was not Piloto or Francesco Lippi. "What has *Ser* Cellini done now?" he asked.

"The moment food and mirth lulled, needs be he must leap up and bring to table a piece of his own to hand over to the young man who commissioned it, Federigo Ginori. Thus Cellini can show off his work to his peers and at the same time belittle our modest efforts by way of comparison."

"Which piece was it?" asked Pagolo di Arezzo.

"A golden medallion, with Atlas chiseled into it. Rather than the world upon his back, Atlas bears heaven itself, in the form of a crystal globe, engraved with the zodiac, all upon a field of lapis lazuli. It is quite fine," Zuccone grudgingly admitted. "The other artists and patrons are most impressed. Carried away by the occasion, Ginori handed over in payment a purse of more florins than he'd originally intended, I'm certain."

Tommaso guessed that Cellini had another agenda besides vaunting his prowess, humbling the apprentices, and gathering a better wage.

Ginori had originally entreated Michelangelo to take the commission. Michelangelo, already overworked and always looking to help his friends by steering employment their way, recommended Ginori approach Cellini to make a model for the project instead.

At the same time, so as not to offend Ginori, Michelangelo said that he'd also submit a sketch and Ginori could take his pick of the two.

Ginori had chosen Cellini's model over Michelangelo's sketch. Now, with the task completed, Cellini could take satisfaction that for at least once in his life he'd bested his idol.

But what Tommaso knew—for he had woken one morning in Michelangelo's bed to find his lover up and working on the sketch for Ginori's assignment—was that Michelangelo had deliberately executed the weaker submission. Watching Michelangelo work, Tommaso saw that it presented a greater challenge for the artist to create a convincing lesser work than to dash off a masterpiece.

This is the man that all of Florence, while conceding his brilliance, criticizes behind his back for miserliness and a choleric nature, Tommaso thought. *Yet his spirit is so great that he goes to such lengths to protect the pride of even a man like Cellini.*

"We'll never change Cellini's nature," he told Zuccone. "Just be grateful that at least the man has talent. All of us know too many who are as boastful as Cellini, yet their bragging is more grievous because it has no substance." He glanced about to see who was nearby. "Of greater importance, have any latecomers chanced to arrive?"

Zuccone took his meaning. The homely youth waited till Elissa Pecorino went to fetch more water for washing the dinnerware before answering in a whisper, "Yes, in the last few minutes. We've taken care to hide him."

"Excellent. Then as soon as Madonna Pecorino returns we're ready to present the *dolci.*"

Tommaso had planned things so that by the time Elissa Pecorino set down her buckets of fresh water, all the dessert platters had been taken out but two. Tommaso hoisted one. "Madonna," he said hesitantly, "all the other apprentices are either preparing for the final skit or else are busy helping me. Would you mind bringing in the last platter? It would hurry the event along so I could send in the younger boys to start cleaning up in here that much sooner."

He asked so pleasantly that Elissa Pecorino could hardly grumble. She picked up the plate with the *castagnaccio* cake.

In the studio all the other dessert bearers stood queued up in front of the table. Tommaso hurried to the front of the line and set down his platter. "For this, our last course, I would like to assert the cook's right to make a toast," he said.

The crowd raised their goblets.

"What is a dessert course without the sweetest thing of all, the presence of a woman? I present to you the muse of this banquet, without whose labors it would not have occurred, Elissa Pecorino."

All the other *dolci* bearers stepped aside, leaving Elissa Pecorino standing alone. She glared at Tommaso while the group cheered her.

He ignored the look. "Madonna Elissa, we apprentices took up a collection and gathered together a purse of *scudi di moneta* for you; more for honor's sake than an actual payment, for we would never be able to adequately reward your unstinting efforts."

Elissa Pecorino appeared somewhat mollified.

"Now, it so happens," said Tommaso, "that a hungry latecomer has just arrived for the festivities, far too dilatory to partake in the main courses of the dinner. We've told him that if he wishes to dine from the leftovers back in the kitchen he must throw himself at your mercy. To that end we've given him the purse to present to you, in the hopes that this will soften your heart to his plight."

Elissa Pecorino began to look peeved again.

From the shadows at the back of the studio came the jingling of coins. Bugiardini's laconic assistant, Marcantonio, slid out of the shadows, holding a coin-laden purse before him like a shield.

Elissa Pecorino favored Tommaso with a murderous glare so patently false that it was all Tommaso could do to pretend to quail instead of bursting into laughter.

"Well," Elissa Pecorino snapped. "I suppose something could be

thrown together, if he can convince me he's starving." By the time she'd
relieved Marcantonio of the purse and herded him before her in the direction of the kitchen, she'd given up all pretense of acting the curmud-
geon and was beaming.

Tommaso threw his arms around Zuccone and Pagalo di Arezzo's
shoulders. "Pass the word to all the others helping with the banquet that
they're released from their duties for now. They should stay out here and
enjoy the rest of the festivities. By all means tell them not to enter the
kitchen, as I believe that *Ser* Marcantonio may be dining for a goodly long
while."

29

November 22, 1528

Tommaso eyed the chunk of alabaster with a critical eye. He lined up his chisel and tapped it sharply with the mallet till a large piece fell cleanly away. He tried to do just as Michelangelo had admonished him: to see the figure of his subject, the beautiful dancing girl St. Pelagia the Penitent, hidden within the stone.

Bertino looked up yawning from the wax relief he worked on. "Aren't you ready for bed yet, Tommaso? We're the last two awake."

Tommaso's gaze never left his piece. "Not quite yet. If I finish blocking this out tonight I can start fine-chiseling it on the morrow." It was at these times Tommaso did his best work—when the studio work and kitchen chores were finished, when Il Tribolino had returned home to his wife and children.

Bertino waved at him in mock disgust. "Do as you like, then. My sainted grandmother always said that red hair was a sign of madness. If our meal tomorrow morning is a disaster, I'll tell the others who is to blame—the cook-apprentice who exhausts himself to mindlessness."

Tommaso let him go without counter-bantering, since there was some truth to Bertino's words.

The hectic preparations leading up to the apprentice's gala had allowed Tommaso little time to remember and dwell on the fact that it had been a year since his brother and sisters' exodus from Florence.

But in the two weeks since the party Tommaso suffered far too much time for reflection as the anniversary of their deaths rapidly approached. At night he dreamed of Pietro running to him with outstretched arms, of Beatrice's doleful eyes, of Ginevra's enigmatic smile. Tommaso woke thinking they still lived and that he would visit them that very day. Then reality coldly seeped in. He'd lie in bed surrounded by the other sleeping apprentices and feel tears fill his eyes. And like those tears, his three little lost ones filled his thoughts the rest of the day.

The only respite came with busy-ness. If he worked hard and long enough, till he was just a stagger away from unconsciousness when he fell at last into bed, he slept so deeply he didn't dream of them. Or, if he dreamed, did not remember.

So when he struck his chisel to the alabaster and almost cut away the flowing shawl St. Pelagia whirled behind her, Tommaso knew he'd find peace in sleep that night. He put away his tools.

As he passed through the edge of the kitchen on the way to the sleeping quarters, he found he was not the last to retire after all. Elissa Pecorino sat talking in low tones to two other women, who huddled in black hooded cloaks before the kitchen hearth's dying embers. The visitors' backs were turned to Tommaso. He raised his hand to bid a silent good night to Elissa Pecorino without unduly disturbing her or her company.

Elissa Pecorino looked up. "Wait, Tommaso. There is someone here to see you."

A small form scrambled out from the folds of one of the women's cloaks. It tottered around to stand in front of Tommaso and stare up at him. It was a girl child of about a year and a half, with hair an even brighter red than Tommaso's. The expression on her face was both blank and penetrating.

Tommaso felt a heavy, dropping sensation in the pit of his stomach. All his hard-sought exhaustion vanished.

One of the women turned toward him, the hood on her cloak slipping back to uncover black, silver-shot hair.

"So, my son. Apparently it proves necessary for your mother to traverse Florence's streets late at night to enjoy the pleasure of your company," Piera said reproachfully.

Tommaso knelt to kiss his mother's hand. Melchiora lay curled on her lap, purring.

"A year ago this day three of my children died. For months now it's seemed as though I've also lost a fourth, my eldest."

"I've come by," Tommaso stammered.

"Of substance and duration much like a ghost," Piera said.

Tommaso flushed, unable to answer the accusation. It was true. He didn't visit his family on all his days off. He'd been able to beg off any number of times because of preparations for the apprentices' gala. And when he did return, he spent most of the time in the storeroom helping pack up and then deliver Ruggiero the Old's regular benefice to the Murate.

Tommaso didn't go to such lengths of avoidance because he didn't want to see his mother. It was his father he couldn't bear to be near. Whenever he was in Gentile's presence Tommaso felt himself boiling with rage. His manner became curt and brusque to keep his anger tightly lidded in. Tommaso was sure his father didn't know he'd seen Filomena abused. Gentile probably assumed Tommaso's estrangement was for the same reason as Piera's: the exile of Ginevra, Pietro, and Beatrice that led to their deaths.

Then there was Filomena herself. Tommaso almost never saw her. Knowing on what days he was expected to visit, she always seemed to be busy elsewhere. When they did chance upon one another it was more than Tommaso could bear. Did she look at him reproachfully, wondering why he didn't speak on her behalf? He couldn't be sure. But what he did see in her eyes, before she quickly looked away, was pain, fear, and horrible shame. The humiliation Tommaso felt in her presence was even greater than the anger he felt for his father.

But in sparing himself the excruciation of returning home, Tommaso now realized he'd inadvertently punished his mother, who had already suffered more loss than any of them.

Tommaso kissed Piera's hands again. "Forgive me, Mother. Nothing is as it was at home. I can hardly bear it, so I confess I've done what I could to stay away. I've been childish and selfish. I didn't mean to add to your sorrow."

He looked up to find his mother smiling at him. She stroked his hair.

"I know you didn't, Tommaso. And I shouldn't blame you for trying to find some ease. You aren't responsible for our family's woes. I'm ashamed of myself for rebuking you for what is your right: to seek some joy in your youth. My own childhood was happy and without the travails you've suffered. It's just that I miss you."

Tommaso laid his head in his mother's lap next to Melchiora. "Then on this day, when you lost so much, I vow a son returns to you." He whispered his promise. With his head turned to the side he could see Luciana leaning against Cousin Francesca's legs. The toddler still fixed him with her curious stare.

"Come and sit beside me. Now that we've made amends I have something to ask of you." Piera drew him up to sit beside her on the edge of the hearth. Francesca picked up Luciana and gave the child her breast to nurse on. Elissa Pecorino bounced Paolo on her knee. Paolo favored Tommaso with a cherubic smile. Tommaso had to smile back. The hearth's embers felt pleasantly warm at his back.

Piera pulled at the chain around her neck, drawing out the curious crucifix. She turned it over in her palm, examining it. "You did excellent work when you repaired this. Have you learned other jeweler's skills during your sojourn here?"

"Of course," said Tommaso. "Some beaten work, some wire and gold bead work, but mostly castings."

"Perfect," said Piera. "In time, do you suppose you could make me a casting of this?" She reached over to Elissa Pecorino, who handed her a piece of paper with a drawing on it. Tommaso realized that this was what the three women had been gathered around when he entered.

Tommaso took the sketch from his mother and scrutinized it. Drawn in pen and ink, it pictured a large but simply shaped talisman. In the center a plain oval had been etched. Drawings, numbers and symbols embellished the pendant's broad edges.

In spite of the hearth's heat behind him, a wave of chill shivered inward from Tommaso's skin all the way to his bones. The signs reminded him of those of the Ruggieros' recondite profession.

He covered his uneasiness with a professional demeanor. "I can do this. I'll make a wax model. What size do you wish it?"

"Exactly the size of the drawing," Piera said.

"And in what metal? Pewter? Bronze?"

Piera passed him her crucifix. "In silver. Melt this down. It should be enough, shouldn't it?"

Tommaso stared aghast at the crucifix. Besides his reluctance to destroy a fine though unusual piece, he balked at the transformation of a holy object into something as arcane as the proposed talisman.

"Mother, I can't melt down an image of Christ's blessed cross to recast it into something so, so . . ." he scrambled for words, "so profane."

Piera stared at him in astonishment. Then she started laughing, a clean merry outpouring of good humor that Tommaso had thought he'd never hear issuing from his mother again. His fears melted away.

"Rest easy, Tommaso," Piera said when she finally regained her composure. "This piece of jewelry will lose none of its sacredness in the metamorphosis."

Tommaso felt as though he'd been caught out in some childish witlessness. "Then the amount of silver should be just about right. What about the unadorned oval in the center?"

"I was about to speak of that. It's the setting for a stone." Piera drew something else from about her neck—a narrow cord attached to a small purple velvet pouch.

Taking the pouch from her, Tommaso felt that whatever was within was curved and smooth.

"Take it out," Piera said.

Tommaso slid the object into his palm. It was a beautiful dark-red cabochon.

"It's too dark to be a ruby," he said, tactfully avoiding the fact that his mother couldn't afford any sort of precious gem, let alone one that size. "Is it a garnet?"

"It's just a simple, colored stone," Piera said, "but precious beyond words to me."

Lying in Tommaso's hand the gem gave off a pleasant heat. It must have picked up the warmth lying against his mother's skin. Tommaso placed it in the center of the drawing. It fit perfectly. Piera had traced carefully around it.

"By when do you need this done?" he asked. "With Christmas festivities looming . . ."

"Not until the spring," Piera said. She picked up the gem from the sketch, slid it back into its pouch, and settled the cord around Tommaso's neck. "If you keep this you can set it accurately into the wax mold."

The weight of the stone rested against Tommaso's chest. It was somehow comforting.

Piera put her crucifix back on. "I'll give you this when you're ready to cast the piece." She stood. "We must return home now. The household thinks we've taken the children to see Leonora. But I felt I had to meet with you and make peace." She looked at him. "We have made peace, haven't we?"

Tommaso hugged her. "Yes, though no ill will ever existed between us. I promise I'll return to see you more often." Tommaso still didn't feel comfortable at the prospect of spending time in his childhood home, but it shouldn't be that hard to cloister himself with his mother. "Let me fetch a cloak and I'll walk you back."

When he'd gone, Francesca leaned over toward Piera, her eyes wide. "Does he really think you wear the Father's emblem? He doesn't recognize a disguised *cimaruta?* Have you taught him nothing?"

Piera looked pensive as she fingered the crucifix. "No. I thought Ginevra would be my heir in such matters. But perhaps it's just as well. When the time comes, he will learn." She sighed. "But he may have to learn very quickly."

That night Tommaso enjoyed the first truly restful sleep he'd experienced in two weeks. He dreamed about Ginevra, knowing she was dead but still feeling her tranquil presence all about him. He woke, comforted, the jewel in its pouch nestling against his heart.

30

Spring 1529

By the beginning of February, Tommaso found time to make a wax model of the pendant. On his next visit home he drew his mother aside and showed it to her.

"It's just what I hoped for," she said. "And the stone? Does it fit well?"

Tommaso took the gem out of the pouch hanging around his neck. He set it into the oval depression in the middle of the talisman. It fit perfectly.

"You've done a beautiful job," Piera said. "Il Tribolino taught you well."

A few weeks later Tommaso cast the model in plaster. When the plaster finished drying he carefully burned out the wax investiture.

"I'll do the silver casting within a month," he promised Piera one afternoon as he hauled sacks of spelt and chestnut flour from the Ruggiero storeroom for transport to the Murate.

Piera started to draw out her crucifix to give to him. Just then Gentile and Old Taddeo walked into the storeroom. Piera dropped the cross back down her bodice.

"The day is so pleasant and warm for this time of the year, I think I'll ride out with you to the Murate," she said loudly enough for the two men to hear.

Over her shoulder, Tommaso saw his father give a resigned, bitter shrug. In the last year Gentile had grown accustomed to his wife's avoidance.

And ever since her clandestine visit to the *bottega* in November, Piera frequently accompanied Tommaso and Old Taddeo as a way both to visit with Caterina and to see more of her son outside the tension-filled kitchen compound.

Caterina skipped into the Murate kitchen almost as soon as they arrived. "Darling Piera!" she cried, throwing herself into Piera's arms.

Piera fell back a little under Caterina's embrace. The *Duchessina* had grown much taller in recent months.

"Am I taking her away from her studies?" Piera asked the nun following slowly behind the *Duchessina.*

The sister shook her head. "If it's possible, the *Duchessina* is almost too serious a student. At her age she needs more laughter and friendship. We welcome any who are willing to visit and provide that, and happily release her from her lessons on such occasions."

Caterina stood on tiptoe to whisper in Piera's ear. "Do you see why I love this place so?" she said in an overly loud whisper.

The sister smiled at the compliment.

As he slung the sacks of grain into the convent pantry, Tommaso reflected on how much merrier Caterina was here. Certainly the good-natured well-educated nuns of the Murate provided a welcome change from their dour austere counterparts at the Convent of Santa Lucia.

But Tommaso had noticed a transformation in Caterina since even her days in what should have been her God-given surroundings—the de' Medici palazzo. He realized now that there she'd worn her precociousness like a stiff, supporting shell. She'd had to fortify herself to meet and go beyond her family's expectations. And then, too, there'd always been Alessandro hovering nearby to keep on guard against.

Here she could be at last, for a while, what she wished to be: a bright eager student and happy young girl. A pleasant sensation spread across Tommaso's chest. It seemed to radiate from where the red gem hung next to his skin.

Back in the kitchen Piera waited till all the nuns and novices were busy with chores. She slipped Caterina a tiny glass vial with a tightly fitted stopper. "You know what to do with this, and when?" she asked the girl.

Caterina nodded gravely, all traces of girlishness vanished. "Yes. Madonna Leonora contracts to bring wild game here every week. I'll return it to you through her auspices."

On the cart ride back to the Ruggieros', Piera turned to Tommaso, her shoulder blocking Old Taddeo's view to the side. "Don't forget that pretty you promised to make me, my artist son," she said. She pressed one of her hands into his. When she withdrew it Tommaso curled his fingers around and covered what she'd left behind: the silver crucifix with its chain wrapped tightly about it.

On the night of the next full moon Caterina waited until the convent slept to slip out into the gardens. It was easy to see in the silver radiance that washed evenly over everything; easier to see than in the day, with daylight's distracting colors.

On a garden bench Caterina set out two clean rags and the vial Piera had given her. Then she drew out a dining dirk from a scabbard at her belt. She raised hands, face, and dagger to the moon, bathing in its light for a moment. "With Your favor, bless this undertaking, Mother Diana," she whispered. She took a breath and slashed a shallow cut across the end of one finger.

When the blood welled up Caterina turned her hand over to drip it, drop by drop, into the glass vial. When the vial filled she stoppered it tightly. She bound her finger with one clean rag and wiped the top of the vial and the blade with the other.

Over at the Ruggieros', Piera sat cross-legged with her back against the well in the middle of the garden. The herbal bed's twists and turns formed a huge knotted circle around her. Gattamelata sat facing her. Between them, on a linen cloth laid on the ground, was another glass vial, a small clean wad of spiderweb, a fresh rag, and Piera's newly sharpened *athamé*. Piera too gazed up at the moon.

"Mother Diana, with Your favor, bless this enterprise. The Little Kitchen Goddess has consented to this deed."

Piera picked up the blade, consecrated it to the moon, then leaned over and sliced a tiny nick in Gattamelata's ear. The cat barely flinched. Piera caught the blood in the glass vial as it oozed up. When the vial was full she stoppered it. She pressed the spiderweb wad to the cut until the bleeding stopped.

"Come, Little Holy One," Piera murmured to Gattamelata as she gathered everything up. "Let me honor and thank you with some cream." She slid the vial into a pocket. Cousin Francesca would take it to her mother Leonora on her next family visit. And Leonora would see that it reached Elissa Pecorino.

31

Tommaso tried to find the time to cast the pendant for his mother, but at every turn events conspired against him. Florence was in a frantic uproar of fear and preparation.

Pope Clement's plotted assault on Florence was moving toward reality: the pontiff had negotiated with his former nemesis Emperor Charles for an alliance through a proposed marriage between Alessandro and the emperor's illegitimate daughter. Clement was also attempting to raise large sums of money.

"Enough to hire an army," Bembo pointed out to Il Tribolino in the sculptor's office one afternoon. "Do you suppose your esteemed patron might be trying to hire troops to invade his native city?"

Tommaso looked up from the set of scales where he was weighing chemicals for a bronze patina formula.

Il Tribolino looked uncomfortable and shrugged. He shoved a large flat wooden box into a cabinet. The carton was so large he had to wrestle it into place. Tommaso stopped his own chore to help him. But when Il Tribolino gestured him away, Tommaso understood that his master needed to look too occupied to be expected to respond.

"How would I know what's in the pontiff's mind?" Il Tribolino finally muttered. He slammed the cabinet door shut and snapped its lock shut. "I just care that he pays his bills. If artists rejected patronage from

a high moral ground, we'd have starved to death as a profession even before the ancient Etruscans ruled."

And Il Tribolino seemed determined to avoid death by starvation. He
was rushing to complete all outstanding commissions he'd contracted
from Clement while there might be time to get the works out of Florence
to Rome and payment from Rome back to Florence. Although they were
tempted to resent their master for the extra work and long hours, all the
apprentices agreed that Il Tribolino was wise to make his florins while he
could before the next set of skirmishes between Florence and the most
powerful de' Medici in the world began again.

Tommaso had only two objections to the accelerated work pace. The
first, he knew, was purely selfish. Weeks had passed since he'd last had a
chance to be alone with Michelangelo.

The second objection was the inability to complete the promised
project for his mother. Every time he returned home he apologized to her
for the delay. She accepted his excuses calmly and with good humor.

To make matters worse, the usually hale Elissa Pecorino fell ill with
some mysterious women's malady. Every time it appeared that Tommaso
might find the hours he needed to cast his mother's pendant, Elissa
Pecorino took to her bed and Tommaso found himself working double-
duty in the kitchen.

On March 22, Tommaso finally found his opportunity. Il Tribolino declared the whole day a work holiday so the entire *bottega* could attend
spring equinox festivities. Tommaso alone begged off, saying he wished to
remain behind to complete some outstanding projects. He knew if he'd
been any of the other apprentices his statement would have met with de-
rision. But, in his case, the other boys looked at each other with sly smiles.
They expected that as soon as they left he'd slip away to meet Michelangelo.

They were wrong. Before Il Tribolino finished locking up his office
Tommaso began stoking wood to a small hot fire to heat a crucible. Il Tribolino waved to him as he walked out the door.

At last completely alone, Tommaso drew the crucifix from around his neck, relieved he'd no longer have the weight of it banging against his chest. Now only the stone in its velvet pouch nestled, far more lightly, against him.

Tommaso put the crucifix into a burlap sack and picked up a hammer. He'd known he couldn't break the Holy Cross into pieces in the presence of others. His hands shook. It would be hard enough doing the deed alone with only his own conscience as witness.

"Would you like some help?"

At the sound of the voice at his back Tommaso dropped the hammer. It bounced several times.

Elissa Pecorino stood behind him, her arms folded on her chest.

"I thought you were sick," Tommaso stammered.

"I was." She shrugged. "Such illnesses last a long time, then pass quickly." She pointed to the cross in the sack. "Your respect for the sacred is admirable but in the end could stop you from action. Would you like me to finish the chore? It would free you to ready the more difficult parts of the process."

"Yes. I'd be grateful." And he was. Tommaso bustled about, readying the plaster mold and setting up the crucible so it would balance evenly over the fire. He heard Elissa Pecorino mumble something in a singsong voice that was followed by a loud *crack* as she brought the hammer down. This seemed to be her preferred procedure, for she repeated it a number of times: a muttered lilting chant, a sharp report. A muttered lilting chant, a sharp report.

"What do you think?" she asked as she carefully turned the bag inside out and emptied the silver chunks into a bowl before him. Here and there elements of the crucifix were still recognizable: the tiny moon almost intact, the fish broken cleanly from the base.

"Excellent." Tommaso worked his fingers along the fibers of the sack to be sure no fragments of silver remained caught there. Elissa Pecorino had done a good, clean job. Tommaso couldn't find a single errant sliver.

He placed the silver in the crucible and set it over the fire. The pieces softened at their edges and began to pool together from the bottom up as the heat rose through them, warmly reflecting the glow of the flames below. It could have been clumps of the palest butter melting together. Except that this braising exuded an entirely different aroma than the rich, unctuous perfume of poaching butter. The pooling mass before him stank of searing metal.

When the silver was almost molten, Elissa Pecorino gestured to where the mold sat anchored in a bed of sand. "Might that not shift as you pour? It's such a small mold, easily knocked over. In such cases does not Master Tribolino have one person brace the mold while the other decants the metal?"

"Yes," said Tommaso, somewhat surprised that Elissa Pecorino knew the procedure. "But it's possible to do it this way if one is alone."

"Don't look so gape mouthed," said Elissa Pecorino. "I've been working and living in this *bottega* since you were a fledgling. Do you think me completely ignorant of the work that goes on here? You're *not* alone, so go fetch me an extra pair of work gauntlets and tongs from the cabinet. I'll hold the mold steady for you."

"I'll have to fetch the key to the cabinet," Tommaso said. "Can you watch the silver for me?"

Elissa Pecorino snorted by way of reply.

As soon as Tommaso crossed the length of the studio to get into the office, Elissa Pecorino took two tiny glass vials from her bodice and pulled a long thin wire of a pale metal neither silver nor gold from her cap and straightened it. She poured the contents of the vials together into the crucible. The blood sizzled, scorched, charred, briefly reeked. Elissa Pecorino stirred the black flakes into the puddled silver with the wire, which itself melted and sank quickly down into the increasingly incandescent mass.

"This day, as in ancient times, the Goddess begins Her ascent from the underworld to arise to guard and protect us all," Elissa Pecorino murmured. "And this day the Little Kitchen Goddess and the Maiden join together to prepare to receive Her as She begins Her journey."

By the time Tommaso returned with the extra pair of tongs and thick leather work gloves, everything in the crucible had melted together into a thick pristine fluid.

"It's perfect," he said after inspecting the crucible's contents.

Elissa Pecorino smiled to herself. "Yes. It appears so." She donned the leather gauntlets. They reached up past her elbows. She braced the mold with the tongs as if she'd done it a hundred times before.

Tommaso put on his own work gloves, grasped the other set of tongs and with them lifted the crucible from the fire. He gently poured the molten metal into the mold. He'd calculated its size perfectly; the silver reached just to the top.

32

May 1, 1529

With his spare hand, Tommaso leaned over and reached down to help his mother up into the cart.

"You have it?" she asked as she settled in beside him. "You promised you'd bring it today."

"Of course. I said I would," he replied.

Piera glanced behind to be sure Gentile and Old Taddeo were still busy loading the back of the cart. She held out her hand to Tommaso.

He had to first untangle the *Calendimaggio* branch he carried from the cart reins, then give his mother the festive bough to hold before he could pull the pouch cord from around his neck.

Piera handed Tommaso back the bough and looked over her shoulder again before she risked opening the pouch and sliding the pendant out.

"Tommaso, it's exquisite. It's everything I hoped for." The cabochon fit so perfectly it appeared to grow out of the pendant's center. The soft glow of the surrounding silver, which Tommaso had labored over so many hours to bring to a flawless polish, set off the gem's satiny winelike depths to perfection. In the spring's fresh morning light the esoteric symbols looked charmingly decorative. Tommaso had cast the piece with a built-in loop for the crucifix's chain to draw through.

"It's just as I imagined, and more," Piera said as she settled the chain about her neck and slid the pendant down her bodice.

Old Taddeo came around on the left side, clambered up, and took the reins from Tommaso. Balancing the *Calendimaggio* bough carefully, Tommaso scrambled around the backboard of the cart and exchanged places with his mother, so that she was wedged in safely between himself and the older man. Tommaso was glad for the distraction. The moment he'd taken off the pendant in its pouch the sensation of comfort and well-being he'd felt for months started to disappear. The May sunshine seemed thin all of a sudden.

"That's a beautifully wrought branch," Gentile said, coming up on the right side of the cart. Tommaso had stained it with the soft gay pigments of peach, pink, and plum. Gold-colored ribbons wound about and bound it. Tommaso had purchased them with part of the purse he'd won at the apprentices' gala. Multihued praline crystals sprinkled the nuts attached to the bough. Here and there among the nuts peeked modeled almond-paste figurines shaped to look like lions and Florentine lilies.

"I made it for the *Duchessina*." Tommaso couldn't keep the edge from his voice. "As I did last year."

Gentile blinked. "I'm sure she'll enjoy this one as much as Taddeo told me she enjoyed that one," he said humbly, though he looked about nervously to see that nobody else was near enough to hear them. Since the reestablishment of the republic it was dangerous to refer to Caterina as any kind of royalty.

Tommaso didn't know how to respond to his father's words so he said nothing. He knew Gentile was reaching out to him. But every time Tommaso longed to pity this sad, lonely man who'd once been the center of his world, Filomena's crumpled, pain-stricken face rose like a blotting fog to coldly fill Tommaso's mind.

The cart moved off, leaving Gentile standing behind.

They turned onto wider boulevards. The streets filled with revelers. To the music of strolling lutists, columns of girls dressed in spring frocks and bedecked with garlands of flowers danced their way to the Piazza Santa Trinitá. Brothers or suitors carried the girls' boughs along behind them. Older citizens wearing masks and costumes cheered the procession of youthful beauty from windows and doorways.

A frantic undercurrent eddied beneath the joy. Florence had spent over a year recovering from the plague. Before that, the city suffered through that pestilence in human form, Cardinal Passerini. Now the pope plotted with the emperor against the city. Disaster might strike at any moment. So, while peace endured, the citizens lived as though it were best to stuff each moment with happiness till it burst at the seams.

Ever since his vision of phantoms prior to the aborted Saint John the Baptist's celebration Tommaso felt uneasy in the presence of masquers. He stared at the cheering crowds and relaxed when he saw no bone-faced apparitions, no spectral *obby oss.*

Still, here and there he glimpsed tall men garbed in traditional black *lucco* wearing raven's masks constructed like helmets. Their eerie visages punched abyssal silhouettes in the pastel frieze of merrymakers. Tommaso would have felt less chilled if the masks had not been so realistic. What sort of man put on a gloomy scavenger's face to watch such gay proceedings?

Tommaso glanced at his mother to see her reaction: Did she share his apprehension, or was she cheered by the festivities?

Neither. Piera sat on the hard cart seat with her eyes closed. She seemed oblivious to everything going on about her. One hand pressed her bodice where Tommaso knew the pendant must be nesting. She had a curious look on her face, as of great loss assuaged, of hard-won serenity restored.

Tommaso felt a not-unwelcome ache in his heart as his mother's features relaxed and transformed into a tranquil beauty he hadn't seen in over a year and a half, since that long ago summer day in June. He forgot about the raven-headed men, the *Calendimaggio* festivities, and all else but this glimpse of his mother as he remembered her.

She opened her eyes to find him watching. "Thank you, Tommaso," she said quietly. She pressed his hand with her own.

Caterina was standing in the convent courtyard when they arrived. She was chaperoned by a novice and talking to a young boy of her own age and a pale, severe-looking woman. She waved when she saw Piera and Tommaso.

"Tommaso, give your bough to the *Duchessina* and then excuse yourself," Piera said. "You can see her later when the cart is unloaded."

Tommaso hopped down and approached Caterina and her company slowly, with deference. They ceased their conversation to allow him to present the bough to Caterina.

"Tommaso, it's lovely," Caterina exclaimed. The stern woman beside her smiled just a little at the extravagant branch. The young boy's expression remained unchanged: His face was still as a stone, his calm eyes hooded, secretive, far too old for their years.

"Who are they?" Tommaso asked his mother once they were inside the kitchen's domain.

"The woman is Maria Salviati, widow of the great war hero Giovanni delle Bande Nere. She is a granddaughter of Lorenzo the Magnificent—one of his daughter's daughters. I only saw her once before, years ago at her wedding procession, but one cannot mistake her eyes and skin."

That was true, Tommaso thought. Like Clarice Strozzi, Maria Salviati had a raptor's gaze. But unlike Clarice, Maria looked like a captured hawk who'd been overly tethered into bitterness and defensiveness. And her skin was not only the palest Tommaso had ever seen, but it shone with an unnatural pallor.

"And the boy?" he asked.

"Must be her son Cosimo. I've heard they live well out of town at Il Trebbio when they're not traveling between Bologna and Venice. They must have come in from the country for the festivities and to pay their respects to Caterina."

Tommaso and Old Taddeo were still unloading supplies when Piera heard the carriage rumble away. She walked back to the courtyard to meet Caterina. The *Duchessina* held out her hands to her.

"Piera, would you stroll with me in the garden to celebrate the day? I hate to detain Sister Anna Maria here from her devotions any longer."

"Of course. It would be my pleasure," Piera said.

The novice smiled her thanks. With Caterina chaperoned by a respectable older woman she could relinquish her duties with a clear conscience.

Caterina waved her *Calendimaggio* bough about coquettishly. "What do you think of my cousin Cosimo? He's usually so serious that you wouldn't know he's great fun during a hunt or out fowling. Have you yet seen the festivities in the piazza this year? I'll wager no other girl possesses a branch as fine as mine."

Between these bits of inane conversation Caterina kept looking up at Piera expectantly. But it wasn't till they were alone in the garden that Piera turned to her. Caterina fell silent.

"You know what today is," Piera said.

Caterina nodded. "Since March She has traversed the labyrinth up from the underworld. Today we rejoice in Her return. Today She has come to join us." Caterina pushed the base of her *Calendimaggio* bough firmly into the damp spring soil. "The Tree of Life grows again."

Piera smiled. She lifted the necklace up and over her head to settle it around Caterina's neck. "Yes, Caterina. And today I dedicate my two oldest children, Tommaso and Ginevra, to your service. Before birth they were already consecrated to the Holy Three. They will guide, guard, and protect you. Love and protect them in kind."

Caterina gasped as the pendant touched her. "By all that is holy," she whispered, "it really is her, come back to us." Caterina's eyes brimmed with tears. She couldn't keep herself to the formality of ritual. "Oh Piera, how can you give up so much? How can I take your children from you? I've already failed you once: I was so young, I could do nothing."

Piera kissed both her cheeks. "How can a fledgling who can't yet fly be expected to carry the world on its wings? You *were* young. You didn't fail—I did. And my children aren't my children. Like all children everywhere, they are spirits I was privileged to give form to. You are older now and ready. As are they."

Caterina shut her eyes tightly and clutched the pendant. "I vow that until the day I pass from this life the bond between myself, Ginevra, and Tommaso will not be broken again," she said.

Tommaso finished unloading and went looking for his mother and Caterina. He arrived at the top of the garden just in time to see Piera place the necklace about Caterina's neck. He dropped to squat on his heels, confused.

He'd made the pendant for his mother. For an instant it hurt him that Piera would give it away so quickly. But when he saw the look on Caterina's face, when it cleared from a grief he didn't understand to radiance, he understood that it had been meant for her all along. Suddenly the barrenness Tommaso had felt since relinquishing the necklace eased. He slipped quietly back to the cart.

33

May 2, 1529

The light from the candle Piera carried wavered along the dark kitchen walls and shadowy forms of stacked bowls and *tondi* as she approached the pantry. *The flame falters and sways about like the future,* she thought.

Of late she'd only been able to see two things. The first was Caterina's uncertain future swelling like a river rising to flood, threatening to jump its banks and find an unpredictable new course. The second was Ginevra's slow reemergence.

Everything else was as concealed to Piera as the corners of the kitchen unreached by the candle's inconstant glow. And she didn't know why. Piera shielded the taper from a draft with her spare hand as she opened the pantry door.

She hadn't been in the pantry alone at night at all since her miscarriage, and seldom in the day. She herself felt no fear of the place. But everyone else in the kitchen except Cousin Francesca became nervously busy whenever she headed for supplies from there. They fell over themselves volunteering to fetch whatever she needed, except for Filomena. The young slave would turn pale and scramble away from the pantry door, no doubt from some superstition of her mother's people. Piera shrugged. Or perhaps it was just one more reaction to her condition. As Filomena grew into womanhood slavery seemed to be wearing her down. She'd grown thin and pale although she was well clothed, ate the same food as the rest of the kitchen staff, and no one spoke to her cruelly.

No, in spite of the other servants' and Filomena's reactions, there was nothing to fear from the pantry. And little risk of being caught there. The only other person that Piera knew for certain was awake was Francesca, standing guard just inside the door to their sleeping quarters. If anyone should stir, Francesca would fetch Piera or, lacking time, create a diversion.

Piera still would have preferred to conduct her rituals this night out of doors. She might take a goodly amount of time, though, and she was more likely to be discovered in the garden. Piera's nervousness stemmed not so much from a fear of being found out as what she herself might unearth in the next few hours.

The day before, as she'd ridden the oxcart to the Murate, all of Piera's senses had been engaged in celebrating Ginevra's return to a consciousness of this life. Her daughter still felt confusion in her new form, yet was aware of her powers and the manner in which she was girded and protected by metal, symbols, and blood.

Mother, am I waking from a dream, or waking into a dream? Ginevra's thoughts expressed themselves as sensations emanating from the pendant through to Piera's breast and straight into the very bone.

You are half-waking from half a dream, Piera thought in reply. *You lay within your brother's protection for many months as you slowly returned to us. Today you are fully ascended into your new form. Did you know that?*

It was a long time before the gem responded. Piera fought back fear. It was possible Ginevra might prove unable to accept her new form and slip away into madness. Piera had heard of that happening before with others. Those who existed in the near-immortality of stone experienced temporality in a fashion mortals couldn't conceive of. It would take Ginevra a while to comprehend and adjust to this, if she could at all. Piera prayed while she waited.

Yes, Ginevra at last answered. *Even though I felt myself floating in some distant vision, I sensed Tommaso always near me. I feel him still close by.*

He is, Piera assured Ginevra. *And now I am carrying you to Caterina.*

Just then Piera felt Tommaso's gaze. She opened her eyes to find his beautiful face filled with love and concern. "Thank you, Tommaso," she said. He hadn't understood what she was thanking him for but he looked relieved.

With that breaking of the link with her daughter, many moments passed before Ginevra returned.

There are so many things I no longer see, Mother. And so many other things reveal themselves that I never knew before.

Ginevra, that is the gift of your new form. What do you see?

I see this: Mother, you cannot balance the great things far away, no matter how much you try, while that which is nearby is unbalanced and tumbling to the ground.

Piera didn't know what to make of that.

And watch for the Watchers, Mother. Surely you see them all about us.

At that Piera's eyes flew open again. And saw them. They were everywhere: peering from alleyways, balconies, from among the throngs. Not since just before the plague had Piera seen so many of the scavengers from Ammon.

But here and there, too, was evidence of the Grigori, the guardians. Piera saw servants of Settrano, who protected the southern portals; of Meana of the western doorways; of Alpeno of the eastern entrances; and the servants of the most powerful Grigori of all, Tago of the northern gateway. She saw them in cats patrolling alleyways, flowers blooming in pots on sills, the dust kicked up by the light spring breeze. The Grigori seemed to be preparing for a grievous assault from all sides.

Piera was disturbed that the situation had caught her so unawares. She must know how things stood before she acted.

Piera opened the pantry with some reluctance. Gattamelata tried to slide between her ankles but Piera blocked the cat out. Tonight's ritual was one she needed to perform alone. Piera closed the pantry door tightly behind her and set the taper on the stone floor. She wished she could hazard flying. She longed for what she'd had too few times in her life: an open meadow under the moon with Leonora and Leonora's daughters circled about her for protection.

She extricated the black scrying bowl from its hiding place. A rag soaked in white wine wiped it clean enough to gleam even in the dim pantry. Piera put the bowl on the floor in such a position that the candle's flame reflected into its glossy sable center. Then she placed a small white shell in the middle of the bowl. "The Mother, and in Her womb, the Daughter," she murmured.

More shells were set in a circle around the bowl. "In their places, guarding, stand the Grigori."

She decanted a volatile oil into the bowl. Its heavy thick fragrance of clove, cinnamon, and rue clashed with the harsh clean smell of the white wine used in the cleaning.

"You, the blessed spirits of the portals to our land—children, like myself, of the Mother—I entreat you to show me what I need to see."

Who would come to her? Piera wondered as she lit the end of a long sliver of kindling in the candle's flame. Would her vision be transported through Meana's western portal to the undine's watery, lightless world? Or perhaps Tagos's cold doorway, opening up to a realm were the simple sight of eyes alone was insufficient before the constant blurring of whirlwinds and rushing air. It was even feasible that the stars themselves would respond and Marax would fly to her from his distant home in the heavens. Or would her entreaty remain unanswered and leave her sight languishing in blindness?

Piera touched the glowing end of the kindling to the oil. With a soughing noise a low blue flame spread across the bowl's surface and the spicy scent intensified.

Piera cleared her mind of fears, hopes, and expectations, concentrating only on the flame. Around the edges of the bowl she imagined five points. The fire followed her thoughts: Five flecks of a brighter blue materialized where she desired them. Equidistantly inward from those points, she visualized five more, the inner angles of the star shape she was building. They appeared.

She pictured the spots connecting to each other with lines, then the lines expanding upward into planes. She pulled gently on the planes with her imagination. A foxfire pentagram arose from the oil. Piera waited till it was crisply complete and self-sustaining before peering into its center.

"Show me what I need to see," Piera murmured again. She felt, deep within every one of her sinews, every one of her muscles, the marrow of hard-grown bone, the overwhelming presence of the dormant life stored around her in the pantry. Each separate grain of spelt and buckwheat, each broad bean and pea, each spore-laden dried porcini and each withered root held a small slumbering flicker of life, much as the blood-red cabochon safely contained Ginevra's dormant spirit.

Every single one of those tiny life glimmers could and would grow to help fill the world; either planted in the soil to become an individual life, or transformed through cooking to join and enforce the soul and body of another. Piera saw, emerging from sacks and barrels and crocks, thousands upon thousands of infinitesimally small flames gather about her as thickly as the stars that freckle the sky.

Clear your mind, she told herself. *Let your palms be open and empty to receive whatever gift might be offered.*

The tiny specks whirled about the candle, bleeding into it, feeding it. Yellow flame flared upward. The candle's flaxen brilliance reflected down into the center of the glowing blue pentacle. Bright, buttery light spread until it filled the center of the blue-outlined star. Images began to move within the pentacle.

Piera peered over and saw inside the star—the pantry. And a face. A face she knew, wailing in soundless pain. The face buckled, crumpled, bled away into tears. The tears gathered and ran together, forming rippling waves that washed together to contour into the face again. Piera knew she was seeing not one instance of misery but many, dozens. She scrambled back till her back hit the pantry shelves.

The face pulsed, enlarged, became another visage, contorted with lust but no less in pain, no less helpless than the first. Gentile. Piera whimpered.

Filomena. Gentile. Filomena. Piera tried to turn away but they were all about her, filling the pantry with outrage. Piera batted her hands against the images. Finally, she gathered her wits and blew the candle out.

The pentacle slowly emptied of its heinous vision, leaving Piera sobbing alone with only the thin flickering blue lines of the five-pointed star for company. Outside, Gattamelata scratched at the door, mewling her distress.

What was it that Ginevra had said? *Mother, you cannot balance the great things far away, no matter how much you try, while that which is nearby is unbalanced and tum-bling to the ground.*

Yes, tumbling to the ground all about her, and she'd been too blind to see.

34

❧

Cosimo paced his father's study anxiously. With so many portents nipping at their heels like hungry curs he'd expected that when his father summoned him that night it was to construct a great magick to counter all the omens.

Instead, the scrying mirror remained turned to the wall. His father sat silent at the great table with no other apparatus before him but the square of four interconnected rods. Every once in a while the old mage picked up this simple tool, flexing and studying it.

Finally, Cosimo could bear it no longer. "Father! The Ammonites gather more thickly with their watching. Surely events are coming to a crux. Are we going to do nothing?"

Ruggiero the Old looked up at his son through a gray thatch of eyebrows. "There is doing nothing, and then there is 'doing nothing.' Holding still, staying quiet, watching and waiting is not 'doing nothing.' He who rushes into action willy-nilly, all enthused and uninformed, often causes more harm than he who hesitates." He flexed the rods again.

"Suppose we were ants, my son, and lived here," he indicated one side of the apparatus. "And our foes were also ants and lived over there," he pointed to the opposite side. "How would they reach us? They might be able to contrive some means to spy on us across the abyss," he moved his hand within the square's empty interior. "But they are ants, not frogs, so they cannot simply leap over upon us."

Cosimo stared. Did his father think him stupid? "They'd reach us by creeping along the two connecting rods, as any ant would."

Ruggiero the Old nodded. "So we could say the connectors form roads or passageways, even, in a sense, doorways, since they constitute a means to enter our realm."

"Yes," Cosimo said.

"This would be an easy task for them, but for two things. The first is that these entryways are known. Or, at least many of them are." The old man sighed. "This tool is the simplest model possible. Imagine a more realistic representation where there are dozens, even hundreds of connecting rods leading to us. We cannot detect them all. What we *do* know is the general 'direction' of their approach. We can guard and lay traps there. That is the first great advantage that hinders our foes."

"And the second?" Cosimo prompted his father when it seemed as though the old man might not continue.

"Think on those connecting rods for a moment. If there are ants on our rod, and enemy ants on the opposite, who is to say there aren't yet more ants on the rods in between, or even creatures other than ants?"

Cosimo struggled to restrain his impatience. For over a year a good part of his study had been concerned with just those "creatures" of the interlocking existences. "I know that well, Father."

"Of course you do. You're an apt student. And you know that these 'ants' of the interim realms can be neutral, or allies, or even, if we force them into situations threatening to their own worlds, reluctant adversaries. At this moment they are guarding the passageways as best they can and alerting us to the approach of our enemies."

"To keep them at bay and turn the tide," Cosimo ventured.

His father shook his head. "A few scouts, spies, and guardians cannot turn the tide of a great army. At best they can hinder, buying us time, and gather information so that when the foe arrives we are prepared. It is time to prepare strategies for feigning surrender, for surviving a hostile occupation and weakening its forces from within."

Cosimo's spirit plummeted. Was the battle lost before it was even joined?

"Don't look so heartsore, my son. In the end we'll survive, even triumph. But tonight we must plan and prepare to forfeit where we must.
You love the game of chess, do you not?"

Cosimo nodded.

"Then think of this as a great chess game. Florence and all of Tuscany around it is the king: rich and powerful, beloved, our very wellspring,
but also slow-moving and vulnerable. The rest of us move about the board
of conflict as best we can. We are much like chess pieces acting in whatever fashion our station in life designates: rooks up and down, bishops di-
agonally; mages with magic, soldiers with arquebuses and lances. All of us
moving in service of the protection of the king." Ruggiero the Old flexed
the rods again. "We will do anything we must, up to and including the
sacrifice of our most able player, the queen."

35

May 15, 1529

Michelangelo rolled away from Tommaso to perch on the edge of the rough pallet that served as the sculptor's bed.

"I can't be selfish and hold you in my arms all day," he said as he pulled on his drawers and buskins. "You haven't seen your family since *Calendimaggio*. It would serve us both ill if they missed you and began to query Il Tribolino."

Tommaso, always secretly fearful of the day Michelangelo would tire of him, reached over and stroked his lover's back. When Michelangelo closed his eyes and shivered with pleasure, Tommaso's heart sang in relief. Michelangelo was not rejecting him.

"Surely there is more time," Tommaso said. "My family grants me my youth. It's expected I spend some of my free day playing, gambling, dancing, looking for love. As long as I arrive before supper they're not concerned. And your apprentices won't be back for hours."

Michelangelo had lent his workers' services to Bugiardini for the day. The muralist needed help laying down a large expanse of plaster and pigment. Since Michelangelo often desired solitude to labor on his own work, Tommaso was fairly certain that Antonio Mini, Ascancio, and the rest didn't suspect that on this occasion—as on others before—Michelangelo had emptied his studio for trysting, not working.

"There is more time for us together," Michelangelo agreed. "With your permission, I'd like to spend it on another pursuit than the bed."

"Whatever you desire, I'm willing," Tommaso said. He slid off the pallet and snatched up his clothes.

"No, not that." Michelangelo laid hold of Tommaso's shirt before he could pull it on. "What I wanted to ask of you . . ." he hesitated. "May I draw you? Would you pose for me?"

Tommaso stopped trying to dress, shocked. His fingers, holding the shirt, felt suddenly weak and numb. He knew that Michelangelo had known lovers before him and undoubtedly would have lovers after him. But Tommaso'd never heard of Michelangelo drawing a lover or hardly anyone else directly from life.

"It would be an honor," Tommaso mumbled. The words buzzed through lips as insensate as his fingers.

"Nothing elaborate or difficult," Michelangelo assured him, pushing forward a sturdy crate for him to pose on. "Just stand simply, naturally. Balance your weight equally on your feet so you don't tire."

Tommaso did as he was told. He thought he must present an uninspired, lackluster picture, but after a few adjustments to the pose Michelangelo seemed satisfied. The artist selected some charcoal sticks and *conté* crayons, arranged a sheath of papers on a board. He made himself comfortable on the pallet and began to sketch with rapid motions.

"You understand that my duties as Commissary General have passed from designing fortifications to building them," Michelangelo said conversationally.

Tommaso knew it was permissible for models to occasionally speak as long as they didn't move their heads or alter their facial expressions. "Yes," he responded.

"Recently, you and I were parted when the *Signoria* sent me to Duke Alfonso of Ferrara to study his fortifications," Michelangelo said. "Now I walk down to the lower part of the city almost every day to oversee the construction of the barriers around San Miniato, using what I learned in Ferrara."

Tommaso could think of no response that might be expected of him so he remained silent. For a long while there was no sound except for the scratching of charcoal on paper.

"Besides my duties in the defense of Florence, I still also work for the

Medici family on the sacristy of San Lorenzo, on various private commissions, and on the Leda in tempera."

Tommaso fought the natural impulse to nod in agreement to Michelangelo's litany of responsibilities. He wondered where it was leading.

"What I'm trying to say . . ."—ah, there it was: that slight edge of irritation that crept into Michelangelo's voice when he began to feel frustrated—"is that we'll have fewer opportunities to be together like this."

Tommaso felt the center of his being drop away to land heavily in the bottom of his belly. He felt suddenly nauseous.

"Tommaso! Don't clench your jaw like that. It ruins the pose. And relax your brow." Michelangelo laid down his sketch, rose from the pallet, and walked around to meet Tommaso's eyes.

"I'm not telling you this to hurt you. Nor to suggest I no longer desire you. Quite the opposite. If I didn't warn you what the immediate future holds for us, then you might indeed have cause to doubt me when our time together, rare as it is already, dwindles away to almost nothing." Michelangelo ran his hand along the outside of Tommaso's thigh. "I'm telling you this to confirm my love."

Tommaso was a little reassured, but he still felt weighed down by a shadow of depression. He couldn't stop himself from muttering, "But someday we will part."

"Yes, someday we will," Michelangelo agreed, his smile infinitely sad. "But I'll wager in the end that it is you who leaves me."

"Never! I would never leave you!" Tommaso was shocked.

"Events will take you away from me," said Michelangelo. "Or the adoration of a woman. You are not one made for the affections of men only. A day will come when you'll feel drawn to some pretty dove-breasted girl or another."

Tommaso flushed, thinking of his desperate yearning after Filomena in what seemed a lifetime ago.

"Aha!" Michelangelo laughed. "Look how your color rises. You've already experienced just those sentiments." The sculptor sat down and picked up his drawing tools again. "Keep blushing, Tommaso. I think I can capture the charming effect with this sienna *conté*."

Tommaso was confused with embarrassment, but at the same time felt, with perfect clarity, in this moment of relaxed intimate banter, the assurance that the love he and Michelangelo shared was still solid and fine as Carrera marble.

"What about you? Have you ever loved a woman?" Tommaso dared ask.

"Love?" Although Tommaso couldn't see Michelangelo's face without turning his head and breaking the pose, he knew his lover well enough that he was sure Michelangelo's eyebrows were cocked in a sardonic expression. "I've lusted after, bedded, and adored my share."

"Then—"

"Stop. I know what you're going to ask. Why didn't I ever marry? Tommaso, I am married. My whole life I've been wed to a single most demanding lady: my Art. Rare is the mortal woman who could accept the fact that—in spite of wedding ceremonies and the sacraments of the Church—she would never be more than a minor mistress in the face of my true wedded wife.

"Look at our good Tribolo. Every day he dashes back and forth between his house and his studio, torn between the demands of his lady Art and those of his lady wife and children. Can you imagine me living such a life?"

Tommaso had to admit he could not.

"So instead I've found—a very few times in my life—a youth such as yourself: lovely as any maid, and more understanding and accepting."

Tommaso thought of the closeness his parents once shared and the way they'd worked happily together at the same trade and in raising their children. His chest collapsed a little in sadness that Michelangelo would never experience that. And suddenly he understood just how well Michelangelo knew him, and why the sculptor had said that the two of them were fated to someday part.

"Straighten up, Tommaso. Are you tired? Would you like to rest?"

"No." Tommaso raised up through his spine and sternum. "Is there no woman for you then anywhere who could be the same to you as me?"

"You mean a woman who could understand my obsession and not be jealous? A woman who could let me be?" The sounds of charcoal against paper came more slowly as Michelangelo's strokes matched his thoughtfulness.

"Yes, such women exist," he finally said "They are of a type: well born, ferociously well educated, in possession of exquisite taste, both in intellect and capability the equal and possibly the superior of any man. Such women as Lorenzo the Magnificent's daughters, and Isabella d'Este, Clarice Strozzi, my beloved Marchioness Vittoria Colonna, and I am sure someday your little *Duchessina*. Such a woman would understand me perfectly, take what love I could offer her and not begrudge the lion's share I tithe to my art.

"But alas, they have a tithe of their own they must pay. The price of their exceptional development is the use their families make of their bodies. They are married out to those families' economic advantage or to strengthen political bonds.

"My entire life I have not let anyone compromise my destiny. With the high regard in which I hold these women, how could I compromise theirs?"

"But you are as highborn as any of them," Tommaso protested.

"My family is from a minor and fading aristocracy. I turned my back even on that when I declared myself for my lady Art. Tommaso, I wish you could have seen my father's face when I told him I wouldn't follow him into law and begged him to apprentice me to the painter Ghirlandaio." Michelangelo's chuckle was bitter. "That good man at last gave in, but he only came to forgive me the least little bit when I gained Lorenzo Magnífico's favor and went to live in the de' Medici palazzo."

The sound of the charcoal and *conté* strokes came furiously again. "You must understand that above all else the highborn live for the consolidation of power. I am now not a poor man by any means. Still, I'm nothing more than a humble artist. In the arena of human affairs, my breath would not stir a feather, my strongest blow not kill a fly. Great women are not married to such powerlessness."

"Such powerlessness that popes beg for your favor," Tommaso muttered. "You are so powerless that men have been known to drop to their knees and weep before the beauty of your paintings. Women find their dreams haunted by your sculptures. Statesmen have found enlightenment in your images and changed the course of nations. You have altered the way three generations of men look out of their very eyes and see the world."

Michelangelo said nothing for a moment, apparently taken aback by Tommaso's outburst.

"If even a tenth of such high praise is true, then I owe what power I do possess to my devotion to my one true wife," Michelangelo finally said dryly. "Save your compassion for others, Tommaso. I can count the men as fulfilled in their lives as I on the fingers of one hand. Would you truly have me be other than just as I am?"

"No!" Tommaso hastened to reply. He was horrified that Michelangelo might think he pitied him. "I just can't bear to see you denied any measure of happiness."

"You have a generous heart. And *you* are one of the measures of happiness I haven't been denied." Michelangelo set his drawings aside. "That's enough for today. If I keep you here longer I'll be cheating your family." He offered Tommaso a hand to help him down from the crate.

Tommaso was surprised how stiff he was from simply standing. He stepped down awkwardly, averting his eyes from the sketches as he did so. He knew how Michelangelo hated people prying at his unfinished work.

"It's all right. You can look." Michelangelo's voice was amused.

The drawings were exquisite. Given Michelangelo's skill and genius, Tommaso knew they must be completely accurate, yet he didn't recognize the long-limbed youth they portrayed at all.

Whenever he looked at himself in a mirror, Tommaso still saw the face of a young boy whose features were overwhelmed and camouflaged by his high coloring. But stripped down to fine lines and simple shadow by the monochromatic effect of *conté* and charcoal, the figure in the drawings displayed the architecture of bone structure, musculature and bearing of an utter stranger.

"Is this me?" he whispered. "I do not know myself."

"An honest response," Michelangelo said, handing him his clothes.

Tommaso left Michelangelo's *bottega* with his mind dazed from grappling with this new image of himself. But his heart was sure and glad, remembering the tenderness with which Michelangelo had helped him draw his shirt over his head, the manner in which the sculptor's hand lingered on his skin, how Michelangelo urged him to take care on his way.

Michelangelo had set the sketches aside as if he were going to put them away. But as soon as Tommaso left the sculptor propped up his board and began working on the drawings again. Deft strokes of *conté* added extra musculature emerging from Tommaso's scapula, substantial enough to support the graceful wings Michelangelo next drew in with long sensual strokes. Michelangelo needed to do little else: The inviolable beauty of Tommaso's face contained all the natural sacredness an angel's visage required.

Even if not grown so tall, Tommaso would have had little to fear from the city's *brigate* on his way home. They were far too busy with civic responsibilities to spend time harassing apprentices these days.

Militia were being organized in every quarter of the city. Although all the young men had been called out, there'd been little need to demand them to serve. With Florence itself threatened and its defense a noble outlet for their hot blood, they flocked to enlist.

Every street corner seemed infested by swarms of gallants, buzzing like so many indignant wrathful wasps. How could the pope possess the temerity to attack his native city? Had the holy traitor been gone so long that he'd forgotten that this land was the birthplace of warriors as much as it was of artists, bankers, and weavers? Let the pontiff bring on the *Reiters!* Let them do their worst! Florentines weren't the lackluster citizens that the Romans were.

Tommaso guessed all this bravado stemmed in part from the fact that in Pope Clement and any armies he might muster, the young men of the city had at last found an enemy they could fight. During the months of the plague they'd had to stand by, helpless and vulnerable, their youth, courage, and strength useless against *that* deadly but intangible foe.

"The godless Germans? Bah! One good Florentine is worth one hundred of their sorry ilk."

Tommaso recognized the loud voice issuing from the center of a crowd gathered in the shadow of the campanile. Tommaso sidled a little ways into the press of people. By peering over a few shoulders he could see Benevenuto Cellini.

"All one needs is a little height over them—as I did on the balustrades of Sant' Angel and which we have here also in our own stout city walls—and *Reiters* tumble like molting ducks before my musket and artillery. Believe me when I tell you they are nothing to fear."

Tommaso bit his tongue to fight from calling out a retort. Michelangelo's friend, the sculptor Rafaello da Montelupo, had also served as a gunner in the defense of Sant' Angel. The story Rafaello related was very different from Cellini's. Rafaello spoke of weeping men unable to fire on their own houses for fear of killing their families, and so were forced to witness the unimaginable cruelties the *Reiters* perpetrated on their loved ones. Cellini was doing his fellow Florentines no favors by leading them to believe that the Germans posed no danger.

"The Spanish soldiers offer even less of a threat," Cellini continued. "Did I not tell you how easy it was to convince my young Spanish neighbor in Rome to dress up like a maiden and play the part, so womanish is their natural disposition?"

This anecdote was met with gales of laughter by the young men assembled. By now Tommaso thought all of Florence would have tired of the story.

Cellini was dressed in a military outfit apparently of his own design. Its rich ornate brocade and satin were hardly practical for any form of fighting. Cellini leaned against a scion of the Orsini family and draped an arm about the shoulders of one of the young Soderinis. The goldsmith was using the looming conflict to ingratiate himself with the highest echelons of Florentine society.

The Orsini youth decided to follow Cellini's lead. "And besides our strength, valor, and prowess, we have intellect and cunning on our side," he said. "There are enough loyal Florentines in Rome that we'll be apprised of every move Clement might make days before he makes it."

The crowd cheered the logic of this statement.

"Why, just the other day when we visited good Benevenuto here in his *bottega*, did not a letter arrive for him from Giacopino della Barca? Now *there's* a worthy expatriate, who with honeyed tongue has the pope well charmed."

Was it Tommaso's imagination, or did Cellini pale at the aristocratic youth's words?

Orsini slapped Cellini's shoulder. "Surely della Barca sent news to help us. Tell us, good Benevenuto."

Cellini coughed as though something had suddenly caught in his throat. "As you know, della Barca used to be a major designer of patterns for Florence's textile makers," he said. "Alas, all he wrote of on this occasion were artistic matters."

Tommaso grinned. Cellini *was* nervous. The tenor of his voice skittered like a dancing cat.

"No doubt, in future missives, della Barca will have something more substantial to offer our cause." Cellini tried to rally, but looked as though he'd rather be elsewhere. The goldsmith disengaged his purchase on Francesco, the Soderini heir.

"It's all well and good to gather like this, discussing strategy and raising our morale in the public forum," Cellini said. "But as one perhaps more tempered in battle's fire than many of those here, I recommend that we also need to act, to prepare ourselves. Those of you with less experience need to go practice your marksmanship, so that the *Reiters* will be easy targets for you from the city walls. I, with my familiarity of battlements, shall go and tour this quarter's share of those walls."

By the time he finished, Cellini sounded like his usual boastful self, but Tommaso could see he was flustered as he hastily maneuvered his departure.

Tommaso slipped out the edge of the crowd and resumed his way home. What had that been all about? If Giacopino della Barca had the pope's ear, might not information be just as likely to pass through *to* the pope as *from* the pope? Cellini himself stood in Clement's favor. Had della Barca written asking Cellini to spy for Clement? That would explain the goldsmith's sudden anxiety.

The Ruggiero kitchen compound bustled with activity, not all of it directed toward cooking. No one's hands were idle, but all wore stunned looks on their faces. Everyone except Cousin Francesca and Piera. Piera, in fact, was ordering everyone else about like a distaff *Priori*.

"Ah, at last you've arrived. I'd begun to fear you ordered up for some quarter's militia," she said briskly when Tommaso walked in. "You may lack a few months of fourteen, but you're tall enough to appear fifteen or sixteen to some overeager officer. Make yourself useful. You have a choice: You can either help Ottaviano in the women's room or dress the chickens and clean the fish for supper."

The latter tasks were usually assigned to Massolina.

"Why doesn't Massolina dress the chickens?" Tommaso asked.

"Because she's not here. She's gone home to her parents for a while."

"Why?"

"Because she has a wedding to prepare for. Her own."

Tommaso was astonished. "To whom?"

"One of *Ser* Ruggiero's men-at-arms, Enzio."

Tight-lipped Enzio? No wonder everyone looked so stunned. "When? How?" Tommaso was beginning to feel stupid with questions.

"The bans have been posted. They're to be married in three weeks. Don't stand there with your mouth hanging open, Tommaso. Love's signs may be subtle, but they're there for those with eyes to see them."

Tommaso wondered if one of those signs might be a growing belly on Massolina's slender frame. "What is Ottaviano doing in the women's quarters?"

"Converting it into an appropriate chamber for a newly married couple. With Florence threatened, now is not the time for one of the master's most trusted men-at-arms to take up residence away from the palazzo, but there's no space in the main house for a room of their own together. So until the danger is past and other arrangements can be made, this is the best solution."

Where then was Filomena to go? Tommaso's heart froze. He hadn't seen her anywhere in the flurry going on about them. Had she been sold away? "What about the slave girl, Filomena?" he forced himself to say.

"Well, she couldn't stay in the women's quarters during its conversion. And certainly not after the wedding. I moved her in with myself and Francesca over a week ago. She's in there now looking after the children in order to give Francesca time to go bargain for some venison from Leonora. Are we going to continue to stand here talking? Are you going to help with this madness or add to it?" Piera snapped.

There was an edge to Piera's voice besides the impatience of a set-upon overly busy woman. It was the edge of someone close to being cornered into answering questions she didn't want asked.

Tommaso was stunned. Somehow his mother had discovered the truth about Gentile and Filomena.

He tried, too late, to step back from his horror and confusion. "I'll go help Ottaviano," he said and hurried away.

Had Piera taken Filomena in to protect the slave, or did she think Gentile seduced by Filomena? Was Piera Filomena's guardian or gaoler?

Tommaso sidled up to his mother's room. The door was slightly ajar. He peered through the narrow view afforded him.

Filomena sat propped in the middle of the bed, Paolo nestled up to her on one side, Luciana on the other. The slave was singing softly, lulling the children into a nap. She was looking out through the open window, facing somewhat away from Tommaso. But enough of her profile showed that he could see how the fear and tension that had strained her face for so long were gone.

Tommaso pushed himself away from the door and leaned against the hallway door, weak with relief. His mother had chosen to be Filomena's protector.

Amado, an apprentice Gentile had accepted shortly before Tommaso had moved to Il Tribolino's, was applying a coat of whitewash in what had been the women's quarters. Chests, a bench, and a cracked old mirror were pushed together in the middle of the room to clear the walls for painting.

Amado turned and waved when Tommaso entered. Ottaviano looked to see who it was, frowned, then went back to painting. He and Tommaso had been no more than civil to each other since Tommaso had first noticed Ottaviano's interest in Filomena.

"I'm here to help you," Tommaso said.

"There are more brushes in the storeroom. Fetch one for yourself," Ottaviano told him.

Ottaviano may not have welcomed Tommaso's presence, but Amado was happy for his help and company.

"What a surprise to come home to, eh, Tommaso? The whole household is celebrating these forced-march nuptials."

"Is Massolina pregnant? Is that the hurry?" Tommaso asked.

The younger boy laughed and slapped more white on the wall. "Not that anyone can tell. Massolina swears not. But after your mother walked in on her and Enzio and sounded the alarm, there was nothing to be done for decency's sake but call the priest and post the bans. With war pending, the sooner their hands are joined before God the better. Especially considering how well, uh"—Amado averted his eyes downward suggestively—"other parts of them have already joined."

Ottaviano snorted. "A joining almost knocked apart by near blows."

"How so?" asked Tommaso.

Ottaviano didn't look inclined to answer so Amado jumped in. "There was a furious row between the lovers after their exposure," he said. "Massolina professed to be quite wounded. She said she was sure your blessed mother knew of their liaison and had acted the accessory for months by winking and turning her gaze from their embraces, and that then she turned about and betrayed them.

"Enzio, for his part, accused Massolina and your mother of complicity against him to trick him into the loss of his freedom. He went on at great length." Amado shook his head so vigorously paint began to splatter about. "I didn't know that man had so many words in him. That, as much as anything, amazed the household, who had all come running. Even Dr. Ruggiero was struck as dumb as Enzio usually is. I, for one, would have not been so foolish to accuse your sainted mother, had I been in Enzio's shoes."

Tommaso noticed how Amado clenched his thumb intertwined in his fist in a *mano en fica* to ward off evil. Did the servants still fear his mother as a witch?

"At Enzio's accusations Massolina burst into copious tears, asking Enzio if all his protestations of love were, after all, false," Amado continued. "Massolina's grief completely unmanned Enzio, who froze back into his customary silence in shame."

Tommaso realized that some while back in Amado's narrative his jaw had dropped. He rubbed it and closed his mouth. No wonder the whole kitchen seemed in shock. "What did my mother do?"

"That amazing woman just folded her arms and said, 'Listen to how the two of you fight, just like husband and wife. You're already married in spirit, if not in fact. I'll call the priest.'

"So here we are preparing for a wedding. To everyone's great surprise, Enzio and Massolina seem ecstatically happy now that all is settled."

Tommaso's head was spinning. Amado's tale sounded a little like his practical and spirited mother of old, not the wounded creature she'd become. But even in yesteryear Piera had never been wont to meddle in this fashion in the affairs of others.

Why had she done this? Tommaso dipped his brush into the whitewash and began to slap the coat of new beginnings on the wall. He couldn't believe Piera truly cared whether Massolina and Enzio's union was sanctified by the Church. Her actions seemed to serve no purpose but to put the household in an uproar. Except—Tommaso lowered his brush again—that it also emptied out the women's quarters, making it necessary for Piera to take Filomena in. Could all these absurd machinations have been put into motion to discreetly salvage a slave?

Piera worked quickly at the chore Tommaso had rejected—dressing and trussing the chickens. In the last two weeks she had moved back and forth between fear and resolve. To manipulate events in such a crude fashion, where, as if cast in some overplotted *commedia*, she played an acted part, felt slippery and unreal to Piera. She was used to affecting events in her own way. That way might be clandestine and arcane, but it arose from the core of her being and was true.

Still, the results had proved satisfying. She sensed the beginning of a return to balance in her home.

Except for that ghastly look on Tommaso's face.

He knew. He'd known of Filomena's abuse by Gentile. Piera shuddered. How long had he known? She'd assumed he'd absented himself from the family because of the circumstances of his brother and sisters' deaths. But when had he truly begun to avoid his home?

Piera thought back. Not when the children died. Not immediately.

Later. Sometime early last spring. That was when Tommaso had begun acting as though he couldn't bear to be in the same room as his father. Piera whispered a prayer to the Holy Three that balance could indeed be returned to Florence and to her family.

36

First Week of July, 1529

Have you heard?" asked Batista, one of Giuliano Bugiardini's students, as he joined the other boys behind the cathedral. The apprentices often met there before Mass to gamble.

"Heard what, that Salvatore is even more luckless than I when it comes to throwing dice?" asked Giorgio Vasari from where he knelt on the cobblestones.

"No. You should wager against the city, for Florence is more luckless than you. Emperor Charles signed the treaty with the pope to march against us."

That got the other apprentices' attention. "No!" "When?" "Where?"

"The where was in Barcelona. The when was last week, at the end of the month. The news just arrived," Batista said. "My father serves the current *Gonfaloniere*. I'm one of the first to hear."

"What can that bankrupt holy bastard offer the emperor?" asked Salvatore. "He couldn't even ransom Rome."

"The pope proffers items of greater value than mere coinage," Batista replied. "Besides marrying off that monster Alessandro to Charles's natural daughter and declaring them Duke and Duchess of Florence, Clement promises to place the crown of Charlemagne on Charles's head, once the Medici are returned to power here."

"That is all well and good, but besieging troops don't dine on crowns and promises. They must be fed and paid," Michelangelo's youngest apprentice Baccio said naively.

The other boys stared at him.

"What? Is my reasoning faulty?"

"How do you think they'll be paid?" Salvatore snapped. "They'll be let loose on Florence and take their wages and victuals out of our hides, just as they did to the poor citizens of Rome when *that* siege was broken."

Baccio turned pale.

"Ho! Here come Paulino and Cencio. By the length of their faces they must have heard the news too," said Donato, a student of Francesco Lippi. "Paulino, Cencio, are you melancholy at the news of the pope's treachery?"

Cellini's two apprentices looked at each other. "Yes. That and our abandonment by our master," said Cencio. "When he left for Rome he told us he needed to attend to business at his studio there and would soon return. Today his friend Piero Landi arrived to pack up the furniture at Master's house and from his studio return gems and gold to the patrons of unfinished commissions.

"In this fashion, we discover that all those letters our master received from Giacopino della Barca conveyed threats and promises directly from the pope. The pontiff swore if our master wished to retain a head on his shoulders, let alone the favor of papal commissions, he must hie himself away from Florence before the emperor's forces move on the city."

"We came today not so much to gamble or pray, but to see if there might be work for us with your master, Donato," said Paulino. "Or perhaps your good *Ser* Piloto, Lapo."

"I'll speak to Piloto," said Lapo. "Signor Buonarotti is always passing along extra commissions to him. There's a good likelihood you could join us in our *bottega.*"

The other boys were subdued by this travesty of contracted apprentices left to fend for themselves.

"Cellini is not the only citizen running to Rome," Batista tried to comfort the two boys. "According to my father, even Francesco Gucciardini left precipitously."

Giorgio Vasari rolled the dice. He cursed. As usual, fortune failed to favor him. "Gucciardini might as well flee. He's such a favorite of Clement's that, highborn statesman as he may be, he'd surely land in prison if he stayed."

The cathedral bells started chiming. Giorgio stood up. He brushed his hands clean against his surcoat and pocketed the dice. "Bless the Almighty. He's saving me from my own poor luck by calling me to Mass."

Tommaso had stood by silently during the entire exchange. He lingered behind the other boys as they filed around the corner of the cathedral to its massive front doors.

"Ascancio." He tugged on Michelangelo's older apprentice's sleeve. "What Cencio said about Cellini and the pope's threats . . . What will happen to Michelangelo? If Clement values Cellini even a little, it could be said that he esteems Michelangelo as a pearl beyond price. Has the pope pressured your master to leave Florence?"

Ascancio shook his head. "Not to my knowledge. Unlike Cellini, Michelangelo considers discretion a point of honor." Ascancio looked at Tommaso pointedly. "As well you know."

Tommaso blushed.

"I understand and share your concern, Tommaso. Michelangelo already lent a thousand crowns to the republic toward protection for the city. I've heard he may be appointed to the war council of Nine of the Militia. Add to that the fortification work he's accomplished as the Commissary General. Should Clement triumph, I fear for my master's life. The world knows of the pope's vengeful obsession with those he feels have betrayed him."

Every step toward the front of the cathedral dragged at Tommaso's heels. How could his friends and fellow students genuflect at the altar where Christ's representative on Earth actively conspired to destroy his own native city and those within it?

Tommaso lagged farther and farther behind. Ascancio looked back at him. The older apprentice recognized his mood and smiled in sympathy. Ascancio turned out of sight around the corner of the building. Tommaso raced away from the cathedral.

Back at the *bottega*, Tommaso risked encountering Il Tribolino. Tommaso liked his teacher, but the man was a master apologist. Tommaso couldn't bear to hear what excuses for Clement Il Tribolino might strain to come up with.

Where did Tommaso then have to run but to that place his whole life he'd called home? The Ruggiero kitchen compound.

Only his mother was in the main workroom, concocting one of her herbal infusions in a kettle boiling in the fireplace. She smiled at Tommaso. "What a pleasant surprise. It's not your afternoon off. Is all well at Il Tribolino's?"

"Yes. There is nothing amiss at the *bottega*," Tommaso assured her. She must not have heard yet.

"Good. Then sit and have a cup of tea with me."

"Mother, grave news has arrived from Rome."

Piera ladled the tea into two mugs. She handed one to Tommaso. "Of late, news from Rome is never anything but grave. Moments of peace and quiet are rare in this kitchen. Your father has been called to the mansion. Everyone else is away at Mass. Surely your tidings can wait till their return. Enjoy the stillness with me."

Tommaso admitted to himself he didn't relish having to break the news twice. He made himself drink the tea and tried to relax.

The tea tasted more peculiar than unpleasant. To Tommaso's palate, accustomed to even the simplest fare made savory, the weird overlap of flavors jangled.

How could he possibly sit still? For months the city had waited. Now what Florence feared most was come to pass. Tommaso closed his eyes, trying to find a place in that darkness where he could calm himself.

Instead, he remembered hiding in the chapel with Caterina and Ginevra, forced to listen to Lazaro the messenger's account of the sack of Rome.

"Tommaso? Have you fallen asleep?" Piera's voice sounded far away.

"No, I'm not asleep." His answer came from a place equally distant. Perhaps he *was* drowsing off. Pictures filled his mind.

"Can you tell me what you see?"

Tommaso could barely hear his mother. He saw laid out before him the fortifications Michelangelo planned. They erected themselves piece by piece: interwoven bastions of oak and chestnut, bricks of tow and dung.

He saw each quarter of Florence organized into watches, artillery hauled up to the walls, river entrances secured. Florence secured itself as tight as a wine cask. But outside there were long, dark shadows watching the city.

The enemy arrived. Thousands of troops crawled over the hills like an infestation of ants. Cannon shot pounded Florence. Here and there parts of the city walls blew inward but never crumbled enough for the foe to breach them.

Tommaso heard wailing in the streets. Florence might stand strong and unbowed, but the lives it sheltered were not so sturdy. Faces grew thin and hungry. Bodies lay half-buried under rubble. Tommaso saw it all. In the wreckage were faces he knew. He moaned. Il Tribolino's newest apprentice, Simone, lay on a battlement with a bullet in his chest. One of his Befanini cousins, Onofrio, limped down the street on crutches, one leg gone. And there, under a collapsed stone casement, a glimpse of long black hair and a bruised and broken bare arm. Was it his mother? Tommaso drew closer. Dried stream beds of caked blood ran from the woman's nose and open, unblinking eyes. Bright blue eyes. Filomena.

"What is this? Does Master Tribolino work you so hard that you need to flee here for rest?" Cousin Francesca swept into the kitchen, leading an entourage of children, apprentices, Massolina, and journeyman Ottaviano back from Mass. And Filomena, very much alive.

Tommaso's heart pounded with relief.

"Tommaso came by to bring us news. I made him wait till your return," Piera said, swiftly clearing away the two cups. Tommaso noticed that though his was empty, she'd barely sipped at hers.

"Well, what is it?" Massolina said smiling, rubbing her growing belly.

They don't know, Tommaso realized. News of Clement's treaty would have spread quickly as the plague in the great cathedral. But the Ruggiero household staff attended Mass at a small church just down the street.

"The pope and emperor have joined forces to march on Florence. They clasped hands in Barcelona."

Just as with the apprentices earlier, the kitchen staff let loose a barrage of questions. Gentile returned from the mansion to a scene of tumult.

The master carver held up his hands. "Quiet! Quiet! I see you've heard.

Calm yourselves. Florence has been readying itself for months and will continue to do so. I have spoken with Master Ruggiero. The firmament has assured him Florence will not share Rome's fate."

Gentile's words acted like a balm. If *Ser* Ruggiero saw it in the stars, then the servants believed surely it was so. But Tommaso saw the calculated look in his father's eyes.

Gentile sat down on a stool. "Attend to me, all of you. There are other matters at hand." He spread out a piece of paper on his lap. "The master and I received a letter from the country estate. This spring my father managed to find again sufficient laborers for the farm. The crops are doing well. He expects a fine harvest."

Gentile refolded the letter, then unfolded it again. "However, he still lacks skilled and knowledgeable help. If we are besieged here, I don't need to tell all of you the importance of laying in a goodly store of supplies. My father is feeling the burden of his years. He begged *Ser* Ruggiero to send him someone who could manage the property with him.

"At the same time, *Ser* Ruggiero foresees that with the impending crisis there will be less need of a full staff here. To that end we agreed—if it pleases you, Ottaviano—that your journeyman status is completed. You are invited to become my father's partner and eventual successor. How say you?"

Ottaviano stood blinking, caught completely unawares.

"This position means you'll have less chance to practice fine cuisine," Gentile continued. "Balancing that loss, you'll have greater responsibilities. And the Ruggieros take holidays in the country several times a year, so you'll have opportunity to maintain your cooking skills then. If you accept, you need to leave within the week."

"I accept," said Ottaviano, still looking stunned.

Tommaso wondered what the journeyman was thinking. That with Gentile hale and hearty, he might never rise any higher here? That with a siege imminent, he might be safer in an isolated farmstead?

"Massolina, be kind enough to fetch a bottle of wine and some glasses. Ottaviano's new position must be celebrated," Gentile said.

While the rest of the kitchen crew gathered around to congratulate the journeyman, Tommaso drew his mother and father aside.

"If Master Ruggiero sees the need to reduce the staff here and increase it at his country property, I have a further suggestion," he said.

"There's no one else," said Gentile. "At least not in my jurisdiction. Now that Massolina is wed to Enzio and with child, nothing could make her leave. The apprentices and Francesca call Florence home. There's nowhere else for them to go."

Tommaso knew that nothing, not even death itself, could induce his father to send a member of their own little family away again.

"Filomena," said Tommaso. "The farm needs a woman's touch."

"Filomena is a slave," Piera reminded her son. "It would be cruel to dispatch one so powerless and helpless to dwell in a place filled with nothing but men." Her glance at Gentile was pointed.

Gentile possessed the grace to look away.

"She could be freed. She *should* be freed," Tommaso insisted. "Surely that can be arranged." He tried not to glare at his father.

"And if she's to be out of the Ruggieros' direct protection, she must have the power to protect herself," Piera chimed in. "I'm sure if they free her so early in her life that she'll remain a loyal servant."

"Let me propose the idea to *Ser* Ruggiero," Gentile mumbled. "Since he'd not be losing an able worker but rather just placing her elsewhere within his domain, I doubt he'll object." Tommaso saw the relief in his father's eyes that the subject of his shame might so easily depart the scene.

Within a week, Ottaviano and Filomena left for the countryside.

The imperial forces arrived in early September. Tommaso and Tribolino's other apprentices clambered to the guard posts along the city wall with most of the rest of Florence to watch the foreign troops surround the city.

Neither side fired on the other. No action seemed imminent. Philiberte of Orange, the imperial commander, was trying to negotiate a surrender, though he knew Florence would reject it at this early date. The process gave him time to situate his troops around the valley and send scouts to ascertain Florence's exact state of preparedness.

The current lack of scrimmage didn't stop the army from shouting up at the walls. "Get your brocades out for us, Florence. We're coming to measure them with our pikestaffs." The citizenry responded by hurling down catcalls of their own.

"Which are the *Reiters?*" Tommaso asked.

Bertino studied the encampment being raised. Each cluster of tents sported its own distinctive flag. "I think there, and over there," he pointed. "Most of the troops are Spanish."

Tommaso felt relieved. Spaniard might be severe, dour people, but they were civilized.

"How many are there?" asked little Simone. The boy came from the small village of Gavinina near Pistoia. Florence alone was almost more than he could cope with; the drama of the siege overwhelmed him.

"Between thirty and forty thousand, I would guess," said Salvatore.

"How can we withstand so many?" Simone wailed.

Salvatore laughed. "Easily. The city is well prepared. We've stockpiled munitions, established supply lines, organized watches along the walls, set up commanders at garrisons outside the valley to harass the enemy at their rear. Florence is sealed as tight as any virgin. Let them pound away at her. They shall not lay her down."

"But first they'll try coercing her into submission with a show of force. Only when that proves unsuccessful will they assault her," Bertino predicted.

Bertino was right. The imperial forces didn't start shelling the city walls until several days later.

At night Tommaso tossed and turned, dreaming over and over his vision of Florence under siege. He saw again little Simone lying dead. (Each morning when he woke he could not make himself look at the young boy.) He saw again Onofrio struggling with a stub of a limb. And he saw again the collapsed stone casement. But no lovely young girl with blue eyes lay crushed beneath it. No one lay under it at all.

37

❧

Not long after the siege started, Tommaso and Old Taddeo arrived at the Murate one afternoon with their cartload of supplies to find Caterina waiting for them in the kitchen. Tommaso was instantly alarmed. Caterina's face was drawn and pale, her eyes as enormous as any owl's.

The words she greeted him with didn't allay his fears. "Tommaso, I must speak with you on a matter of grave import. Please meet me and Sister Anna Maria in the garden when you're done with your work here."

Tommaso rushed through unloading the cart. Caterina and her chaperone waited for him in the garden near the river's edge, pacing with tight, agitated steps. They weren't far from where Michelangelo had created the magnificent snow sculpture.

At a gesture from Caterina, Sister Anna Maria moved away a discreet distance. Caterina clasped both of Tommaso's hands in her own. In spite of the drowsy warmth of the garden her hands were cold. "One who is a friend to both of us is in grave danger. I need your help in warning him."

"I'll aid you in any way I can," Tommaso said. "Who is this friend?"

"Michelangelo Buonarotti. His integrity, his life, his very soul are in jeopardy."

Tommaso froze with dread. "Who threatens him? In what fashion? How do you know?"

Caterina answered only his last question. "I have seen—" she began, then faltered. "I have seen," she began more strongly, "information that could be construed as a plot against Michelangelo. Please tell him to flee the city immediately. In two nights the new moon arrives in the sky. Its light, as it shines down, should not find him in Florence."

"But Michelangelo is the Commissary General of Florence, in charge of the city's fortifications. Besides that, he is one of the Nine of the Militia. He would never turn his back on those responsibilities."

"Tell him he can and shall return to Florence," Caterina said. "But you must persuade him to depart for the present. If he does not, he won't survive to discharge his duties. Tell him we'll arrange to send him a signal when his safety is once again assured."

Since it was his free afternoon, Tommaso had a certain leeway in time before he returned to Il Tribolino's. He made an excuse to his parents about needing to confer with the commander of the section of city wall he'd been assigned to—it was his turn to assist on the watch that evening. Then he ran all the way to Michelangelo's.

He racked his brains for a way to convey Caterina's dire yet obscure message in a way his lover would take seriously. His mind kept filling with the image of Caterina in the garden: her features blanched with anxiety, her hands alternately twisting at the pendant chain hanging from her neck or pressing against her breast.

At Michelangelo's *bottega* all was hustle, bustle and controlled chaos.

"Ho there, Tommaso," called Ascancio. "Are your hands so idle on your day off that you've come to help us, or are you like everyone else and just bring us news of more work?"

Tommaso glanced about the studio. None of the sacristy sculptures looked any more finished than the last time he'd stopped by—not the female figures of Dawn or Night, or the statues of Lorenzo the Magnificent or his doomed brother Giuliano. Not the capitals or cornices the apprentices worked on. And probably not the figures of Day and Dusk, though, since they were draped over, he couldn't tell.

Instead, everyone labored on carving huge wooden joints and hinges, no doubt part of the protective mechanisms being engineered into place at San Miniato.

"Forgive me, Ascancio. I *do* bring urgent news of the siege, though whether you will suffer more or less work because of it is not my place to say. I must, however, convey it to your master immediately."

Looking skeptical, Ascancio waved Tommaso toward the back of the studio.

"Approach him at your own risk. He's not in the best of tempers."

Michelangelo was embroiled in an argument with a drayage master regarding the delivery of timbers to the fortification sites. He looked up as Tommaso approached, obviously peeved at the interruption.

Tommaso took off his apprentice's cap and stepped back several paces to wait until the sculptor finished. He sensed that he might at last experience the sting of Michelangelo's infamous irascibility.

When the drayage master at last stomped off, Michelangelo turned to—or rather, from the expression on his face—turned *on* Tommaso; Tommaso rushed to speak first.

"I bring you an urgent message from Duchessina Caterina Romola de' Medici," he blurted.

That deflected Michelangelo. Tommaso delivered Caterina's message almost word for word.

Michelangelo's mood changed from irate to thoughtful and troubled. "How can I leave now? Once before, I fled Florence. It was when the *Duchessina's* grandfather Piero was exiled. The city branded me a coward for a while, though, afterward, all admitted my actions were wise. I was young then and my flight made no difference to Florence's fate. Now, if I left, I would leave my city helpless."

"But Caterina promises that if you stay you shall be lost forever," Tommaso said. "How would that benefit Florence? If you leave she vows you shall shortly return once the danger is past. Then you can take up your work defending the city again."

Michelangelo still wasn't persuaded. "I could better make a decision if I knew what threatened me, and how the *Duchessina* discovered this danger."

Tommaso shook his head. "She would not say. But consider this: Caterina is not as isolated in the Murate as one might think. Besides her aunt and Strozzi cousins; the Ruggieros, who frequently visit her; other diverse relatives who stop by to see her out of concern for her welfare; she is also privy to any news that passes among the nuns there. Most of the sisters of the Murate come from influential and powerful families. Just because they've chosen to lead the cloistered life doesn't mean they aren't still well informed. With those resources, Caterina may know more about the city's very heartbeat than even the *Signoria.*"

Michelangelo still looked unconvinced.

"If you could only have seen her face, as I did!" Tommaso pleaded. He was beginning to feel desperate. "I curse myself that I so poorly convey her concern for you! If you choose not to leave I'll run away from Il Tribolino's and become a vagabond in the nearby streets so that I may guard you day and night."

Michelangelo looked both amused and alarmed at Tommaso's outburst. "Calm yourself. I believe you and the *Duchessina* that I am in some way imperiled."

"It's not for your own sake but Florence's that you must depart." Tommaso didn't know why he said that. The words came from nowhere in particular, but seemed exactly right as they poured from his mouth.

Michelangelo looked at him sharply. "What did you say?"

Tommaso repeated himself, more hesitantly this time.

"All right. You've convinced me. I'll leave. Go help my apprentices with their work while I decide what to do."

The next night Tommaso crept away from Il Tribolino's *bottega* to accompany Michelangelo, Antonio Mini, and the goldsmith Piloto. They walked to the hill of San Miniato on the pretense of inspecting the strengthening of the fortifications there. Each of the three men possessed a quantity of gold crowns sewn into their clothing. Michelangelo and Piloto had made sure their apprentices were cared for and employed in their absence.

Michelangelo led them to a secret exit in the balustrade. It was one of the many ways that the Florentine commanders were able to leave and return with supplies.

While Piloto and Antonio Mini slid out Michelangelo showed Tommaso how to bar the way behind them.

"Tell the *Duchessina* we'll first make our way to Ferrara, then on to Venice, so she'll know where to send word when it's safe to return." The sculptor looked over his shoulder. The two other men were gone. Michelangelo took Tommaso in his arms and pressed his lips to Tommaso's. Tommaso thought he might drown in that kiss.

Michelangelo released him and smiled wryly. "You're almost as tall as I am. I pray the *Duchessina* recalls me before you grow to loom over me."

"I'm sure I won't have the heart to grow an enth until your return," Tommaso whispered.

"Do you know what finally convinced me to go?"

Tommaso shook his head.

"Those last words you said, about departing for Florence's sake. When I fled that time before, so many years ago, I was warned with those very same words.

"I'd gone to the de' Medici mansion to see if I could aid the beleaguered Piero in some fashion. A woman servant apprised me as soon as I stepped through the door. It was as if she knew I was coming and waited for me, though that was impossible. I'd come on a sudden impulse without telling anyone.

"There was something about her manner that, young and impressionable as I was, put the fear of God in me. To this day I don't know what I dreaded more—her warning or the woman herself.

"After all these years I'd forgotten the incident. But when you spoke, I felt as though I'd been hurled back in time. Her words were exactly the same and her hair was the same amazing hue as yours. It framed her face like a saint heralding the apocalypse."

It was late by the time Tommaso returned to Il Tribolino's *bottega*. All was dark in the studio, except for a wedge of light shining from under the office door. With the entire citizenry working double duty to defend the city, Tommaso wasn't surprised that Il Tribolino lingered longer than his wont to catch up on his paperwork.

Tommaso crept inward. He prayed he wouldn't disturb the other apprentices or Elissa Pecorino.

Melchiora pounced at his feet the moment he entered the kitchen's confines. She leapt back as if astounded to find shoes rather than mice under her paws.

"Shhh, my little lioness. Don't wake anyone," Tommaso scolded her in a whisper.

Melchiora laid back her ears at the reprimand, bunched her hindquarters beneath her, and commenced racing about as if Satan himself were after her.

Tommaso stifled a laugh. After a day of worry and tension, the cat's fey outburst charmed him.

Out of the corner of his eye and through the portal from kitchen to studio, Tommaso observed the office door opening. Il Tribolino, a bulky shadow bearing an oil lamp, left his office.

Melchiora also noticed Il Tribolino's exit. Like a demon possessed she dashed straight for the sculptor. Tommaso had only time to cry out "Master! Watch out!" before the cat collided with Il Tribolino's legs.

The cat sailed in one direction and everything that Il Tribolino carried—sheaths of paper and the bulky box he'd been toting between house and studio for months—went flying in the other. Miraculously, Il Tribolino bandied the oil lamp like an expert *jongleur* till it came to rest in his trembling hands.

"I'm so sorry, Master," Tommaso said, hurrying over. "I think that cat is infected with—" and he fell silent at what the lamp's glare revealed.

Il Tribolino's papers lay scattered like autumn-blown leaves. The box sat open and revealed in one piece where it had fallen.

Il Tribolino's clandestine project was a miniature model of the city of Florence, sculpted in cork. The piece was a miracle of intricacy. For a brief instant Tommaso's artist's eye admired its meticulous beauty. Then he took in the full detailing. Besides the delineation of every street and building, each siege command post, each balustrade, and every item of Florence's defense was rendered minutely. Even the secret exit by which he had conducted Michelangelo to safety that very night.

"Who commissioned this maquette?" Tommaso breathed more than asked. "Tell me that it's for the *Signoria* or the Militia of Nine."

Il Tribolino said nothing. He refused to meet Tommaso's eye. Tommaso knew therein lay his answer. Just as Tommaso had helped smuggle Michelangelo out of Florence, so Il Tribolino was prepared to smuggle this model out, now that Florence's defenses were in place and almost fully implemented.

"Clement. You were going to deliver this to the pope, weren't you?" Il Tribolino turned his head away.

Tommaso was aghast. The maquette embodied, in every exquisite excruciating detail, Michelangelo's master plan for the city. Only Michelangelo, the Militia of Nine, and Michelangelo's closest friends knew of those designs in their totality. If the enemy laid hands on this model, Florence would be lost. And it would appear that Michelangelo, by design or indiscretion, was the author of the city's destruction. What was it that Caterina had said? "His integrity, his life, his very soul are in jeopardy."

Tommaso lifted up the model from the floor. "Michelangelo calls you friend. Is this how you serve him? By betraying him to Florence's enemies?"

"No! No!" Il Tribolino put up both his hands in protest. "No matter what the outcome, I vow Michelangelo will come to no blame. On the lives of my wife and children, I swear it!"

"There is only one way to assure your promises." Filled with cold rage, Tommaso raised the model higher, then smashed it to the ground. He picked up a mallet and pounded what was left into unrecognizable chunks of cork.

Il Tribolino slumped against a workbench, his head in his hands, weeping. Tommaso swept the remains of the model into a bucket and fed it into the foundry fire. The smell of burning cork made him gag.

38

❧

While Il Tribolino spent a sleepless night tossing and turning wondering if Tommaso would report him to the *Signoria*, and Tommaso spent a sleepless night wondering if he would be driven from the *bottega* in the morning, Caterina sat awake and tranquil in her cell at the Murate.

She took off the pendant and held it so the light from her single small lamp fell into the gem's blood-red depths. She peered at the stone, just as she had a hundred times before. But no matter what visions greeted her eyes, Caterina never found the one image she hoped for.

She couldn't remember Ginevra's face whole-cloth anymore. She had to rebuild it feature by feature in her mind. First, always, the dove-shaped gray eyes. Next, the tender mouth with its gentle smile. Then, the finely sculpted nose, velvet complexion, and smooth doe-colored hair.

Caterina sighed and put the chain back on over her head. The apparitions she glimpsed in the stone always clarified when the pendant rested against her skin again.

Caterina closed her eyes and saw the inner sanctuary of Michelangelo's *bottega*—the room that served as both the sculptor's office and sleeping quarters. It was empty. Tommaso had succeeded in persuading Michelangelo to leave the city. Caterina allowed her lungs to fill and then slowly, luxuriously, empty in relief.

He is safe and Florence, therefore, also that much safer. Ginevra's voice echoed in Caterina's mind.

Because he is part of Florence, Caterina thought in response.

Part of its very underpinnings and soul, Ginevra confirmed. *He serves as a balance point. If he were corrupted or destroyed, the city could fall.*

Caterina giggled. *They'll be vexed when they come for him tomorrow and find him gone.*

Don't laugh, Caterina. They'll search for the reason why. If they discover the cause they'll move against you.

The thought sobered Caterina. *I miss you, my gossip,* she thought wistfully.

The gentle smile Caterina had futilely sought to glimpse in the gem warmed its way from the stone to wrap about her heart. *How can you miss me? I am always with you.*

39

❧

The following night a new sliver of moon sliced its sharp way into the autumn sky as it rose. Its light entered the single window that illuminated Michelangelo's sleeping quarters—a window as narrow as the moon itself.

With such a thin moon and such a thin window, what little radiance able to enter laid only the barest sheen upon Michelangelo's simple cot, the crates Tommaso had stood on to model, a cabinet to hold sketches, and a chest for Michelangelo's clothes. It barely glinted off the sharp angles and grotesque curves of shadowy shapes growing out of the corner of the room.

The creatures, if creatures they could be called, detached themselves from the walls and flooring. When they unfolded themselves they half filled the room. Though they possessed no eyes, they commenced to search the space, sliding indescribable limbs about the place, sniffing the air with nostril-less members that might have been noses.

Their prey had flown.

They began to quiver, causing the air to vibrate with a low grinding growl. At the opposite end of the *bottega,* in the apprentices' quarter, young Baccio cried out in his sleep.

The creatures compressed themselves back into the shadows. They settled in to wait. They would emerge the next night and the night after, until the moon ran its course and began to fade again.

Michelangelo was a foundation stone. Their task was to dislodge him if they could. Only one other time, long ago, had all the precise elements necessary to seize him aligned. The hour, the place, the temper of the air, the weakness of the city, the disposition of things and people—all must be just so. They might never have the chance again.

40

Tommaso was astounded by Giorgio Vasari's concentration. The two youths sat on a knoll high on a hillside overlooking Florence. Below them sprawled the enemy encampment.

Tents were pitched everywhere, like a carpeting fall of sharp-pointed white flowers blooming furiously under the blue autumn skies. Cannons fired from enemy positions close to the city and from the city walls back at the enemy. Distance gave lie to the damage being inflicted: From here it appeared a toy battle of smoke puffs. More ominously, just beneath them—so closely Tommaso could make out the brass of their belt buckles—a regiment conducted target practice with their arquebuses. Tommaso felt barely hidden by the sparse brush he and Giorgio crouched behind. Yet, through it all, Giorgio calmly sketched the entire scene.

Tommaso thought the other apprentice quite mad. Yet he had to admire Giorgio's simpleminded dedication to his art. Tommaso could not sit still. Since he and Giorgo had slipped away from Florence with Francesco Ferrucci and his men the night before, Tommaso had hardly been able to contain himself.

"Tommaso, stop fidgeting about," Giorgio whispered. "I'm keeping adequate watch here. Why don't you go look out for the wagon?"

Tommaso crept over the edge of the rise to the other side of the knoll, where a rough track ran down from the mountains. The position of the sun in the sky told him it was already past noon.

The sun moved very little, but it seemed as though hours had passed when at last Tommaso glimpsed a film of dust rising through the pass. A moment later he heard the clattering sounds of an ox-drawn cart. Tommaso slithered back to Giorgio.

"I hear them approaching. Come, it's time."

Giorgio folded his sketch and tucked it into his workman's smock. Beneath his heel he ground what little was left of the stub of charcoal he'd used.

Tommaso started to rush down the hillside. Giorgio pulled him back. "Wait. It's likely it's our men, but we'd be foolish to show ourselves before we're certain."

A cart drawn by two sweat-stained oxen lumbered into sight. Brushwood was piled high in the back of the cart. Two men in woodcutters' garb sat on the buckboard. A third man helped lead the oxen on foot. A man riding a donkey brought up the rear.

The wiry weather-beaten man leading the oxen could only be one person. "It's them," Tommaso said. He ran to meet the cart.

"Ah, here are our assistants." The donkey rider trotted up. "I believe you know these youths, messers. They were most anxious to volunteer for this mission."

"Oh, yes. I recognize those ruffians," Piloto called from where he sat next to Antonio Mini on the cart seat.

"Good. I'll be brief. My men await me. The boys here know the route downward and where you'll be stopping. I doubt you'll be questioned. With the distracting raid my men and I intend to provide on the opposite side of the valley the troops below will have more pressing matters to concern themselves with than scrutinizing you.

"You know the rest of the plan. When you arrive at the entry point, our munitions officers commanding that section of city wall know to look out for you. They'll direct the attention of enemy sentries away from you with a covering fusillade. Piloto, since you speak Spanish, you are the chief merchant here, but don't speak unless you need to. The rest of you say nothing. Or if you have to, just say '*Sí, sí, sí*' in the most bored, put-upon fashion you can muster. In that wise you'll appear the epitome of long-suffering laborers."

"*Ser* Ferrucci, we owe you a debt of gratitude," said Michelangelo from where he stood by the oxen.

The man on the donkey flashed a brilliant smile. "Which you'll repay me by repairing the havoc visited on San Miniato in your absence. The tower there has been our most effective ordnance post, inflicting much damage on the enemy. Which is why they've worked so hard to destroy it."

"I already know how I'll mend it," Michelangelo promised.

"Then I bid you farewell. I regret that neither I nor one of my men can accompany you, but we need all hands for our raid." Francesco Ferrucci slapped the reins against his donkey's neck and turned the beast back up the mountain road. "For which I must exchange my steed for one swifter, if not wiser, than this one."

The cart wound its leisurely way down the valley. It stopped at the kitchen of each enemy encampment on its route. Antonio Mini and the two apprentices unloaded bundles of brushwood while Piloto played the grand master of the enterprise and Michelangelo continued leading the oxen. Tommaso couldn't help but try to analyze the smells drifting from the camp pots. The kinds and balances of spices the Spaniards used differed from those he was accustomed to.

"Ho! Your boy there looks hungry," the cook at one campsite shouted. Spanish is close enough to Italian that Tommaso could make out the man's meaning.

"*Sí, sí,*" Michelangelo replied, the very picture of boredom.

All went well until they'd made their way halfway down. They were unloading wood before a battery of camp ovens when Tommaso noticed an almost shapeless, dark-cowled figure lingering nearby. Tommaso was at first surprised at the unusual raven color of the man's apparel, then he shrugged. *Spanish monks might wear black instead of brown robes,* he thought. *But like clergy everywhere, though their souls may linger near the church, their bellies can always be found close by the kitchen, their sniffing noses practically buried in the soup pots.*

The monk did appear to be sniffing, though his face was so sunk in the copious cowling that Tommaso couldn't see his nose.

But the more Tommaso watched, the more he realized the friar wasn't whiffing about in the direction of the wafting aroma of the cooking food. Rather, he appeared to be casting for a scent.

Then Tommaso realized he was blind. *He's looking for something. This is the only way he can find it. And he's lame too,* Tommaso observed, watching the figure lurch about with such a strange gait that it hardly looked human.

How could the cooks and scullions and nearby soldiers let their chaplain wander about helplessly in such a fashion? No one seemed to notice the monk, as if they too suffered from some sort of deficiency of vision. Tommaso watched as a burly man laboring under a side of beef almost overran the stumbling figure, yet didn't even break his stride.

Tommaso took several steps forward, ready to reach out a hand in case the monk fell. One corner of his mind shouted at him not to risk attracting attention. *Surely even a woodcutter's assistant would help a holy man,* he told himself.

The monk swung in his direction. Tommaso could still see no face in the depths of the cowling. He was seized by a sudden strange notion. *It's looking for Michelangelo. It's so close and knows it, yet can't see him.* Tommaso's hand dropped to his side. He held perfectly still, not daring to breathe. The eerie figure cast about for a moment, then moved on.

"Tommaso, why are you standing there in a daydream?" Giorgio hissed under his breath. "I can't unload this brushwood by myself."

Tommaso shook himself and turned to Giorgio. What sort of delusion had he suffered? "It was that monk, the blind monk," he whispered back, pointing.

"What monk? I see no monk."

Tommaso looked over his shoulder. The monk was disappearing into the darkness of a tent shadow—not rounding the corner of the tent, but melting down and into the angular black shape. Tommaso leaned heavily against the wood cart and wiped a hand across his sweating brow. "Pass me some water, Giorgio. I think I've toiled overly long in this sun."

The little group reached the bottom of the valley shortly after dark. The air had mercifully turned chilly. The cook at the last kitchen scolded them for their lateness: Didn't they know troops were waiting to eat and the kitchen had almost run out of fuel?

The faux firewood mongers led their empty cart and oxen out past troops crowding in to dine and headed toward the stockade, as if to make camp there overnight before returning over the hills to cut more firewood in the morning.

They turned off abruptly and rounded the edge of the palisade. The route to the city gate lay deep in shadow. As they approached it, a burst of cannon fire thundered overhead, lighting up the opposite quadrant of the sky. For a brief instant, enough light cast into the blackness before them that Tommaso saw that no strange shapes lay waiting for them there. His heart slowly stopped its painful pounding. Tommaso was sure no one noticed them slip in through city gates opened barely wide enough to drive the cart through.

As soon as the gates closed behind them a gang of men leapt into the back of the cart. To Tommaso's amazement, they started yanking up its floorboards. Beneath the false bottom lay boxes of rifle shot, small casks of gunpowder, and jars of potted meat.

Michelangelo chuckled at the expression on Tommaso's face. "Do you think Francesco Ferrucci would risk so much to only smuggle a simple errant sculptor back into the city? Besides what you see here, think of the florins he earned today from his kitchen fuel concession. The profit from that buys the very ammunition Florence fires down on its enemies."

All five artists—masters and apprentices—returned to Michelangelo's *bottega* to celebrate their safe return. Tommaso noticed the way Giorgio Vasari pulled out his battle landscape sketch and studied it, in the vain hope Michelangelo would notice it and him. But Michelangelo was too busy greeting the young apprentices he'd left behind.

Then the sculptor went into his private quarters to clean up and fetch fresh clothing. When he came out he wore a puzzled expression on his face.

"What is it, Master?" Antonio Mini asked.

"Nothing, I think. Ascancio, did anyone enter my room while I was gone?"

Ascancio shook his head vehemently. "No. It has remained locked since you left. Why?"

"There's a faint, peculiar smell in there, as if something lingered for a while and then left." Michelangelo shrugged his shoulders. "No matter. Perhaps mildew is settling in. We'll fumigate the place."

He hoisted a wine bottle. "Drink and eat well tonight, but not to excess. We rise early in the morn to repair the tower of San Miniato."

41

June 1530

Tommaso stumbled back to the *bottega* after another long night on the walls assisting the bombardiers. His eyes felt as gritty as if cobblestone dust had worked its way behind their lids. His stomach grumbled, but he was too tired to hunger. As she had for the last eight months, Elissa Pecorino would greet him with food and force him to eat. He always ate quickly to please her, because, once finished, she released him to his one true desire: to fall into the big apprentices' bed and experience blessed black nothingness for a few, too-brief hours.

For months he had feared sleeping. Slumber cruelly deprived rather than provided him with rest. Dreams tormented him with all-too-possible futures.

Then, three weeks ago, young Simone caught a round of shot as he worked beside Tommaso on the balustrades. He died at Tommaso's feet before Tommaso could stoop to hold and comfort him. After that Tommaso never saw the boy in his dreams again and finally found solace in sleep.

But when he mounted the battlements now to help with the artillery, every time a cannon flared he glimpsed an illusion of a face whiter than bone, its open mouth filling with blood so dark a red it could pass for black, and all of that only a frivolous decoration topping the gaping spurting ruin of Simone's chest. Tommaso shuddered, remembering.

"Mice. Juicy, plump, freshly killed mice." A ragged man dangled his wares at Tommaso. The sad little creatures dangled by their tails from a long stick. "Delicious delicacies. Savory in stews, pleasing in pies."

The poor already suffered from food shortages. Meat, especially, was in short supply. Staples like spelt, broad beans, and dried figs were sure to follow next. The provisions patrols found it increasingly difficult to make their way in and out of Florence. Soon more than the indigent would feel hunger's pinch.

Looking at the mouse vendor, Tommaso supposed that dusty and gaunt with fatigue as he was, he must seem a promising customer to the fellow. The man would be better off eating his own wares. The pauper's skin stretched skull tight across his face. His teeth-baring grin, meant to entice, discomfitted Tommaso. Tommaso waved him away.

The man shrugged off Tommaso's declination and turned to accost three men turning into the street from a doorway up ahead.

He was doomed to failure. Tommaso recognized one of the men as the *buffon* who entertained the *Priori* at the Palazzo de la Signoria. The jester performed at many of the city's festivities. Another of the men sported the green livery of those who worked as servants for the *Signoria*. The third wore a scholar's cloak and carried an armful of ledgers. Considering the company he kept, Tommaso guessed him to be a clerk for one of the *Priori*. All of them looked well enough fed.

The *buffon* capered beside the poor man, trying to snatch his wares from him. The mouse vendor tried to take it in good grace. Still attempting a sale, he continued to extol his "delicious delicacies" while holding the stick as high above his head and out of reach as he could.

The other two men followed at their leisure, more interested in conversing than in the clown's tired antics.

Tommaso, too weary to generate enough energy to pass them, strolled slowly behind.

"I believe the *Signoria* justified in their concern," the clerk said. "A mob marched down the Via Largo yesterday shouting 'Surrender for bread! Bring back the Medicis!' It's intolerable that through the very suffering that miserable family has caused the city that they should regain respect. So, while the rumored measures seem extreme, I believe them warranted."

"Warranted? The outrage of an innocent girl is warranted? Even if she were the daughter of the devil himself I would object," said the other man. "Why not take her from the convent and intern her in the Bargello with those of her family's supporters already imprisoned there? Wouldn't that be more appropriate?"

Tommaso came completely awake, shedding his exhaustion like an old skin. They were discussing Caterina.

"In the Bargello she might become a rallying point, just like that." The clerk snapped his fingers in disdain. "As she apparently has done already in that den of supercilious, imperious nuns. Have you never noticed the tidy resemblance those baskets of six buns the sisters send around bear to the six *palle* of the Medici coat of arms? That's why many of the *Priori* are beginning to realize she must be removed from the Murate."

"But to put her out to market in a brothel? I understand she is barely eleven," the green-liveried fellow protested.

"That solution bothers you? Then perhaps to save her honor, you'd prefer the proposed alternative: hang her within a cage slung from the city walls for the enemy to fire upon. No? Oh, I forgot. You have three daughters. That explains your squeamishness." The clerk clapped the other man on the back.

Shaking with horror, Tommaso began to fall back and away from them.

The servant shrugged the clerk off angrily. "You think yourself as witty as our *buffon* there." He gestured to where the clown still tormented the mouse merchant. "But you haven't seen service at the Palazzo de la Signoria for very long. I've worked there for years, and I tell you, I've never seen such an air to the place as that which blew in with the Arrabbiati when they came to power at the start of the seige."

The clerk laughed. "You take me too seriously. I said these measures are only rumored. No doubt the idle rumblings of frustrated men looking to vent some spleen."

Tommaso let them pull ahead to where he could no longer make out their words. Only rumored measures. Surely that was so. Most Florentines were like the green-liveried servant: too decent to consider such actions. Tommaso just prayed Caterina never had cause to hear of them.

What was it Filomena said her mother's people believed? That somewhere there existed an exactly opposite world, where if all was fair here, all was tragedy there, and the inverse. If that were so, in that ghostly, contrary realm surely today its citizenry feasted in their dining halls, reveled in the streets, and death was in abeyance.

42

❧

The Meraks's golden presence filled the room, obscuring everything within it, even the great speculum that was the source of its arrival. In the glare Cosimo could barely make out his father standing before the great creature.

Now I understand perfectly how the ancient Egyptians came to worship the sun as a god, Cosimo thought.

"What is it that you see?" Ruggiero the Old asked the shimmering image.

"They have found her and know she is no longer merely a pawn. They know she moves against them. They will, in turn, move against her. They must."

"What can we do?" Cosimo asked.

The Meraks turned enormous, liquid eyes toward him. *The creature is all gold,* Cosimo thought. *How is it then that its eyes seem blacker and deeper than the space between the stars?*

"There is little you can do with arcane measures. Your foes—*our* foes," the Meraks amended itself, "are watching and ready for just such a response."

"Is there any manner in which you might affect the outcome?" Ruggiero the Old asked.

The Meraks shook its head. "I can be summoned or visited. The one time before I attempted to intervene directly, my efforts came to naught. "Rest somewhat assured in this—their own esoteric measures cannot affect or destroy her. She is too well guarded by her own strengths and the guardianship of higher powers for that. They will have to move against her on the battlefield of earthly events. And it is there that you must be ready to act when the time comes."

Hours later, after the Meraks departed and the great speculum was put away, Cosimo decanted some wine for his father and himself.

"What did the Meraks mean when it said it had attempted to intervene once before?" he asked as he handed his father a goblet.

His father accepted the goblet with one hand as he rubbed weary eyes with the other. "When Lorenzo the Magnificent lay ill and dying, an unprecedented event occurred: The Meraks reached out to try to save him.

"Many omens and portents were observed at that time. Mysterious lights appeared in the sky. Lorenzo's friend Marsilio Ficino saw phantom giants fighting in his garden. And a woman praying in Santa Maria Novella ran deranged from the building, screaming that a burning bull with flaming horns had appeared and was annihilating the church."

43

July 19, 1530

Someone was shaking him hard, shaking the whole bed. "Stop, Madonna, stop," Bertino muttered on Tommaso's other side, trying to turn away from the disturbance.

"Tommaso, wake up," Elissa Pecorino hissed. "A messenger from *Ser* Buonarotti is here to see you."

At that, Tommaso sat bolt upright, disoriented but awake. "What time is it?" He looked about him. Past Bertino, Pagolo di Arezzo lay sound asleep, undisturbed by the commotion. The rest of the wide bed was unnaturally empty. Then Tommaso remembered: The other apprentices were away at night sentry duty on the city walls. "How long have I been asleep?"

"About two hours," Elissa Pecorino said.

Only two hours. Tommaso had stood night duty the evening before, then returned to a full day's work in the studio.

"Tommaso, you *must* hurry. It's Ascancio. He says it's urgent."

"Tell him I'll be right there." Tommaso scrambled out of bed. He pulled on a pair of drawers and a work tunic. Carrying buskins and boots he trotted into the studio.

Ascancio paced by the alleyway door. "Caterina de' Medici is in danger," he said as soon as he saw Tommaso.

"How? What's happened?" Tommaso hopped on one foot, then the other, pulling on his leggings.

"Master met tonight with the *Signoria*, as he must as both Commissioner General and a member of the Nine of the Militia. Among other things they discussed, several of the *Priori* fear the pro-Medici factions may use the *Duchessina* to force the overthrow of the government and lead a capitulation attempt with the pope and the emperor. They decided she must be removed from the Murate."

So the rumors had become truth. "And taken where?" Buskins on, Tommaso struggled with his boots. All he could think about were the threats to put Caterina in a brothel.

"They wouldn't say in front of Master Michelangelo. He fears she could just disappear." Ascancio made the motion of drawing a knife across his throat. "Master stayed behind to see if he could find out more. And also because he feared that if he left the *Signoria* would become suspicious of him. In spite of his defense of the city, they haven't forgotten his lifelong alliance with the de' Medicis, or his little, uh, vacation away. But he managed to speak with Antonio Mini in private and sent him out with the news."

"When is the *Signoria* going to act?" Tommaso asked.

"This very night. They're organizing a party to fetch her even now."

"She must be warned," Tommaso said. "And the Ruggieros and Madonna Strozzi alerted."

Ascancio nodded. "Master sent Baccio to the Strozzi palazzo. Antonio Mini ran to tell the Ruggieros."

Tommaso thought of the distances between those places and the Murate. Like the members of the *Signoria*, the Strozzis and Ruggieros would take the time to arm themselves.

"If we run we can reach the Murate first. It might give Caterina time to hide or at least prepare."

In all his life Tommaso had never run the way he ran now through Florence's streets. Somewhere in the back of his mind he remembered the day he'd fled from the Arrabbiati: how leaden his legs had felt toward the last, how his lungs had strained for air. Tonight he felt nothing except the length of his stride and the hard fast slap of the bottom of his boots on the street's stone pavers. Before, he had been running *from* danger. This night, he ran *to* Caterina. The desire to save her drew him forward effortlessly as if he were pulled by an immense lodestone. Although older and still a little taller, Ascancio was hard pressed to keep up with him.

The Murate was silent, dark, and peaceful when they reached it. "To the back, to the kitchen," Tommaso said. "The nuns there may still be up, baking for the morrow."

Tommaso pounded on the kitchen door. "Let me in, please, good sisters. It's Tommaso Arista. I have urgent news."

He was still pummeling the door when he heard galloping hoofbeats coming up fast. He and Ascancio whirled around. Tommaso cursed himself for not bringing a weapon from Il Tribolino's. All he carried was his dining dirk in his belt. He pulled it from its scabbard and held it ready.

Two horsemen rounded the corner of the building at a fast clip. They hauled back on their reins and dismounted before their horses came to a complete stop. It was Cosimo Ruggiero and his brother Lorenzo. Tommaso sheathed his dirk.

"Tommaso! Thank God it's you. And good Ascancio! Have you warned them?"

"We just arrived. We've been trying to get in," Ascancio said.

At that moment the latch on the kitchen door's spy-hole shot back. For an instant a small circle of golden light shone there. Then it dimmed as someone looked out at them, blocking the light.

Cosimo strode forward, throwing his reins to Ascancio. "Good Sister, whoever you may be, please let us in. I am Cosimo Ruggiero. The four of us have news of danger both to the *Duchessina* Caterina de' Medici and to this convent itself."

He got no further than Caterina's name when they heard the bolts on the door thrown. By the time he'd finished the door was flung open. Sister Anna Maria, the young novice who often chaperoned Caterina, stood there. Behind her was Sister Teresa Lucrezia, the kind, elderly nun in charge of the kitchen.

"Quick, enter quickly." The older nun hustled them into the kitchen. Three other nuns stood agape at their kneading troughs and mixing bowls as Lorenzo Ruggiero marched the two panting, lathering horses right into the kitchen.

"What danger do you speak of?" Sister Teresa Lucrezia asked.

"The *Signoria* are sending a party of men to take the *Duchessina* away," Cosimo said. "Please fetch your mother superior and Caterina."

"Anna Maria, you go fetch our darling. Young man, please lead your steeds into the scullery. I'll go waken Mother Superior," Sister Teresa Lucrezia said as she bustled off.

Everyone left in the kitchen jumped as someone else began pounding on the kitchen door. The noise stopped as whoever it was left off their thumping and jiggled at the latch. The latch began to lift. Tommaso realized to his horror that in the excitement the door had been shut but not barred when they entered. *But now I'm in a kitchen and therefore not unarmed,* he thought.

He saw Cosimo, Ascancio, and Lorenzo begin to rotate toward the door so slowly it seemed that their motions could be measured in hours. By the time they turned halfway Tommaso had seized a carving blade in one hand and a chopping knife in the other. As the door started to open he let fly with the chopping knife. It embedded itself in the doorsill, just inches away from a white face only briefly glimpsed before the door slammed shut. Tommaso heard one or more of the nuns shriek.

"Holy Mother of God, that was Piero Strozzi. You might have killed him." Cosimo rushed forward across Tommaso's line of fire, then flinched as he realized Tommaso still held the other blade back ready to fling.

Tommaso lowered the carving blade. "Not at all." He was amazed at the calm in his voice. It must belong to another person. "I assumed it was one of the *Priori*. Do you think I wish to murder a member of the *Signoria?* I just wanted to make them jump back so we could slam the door shut and lock it."

Cosimo opened the door on a shaking Piero Strozzi, grabbed him by his sleeve, and hauled him in. Michelangelo's apprentice Baccio sidled in behind him.

"Tommaso thought you were one of the *Signoria.* He was just trying to scare you," Cosimo explained to the Strozzi heir.

"Truly," Tommaso said sheepishly when Piero Strozzi glared at him. Lorenzo Ruggiero ducked out the door to bring a single exhausted horse in. Piero Strozzi and Baccio must have ridden double on it. Ascancio took this horse too back to the scullery.

Jangled, Piero Strozzi might have been, but Tommaso noticed he maintained the presence of mind to bar the door behind him and slide shut the peephole.

"Where's your mother?" Cosimo asked Piero.

"She's on duty on the barricades," Piero said. "I sent Leone to apprise her of the situation."

"Where's Antonio Mini?" interrupted Ascancio, asking Cosimo Ruggiero.

"He returned to Michelangelo, both to report on the errand discharged and allay any suspicions. We can only hope the *Signoria* didn't notice his absence."

"Piero! Cosimo! What is happening?" Caterina ran into the kitchen with Sister Anna Maria at her heels. Although she wore a heavy robe over a night shift and thin slippers on her feet, Tommaso noticed that she appeared neither disheveled nor sleep dazed. He guessed that late though the hour was she hadn't been sleeping. And although she looked frightened, she didn't seem surprised.

Before either Piero or Cosimo could answer Caterina, a contingent of nuns swept into the kitchen, the abbess of the convent in their midst.

Piero Strozzi swept off his cap and bowed low. "My apologies for this intrusion, good Mother Superior. But at this very moment the *Signoria* is sending some of their *Priori* to wrest my little cousin from your guardianship."

The abbess paled. Unlike Caterina, she did appear surprised. But she wasn't flustered with consternation. She turned to the elderly kitchen nun. "Sister Teresa Lucrezia, take the novices and send them about to be sure no lights show at any of the outer windows," she said. "If the convent appears asleep, the *Priori* will expect to take a while to rouse us. Station yourself by the front door. As soon as the *Priori* arrive, send the swiftest girl back here to tell us. Answer the *Priori* eventually, but take your time about it. Tell them you've sent someone to fetch me, which is only the truth, but that they must be patient—seeing how late the hour is, I must be wakened."

Sister Teresa Lucrezia and the novices left.

"Dearest Cousin, why is this happening?" Caterina asked Piero Strozzi.

"As Florence starves and begins to falter, the people are turning away from the *Signoria*. So the *Signoria* fears that as the only legitimate Medici heir, Florence will turn to you and beg you to negotiate with Clement. The *Signoria* must act against you now before that idea is proposed."

"Where would they take me? What would they do with me?"

Piero Strozzi and Cosimo shared a glance. "That isn't known," Cosimo answered. "We were alerted to the situation by Michelangelo Buonarotti. The *Signoria* didn't apprise him of their plans for you."

Piero Strozzi clasped Caterina's hand. "Cousin, I fear for you. Until the party of *Priori* arrives we have time to transport you away. We can slip out this back door here, down to the garden and the river. I can procure a skiff and row us to a safe dock. From there we'll smuggle you out one of the city's gates and deliver you to the safety of the Prince of Orange's camp."

Caterina smiled at him sadly. "It's a credit to your courageous heart that you'd risk so much for me. But even if your plan was successful, think of the aftermath of your actions.

"The *Priori* would believe me hidden somewhere here in the Murate. If Mother Superior doesn't produce me I doubt the *Priori* will respect the sanctity of these grounds. I tremble to think what would happen to this holy place and these good women if mobs from the street were allowed to rush in and search for me."

Tommaso glanced at the abbess and saw by her waxen complexion that these thoughts had already occurred to her.

"Then, not finding me here, they'd turn next to your home, the Strozzi mansion, to look for me. This time perhaps even your mother's valiant nature might prove insufficient to turn them aside."

Tommaso had other concerns about Piero's plan. "Even if you could get the *Duchessina* out of Florence undetected, the chances of delivering her to Philiberte of Orange's camp safely are almost nonexistent," he said. "The *Reiters* would slaughter us all as soon as they discovered us, before we could convince them of our mission.

"The only man I'd trust with such an enterprise is Francesco Ferrucci. I've ridden on one of his forays. He'd be horrified at the *Signoria's* dishonorable actions against the *Duchessina*. But I'm sure he'd also consider it treasonous to help her escape."

Sister Anna Maria ran into the kitchen nearly breathless. "Mother Superior, they've arrived."

Piero Strozzi shrugged his shoulders bitterly. "We've wasted what little advantage we had."

"Not necessarily," Caterina said. "Thanks to you six cavaliers I wasn't caught unawares. That bought time to consider different possibilities. Even if in the end we rejected them, at least it saved us from leaping into recklessness. We still have time to think."

"Sister Teresa Lucrezia is speaking to the *Priori* as slowly as she can," Sister Anna Maria said. "She's feigning slow-wittedness as well as sleepiness. You'd think her in her dotage."

A smile lightened the abbess's grave face. "Trust Teresa Lucrezia's lively mind to think of feigning its opposite. In like manner I'll proceed as slowly as I can to the front door."

"I'm going with you," Caterina said.

"Do you think that's wise?" asked Piero Strozzi.

"I wish to see my opponents. But I'll take care that they can't see me," Caterina assured her cousin.

"Where you go, so go I," Cosimo said.

"And I," said Piero Strozzi. "The rest of you should stay behind to guard this back door."

Tommaso could see by the look on Lorenzo Ruggiero's face that he did not intend to stay behind.

The nuns wheeled about as one and swirled out of the kitchen, the abbess and Caterina in their midst with Cosimo, Lorenzo and Piero flanking them.

A flock of doves going to confront raptors, Tommaso thought.

"That leaves us to guard back here," Ascancio said. "Piero Strozzi is right. Surely members of the *Priori's* command will remember this entrance. They're not fools. They'll send men back here to watch for an escape attempt. And most likely they'll test the door to see if they can broach it."

Tommaso hesitated. He was a cook. This was a kitchen. There was no more natural place in the world for him to make a stand. But with every fiber of his being he did not want to leave Caterina's side.

Baccio grinned at him. "Go ahead, Tommaso. We can see where your heart lies. The two of us should suffice. For once, feel free to relinquish your domain to us." The apprentice pulled the chopping blade from where it still protruded from the doorsill. "You've already indicated the best way to arm ourselves."

"Speak for yourself," Ascancio said. "I prefer weapons of my own choosing." To Tommaso's astonishment the young man reached around and from the back of his belt under his cloak pulled a pair of arquebuses.

As Tommaso hurried to catch up with the nuns he reflected that Piero Strozzi was lucky that it was he and not Ascancio who was first to react when Piero tried to enter the kitchen.

In contrast to the brightness of the kitchen, the hallways winding through the convent were almost completely dark, punctuated by the timid flames of the few candles the nuns carried.

Tommaso initially felt nervous about traversing this place that was both holy and forbidden to men. But he could see nothing other than the dim, silent, shadowed forms of the nuns in front of him and the occasional cell door as he passed. Whatever secrets the convent possessed, it revealed none to him. His passage through it left it undefiled and untouched.

The hallway opened up to a foyer. The nuns doused their candles. The smoke from the wicks censed the air with a dusky smell. Now the only light came from some source outside, staining the curtains and bars covering the front windows with a foreboding flickering glow.

Sister Teresa Lucrezia was talking to the mother superior in a low voice. A number of other nuns clustered about them. Caterina, Piero Strozzi, and Cosimo positioned themselves at the window to the far right of the door. They peered out the crack where the curtains met in the middle. The two youths held the curtain fabric taut so that there was room enough to look out without the curtains folding back and revealing them. Tommaso went to the far end of the window and did the same there with Lorenzo Ruggiero.

"Ascancio and Baccio stayed behind to guard the back," he whispered to Lorenzo. He peeked out the window. The scene that met his eyes didn't reassure him.

A large group of men stood outside positioned close to the door, their torches held high. Tommaso couldn't be sure how many men there were altogether. Their numbers faded out of sight beyond the canopy of light shed by the torches.

Three of the nine *Priori* that made up the *Signoria* led the deputation, resplendent in their official garb of crimson coats garnished with ermine collars and cuffs. Just behind them, Tommaso recognized several of the Council of Eight of Security.

Sister Teresa Lucrezia unlatched the front door's viewing panel and opened it.

"I believe I hear Mother Superior approaching," she announced in a quavering shout, as if she were not only feebleminded but deaf besides.

The abbess waited a moment before stepping up to the panel.

"By what right do you awaken a holy and peaceful convent at this late hour? What is your business here?"

The foremost *Priori* held out a magisterial-looking piece of paper. "By the command of the *Signoria,* we have here an official order. You must deliver up to us the girl known as Caterina de' Medici."

The abbess stepped back from the door and looked at Caterina. Caterina gestured to stall them.

The abbess returned to the viewing panel. "You expect me to release from my care an innocent young girl to a mob of rough men who arrive like thieves in the night? Before I even consider such a demand I must hear the particulars."

The *Priori* looked vexed, but there was little else he could do but acquiesce. He began reading the document. It was couched in the *Signoria's* typically grandiloquent and obtuse style. Every other sentence the mother superior interrupted him with questions until he was so flustered that he had trouble keeping his place.

"Look at their faces," Caterina whispered. "See the shadows within them, looking out from behind their eyes? At this moment they are not men of Florence."

"I grant you that they look frightening. But it's just the play of the torchlight on their features," Piero Strozzi tried to reassure her.

Tommaso was not so sure. To him the mob looked like revelers at some funereal festival. The faces and bodies of his fellow citizens seemed merely skins worn as costumes by creatures he couldn't imagine; didn't want to imagine. At the same time there was something horribly familiar about that darkness in their faces.

"Cosimo, you see it, don't you?" Caterina pleaded.

Cosimo Ruggiero muttered something. To Tommaso's ears it sounded like a name. And for no particular reason Tommaso recognized what the crowd reminded him of. He'd seen exactly that same effect, like a contrary penumbra, playing about and within the person of Alessandro de' Medici.

It was a darkness he now realized was shared by the friar-mimicking creature searching through the enemy encampment for Michelangelo.

"If I leave with them my life ends tonight," Caterina whispered.

Tommaso saw Cosimo and Piero exchange a glance above her head. Neither of them responded. They could not refute her.

The abbess had drawn out the *Priori's* spiel as long as she could. "Allow me a few moments to consider your words," she said, shutting the latch.

Caterina went to her. "Mother Superior, I do not want to endanger the Murate, but if I go with those men I fear I shall suffer death in the dark. Can you tell them you'll release me into their custody in the morning?"

The abbess nodded. "I can, but I'm not sure that it would be advisable to let you go, even then."

"True," said Piero Strozzi. "But at least we gain more time to plan."

"I know how to deal with these men," the abbess said. She opened the panel again and spoke loudly so the entire crowd outside could hear her.

"Your document seems in order. Of course I can do nothing but bend to the will of the government of Florence."

At the abbess's words the faces in the crowd responded with identical eagerness.

"However," the abbess continued, "I would be remiss in my duty if I released an innocent young girl to a company of men at this late hour without even appropriate chaperonage. Therefore, I will be pleased to relinquish her tomorrow morning under the blessing of God's honest sunlight."

The mob coiled to strike as if it were a single entity. Tommaso was seized by such a cold, strong shiver that he felt his skin might leap from his body.

The abbess's voice sharpened. "Within this convent we are simple brides of Christ. But outside these walls, do not forget that many of the nuns of the Murate are daughters, sisters, and aunts of the wealthiest and highest-born families of Florence.

"During the sack of Rome the barbaric *Reiters* breached and violated nunneries. Would you risk the same censure by God and men that they face? At the very least, such actions would ensure the downfall of a government that would send you on such a mission—surely a foolish chance to take when you shall attain your purpose in just a few brief hours."

The crowd wavered, a great uncertain beast. Seeing their resolution bend, the abbess drove her point home.

"By now word of your endeavor must have spread throughout the city. Men of common decency will be on their way to confront you."

Tommaso thought of how Leone Strozzi by now would have reached Madame Clarice. She'd be gathering her forces even as they stood there.

"Surely, with the enemy threatening at our gates, you wouldn't want to turn Florentine against Florentine within them?" the abbess ended.

Tommaso wouldn't have cared to guess at what was in the hearts of the men before them that moment. But there was little they could accomplish against the abbess's calm, rational words and her almost impregnable position behind the barred doors.

"We'll return at morning's first light," the foremost *Priori* announced. "Have Caterina de' Medici prepared to leave at that time."

From his vantage point at the end of the window Tommaso watched the crowd disperse. A few men remained behind to watch at the front doors.

"The immediate danger is over," the abbess told Cosimo and Piero. "Grateful as I am for your aid, it is inappropriate for those of your sex to remain in this part of the convent. Sister Anna Maria will escort you back to the more profane and acceptable environs of the kitchen. As long as there are men standing guard outside it isn't safe for you to leave."

Piero Strozzi bowed to her. "Of course, Mother Superior. But you are still threatened. What do you intend to do?"

The abbess stood very straight and tall. "The little that can be done. A few of the youngest sisters will stand watch at all possible entrances in case the *Signoria* resorts to treachery and tries to breach the convent after all. The rest of us shall retire to the chapel and spend the rest of the night praying to God for strength and guidance."

44

Sister Anna Maria lit a candle. She and Caterina led the way to the kitchen. Tommaso found himself again bringing up the rear behind Piero Strozzi, Cosimo, and Lorenzo. They'd only turned one corner, however, when Sister Teresa Lucrezia bustled up from behind to join them.

"I can pray at my baking as well as I can kneeling in the chapel," she told Tommaso. "In the morning the walls of the Murate will either come down or not. If they come down, God won't care where I've prayed. But if they do not, God might not forgive me over-risen bread and burnt pastries. My baked goods will be all the holier for the prayers recited over them this night."

Tommaso had to smile. It mattered not what vocation might call to one, even God's very service: A cook was always a cook.

In the kitchen, Ascancio and Baccio looked relieved to see them. "What's happening?" Ascancio asked. "Almost as soon as you left five *brigate* came to the door, tested it to see if it was locked, then pushed against it, thinking no one awake back here. Baccio had to pretend to be one of the sisters. He shouted at them in falsetto. He hurled church curses at them till they stopped. Apparently the ruffians still respect the threat of excommunication."

"Are they out there yet?" Piero Strozzi asked.

Baccio nodded. "A few moments ago a couple of other fellows arrived and spoke to them. At present the lot of them are standing guard."

Lorenzo Ruggiero explained briefly what had transpired at the front of the convent. "Do you know how to use one of these?" He drew out an arquebus.

Ascancio nodded yes and displayed his own two.

Lorenzo looked impressed. "You and Baccio continue to watch. If they try to break the door down again we'll be forced to shoot them. They can't be allowed to get in."

"But shoot *only* if they attempt to ram the door," Cosimo cautioned. "At present they have no inkling we're here. If they find themselves dodging musket shot, they'll conclude there are men in the Murate. We'll lose any advantage surprise might afford us."

Piero Strozzi, Cosimo, and Lorenzo began to discuss different strategies. Cosimo favored Piero Strozzi's earlier plan of hiding Caterina or smuggling her out somehow, then using Clarice Strozzi's influence and men-at-arms to protect the nuns of the Murate.

Piero Strozzi agreed with marshaling his mother's forces but now felt that full-scale confrontation was in order to topple the government.

Lorenzo Ruggiero believed their little group shouldn't wait for reinforcements. He was sure they could slip out of the convent and silence the guards one small group at a time, leaving the way clear for a safe escape by all. "The sisters could return to their families until the danger was over. Imagine the look on the *Prioris'* faces when they return to find their 'watchdogs' gagged and trussed up like so many chickens and the Murate empty!"

Cosimo and Piero started to point out the impracticality of such a plan. They kept their voices low, but the conversation soon grew heated.

"Stop this!" Caterina said loudly, not caring who heard. "This is *my* life!"

When Cosimo looked at the door and paled she softened her voice. "Cosimo, do you so soon forget those words you bade me live by, 'Astra declinant, non necessitant'? I *will* decide my own fate. If you could just hear yourselves! Your bravery is imprudent. Cosimo, you're the oldest here and you're only nineteen. Baccio, you look to be the youngest."

"I'm thirteen," Baccio said. He held up his hands in protest. "But I offered no suggestions, good lady."

"And you are the wiser for it," Caterina said. "But you, my cousin and advisors, you would have such a band of youths challenge the *Signoria* and whomever and whatever it might bring to bear against us." Her pointed glance at Cosimo carried some meaning Tommaso didn't understand.

Cosimo looked chagrined.

"For too long I've been others' puppet. This day at least I decide my own destiny." Caterina turned to Sister Anna Maria. "Sister, will you accompany me to my cell? I need solitude in which to think and pray."

The novice nodded and moved with Caterina toward the hallway door.

"Tommaso, may I speak to you a moment before I go?" Caterina asked. She stood on just the other side of the doorway to the hall leading away from the kitchen. When Tommaso approached her she slipped back a little into the shadow its edge afforded her. "Anna Maria, go on ahead. I'll be with you momentarily," she said over her shoulder to the novice. Then she turned back to Tommaso.

"My friend, I need to decide my fate by myself, with no help from anyone. Would you aid me by keeping this—just for a brief span of time?" Caterina lifted the silver pendant with its red stone from her neck and placed it around Tommaso's, the reluctance in her face clear. She made sure it slid down to hide within his shirt.

"Any wish from you I accept as a command," Tommaso said. "But I don't understand—"

Caterina put a finger to his lips. "I know you don't. If I could explain I would. Can you accept that?"

The pendant bumped against Tommaso's chest. Suddenly he was filled with a warm strange mixture of love, concern, and faith. Caterina trusted him as she trusted none of the others, not even Cosimo Ruggiero. And Tommaso knew, once and forever, that he belonged to and with Caterina. He nodded. "Whatever you ask of me, I will accept and undertake, whether it is the laying down of my life or simple understanding."

"Then I'm going to shortly ask of you one more small favor." Caterina smiled. "One I don't think you'll mind." And she was gone.

Tommaso turned back into the kitchen, wondering if the others were curious about their exchange.

Lorenzo Ruggiero and Piero Strozzi had returned to discussing alternate strategies as if Caterina's outburst meant nothing. "Surely my mother will send reinforcements soon," Piero was saying. Baccio and Ascancio hovered at the door, occasionally peeking out the spy-hole and joking with each other nervously. Sister Teresa Lucrezia punched down pillowy mounds of dough where they'd risen in their bowls. Only Cosimo Ruggiero sat alone and quiet, apparently brooding over Caterina's words.

Tommaso felt awkward and out of place. He went over to help the elderly nun. The dough was ready for rekneading. Even here, with supplies coming in from the wealthy families the nuns had been born into, Tommaso noticed that ground oak bark had been added to the flour to stretch the Murate's supplies.

He and Sister Teresa Lucrezia pulled each batch apart into six equal pieces. These were shaped into balls and set to rise next to each other. In a few hours they'd be baked into the sweet buns the *signoria* had chosen to interpret as representing the six *palle* of the Medici coat of arms.

Tommaso heard light footsteps coming down the hallway. He looked up, expecting to see Caterina. It was Sister Anna Maria. In her arms she carried Balthazara. The cat, seeing unfamiliar faces filling the kitchen, began to struggle.

"The *Duchessina* wishes complete solitude. She asked if you would watch over her small companion for her. She said I should tell you this is the second favor she begged of you," the novice told Tommaso.

Tommaso took the panicking animal. As soon as he held it to his chest it calmed. Sister Anna Maria stared. "I'm an old friend," Tommaso explained. "A member of the family, really. Balthazara's mother comes from my parents' home. Cats sense such things."

He could hardly have told the young nun that the pendant dangling hidden against his breast had suddenly warmed and seemed to reach out to the cat, soothing it.

Sister Anna Maria crossed herself. "That must be the case," she said. "I must return to the *Duchessina* now."

It took Tommaso a while, but he was finally able to convince Balthazara that a stool by the *fornaio* was as pleasant and secure as a place in his arms. He glanced at her frequently as he returned to helping Sister Teresa Lucrezia.

The elderly nun hadn't jested when she said she could and would pray at her baking. Every pummeling of a loaf of bread, every measuring of oak-bark-laced flour added to the batters elicited a muttered plea to the Mother of God for guidance and compassion for Caterina.

The rapid footsteps of at least two people sounded down the hallway. This time everyone looked up when Sister Anna Maria entered. She appeared upset, almost frightened.

"I didn't know," she said. "When I returned to her cell it was already done."

She stepped aside. Caterina was right behind her.

Cosimo Ruggiero gasped. Other than that, there was no sound at all in the room.

Caterina had cut off her hair. What little was left of it hung in wisps about her ears. She wore a novice's habit—no doubt one of Anna Maria's. Tucked up and folded about her it fit rather convincingly. She carried a wimple, which she handed to Sister Anna Maria.

"What have you done?" Piero Strozzi whispered.

Caterina smiled at him, but turned to Cosimo Ruggiero to make her answer. "Will they dare now to remove me? When they come back in the morning it will appear to everyone that they are guilty of carrying off a nun from her convent."

Cosimo looked nonplussed. Then he bowed to her. "We should have trusted in you," he said. "You have saved yourself, saved the women of this convent, and saved us from our impetuous selves."

"But I don't see how—" Piero Strozzi began.

"The *Duchessina* is keener then all of us put together," Cosimo said. "She saw that her very weaknesses are her strengths and chose to amplify them: She already possesses youth and innocence. Now she has annexed holiness to her cause. In the light of day, with all the city as witness, the *Signoria* will be helpless to maneuver her. She has checked their move."

While Cosimo's explanation held the rest of the room's attention, Caterina asked Tommaso softly, "Those items you safeguarded for me . . . ?"

Tommaso slid the pendant from his neck back to hers. He picked up Balthazara and handed the cat to Caterina.

Caterina had seemed full of confidence when she sailed into the kitchen. But it wasn't until the pendant lay hidden against her heart and the cat nestled purring in her arms that she relaxed, as if in those simple actions she found confirmation for her decision.

"Sister Anna Maria, will you help me place the wimple on my head?"

When they were done, Caterina looked exactly like any other fresh-faced novice.

"A convincing imitation," Piero grudgingly admitted. "But I still don't believe anyone will be convinced you've taken vows to live the cloistered life."

"Why not?" asked Caterina. "The whole world believes my cousin Giulio in the holy role of Pope Clement, and before him Great-uncle Giovanni as Pope Leo. Surely my bit of play-acting is more reasonable than theirs."

Behind her, Sister Anna Maria paled and crossed herself.

"Now we must go join our sisters in prayer in the chapel," Caterina said. She reluctantly put Balthazara back on the perching stool near the *fornaio*.

"I'll finish up the baking," Tommaso assured Sister Teresa Lucrezia, who looked torn between going and staying.

The days in July are long, the nights short, and a good deal of time had already passed in the course of events. But, to Tommaso, the remaining hours till daybreak stretched like an eternity spent in purgatory.

The six youths traded off watching at the door. Cosimo insisted each try to catch some sleep. "Even half an hour will refresh you, and we may need our wits about us in the morning."

Tommaso dozed lightly between his rounds of sliding bread, rolls and pastry into the ovens and standing guard. Like any good cook, he woke instantly to the odor of food when it reached the point of baked perfection.

In between he dreamed: Gliding like a bird up near the ceiling of the Murate's chapel, he looked down on the praying nuns. Their prayers rose up as songs. He tried to spot Caterina, but from his vantage point all the sisters looked the same. Tommaso swooped lower so he could see their individual faces. Still he couldn't find her. He didn't recognize any of these women. The walls of the chapel appeared to go on forever; their edges disappeared into sable night. He would have been grateful to at least come upon Anna Maria or Teresa Lucrezia.

Finally Tommaso spied someone familiar. So relieved was he that he didn't think it odd that the face belonged to his cousin Francesca. Tommaso looked about. He knew the next woman too—Francesca's bold mother, Leonora. And here was his own mother. And Elissa Pecorino, although in some corner of his mind Tommaso knew Elissa must have gone to bed back at Il Tribolino's hours ago.

The walls of the chapel moved closer. The space became small and compressed. He shouldn't have trouble finding Caterina in here, for now he knew all the sisters praying. They were the rest of Leonora's daughters, some of them girls younger than he. *When did Leonora send them to be novices?* he wondered. It seemed unlikely for such an idiosyncratic near-heretical family, but he didn't question it, for they all prayed for Caterina.

Then he saw that he no longer floated through the chapel but rather hovered near the ceiling of a crowded antechamber, the kind that led into a shopfront or out to a roadside stand. Pelts and bird skins hung on the walls. Butchering and carving knives sat tidily as cats in their proper slots along carving blocks.

A window somewhere was open. Through it Tommaso heard a river's murmuring. Even the rushing water added hopes and prayers for Caterina's future.

Tommaso woke confused to a pattering sound and saw that he sat on a stool in the Murate kitchen. Balthazara lay curled on his lap. Cosimo and Lorenzo Ruggiero stood guard at the back door. The oil lamps had almost guttered out, the glow from the *fornaio* was almost dimmed, but none of that mattered because morning's earliest light had begun to brighten the kitchen. Ascancio and Piero Strozzi sat asleep with their heads pillowed into their arms, arms rested folded up on the main worktable, surrounded by the dozens of rolls, pastries, and bread loaves Tommaso had pulled from the *fornaio* in the course of the night. Baccio slept seated on the floor, leaning back against the wall near the fireplace hearth.

The fire in the hearth needs to be lit, Tommaso thought. *By now it should be blazing and water set to boiling.*

He'd begun to rise and put Balthazara on the stool when he realized that the pattering noise was real and not a part of his dream. Out of the corner of his eye he saw Cosimo's head turn toward the sound.

Sister Anna Maria trotted into the room. "They've returned," she said. "They're shouting at the front door for the *Duchessina* to come out."

Tommaso was impressed at the way Piero Strozzi woke: smoothly, with an instantaneous transition between deep sleep and complete alertness. In contrast, Baccio and Ascancio fumbled their way up from slumber looking as confused and disoriented as Tommaso had felt.

"How do the *Priori* seem?" Piero Strozzi asked the novice. "As antagonistic as the night before? Are there more or less of them?"

"They seem as belligerent as last night," Sister Anna Maria said, "but perhaps less brave in the daylight. I couldn't be sure then of their numbers because of the darkness, but I would say there are more of them now. And already the commotion is attracting the attention of passersby."

"What is the mood of those folks—those passing by?" Cosimo Ruggiero asked.

"Just curious so far, since nothing has happened and the *Prioris'* men won't answer their questions. But more and more of them gather every moment."

"We can only hope they'll become angry with the *Signoria* when they find out what's afoot," Piero muttered.

"More men have just joined the guards back here," Lorenzo Ruggiero called in a low voice from his position by the door.

"The *Priori* fear Caterina may try to slip out this way," Cosimo said.

Sister Anna Maria shook her head. "She's at the front, preparing herself to talk to them."

"We need to be there. Please lead us back to her," Cosimo said. Piero Strozzi and Lorenzo started to head out of the kitchen. Tommaso moved into Lorenzo's post at the spy-hole.

Piero Strozzi stopped Lorenzo. "My friend, I know you like to be in the forefront of any fray, but would you stay back here and lead these youths? I fear the *Signoria* may still attempt to breach the Murate by stealth. From what the good sister has told us, they've lost the advantage at the front, but they may still try something back here."

Lorenzo reluctantly agreed.

A few moments after Cosimo and Piero departed it appeared that Piero had been wise to be cautious. Several men joined the guards outside.

"We have new arrivals," Tommaso reported.

"Piero could have been correct in his fears," Lorenzo said, joining Tommaso at the small window, "or they could be replacing the current watch."

The group outside huddled together briefly. Then they all marched off around the corner of the building.

"Why did they do that?" Tommaso asked.

"A pox on the *Signoria*," Lorenzo cursed. "There can only be one reason. Caterina walked out the front doors and the *Priori* have her. There's no longer any need for their men to wait back here."

Tommaso's heart filled with horror. "We must reach her. What if they lay hands on her?" In his mind's eye he saw Caterina huddled in a cage hung from the city's walls, or tied up in some dark corner of a bordello.

"Don't panic," Lorenzo said. "That's the most dangerous action we could indulge in."

Tommaso blinked in surprise. Was this the same brash youth who had advocated their little band somehow take on all the *Signoria's* guard? Sometime during the night Lorenzo had begun to grow up.

Lorenzo chewed on his lower lip, thinking. "At least two of us will have to stay back here," he decided. "Who knows what could happen in front? A back escape route might prove necessary. Someone should remain to open the door in that case."

"Or protect it if need be," Ascancio pointed out.

Lorenzo nodded.

"Lorenzo, you are well known about the city," Tommaso said. "So are your brother and Piero Strozzi. If any of you shows yourselves the *Priori* and their men might become suspicious. The three of us, however, are humble and therefore anonymous apprentices. With the guards gone back here, we could slip around to the front and join the gathering crowd and watch."

"Don't forget your three valuable horses still tied up in the pantry," Ascancio said. "If you need to effect a quick escape they'll be indispensable, but you can't march them out inconspicuously from the back of the Murate. Tommaso's right. It will be up to two of us apprentices to reconnoiter on the outside."

"But as Michelangelo's senior apprentice, you are also quite familiar,"

Baccio pointed out to Ascancio. "I'm the youngest here. I'll be the least noticeable." He and Tommaso were out the door before the two older boys could react.

"One of us will return to report to you," Baccio called back.

Balthazara tried to slip out with them. Tommaso blocked her with his leg. "Don't let the *Duchessina's* cat escape," he said. The look on Lorenzo's face told him the Ruggiero youth was just realizing that his newfound wisdom had deprived him of a chance at action. Ascancio was still scratching his head.

"That was neatly done," Baccio snickered as they ran around the building. "You didn't give Lorenzo a chance to realize that as far as anonymity goes, with your hair you might as well be wearing a flag on your head."

"I'm not the only redhead in Florence," Tommaso protested.

Then they rounded the corner and plunged into the edges of a huge crowd. They slipped, pushed, and prodded until they had a clear view of the unfolding drama.

Caterina stood alone facing the *Priori* and their men. The abbess and several other nuns lined up along the Murate's front doors and windows behind her.

The *Priori* looked aghast and confused at Caterina's transformation.

One of the *Priori* held the reins to a saddled horse. "Behave yourself. Change back into your clothes," he scolded at Caterina as if she were a recalcitrant daughter.

"These are my clothes." Caterina stared him down.

"Your little scheme will avail you nothing." Another *Priori* spoke, a tall man made even more imposing by his scarlet robes of office. He waved the document they'd brought the night before at her. "This official order states that you *will* leave this place and come away with us."

"If it comes to that, then at least all the world shall see I'm a nun taken forcibly from my convent."

Like the murmur of flood waters rising, the wave of sound from the crowd was low and ominous. Tommaso shivered. It reminded him of the mumbling river noises in his dream. The *Prioris'* men glanced about nervously.

Tommaso looked into their faces. *How could I have found them so terrifying last night?* he thought. Piero Strozzi was right—it must have been the lateness and darkness of the hour and the way the torchlight played about their countenances. Daylight revealed them as a sorry mob of ineffectual men, easily thwarted by the will of an eleven-year-old girl.

The *Priori* stepped away from Caterina to confer with each other, whispering angrily as they huddled.

Tommaso wondered what Cosimo Ruggiero and Piero Strozzi thought of the standoff. They must be pressed against the curtains of those windows just behind the abbess. It occurred to Tommaso that he had a way to at least let them know that the back entrance was no longer guarded.

"The guards have left the rear of the premises. That way at least is clear, should we need it," Cosimo Ruggiero told Piero, his eyes never leaving the tableau playing out before them.

Piero leaned back from the curtain crack to stare at Cosimo. "I swear on the head of Saint John the Baptist himself that you shall surpass even your father as a mage," the Strozzi heir said in fearful admiration. "Your second sight is nothing short of amazing."

"Nothing of the sort, at least in this case." Cosimo grinned at the sight of Tommaso's bright hair bobbing up and down, the young cook's gaze locked fixedly at the windows as if he could actually see Cosimo and will into Cosimo's brain the message his appearance in the crowd conveyed.

"Though there are some things I see here that others will not," Cosimo muttered to himself as much as to Piero Strozzi. The shadows cast from within the faces of the *Priori* and their men the night before were almost entirely gone. The portal by which the enemy had entered was closing, almost closed.

Whatever the outcome of the day might be, Cosimo knew Caterina would be safe. The foes of Florence had struck at her too late. She had come into her power. Cosimo couldn't wait to tell his father. Their queen could still be driven from the board but she could not be captured or destroyed. "Be prepared to race to the kitchen to fetch our horses," he told Piero.

Cosimo watched as scarlet-cloaked men approached Caterina again. The tall one acted as spokesman. "Do as we say. Change into lay clothing. For where we are taking you, your current garb would be unseemly."

"And where would that be?" asked Caterina. "Some months ago I heard that one of your number proposed putting me in a brothel. Is that how the government currently treats young brides of Christ?" Her voice carried like a high clear church bell.

The *Priori* recoiled from the ugly rumble that rose from the crowd. They hastily regrouped to confer again.

"This may take a while," Tommaso said to Baccio. "We have two compatriots who might like to know of these goings-on. I'll wait for you here if you'll go tell them."

Baccio took his meaning and slid out to report to Lorenzo and Ascancio. He returned some minutes later.

The standoff went on for more than an hour. The crowd, rather than losing interest and drifting away, grew larger, until it seemed that half of Florence watched and waited for the outcome of the drama.

"The blood of Il Magnífico runs strong in that little maid's veins," an elderly man standing near Tommaso said.

At last the *Priori* gave in, at least in part. The eldest, the one who'd first spoken to Caterina, led a horse up to her. "Wear whatever you like," he said, "but get up on the horse."

"Where are you taking me?" Caterina's voice was strong enough for the whole crowd to hear her.

The old *Priori* made a sour face. "To a convent, of course. Where else would we take an avowed nun? You're going back to the Convent of Santa Lucia."

If Caterina felt dismayed at the thought of returning to that dour, plebeian place she showed no sign of it. "In that case, I acquiesce to your wishes," she said. "Wait a few minutes more. One of my sisters here will a fetch a few of my things."

She spoke briefly to Sister Anna Maria. The novice returned a while later with a number of parcels stacked in a pile and strapped together with several leather belts. The topmost item was a Bible, prominently displayed.

One of the *Priori* offered to help Caterina mount. She ignored his proffered hand. The stirrup was high, but once she'd managed to get a foothold,

she leapt lightly into the saddle, her bulky novice's robes not hindering her
at all. Sister Anna Maria handed her her things.

"What's in that?" The tall *Priori* pointed to a square, open-wickered
basket that was next to the Bible.

"When I last resided in Santa Lucia it was overrun with vermin," Caterina said. "So I am bringing a cat with me to protect me from whatever
form of rat I might find there this time."

The crowd laughed at her comment, but Tommaso noticed how the
Priori flinched away from Caterina.

Sister Anna Maria must have run back to the kitchen to fetch Balthazara. It gave Tommaso comfort to know the creature would be keeping
Caterina company in the grim old convent.

"Shall we go?" Caterina asked the *Priori*, all politeness now.

If the *Priori* thought the crowd would dissipate, they were wrong.

"Are we going to let those men go wherever they like with that child?
I hear they tried to spirit her away in the middle of the night," a woman
on the other side of Baccio said. "I intend to see with my own eyes that
she's safely installed in the convent."

Some men nearby voiced their agreement.

"Go tell Lorenzo and Ascancio," Tommaso whispered to Baccio. The
crowd began to move off as a solid mass, following the *Priori* and their
captive. All around could be heard support for Caterina and the desire to
see the affair to a proper and decent end.

In their hearts, the people of Florence know what is right, Tommaso thought
proudly.

Then he realized that the woman who'd spoken nearby seemed familiar. Where had he seen her before? He tried to recall as he let the crowd
carry him along. He caught a glimpse of Cosimo Ruggiero on the crowd's
outskirts, leading his horse. Beyond Cosimo, Piero Strozzi was trying to
appear inconspicuous.

Piero Strozzi! Tommaso suddenly remembered where he'd seen the
woman who'd spoken up for Caterina. Surely she'd been one of the servants helping to strap the men-at-arms into their armor that day so long
ago at the Strozzi mansion, when he'd run to fetch help for the beleaguered
Medici palazzo.

Tommaso looked about the crowd more closely. Now he saw them: Strozzi men-at-arms and servants dressed as day laborers, de' Medici retainers disguised as tradespeople. Had they been waiting half the night to join the crowd when it gathered?

When Tommaso saw Piero Strozzi's brother Leone outfitted as a humble wool-comber he knew his guess was true. Involved as she was with the defense of the city, Clarice Strozzi had not sat idly by while her niece was threatened.

The next night an exhausted Cosimo met with his father before the great mirror. Cosimo began to draw the velvet away from the polished black surface. His father stayed his hand.

"Do we not need to look for the outcome of today's actions?" Cosimo asked.

Ruggiero the Old shook his head. "No. Our opponents now know that the fates of their bishop and king are tied to our queen. They'll try to move her about the board, but they understand they can't destroy her without destroying themselves."

45

❧

Two weeks later, on August 3, Francesco Ferrucci was captured by Spanish soldiers in the mountain village of Gavinina, birthplace of the apprentice Simone, and hacked to death.

It was the last blow. With Florence disheartened and starving, a delegation of citizens assembled the next week to negotiate a surrender. The price Clement and the emperor demanded proved high: an enormous sum of money, with fifty prominent citizens held hostage till it was paid in full. And although Clement promised leniency toward his native city, Florentines knew that the future promised the banishment of many families and the execution of at least the most prominent anti-Medicean leaders.

In the meantime, the countryside for miles around was stripped bare by besieging troops. Villas lay leveled. Peasants who'd worked the small productive farms that provided much of Florence's sustenance were either murdered or fled. Impendent in the future was the return of Alessandro de' Medici, this time as the Duke of Florence. But, by acquiescing, Florence avoided the terrible sacking and pillaging that had ended the siege of Rome.

Among the first acts by the Prince of Orange after the surrender were the freeing of all pro-Medici supporters imprisoned in the Bargello and the return of Caterina to the Murate.

Tommaso was overjoyed for Caterina. As for himself, as an apprentice to Il Tribolino, and with his family employed by the de' Medici physician and astrologer, Tommaso had no reason to fear for his own safety or that of his family.

Michelangelo was another matter. Who knew how the vengeful pope might retaliate against the favorite artist and companion of his youth who had defied him by rendering Florence physically impregnable? Not knowing where the sculptor was from day to day, whether he was safe or captured, drove Tommaso almost out of his mind with worry.

Therefore, he was so distracted the morning Il Tribolino summoned him into the *bottega* office that he didn't hear his master calling him. Pagolo di Arezzo had to nudge him to get his attention.

"Tommaso! What ails you? Answer *Ser* Tribolino before he deafens us with his shouts."

Tommaso looked up from polishing a marble bas-relief. Il Tribolino stood by the office door with his hands on his hips.

"My apologies, good Pagolo. I was in some sort of a daze." Tommaso set his work aside.

Il Tribolino had every right to be testy with Tommaso for his inattention. But when Tommaso approached him the master artist's eyes dropped. Since the cork model incident he'd never been able to look Tommaso fully in the eye for long.

"Please step inside, Tommaso," he said. "I need to talk to you in private."

He looked so ill at ease that Tommaso's first thoughts were of Michelangelo. Aligned as he was with the pope, Il Tribolino would be one of the first to hear if Michelangelo were caught.

"A visitor stopped by my home last night," Il Tribolino began. "On a matter of some concern to you."

Tommaso felt the blood draining from his face. His guess was correct. Philiberte of Orange's men had discovered Michelangelo. A wave of dizziness washed over Tommaso. His lips turned numb. For a moment it was a struggle just to stay standing.

"It was Cosimo Ruggiero who came to call," Il Tribolino continued, "in the role of your contractual proxy. He pointed out that three years and a little more have passed since the beginning of your apprenticeship. The obligations of both sides having been fulfilled, the Ruggieros and your father call you back to service."

So great was Tommaso's relief that the news was not of his lover's arrest that it took several moments for Il Tribolino's words to sink in. When they did, Tommaso felt suddenly hollow.

"When am I to leave?"

"Today."

An image floated into Tommaso's mind. He recalled once seeing a skiff broken loose from its moorings during a flooding of the Arno. The little boat had drifted along forlornly, bumping against debris and other boats, helplessly picking up speed till it disappeared from sight around a bend in the river. *I am that boat*, Tommaso thought.

"But I haven't finished polishing the equestrian relief sculpture," he protested. "And there are my own incomplete pieces."

Il Tribolino waved a hand to silence him. "Gherardo or Bertino can finish the marble. Take your projects with you. Perhaps you'll have time to complete them later. Now you must pack. The Ruggieros just sent a man-at-arms with papers for us both to sign. He'll be back shortly to help you transport your things."

Only then did Tommaso realize how unconscious with worry he'd been. He hadn't noticed anyone entering or leaving the *bottega*.

Il Tribolino walked him out into the studio. The master clapped his hands to get the other apprentices' attention. "Please leave off your work. I have something to tell you."

When all was quiet he cleared his throat. "On this day, Tommaso Arista is formally acquitted of his apprenticeship at this *bottega*. He conducted himself diligently and with honor, but his services are urgently required at the Ruggiero palazzo. He is being recalled today. We will miss him."

Tribolino's assistant Vittorio, along with Gherardo, Bertino and all the other apprentices, just stood there, their faces blank with astonishment.

Tommaso's cheeks grew hot with anger. In spite of Il Tribolino's fine words, it was evident to all he was being summarily dismissed.

"Today?" said Bertino. "But that leaves us no time to put together a farewell celebration."

"It's regrettable, but as I said, his services are urgently required."

Tommaso slunk to the apprentices' quarter to pack. Elissa Pecorino came to help, though other than a few changes of clothes and some tools he owned very little.

"Don't think you've seen the last of me," Elissa Pecorino scolded softly. "I shall come haunt you for the egregious disservice you've done me: First you come and raise the culinary expectations of simple apprentices. Then you depart, leaving me to fulfill those expectations by myself, without your fair company."

Tommaso hugged her good-bye fiercely. When he let her go she dabbed her eyes with the edge of her apron.

Crating up his work in the studio proved an even worse experience. The other apprentices stood about awkwardly. Under the circumstances, Il Tribolino didn't pressure them to work. Salvatore silently hammered together two medium-sized boxes for Tommaso's pieces. Only Pagolo di Arezzo spoke up. "It isn't right, Tommaso. You can't go back. You're one of us now."

Tommaso bit his lip to keep from agreeing out loud. He knew he would always be a cook, but now he was also an artist. It was wrong to leave. He was a loaf only half-baked; a turning spit roast still too raw; a fritatta unrisen.

Jealousy flared through him, so sour and rancid he could taste it in the back of his throat. Claudio and Pagolo di Arezzo would enjoy the years of training he was being denied. Very soon Salvatore and Bertino would become journeymen, and, after them, Gherardo. He wouldn't be here to celebrate their rites of passage.

The Ruggiero man-at-arms returned. Tommaso wasn't surprised to find it was Enzio. Tommaso made his farewells at the alley door as Old Taddeo backed up the Ruggiero cart. To Tommaso's surprise, Il Tribolino followed him into the alleyway.

"Tommaso, I know we will meet again at another time, in better circumstances," the sculptor said. "I'm a cautious, even timid, man. I hope someday you can forgive me my flaws." He hesitated, clearly uncomfortable in bringing up the episode they both knew he alluded to. And true to his nature, he shied away from it.

"You've been a good student—as talented as any that have studied with me and twice as hardworking as most. I'm truly sorry you have to go. I'd hoped to speak to *Ser* Ruggiero and your father about extending your apprenticeship to the full term. You deserve that. And if you felt uneasy about continuing with me, I would have recommended you to another *bottega*, possibly Rafaello da Montelupo's."

Tommaso stared. The man was completely sincere. Tommaso would have guessed him relieved to be rid of him.

"But since you must go, I know you will find satisfactions upon your return to the Ruggieros' that will balance out any disappointment you feel in leaving." Il Tribolino tried to smile a farewell.

The atmosphere at the Ruggiero kitchen complex was so different from what Tommaso had grown used to and just left. The worktables were covered with dishes. The odors filling the kitchen smelled not only of baking, roasting and boiling, but a subtle perfume that took Tommaso a moment to identify: a bounty of fresh produce. Supplies must finally be making their way into Florence.

"Tommaso! Back not a moment too soon," Gentile called, glancing up from trussing a brace of larks. "Don't worry about your things," he said as Tommaso headed toward the hallway to the sleeping quarters. "Taddeo will unload them and you can unpack later. Right now I need you to prepare the stuffing for the boiled goose."

Piera came in from the storeroom carrying a basket filled with savoy cabbage and bright green broccoli. She beamed when she saw Tommaso, but only took the time to kiss him on the cheek.

"We'll welcome you home properly later," she promised him. "But tonight *Ser* Ruggiero hosts the Prince of Orange's captains. We're in desperate need of your capable hands."

Tommaso went right to his work station. He stuffed the goose, then moved on to wrapping poached pears in sheets of soft beige marzipan. The happy bustle reminded him of his childhood. Massolina cradled her baby with one arm, nursing it even as she stirred a thickening custard cream with a wooden spoon in her other hand. Cousin Francesca rolled out the tart crust that would hold the custard. The apprentices—they'd grown to the point they could no longer be counted mere boys—hoisted a spit-roasting goat with ease. Several new and very young scullery maids cleaned a pailful of pike. *Ser* Ruggiero must have hired them on just since the end of the siege—a hopeful sign that the old mage foresaw prosperity looming again in the future, and with it the duty to entertain lavishly. In a corner, Paolo and Luciana sat quietly hulling peas. Tommaso marveled how the contented little boy tempered Luciana's disposition. Even Gentile and Piera bantered with each other.

This is my proper welcome home, Tommaso thought. *Nothing else is necessary.* He could almost forget the abrupt end to his life as an artist, his worries for Michelangelo, and the phantom presences haunting the kitchen with their absence: the scullery maid Maddelena; Filomena and Ottaviano; Ginevra, Beatrice, and Pietro. He could almost forget them, but not quite.

46

Cosimo Ruggiero appeared when the meal was almost ready to be carried over to the mansion and arranged on the great sideboard in the banquet hall. He drew Tommaso aside.

"It's good to see you returned, my friend. I'm pleased Tribolo released you as promptly as I requested," he said. "As you can see, life has abruptly returned to the frenetic pace of the old days. We need all the able help we can get." Cosimo glanced about, as if checking to see who else was nearby.

"I have an errand to send you on. One of the men-at-arms fell ill yesterday. He's cloistered in a room in the back wing. We don't wish our illustrious guests to fear contagion. I want you to take a tray up to him for his supper. I'll pick out the victuals and you can carry them in when dinner is delivered to the banquet hall. Lorenzo will meet you and show you the way to the sickroom."

Tommaso blinked in surprise, but as one well trained in servitude, he said nothing. Surely Cosimo knew that even sick servants were not fed until after the master and guests supped.

But Tommaso was truly astonished as he watched Cosimo heap a large majolica plate with the best morsels from the serving platters. Following behind, Tommaso readjusted the food destined for the serving board so there wouldn't appear to be any gaps on the platters. Whatever the sick

man-at-arms suffered from, it evidently wasn't an infirmity of the stomach.

Cosimo looked up to see Tommaso staring at him. "The poor fellow
was prescribed adequate nourishment for his healing," he said sheepishly.

"Then he should soon be bursting with health," Tommaso observed
dryly.

Tommaso set up a tray with cutlery, two napkins, condiments, and a
water glass. Cosimo added a bowl for handwashing, a goblet, and a small
flagon of good wine. Then he draped a clean linen over the tray. Tommaso barely had time to join the end of the procession leaving the kitchen
with the evening feast.

"I must take my leave of you and run ahead to help my father greet
the guests," Cosimo said. "Watch out for my brother."

Lorenzo waited just inside the back door to the mansion. "This way,
Tommaso," he said and led Tommaso on a winding route up stairs and
along hallways until they were somewhere in the rear of the palazzo, in the
maze of servants' quarters and workrooms. Other than a housemaid or
two, they came across no one on their way. Lorenzo finally opened a door
and ushered Tommaso in.

Tommaso looked about him. Was this some sort of jest? They stood
in a linen room amid cupboards piled with clean sheets and bedding.
Lorenzo closed the door behind them. He smiled at the look on Tommaso's face. "No, this is not the end of our journey."

He went to a section of ornate paneled wall between two cupboards.
"Set your tray down, Tommaso, and come here. What I'm about to show
you is a secret you must reveal to no one." Lorenzo took Tommaso's hand
and slid it into the space between wall and cupboard.

"Do you feel that decoration carved into the paneling? It's a lion's head.
If you just run your hand over it, nothing will happen. Position your first
and index fingers over the lion's eyes. Then place your thumb in its maw."

Tommaso did as he was instructed, though the narrowness of the space
made the task difficult.

"Now press with equal pressure at the same time on all three spots,"
Lorenzo instructed him.

Tommaso pushed. The wall panel before them slid open.

"Bring your tray in here," Lorenzo said, stepping through the opening.

The room inside was small, sparsely furnished with a cot, a washstand with a chamber pot, a clothing chest and a small desk pushed up against the far wall to catch what little light it could from a pair of tiny windows.

A man sat at the desk, hunched over some large sheets of paper. He was so engrossed in his work that he either hadn't heard them enter or didn't care. Tommaso would have recognized that back anywhere.

"Michelangelo," he whispered.

At the sound of his voice, Michelangelo whirled about.

"My father thought you might be hungry, *Ser* Buonarotti," Lorenzo said. "Both for food and for the company of a fellow artist."

Michelangelo hid in the Ruggieros' secret room for almost a week right under the very noses of the Prince of Orange's captains, who Ruggiero the Old had consented to quarter. Those days were among the sweetest of Tommaso's life.

On the sixth morning, Cosimo came to the kitchen. "The man-at-arms recovered his health. It won't be necessary to take him food to break his fast," he told Tommaso.

Tommaso felt as crushed and hollow as he had when Il Tribolino announced the end of his apprenticeship. But now he understood the real reason for *that* occasion's timing. Perhaps Michelangelo's abrupt departure was equally necessary. But he and Michelangelo, not knowing, had not said good-bye the night before.

"Where?" he choked on the word.

Cosimo looked at him with some sympathy. "Walk with me in the garden for a few moments, Tommaso."

Cosimo waited until they stood alone by the well in the middle of Piera's herb garden. At this time of year the basil and mint should have stood as tall and thick as bushes. But because of the siege and famine, they were picked down to almost bare sticks.

"Tommaso, I can't tell you where he hides now. Even I don't know. The pope's men search for him everywhere. They're questioning everyone suspected of closeness to him, especially in the *bottegas,* which was one of the reasons we retrieved you from Tribolo's. For his safety, and yours, and mine, it's better that we don't know."

Cosimo threw an arm around Tommaso's shoulders. "Don't look so glum, my friend. I can tell you this—he'd been moved from place to place after the end of the siege, but now I'm told he's safely ensconced in a place that will amaze us someday when we can learn of it. Try not to worry."

47

⌘

B ut Tommaso did worry, for weeks. On September 24, Francesco
Gucciardini returned from Rome to expedite the rebuilding of Florence's government and pave the way for Alessandro's arrival as duke of
the city.

If Florentines expected mercy from a fellow citizen, they soon suffered
sore disappointment. Gucciardini's own villa outside the city walls had been
leveled during the siege. He was in no mood to employ mild measures.
Dozens of families were exiled in perpetuity and their properties seized.
Francesco Carducci, the leader of the Arrabbiati, was tortured and executed. The last *Gonfaloniere* elected to lead the *Signoria* during the siege's end
was also condemned to death, though his sentence was eventually com-
muted to lifetime imprisonment in the Bargello.

All this served to throw Tommaso into a perpetual state of terror for
his lover, far worse than the fears he suffered prior to Michelangelo's secret sojourn at the Ruggieros'.

Shortly after Gucciardini's return, the papal agents who'd been searching for Michelangelo, frustrated by their lack of success, publicly announced that they were simply trying to serve Michelangelo with a full
pardon and provided the documentation to prove it. Michelangelo emerged
from hiding.

Tommaso's joy at the turn of events was short lived. In exchange for the pardon, the pope expected Michelangelo to return to Rome almost immediately to continue working on his Vatican commissions.

No sooner had Tommaso absorbed that news than he discovered that the pope was also recalling Caterina to Rome at the same time, the better to decide her future.

So, one day at the end of October, Tommaso found himself sitting at the main kitchen worktable, his head in his hands.

"Don't you want to see Caterina one last time before she goes?" Piera asked him. The *Duchessina* was stopping by to meet with Ruggiero the Old on her way out of the city, no doubt for an astrological consultation. The whole household had assembled in the mansion to wish her farewell. Only Tommaso lingered behind, not wishing to pull a long face in Caterina's presence.

"I saw her last week when Taddeo and I went to the Murate. I had good cheer of her then, before I knew of her departure. She'll not miss me in that sea of faces up at the house."

"Perhaps not," Piera said. "But then you only deprive yourself." When he didn't respond she clicked her tongue in mild disapproval. "Please yourself, then. I, for one, am going to make my good-byes." Although her words were tart, Piera's eyes softened with compassion at her son's misery.

Tommaso sat for a while alone. Then he felt something soft brush against his thigh. He looked down to find one of the cats gazing up at him anxiously. "Melchiora?" He picked it up. The cat snuggled against his chest. Tommaso was embarrassed to admit it, but since returning home, he couldn't differentiate his cat from her mother or sisters, they looked so exactly alike. The only one he recognized for certain was the one that was lame, his mother said, from battling a rat during the plague. He guessed that the cat that sensed his sad mood and came to comfort him was either Melchiora or Gattamelata.

"Thank you," he whispered into its fur. When it began to purr he was comforted. It must not be Melchiora after all. His cat never purred so loudly. The pleasant humming surrounded Tommaso. His memory was tickled by a distant recollection of a time past when he'd been similarly encompassed, but no, his mind couldn't quite retrieve it.

The sound *did* come not only from the cat he held but all about him, Tommaso realized. He looked down. The three other cats sat on the floor spaced about his chair, all of them purring, their eyes half closed and ears tilted slightly back in the expression cats get when they have accomplished some great feat and are particularly pleased with themselves.

"Tommaso. I knew I could find you here."

Tommaso whirled about, still holding the cat.

Caterina stood in the doorway that led out to the garden and the mansion. Behind her stood a lady-in-waiting. Caterina almost mirrored him, for she too held a cat in her arms, the exact duplicate of his.

At least I know that one's Balthazara. Tommaso recognized the inanity of the notion the instant he thought it.

"I bring you a proposal. But you'll need to hurry in the choosing. There isn't much time," Caterina said.

Tommaso couldn't keep up with her. "Hurry?"

Caterina set down Balthazara. "Visit with your mother and sisters a moment, my pet, while I speak with Tommaso," she instructed the cat. She turned to Tommaso and patted her coif. Her hair had grown rapidly. It was now long enough to coil and hide in a headdress. "You know, since the night I cut off my tresses at the Murate I haven't let her out of my sight. Which of course scandalized the sisters of Santa Lucia. They said I must be a *strega.*"

Tommaso was feeling more stupid with each passing moment.

"Perhaps I am a *strega.* I'm hoping to conjure you away with me to Rome. It appears that my relative His Holiness"—Caterina paused to make a face—"wishes me to prepare for imminent ladyhood. To do so I must have my own retainers. I've been busy explaining to *Ser* Ruggiero and your father that if I'm to be a Duchess-in-training, I wish you to be my head-chef-in-training. I impressed upon them that you've amply demonstrated all the proper qualifications: you cook divinely, you're sufficiently witty, you're artistically creative, and you drop everything else at a moment's notice to come to my aid."

Then Caterina shed her arch demeanor. She looked at Tommaso gravely. "In the Murate you vowed that whatever I asked of you, you would accept and undertake. I will not keep you to your word—I know you may not be able to accept or even wish for what I offer. And, unlike the stars that supposedly only guide our fates, I would not compel you. Nor will I bear you any less love if you choose not to leave with me."

Gentile had come up silently behind Caterina and her lady-in-waiting. He said nothing, but in the expression on his face Tommaso read clearly, *Please don't leave, my son. There's much I have to make up for, much between us left unfinished. If you go now we might never make amends.*

Tommaso was torn. He wanted the same thing Gentile wanted, badly. To work toward returning to that happy, fulfilling, peaceful life of the past.

"Ruggiero the Old is drawing up the papers now," Caterina said. "Forgive me, but you'll have to hurry with your choice."

The past, both good and bad, was gone. The future lay ahead.

"I choose to go with you," Tommaso said and watched the light die in his father's eyes. Gentile left the kitchen as silently as he'd entered.

Caterina looked relieved. Had she doubted his answer? "Your mother assured me it would take no longer than ten minutes for you to ready yourself."

Tommaso jumped from his stool, unsettling the cat on his lap. "It will only take me half that time."

Caterina and her lady waited for him. Tommaso returned from the men's quarters with his possessions packed in two satchels. "I have some artwork too," he said. "I never bothered to uncrate it since returning here."

"I'll send someone back to load it into the carts," said Caterina. "Come, Balthazara." She held out her arms for her cat. Tommaso wondered if he should similarly call to Melchiora. But his cat had settled in so well again with her family here. He had chosen not to stay, but he didn't have the heart to dislodge her. Surely one patchwork cat was enough to take on the long hard journey to Rome.

"Balthazara!" Caterina was becoming impatient. All five cats stared up at her impassively.

"By the Holy Mother," Caterina marveled. "They are exactly alike! How could have I forgotten?" She took a deep breath. "My darling, the companion of my life, *please* come to me. We must go. I promise you a roomy basket with a pillow in the bottom to travel in," she cajoled.

A single cat came forward and sat at Caterina's feet.

"At last," Caterina sighed. She picked up the cat. "We must make haste now," she told Tommaso. "We're to be accompanied by another party also recalled, as you know, by the pope. It would be unseemly to make them wait overly long."

Piera waited at the front door to bid them good-bye. At least in her eyes Tommaso saw rejoicing. Gentile was nowhere to be seen.

"Tell Father I'll write to him and be grateful if he writes back," Tommaso whispered in his mother's ear as he hugged her good-bye.

"I'll tell him," Piera promised. "Don't worry about us, Tommaso. I vow we'll be all right."

Caterina's retinue was huge for a girl so recently a simple "novitiate" of the Murate. Besides maids, ladies-in-waiting, stewards, hostlers, a few clerics, and a falcon master, Piero and Leone Strozzi attended on her and brought *their* men-at-arms and a full complement of servants. Tommaso rode in a supply cart up near the front of the line by Caterina's carriage. When the entourage reached the city gate it met another set of carts led by a man on horseback.

"Ah, our companion party." Caterina smiled.

Michelangelo Buonarotti swept off his cap to Caterina, winking at Tommaso as he did so. "A fine day for traveling to Rome," he said.

48

That night, Piera went out into the garden. She took her pebbles one by one from their pouch and murmured a prayer or curse over each of them, as was appropriate. On the morrow she would have to arrange new placements for their changing configurations.

At the same time, in the de' Medici mansion, Tommaso's cousin Umberto was raiding the pantry for a late snack. Like the rest of the household, he'd found himself depressed of late with the specter of Alessandro's impending return. Umberto's response was to eat greater quantities of food more frequently.

He'd just raised a leftover quince pastry to his lips when the most spine-thrilling, shrill, horrid noise he'd ever heard issued from nowhere to bounce off the kitchen walls, the ovens, and rattle about as an echo in the great fire pit. Umberto's teeth shivered in their gums. He spun about to find the ghastly sound's source.

His great-grandmother Angelina sat where she always perched—on her stool. He hadn't noticed her, so much a part of the piece of furniture she'd always been.

She was laughing. And laughing and laughing. Umberto put his hands over his ears to cut out the noise, not caring that he still held the pastry.

When she finally stopped he lowered his hands in amazement. Angelina wiped tears of laughter from her face with the back of her forearm. Then she fixed Umberto with an utterly malevolent grin.

"They should have left me and mine alone to keep changing in peace. But they had to go and meddle. Oh, they'll be sorry now, won't they?"

Gattamelata turned round and round in the carrying basket. She tried to make herself comfortable but she felt every jolt of Caterina's carriage in her bones.

She was older than anyone knew, even Piera, who comprehended her true nature. Gattamelata was ancient before Piera was born, ancient even before the birth of Piera's predecessor, Angelina.

Only recently, though, had Gattamelata begun to feel the accrual of years. She knew her last septennation had been her final one. She hadn't borne even a litter of common kittens since then, and neither had any of her new daughter-selves. That, at least, might change with her leaving.

In all of her long, long life Gattamelata had never left Tuscany before. But her own fate and the fates of the land she served and the boy and the girl were intertwined in a vast intricate knot. For now that knot tightened toward Rome. It wouldn't always. Soon enough, they would all return to Florence.

Gattamelata at last trod the hollow of the pillow into exactly the right shape for her body. She settled down and closed her eyes.

ACKNOWLEDGMENTS

W hy in the bright blue blazes did I decide to write about the late Renaissance? I must have been out of my mind. Once too thoroughly entrenched to back out, I realized that the era is too broad and rich to do full justice to. Without a lot of help I wouldn't have made it through to the end of this volume.

My heartfelt thanks for the help I've received from my editor, Beth Meacham; for helpful comments from Lisa Goldstein, Charles N. Brown, and my "Italian connection" and fellow Clarionite Mickey Massimino (the only other Michaela Marie I know—except she spells it wrong, of course); my mother, Barbara Grutze Roessner, who supplied me with a lot of my source materials by ferreting through Powell's Books for me; Ellen Asher, who in just a few brief moments in Baltimore liberated me from fearing to use historical sources freely; my agent, Merrillee Heifetz; and my husband, Richard, for his limitless patience.

REFERENCES

One of the greatest pleasures in writing this book was researching the food. This research, however, had its drawbacks: I gained ten pounds in the process, either in attempting to reconstruct some of the recipes or in just the general stimulation of my appetite.

The books relating to food that I found most useful in writing this volume included:

Black, Maggie. THE MEDIEVAL COOKBOOK. New York: Thames and Hudson, 1992.

Fisher, M.F.K. SERVE IT FORTH (from the compendium *The Art of Eating*). New York: Vintage Books, 1976.

de' Medici, Lorenza. TUSCANY THE BEAUTIFUL COOKBOOK. San Francisco: Collins Publishers, 1992.

Tannahill, Reay. FOOD IN HISTORY. New York: Stein and Day, 1973.

Visser, Margaret. MUCH DEPENDS ON DINNER. New York: Grove Press, 1987.

Visser, Margaret. THE RITUALS OF DINNER. New York: Grove Weidenfeld, 1991.

FOOD GLOSSARY

Alchermes   a sweet, red liquor
Arrosto morto   a kind of pot roast
Berlingozo   a cake, traditionally cooked for Easter
Brigidini   aniseed wafers
Castagnaccuo   a chestnut-flour cake
Cibreo   cooked cockscombs and chicken livers served on a bed of artichokes
Gobbi   cardoons. A relative of the artichoke plant.
Dragoncello   tarragon
Dolci   sweets, the dessert course
Dulceforte   sweet-and-sour sauce
Frittata (plural, *frittate*)   a sort of omelette
Minestra   a light soup
Panina gialla   traditional Aretine bread, in which olive oil, raisins, saffron, cinnamon, cloves, and coriander are added to the dough.
Pappardelle   wide, ribbonlike Tuscan pasta
Pecorino   sheep's milk cheese
Poltettina fritte   rissoles
Risotto   a rice dish
Silver beet   chard
Spelt   an ancient strain of wheat, reddish brown in color
Torta di verdura   a paté or tart composed of vegetables
Zuppa   soup that is poured over slices of bread

FOOD RECIPES

ALMOND MILK

Take a quantity of almonds such as pleases you. Crush them to a fair fineness with mortar and pestle. Cover with a boiling liquore and then again a third. For a temperate beverage beneficial to women, children, and invalids, let that liquore be clean well water. For a sauce to grace other foods, let that liquore be a good hearty stock.

Let to stand at least one half an hour. Strain through good cloth. If too thick, add more fluid. If mixture be too thin, simmer slowly, all the while stirring, till it be as thick as you please.

[Author's Note: Use a blender instead of a mortar and pestle unless you're rabidly into authenticity and a martyr to boot. After letting the mixture soak, I run it through the blender again and then strain it through a metal kitchen sieve lined with cheesecloth. Another variation is to scald some milk and use that as your liquid. If you're a real hedonist, you could try cream. I've seen variations where if the liquid is too thin, adding some cornstarch or rice flour to thicken is recommended.]

Z U P P A   F O R   L A   M A T T A   C E N A

Set to rest under a roast turning on a spit sufficient bread crusts to catch
the juices. When the roast has been removed, take the crusts and cast
them into a goodly sized soup pot. Lave with excellent green olive oil
and stir. Add vegetable water or a meaty stock. When soup comes to
simmer, add chopped savoy cabbage, chickpeas, and any other *verdura* at
hand.

[Author's Note: If you're striving for authenticity, use vegetables common
to the Florentine kitchens and gardens of the time, such as silver beet
(chard), *gobbi* (cardoons), spinach, or broccoli. Although the turkey became
an instant hit throughout Europe as soon as it was introduced, other im-
ports from the Americas such as tomatoes and corn (maize) took a while
to become assimilated into European cuisine and were not in common
usage at this time.]

C A S T A G N A C C I O

2½ c. chestnut flour   pinch of salt
6 T. extra virgin olive oil   ½ c. pine nuts
1½ c. water   2 T. rosemary leaves

Preheat oven to 350° F.
        Pour flour into a mixing bowl. Stir in 2 tablespoons of the olive oil.
Gradually add the water, whisking constantly. When smooth, season with
salt.
        Pour the remaining olive oil into an 11-inch-square baking pan. Tip
the pan to distribute the oil evenly. Pour batter into the pan. Sprinkle the
top with pine nuts and rosemary.

Bake about twenty minutes, until the top begins to develop cracks. Remove from oven. Drain off any excess oil. Transfer cake to a serving platter and serve warm.

ARTICHOKE FRITTERS

juice of one lemon	*salt and pepper*
2 ½ lbs. artichokes	⅔ c. all-purpose white flour
2 eggs	5 c. extra virgin olive oil

Fill a large bowl with water and add lemon juice. Trim the artichokes by cutting off the stalks and sharp tips of the leaves, and remove any tough outer leaves. Cut artichokes lengthwise into eighths. Remove and discard fuzzy chokes. As each section is trimmed, drop into the lemon water to prevent discoloration.

Beat eggs with salt and pepper to taste. Drain artichokes and pat them dry. Dredge artichokes in the flour, shaking off any excess, then dip in the beaten egg.

Heat olive oil in a deep heavy skillet to 350° F. Slip the artichoke sections into the oil a few at a time. Do not overcrowd. Fry till golden, about three minutes. With a slotted spoon, remove to paper towels to drain. Continue frying until all are done. Serve hot.

PAPPARDELLE WITH RABBIT SAUCE

SAUCE

1¼ lbs. rabbit, cut in pieces*	2 carrots, chopped
3 T. extra virgin olive oil	1 T. white flour
2 oz. prosciutto, chopped	pinch of grated nutmeg
2 small yellow onions, chopped	1 whole clove

2 celery stalks, trimmed and chopped   salt and pepper
⅓ cup rabbit's blood or rich beef stock   1¼ c. red wine

NOODLES
2½ c. white flour   3 eggs
½ c. freshly grated Parmesan cheese

Sauce: Warm olive oil in a heavy pot over low heat. Add prosciutto and onion and cook gently for five minutes. Add celery, carrot and rabbit. Fry over moderate heat about five minutes, stirring occasionally, until rabbit colors. Sprinkle with flour and nutmeg. Add clove and season to taste with salt and pepper.

Pour about one third of the wine and blood or beef stock into the pot. Stir well, scraping any pieces sticking to the bottom of the pan. Lower heat, cover, and cook for approximately one and a half hours, slowly adding the remaining wine. Bone the rabbit. Chop meat coarsely and return to the pot. Add a little water if sauce becomes too dry. Keep warm.

Noodles: Heap flour in a mound on a clean surface. Make a well in the center. Break the eggs into the well. Work the flour into the eggs with a fork until a loose ball of dough forms. Knead dough on a lightly floured surface until soft, smooth, and elastic.

Using a pasta machine, roll out the dough very thinly. Allow to stand for a few minutes. Take a sharp, thin knife and cut into strips I 1/4" wide and 4" long.

In a saucepan, bring 6 quarts salted water to a boil. Add the noodles and cook for precisely two minutes. Drain and tip onto a warmed serving platter.

Spoon the sauce over the noodles and toss. Sprinkle with the Parmesan cheese and serve immediately.

[Author's Note: The actual name of this recipe is Wide Noodles with Hare Sauce. In Italy it can be cooked with either rabbit or hare. In North America, hare (jackrabbit) is not raised as a domestic meat. While

wild hare is common, particularly in the West, it is often diseased
(check for boils on any captured animal) and not considered particularly safe to eat. Therefore, I've eliminated all references to hare in this
recipe.]

CAST OF CHARACTERS

*denotes historical personages

Academicians, Occultists, and Their Families

Ariosto   a poet
Bazile   a mathemetician
Cosimo Ruggiero   Ruggiero the Old's eldest son
Lorenzo Ruggiero   Ruggiero the Old's second son
Madame Ruggiero   Ruggiero the Old's wife
Ruggiero the Old   astrologer, physician, and mathematician

Artists

Andrea del Sarto   a painter
Benevenuto Cellini   a goldsmith and sculptor
Carota   a woodcarver
The Four Crowned Ones   Simpronian, Claudius, Nicostratus Castorius, and Simplicius. Four martyred stonecarver saints
Francesco Lippi   a goldsmith, grandson of Fra Filippo Lippi
Ghirlandaio   Michelangelo's first teacher
Giuliano Bugiardini   a fresco painter
Michel Agnolo da Siena   an artist who worked on Hadrian's tomb with Il Tribolino
Michelangelo Buonarotti   a sculptor, painter, architect, and engineer
Piero Torrigiani   the sculptor who broke and crushed Michelangelo's nose. Called to serve in the court of Henry VIII of England

Piloto   a goldsmith

Pontormo   a painter and draftsman

Rafaello da Montelupo   a sculptor

Ridolofo   a stonemason

Rosso Fiorentino   a painter

Tasso   a woodcarver

Titian   a Venetian painter working in Rome

Il Tribolino   a sculptor, whose real name was Nicolo de Pericoli. He was also nicknamed "Tribolo."

The Artists' Apprentices, Assistants, and Journeymen

Annibale   apprenticed to Rosso Fiorentino

Amerigo da Siena   apprenticed to Andrea del Sarto

Antonio Mini   assistant to Michelangelo

Ascancio   apprenticed to Michelangelo

Baccio   apprenticed to Michelangelo

Battista   apprenticed to Giuliano Bugiardini

Benedetto   apprenticed to Tasso

Bertino   apprenticed to Il Tribolino

Bertoldo   apprenticed to Rafaello da Montelupo

Cencio   apprenticed to Cellini

Claudio   apprenticed to Il Tribolino

Donato   apprenticed to Francesco Lippi

Gherardo   apprenticed to Il Tribolino

Giorgio Vasari   apprenticed to Andrea del Sarto

Lapo   apprenticed to Piloto

Marcantonio   assistant to Giuliano Bugiardini

Pagolo di Arezzo   apprenticed to Il Tribolino

Paulino   apprenticed to Benevenuto Cellini

Pierino   apprenticed to Giuliano Bugiardini

Pietro Urbino of Pistoia   Michelangelo's assistant in Rome

Raeldo   apprenticed to Rosso Fiorentino

Salvatore   apprenticed to Il Tribolino

Simone   apprenticed to Il Tribolino
Tommaso   apprenticed to Il Tribolino (see also "kitchen staff")
Vittorio   journeyman to Il Tribolino
Zuccone   apprenticed to Rafaello da Montelupo

Cats

Gattamelata   the cat at the Ruggiero kitchen compound
Melchiora, Balathazara, Casparina   three of Gattamelata's seven kittens

Clergy

The Abbess of the Murate
*The Bishop of Nocera   saved Pope Clement during the sack of Rome
*Cardinal Cibó
*Cardinal Passerini   sent by Pope Clement to govern Florence
*Cardinal Ridolfi
*The Four Crowned Ones   (look under Artists category)
*Pope Clement VII   (see also Giulio de' Medici in the de' Medici family
   section)
*Pope Leo X   the pope who arranged the marriage of Caterina's parents,
   Lorenzo Duke of Urbino and Madeleine de la Tour d'Auvergne
   (see also Giovanni de' Medici in the de' Medici family section)
*Saint Pelagia the Penitent   a dancing girl who converted to Christianity
   and became a saint
Sister Anna Maria   a novitiate at the Murate
Sister Dominica   a novitiate at Santa Lucia
Sister Teresa Lucrezia   a nun at the Murate

Florentine Citizenry

Agostino   a member of the Arrabbiati
*Antonio Gondi   a Florentine banker and art patron

Bartolommeo Bettini   an art patron

Bernardo   an art patron

Bembo   an art patron

Botello   an art patron

Federigo Ginori   an art patron

Francesco Carducci   leader of the Arrabbiati

Francesco Ferrucci   a commander and war hero during the siege

Francesco Gucciardini   the aristocratic expatriate Florentine who Clement sent to govern Florence after the siege

Francesco Soderini   a scion of the Soderini family

Giacopino della Barca   an expatriate Florentine ally of Pope Clement's

Girolamo Marretti   a Sienese art patron living in Florence

Marsilio Ficino   a scholar and friend of Lorenzo the Great's

Piero Landi   a friend of Benevenuto Cellini's

The Kitchen Help and Other Servants

Amado   an apprentice cook in the Ruggiero kitchen

Angelina Befanini   the elderly matriarch of the de' Medici kitchen

Atalanta   a scullery maid in the Ruggiero mansion who dies of the plague

Beatrice Arista   Gentile and Piera's second daughter

Costanza Arista   Vincenzo Arista's wife

Elissa Pecorino   the housekeeper at Il Tribolino's *bottega,* also a cousin of Leonora's

Enzio   a Ruggiero man-at-arms

Filomena   a half-Tartar, half-Greek slave in the Ruggiero kitchen

Francesca   Leonora's oldest daughter, also the mother of Paolo

Gentile Arista   master cook and carver of the Ruggiero kitchen

Giacomo Befanini   the master carver of the de' Medici kitchen, also brother to Angelina Befanini

Ginevra   Gentile and Piera's eldest daughter

Grandfather Arista   Gentile's father

Grandfather Befanini Angelina's illegitimate son and Piera's father

Grandmother Befanini Piera's mother

Lazaro a messenger of the Ruggieros

Leonora an Arista cousin, owner of a wild game shop on the Ponte Vecchio

Luciana Gentile and Piera's youngest daughter

Maddalena a Befanini cousin

Marsolino the Strozzi mansion watchman

Massolina a scullery maid in the Ruggiero kitchen

Old Taddeo an elderly Ruggiero household servant, the cartmaster

Ottaviano a journeyman cook in the Ruggiero kitchen

Paolo Francesca's son

Piera Befanini Arista Gentile's wife

Pietro Arista Gentile and Piera's second son

Tommaso Arista Gentile and Piera's eldest son

Umberto a Befanini cousin, son of Vittoria

Vincenzo Arista Gentile's half-brother

Vittoria Piera's sister, also Umberto's mother

The de' Medici and Strozzi Families

*Alessandro de' Medici ostensibly Caterina's bastard half-brother, but almost surely Pope Clement's illegitimate son

*Caterina de' Medici *Duchessina* of Florence, great-granddaughter of Lorenzo the Great, and the last legitimate heir along the male line of the family

*Clarice Strozzi Caterina's aunt and one of Piero de' Medici's two children

*Cosimo de' Medici, Pater Patriae founder of this line of the de' Medici family and grandfather of Lorenzo the Magnifcent

*Cosimo Salviati de' Medici a cousin of Caterina's and son of Maria Salviati and Giovanni del Bande Nere

*Giuliano de' Medici Lorenzo the Great's younger brother, murdered in the cathedral during the Pazzi conspiracy in 1478

Giuliano de' Medici   Lorenzo the Great's youngest son, named after Lorenzo's murdered brother

Giulio de' Medici   the murdered Giuliano's only acknowledged, though illegitmate, child. Adopted by Lorenzo the Great and raised as a member of his family

Giovanni de' Medici   Lorenzo the Great's middle son and Caterina's great-uncle, who became Pope Leo X

Giovanni delle Bande Nere   a Medici cousin and a Florentine war hero. Married to Maria Salviati

Ippolito de' Medici   Lorenzo the Great's youngest son Giuliano's only child. Though illegitimate, Ippolito was also an acknowledged member of the de' Medici family.

Leone Strozzi   Clarice and Phillipo Strozzi's second son

Lorenzo the Great (Lorenzo Il Magnifico)   Caterina's great-grandfather, a ruler of Florence, under whose influence the Rennaissance culture flourished

Lorenzo, Duke of Urbino   Caterina's father, only son of Piero de' Medici

Lucrezia Tornabuoni   Lorenzo the Great's mother, from an ancient and aristocratic family that chose to join the merchant class

Lucrezia Salviati   one of Lorenzo the Great's three daughters

Madeleine de la Tour d' Auvergne   Caterina's mother. A cousin of King Francis of France

Maria Salviati   Lucrezia Salviati's daughter. Married unhappily to the great war hero Giovanni delle Bande Nere

Phillipo Strozzi   head of a prominent Florentine family. Married to Clarice de' Medici Strozzi

Piero de' Medici   Lorenzo the Great's eldest son and Caterina's grandfather

Piero Strozzi   Clarice and Phillipo Strozzi's eldest son

Occult Entities

Aradia   daughter of the Goddess Diana

Ammonites   creatures from another realm whose avocation is to watch over events

Grigori Alpeno, Meana, Settrano, and Tago. The spirit guardians of the four directions

Intialo the shadow sorceror from another dimension

Marax/Meraks A demon who is the spirit of a star in the constellation of the Big Dipper

Obby oss Mages or shamans from a realm diametrically opposed to Earth

Undines female denizens of a starless water world

Others

Alfonso of Ferrara Duke of Ferrara, also brother of Isabella d'Este

Diego a Spanish neighbor of Cellini's in Rome

Emperor Charles V also King of Spain

Ferrante Gonzaga son of Isabella d'Este, an officer in the imperial army

Isabella d'Este born to the royal house of Ferrara, married to Gianfrancesco Gonzaga, Marquis of Mantua

Orazio Baglioni a general in the Italian army controlled by Pope Clement

Philiberte of Orange commander of the Imperial forces

Vittoria Colonna Marchionessa of Pescara, a renowned poet and art patron and a good friend of Michelangelo Buonarotti

Von Frundsberg leader of the *Landsknechte*